KENNETH CAHILL

The Ace of Spades

"In all my years of experience I have never come across a more devious, calculated and terrifying criminal mind than that of which Detective Spade faces in these pages. This is a thrilling page-turner that is sure to be an instant classic."

—*Tim Hennessy, Criminal Defense Attorney*
M.A., Criminal Justice

The Ace of Spades

KENNETH CAHILL

Safari Multimedia, LLC

For Swietlana, Justyna, Emilia,
Ashley, Shannon, Mom and Dad

ONE

The white satin blouse is now stained with a dry crimson in the collar and shoulder regions. The lifeless body of a beautiful young girl lies on the sidewalk of this dirty old alley. Alone among the people society forgets about, this beautiful young thing was left to become the same. The only thing disturbed on our victim was the exposed left breast the killer left his calling card to rest against. A calling card that is very familiar to me, left behind by a monster to mark his prey.

The spade. Something I have become a bit of a connoisseur on. I guess that would be expected, growing up with a name like Kenny Spade. Yes, ever since second grade I was the subject of all the mockeries that school kids are so gifted with. The teasing did have its benefits, though. It made me very tough. Tough and thick skinned. People learned very quickly to pick and choose their quarrels with me. Anyone who dared call me ace soon learned that I was more of the king of Spades. Ever since high school I've been known simply as Spade. All of my friends call me Spade. On occasion even my folks let a Spade slip. Of course I have to come back my royal flush in spades remark.

Thusly, I am very intrigued by the card I see before me. The ace of spades. Very, very intrigued. The ace of spades. This one is special. It holds a very sinister secret. The upside down heart, blackened by the touch of its holder, with the stem tucked up underneath just inviting you to dare and try to remove it. Oh yes, this spade has purpose. The dark red smudge across the in-signia in the corner let's you know this is a message. This black heart wants blood. And the breast it leans against, a beautiful girl with a bright promising future, validates its message. The girl is a red head, with big hazel eyes and very well dressed.

"Spade, why are you here?"

"Hey Loot, couldn't sleep." Lieutenant Dan Murphy is Chief of Homicide Detectives for the Orlando Police Department. I have a bit of a reputation as a night owl, so Loot is actually not that surprised to see me. Lieutenant Dan Murphy, whom I call Loot, knows I don't sleep. He is also very aware that this is not my night to be at a murder scene. But like I said, Loot almost expects to see me here, because I always am.

In a city such as Orlando the night life never seems to end. There is a substantial percentage of people in this town who are here for fun. Granted, Orlando is a lot more family friendly than someplace like, let's say, N'Orlans that's adult oriented. O Town, as we like to call it, is still a vacation destination for people of all nationalities, ethnicities, religions and any other type of different philosophy you can possibly imagine. Adults need to unwind on vacation as much as the kids need to have fun. So there are quite a few different night destinations for adults to have their fun. As a young officer working my way through the ranks I had the opportunity to work a fair share of overnight shifts. As I graduated to reach the level of detective my affinity toward the life of a night owl grew considerably. I found it was much more valuable to probe different facets of any investigation either early in the morning or late in the evening. These times have a propensity to be more conducive to snitches and informants. They are a very useful resource in any investigation. I would need them with this one.

The killer was probably left handed judging from how the cut across the victim's jugular ran from right to left. It looks to be a clean single motion slice, judging from the smoothness of the skin on both sides of the fatal cut. It is curious that he stopped two thirds of the way through. The killer was very meticulous. There is no blood on the shirt near the exposed breast. Was the blood put on the card intentionally? Is the killer trying to tell me something? It could be a warning, possibly of more killings to come. Perhaps the killer is taunting us, daring anyone to try and catch him. I'm sorry young lady. OK. Let's get to work.

The victim's wallet indicates she was twenty-three, from Winter Park, a nearby well-to-do suburb. There are no very distinguishing clues among her belongings. A driver's license, some credit cards, a Social Security card and a seasonal pass to some of the local theme parks were present. Three hundred sixteen dollars and forty eight cents have not been confiscated by the killer. A diamond laden Citizens watch was also disregarded. This killer is not in it for the money. This was no accident. I don't know if she was the intended victim or a random one, but our perpetrator was definitely planning on committing this crime. "So Spade, what do you think?"

"Loot, I was going to ask you the same thing." There is nothing here to go on, and we both know this. All the blows inflicted were very meticulous, very skilled. We definitely have a lefty. The cut is too clean. Maybe it was someone who knows how to use a knife. Possibly a doctor or maybe a butcher. A blacksmith? Well it seems my possibilities have been narrowed. To a few million or so. Young lady, it's time to get you out of here. The coroner's office has just arrived. You don't need to be here anymore. I'm sure there must be tons of pictures of you much happier than the thirty or so my colleagues just took. Her wallet is secured in an evidence bag, along with her purse, a cellphone and her shoes. I hold on to the ace, it has more to tell me. I place it in its own evidence bag, for right now I have something else to tell. Now it's time to let her parents know their pretty little girl will not be coming home. There is never a good time or a good way to do this, day or night.

This ace is a tell tale heart. It wants to speak. It wants to reveal the evil that perpetrated this atrocity. Speak to me. Why won't you speak to me? Whatever the message, you will tell me. I have to find your secret. I stare at the card endlessly. The spade expands into a thousand blurs, each one laughing at me, taunting me. Spade. You call yourself a spade. You disappoint me. You are giving us spades a bad name. Are you a real detective? Look at me, Spade. Everything you need is right in front of you.

Open your eyes Spade. Open them! Do you really want a maniac to ruin your streets, Spade. Spade, can you hear me? Spade? Spade? "Spade?" What? Huh? "Oh, sorry Loot." Yeah, yeah I'm OK. "How long was I zoning out for?" Zoning is an understatement.

"A few minutes." Loot replies. "What's up?"

"Nothing boss. Just checking the evidence."

"Spade, you need to go get some sleep. You're shot."

"I know. I will, Soon."

"Spade, go before you faint. That's an order."

"OK, Loot. I'm feeling you." He is not wrong. I'm shot. But this ace is taunting me.

The car operates almost on autopilot. I hardly even remember driving the twenty minutes to get to my house off West Colonial and Hiawassee. I moved here just because I like the word Hiawassee. That should tell you a little something about me. My place probably looks like most others belonging to cops who work too much. Coffee cups that should have been washed weeks ago sit in the sink. There are ashtrays full of butts scattered about. My elegant furnishings include a double bed; torn up recliner, beat up TV and coffee table. It is lit as well as a seedy bar in the worst part of town would be. A collection of DVD's including the policeman standards Lethal Weapon I thru IV, Young Frankenstein, the Godfather Collection and Mad Max. My pride and joy is my collection of Civil War artifacts, including an authentic letter written to President Lincoln notifying him on the progress of the war and a genuine musket from the Battle of Gettysburg. It is probably the one thing I have taken an actual interest in other than my work. And Spades, of course. There are dozens of books on spades scattered throughout the home. Strategically placed is my crown jewel. On the east wall of the living room is an ace of spades. Three foot, beautifully framed, off set on white with a deep burgundy wall as the backdrop. It is my reminder. A reminder of darker times. A reminder of desperation and loss of control. A reminder of the incident.

It was years back when I was a young OPD beat officer. I had a midnight double. It was around 3 a.m. in the Park Lake section of Colonial Drive. Colonial is a main cross fare in Orlando. I was on routine patrol. I received a call for someone screaming in the woods around the lake. I pulled up and started to search the area. I had my lights on in the car but no siren. There was some light being permeated by the moon but most of the light was being created by all of the lights of my car. I had a flashlight in my right hand and my left hand in the vicinity of my nightstick. I had scoured a substantial quadrant and found nothing. I had begun to make my way back to my car when I heard a faint thump or grunt over to my left side. I immediately went in that direction and then could not believe my eyes. There was a balding middle age man raping a girl, probably nineteen or twenty years old. She was unconscious. Her face was brutally broken up and swollen so much it looked like the humps of a camel. Her right eye was the bleeding combination of black and purple with blood streaming steadily down her destroyed cheek. He had restrained her by the wrists to two different trees using nylon restraints. They had dug into her wrists so tightly they went through the flesh rubbing against her bone. From the look of her skin she had been there for a few days as there were maggots already formed and exploring her wounds. Both of her feet had been amputated at the ankle. She had bruises all over her body in the torso and chest area. There was bruising on her inner thighs, obviously from the force of his violations. There were bite marks on both of her breasts and down the left side of her neck to her shoulder. Evidently the perpetrator was enthralled in his venomous activities, for he did not realize I was there until I was almost upon him. My gun drawn, I ordered the man to freeze. Simultaneously he leapt at me. I got one shot off that missed completely. I radioed for immediate assistance. He ran at me again. I got one shot off, hitting him in the side of the abdomen. He stuttered momentarily and came forward with a voracious thrust that knocked me down. He punched and kicked me repeatedly with anything he could. During this whole time both of us were struggling for the gun. I saw no proverbial light before my eyes but concentrated solely on my pistol. Our struggle continued for what seemed to be the better part of an hour but according to the police log from the arriving support officer was probably closer to three or four minutes. The struggle continued until my back up officer smacked the perpetrator on the back of the head with his night stick. He rolled off me and on to his back. My gun was drawn and pointed at his head. Just then Lieutenant Dan Murphy arrived. I was about to pull the trigger and put a bullet in his face. Lieutenant Murphy talked me down. I lowered my piece and turned my attention to the girl. She was not conscious. Her pulse was very faint and there was no way to check her pupils due to the condition of her eyes and face. There was really no way as she passed the shock phase a day or more ago. Come on baby, don't die. Come on, please don't die. Where are the goddamn medics? Hold on. There was a slight gasp. This was followed by a mischievous barrage of everything she could muster; one of what was probably many previous attempts by this brave warrior. "Hold on, hold on I'm a police officer. It's OK. I got you. You're going to be OK."

"What took you so long? What took you so long!? What took you so long!!!!?"

"It's OK I'm here now."

"I needed you three days ago! What took you so long?!!"

"I'm sorry, it's OK now. You're going to be OK. I got you. My name is Kenny."

"I needed you three days ago. Tell my mom and dad I'm sorry and I love them. And Kenny, Thank You."

Such were the last words ever spoken by Miss Elizabeth Downing of Jacksonville, Florida in her last breath of life. The life robbed from her by a monster who to this day I wish I had splattered his face all over my uniform.

It was Lieutenant Dan who prevented this from happening. Lieutenant Dan remanded the prisoner to custody. Lieutenant Dan brought me in and debriefed me. The crime was so brutal brass made Lieutenant Dan, who wasn't even my lieutenant then, give me paid leave and get counseling, a department mandate. Well, counseling I received. After my first visit with the department shrink I was on a plane to Vegas, savior of all. I found every single sin in sin city. And I even invented some sins that mortal man didn't even know existed yet. Houses of ill repute, I didn't miss a single one. I had an international smorgasbord of ladies, I doubt if I missed ten of the countries on the entire planet. As for the nectar of the gods, if it had a kick I had overindulgence. I had some rough trips with several different illegal substances, and even one where I woke up forty-eight hours after the fact. It was three weeks of excess, but it couldn't stop the pain. Every girl I was with had her face. Every bad trip I had involved a replay of the final, fatal conversation of Elizabeth Downing. I could not escape her, I could not forget I was three days too late. My reign of error was capped on my twenty-third day in Vegas. I had run through every penny I had access to, and some I didn't.

I was in the MGM, slightly loaded. I was playing some poker for a few hours and had lost a bunch. Then I got a little lucky I played a hand with two small suited cards and wound up three minutes later with a straight flush, in spades of course. It netted me 10,000. I bailed from the table and decided to go try the tables. I settled on roulette. I was a little more than a little inebriated but I didn't care. I was a little rowdy at the roulette wheel when some of the finest security guards came over and began to shadow me. After one unsuccessful, costly roll I was a little more than a little pissed and more vocal than I should have been. MGM's Grandest were waiting for this and tried to remove me. Well, my bad luck and bad behavior had one more up swell left, and I resisted my escorts as much as possible. In fact, it took seven to subdue me. My next step was a visit to the Las Vegas holding facility.

A phone call to my CO got my ass in a whole lot of professional hot water. It also got me an in person escort back to Orlando. Once I arrived back to work I was besieged with every possible question, regulation, and disciplinary statute they could throw (deservedly so). The end result was twice a week sessions with Dr. Frankenstein. These sessions lasted for eight months, during which time I was still self-medicating to the max. It came to a head at one of the Christmas parties, when I was so drunk I couldn't stumble straight. I hit my car and tried to go. Standing in front of me when I turned my lights on was Lieutenant Dan Murphy, Orlando PD. He stood his ground in front of me, much like the elderly Chinese gentleman in front of the tank in Tiananmen Square. After much swearing and a fifteen-minute standoff, Lieutenant Dan Murphy took my keys and drove me to his house.

I don't remember hitting the couch, or how I got in at all. What I do remember is a pot of hot coffee at 7:30 a.m. and a conversation. Not with Lieutenant Dan but with his lovely wife Kate. She was a lady of simple beauty, the perfect girl next door that every teenage boy wanted to grow old with. She was apparently aware of my indiscretions, for she never acted surprised by anything I did. Loot was nowhere to be seen when I arose, just Kate and that coffee. Kate offered me some of the best tasting coffee I had ever had. Of course, after my night before it is very possible that a pot of pig vomit would have tasted that good. Kate did not preach to me or lecture me. She simply told me what it was like being Loot's wife, being in love with a man so dedicated to his job, and worrying every day whether it was the day of the nightmare. The day she never knew if the two cops would show at the door with the worst news she could imagine. Thankfully that day had not come yet. It could be today. She didn't know. But every day in Kate's life was filled with the inner turmoil of fear versus faith. I sat in Kate's kitchen drinking coffee for hours, just listening. Never had I experienced a woman so wise. But for the first time I understood the final seconds of the life of Elizabeth Downing, a combination of relief and agony no mere mortal person should have to live through. I finally got the answers to questions I didn't even know I had. I understood that the world is not always kind, and you're responsible for yourself and your ability to change it.

I went to find Lieutenant Dan. I found him at homicide. He asked me how I was. No lecture, no judgment. He didn't ask of my morning or how Kate was. He knew. That day I realized that

I was on a path of self destruction. On that day I forged a non-obligatory, endearing friendship with Kate and Dan Murphy. I resurrected my career by throwing myself into my work. It took me years to get off foot patrol. Years of making a difference. Years of fighting the demons I embraced that fateful night. And years of saying goodbye to Elizabeth Downing. I still fight my demons every day, and every night I tell Elizabeth Downing how sorry I was I didn't arrive three days earlier. After I rededicated myself, I had the good fortune of having an open application to homicide when one Lieutenant Dan Murphy was named Chief of Homicide Detectives. It took me eighteen months, but I was finally given the opportunity to join homicide. Loot and I have caught a decent number of murderers and put ourselves in a position to make all potential criminals think twice. As for my friend the Ace of Spades, well my work is not yet done here.

TWO

The image is inescapable. I have followed this pretty girl for three blocks. I selected her while leaving a bar across from the Orlando Arena. You are very pretty. Very pretty indeed. Why would any girl this pretty be leaving a bar all alone? I'm sorry young lady, but I can't allow this travesty to go on uncorrected. Wait for me, I'll be right there. No, no don't walk faster. Don't walk faster. You don't want to get away from me; I can make you feel happy and loved. Don't run from me. I said don't run. Come on now. I said DON'T RUN. The blade runs cleanly across her throat. With a little more effort I could have decapitated her. Oh baby, don't look sad. It's not too bad anymore. Here, let me fix your blouse. We just loosen this button here, and this button here. Oh baby, you're beautiful. Still something is missing. Oh yes, this will do nicely. The perfect accessory. Here you go. An ace of spades. Yes, you'll look divine right there. OK, just a little more skin. Oh, you're perfect! Sleep well, Cinderella. Don't let the bedbugs bite.

AAAAAAAAAAAAHHHHHHHHHHHH! Why is this guy in my head?! Stop! The chills ripple through my body. I had enough sweat in my pillow to fill a gallon milk jug. Two fifteen. Perfect. It's my time of the day. The middle of the night. Why am I seeing this murder in my head? I haven't experienced anything like this ever before. Something is eating at me. I need to work. That's it. It's got to be. I can't let go of the card. I've brought home my work before, but never had any kind of image like this before. There must be something I'm missing. Well shit, this is my time of night, right? So let's get to work. What do

I have to work with? An ace of spades. A bar across from the Orlando Arena, or as us die hard locals call it the O-Rena. A twenty three year old girl. A part time employee at the local amusement park. She's obviously living off mommy and daddy, for there is no college ID or workplace ID. She is an attractive girl, but this is Florida and there are tons of attractive girls here. He likes to pose his victim. He was very meticulous about her appearance. She sits a certain way. He wanted her to be found that way. Him and that ace. He wants to taunt me.

Wwwoooooohhhh. Calm down there cowboy. You're making this personal. This is personal to the parents of a twenty three year old from Winter Park, Florida. Let's stay objective. Focus on what you know. Get an idea of where you want to go. GO! Brilliant! Let's see if any of the regulars at that bar I saw in my dream saw anything. Maybe they saw someone. Perhaps I could talk to the bartender. He probably remembers the girl.

The Hurricane From Hell was a nice new bar in the downtown area just a stone's throw away from the Orlando Arena. It is in the middle of a Florida strip mall on South Orange Blossom Trail with sub places, tanning studios and a grocery store. At three in the morning it's also a barren field of little green lizards in a crossing pattern that would make the world champions of air traffic control feel like they were running a day care at O' Hare. My Corvette glides across the holding pattern while the little green critters scramble. All probably did not make it. The specially designed sign above the door features a hurricane warning sign with the devils horns in the middle. The wooden double doors are accented with deep brick red smoky blown glass inserts designed to resemble someone's interpretation of hell. They are very much locked at this ridiculous hour. There do not appear to be any lights on inside. A quick jaunt around the back tells me the Hurricane From Hell is closed for business this evening/morning. The next thing to do is crash my office I guess.

The office, or the Hole as we like to call it, is fairly empty during the wee hours of the morning. In fact, currently I am the office. Some genius left the coffee pot on when they left so I have a little work to do before I can brew some fresh sludge. Hey, after Kate Murphy's coffee everything is sludge. I have a whole lot of nothing to go on. No eyewitness. No murder weapon. Just a dead girl and a card. A card that taunts me. Forensics determined from a residue powder smudge on the card that the killer probably was wearing yellow surgical gloves like you see nurses wear in a hospital. In these times of blood carried pathogens those rubber gloves are a dime a dozen. We even use them to pick up evidence. Since I didn't touch the ace of spades near the blood spot, I know the residue was not mine. This leaves me with a useless playing card that's some kind of message from a sadistic killer who's doing nothing more than taunting me. It's a shame that this fresh pot of sludge cannot help wake up this mind of mine. I am nowhere. When the rest of the normal world turns on I will go to the victim's place of employment. I continue to look at the card in front of me.

Spade, oh Spade what's the matter with you. You can catch me. Or can you? Maybe you can't. Have you lost your edge? Can't handle it anymore? I'm sure your sweet Elizabeth Downing will forgive you. Couldn't even get to her three days earlier, could you? You are weak. Bordering on pathetic. Come on, you call yourself a spade? How dare you! Look at me Kenny. LOOK! You are not a spade. You are a wimp. I call you Kenny Club. You don't deserve to be a spade. Kenny Club. Dear Elizabeth, your champion is letting you down again. Kenny, I need you. I needed you three days ago. Kenny, don't let me down. Don't let me down again. Hurry, it's going to be too late. Elizabeth, I'm sorry. Don't give up on me. Elizabeth, please. Elizabeth. Elizabeth, don't give up on me. Elizabeth. Elizabeth. Spade. Spade. "Spade. Spade. Wake up there Spade." "Huh? Oh Loot, it's you. What are you doing here?"

" Spade, I could ask you that but I already know the answer."

"Yeah, couldn't sleep."

"Sleep? Do you know what that is?"

"Not really."

"Spade, why are you calling for Elizabeth? I thought you were done with that years ago?"

"Ah, Loot it's the damn case. I can't get a handle on it."

"Spade, what about Elizabeth? Why her, why now?"

"It's nothing."

"Spade, this is me. Lieutenant Dan, remember Forrest? I am not a smart man but I know what BS is.."

"That's funny Loot. I feel ya. I don't know. This spade is taunting me. It brings me out."

"And Elizabeth? It's been four years."

"Dan, I see her. I talk to her. I tell her every night how sorry I am I was so late. And she tells me she needed me three days ago."

"Jesus Spade, why didn't you ever tell me this?"

"Loot, you saved my life and gave it back but I still fight those demons daily."

"Listen, when was the last time you did anything? Come over Sunday. We'll have a barbecue and a couple of beers. Kate would love to see you."

"We'll see."

"No we won't. You'll be there. That's an order."

"OK Loot, I feel ya."

"Yeah, I know."

"So listen, do you have any leads yet? "

"No. I went to the bar, but it was closed. I'll go back later."

"What bar?" Oh shit, insert foot.

"Well, I had a hunch."

"Come on Spade. A hunch? Are you holding out on me? What do you know?"

"A hunch. No lie. There is a bar by the O-Rena called the Hurricane From Hell. So I figured I would go and poke around. But it was closed. I have no other really good leads so why not."

"Spade, should I worry here? Hunches, Elizabeth…"

"I know it sounds weird, but right now it can't hurt."

"All right, run with it. Spade, are you sure you're all right?"

"Yeah boss, I'm gooooood." A feeble attempt at humor, which I'm sure we're both aware of. Damn, how much trouble did I just get myself in? Well, he's right about my lack of a social life. The only true female companionship I've had over the past four years, minus twenty-three days of course, has been the ghost and the memories of Miss Elizabeth Downing of Jacksonville, Florida. Ironically, it was the death of Elizabeth Downing that brought me to life. She made me rededicate myself to my job. She makes me do this every time I close my eyes and sometimes while I am still awake.

Loot is still very suspicious. Maybe worried is a better word. Damn, I hope I didn't put myself in jeopardy. I have to figure this all out. I need to solve this murder. I can do this for you, and for me. It's 7:30 p.m. It's still too early to go back to the Hurricane From Hell. Let's go back to the place we found her. We can follow the day time traffic flow and see how busy it gets. Maybe the killer picked this place specifically. Maybe he scoped it out. He could work in the local area. I could recheck the vicinity for things I missed. I am going to grab a new fresh cup of sludge from Louie the Coffee truck guy and head on that way. I have to be missing something. I have to be. "Loot, I'm going to go check something out. I'll be back."

"Spade..."

"I'm OK Loot. I'll let you know if I find anything interesting. See ya."

I ran out to escape the awkwardness of the situation. I can't believe I let that slip. Damn, that was stupid. Enough of this crap. Let's go catch this SOB! Louie, I am on my way. How's that sludge doing?

The blood stain on the side walk is still fresh. The forensic team released the scene yesterday and I am sure that there have been a few visitors. There are virtually no other indications visible of the brutality that occurred here just thirty or so hours prior. I scan the ground in the vicinity of the stain. There does not appear to be anything screaming at me like the card did. Maybe my approach is all wrong. Maybe the card was put there on purpose. Maybe the killer was talking to ME. Ah, I'm just getting too personal again. Hmmmmm. Maybe not. What's that? I notice on the ground is a concert ticket. The Barenaked Ladies.

Maybe it belonged to my victim. She could have dropped it. Or maybe the killer dropped it. Who did she go with? Isn't anyone missing her? Surely someone went to the concert with her. Most people don't go to concerts alone. It's only three or so blocks from where the Hurricane From Hell is. I'll just walk down that way and see if anybody is home. There are a few industrial buildings and businesses as I make my way down the street but none of them seem to have external cameras. So much for trying to be fortunate. The sun is just starting to break the crest of the city and everything I see on my journey is showered in golden orange sunlight. It is actually quite pretty. I wish my victim could see this particular one. Elizabeth, I know you are with me and can see this one, I wish you had never seen those last two. I'm sorry. The doors to the Hurricane From Hell are still locked tight. It's still before ten. I shouldn't be surprised. I'll just go around back and take one more quick peak and see if it's tight. The strip mall is slightly more occupied than it was a few hours prior, there is a complete void of those cute little green lizards I saw just a while ago. The smell of the dumpster permeates in five feet each way and is rather disgusting as I turn the corner behind the mattress place. There is a door behind the dumpster with the Hurricane From Hell logo we saw above the front doors on some kind of vinyl appliqué. It's unlocked. How can that be? It doesn't make sense. "Hello. Hello. Hello."

"May I help you?"

"Detective Kenny Spade, OPD."

"Yes detective."

"I am investigating a murder that occurred the night before last. I think the victim may have been a patron at you bar that night."

"There were a hundred or so people here a couple of nights ago. It's always busy after a concert." The woman appears annoyed with the imposition.

"Miss, is there a problem?"

"Excuse me?"

"I asked if there is a problem."

"I don't know detective, is there?"

"I'm sorry ma'am but you seem to be slightly upset with my inquiries. I was wondering if there is a problem."

"Look detective, I have a business here. It does not bode well for me to have people come to my bar and get murdered. It is a very competitive industry, especially over here where we cater to the locals. This is not International Drive where all the yahoo tourists go to party. This is my reputation here."

"I'm sorry, could I get your name."

"Why?"

"I feel kind of awkward calling you miss and ma'am all the time. I would just like to be more polite."

"My name is Diane. Listen detective, try to understand me here. A single woman has to fight for everything she gets, even in this day and age."

"Diane, nice to meet you. I certainly did not mean to create any problems for you. I think my victim went to the Barenaked Ladies concert at the O-rena and I thought she may have come here after."

"Do you have a picture?"

"Yes, here." Spade extends his hand holding a wallet size photo of the victim. "Do you have any video surveillance here?"

"I can't afford anything like that."

"I'm sorry. I understand but I had to ask. I need all the help I can get on this one."

"Listen detective, come by after dark. We'll run the picture by my bartenders. Both of them were here the other evening. Maybe I'll buy you a drink."

"Thank you I will. We'll see about the drink. Occupational hazard you know."

"Goodbye detective."

"Goodbye." Wow, she's a hard one to figure. Comes off like an ice queen. I never really thought about it being such a cut-throat industry. Maybe I will get lucky tonight. I wasn't lying; I really do need all the help I can get on this one. I try to stay out of bars as a rule given my past reckless inclinations, but I still responsibly enjoy an adult beverage with my friends on occasion. Elizabeth will help guide me through this situation. I cannot let her down by kicking back to my old ways. I hope the bartenders can remember one nondescript face in an atmosphere that breeds the contempt of invisibility and forgetfulness. It will not surprise me in the least to see the bartenders tell me absolutely nothing. I have to try, like I said I need the help. Bartenders are known to be great listeners by trade, much like children are, so maybe I can get lucky.

The wake was a very emotional experience. I go to the wake of every victim I encounter. Many of my colleagues find this practice morbid, but I find it a show of respect to the victim. I was not allowed to attend Elizabeth's funeral but I did get the message to her parents that she asked me to. I visit her grave religiously throughout the year on all special occasions. It is out of this practice that my pattern of attending wakes was formed. I have no contact with the Downings. This would only bring them more pain and bring me more questions, like why it took me three days to find her. I don't make a big deal about my presence at these gatherings. Today's mother was a little volatile, beating on me and cursing. The father was typically more stoic. I assured both of them that I was doing everything in my power to find the killer. I expressed my sympathies and took my absence. I find that I don't know where to go next. I have no lead except for that damn ace. I'm missing something. I have to be missing something.

The difficulty in catching killers is that you have to find the thread that links the killer to his victim. Frequently this requires that you become irrational. This in itself is an oxymoron, for you need to do what you have to fight and catch to be successful. It is always the one thing that keeps you going. Most serial killers slip only once. It truly is a slip. So it makes the homicide detective stay on his toes, for the tell tale clues are usually few and far between. You cannot afford to miss even the stupidest little piece of cloth or paper, or you will wind up with the Black Dahlia. The Black Dahlia was a famous call girl in Hollywood in the Great Depression era who was brutally murdered but whose case was never solved. This case was heading that way, toward a whole lot of conjecture and no sure fire answer for the family of the last case you worked. Such is the job of homicide detective. And the only sure fire clue I have in my current one is an ace of spades. The death card. That could mean anything to anyone with a demented mind. To me it means more. Why do I take this so personally? I need to remain objective if I am to catch this scumbag. Why can't I get a feel for this guy? What to do, what to do? Let's call Loot and see if he has any insight. Typically, I find him at the office. No, he does not have any new info. There is nothing from forensics. The tickets stub turned up no new leads. The clothes were clean. Right back where I started from. Damn, I know it's there. It's got to be.

Did you ever wonder as you stare at the moon why it never seems to move? And yet you can look at it fifteen seconds after you take your eyes off and it seems to have moved half a continent? Tonight is one of those nights as I zip down Interstate 4 toward the Hurricane From Hell. I fly down the road at close to ninety, and yet the moon does not move. But once I glance down to check the road, well when my gaze returns the moon seems to have grown twentyfold. Oh boy, it's going to be one of those nights. Damn, I hate this shit. I feel like this is going to blow up in my face. Big time. I sit in the parking lot and stare at the moon, maybe it has the answers. Elizabeth, keep me focused. I hit the burgundy blown glass doors of The Hurricane From Hell and ask for Diane. I find myself face to face with the bouncer with arms bigger than the Hulk. He is not amused. I flash the badge. Oh yeah, that was smart. Now he is really pissed. He directs me to the bar to wait for her. OK, that's where I was going anyway. Drink? Yeah, screw it. Make mine a dark beer. Tall glass, thanks for asking. Both of the bartenders look at me suspiciously, as if the bouncer had told them both that I had stolen a cookie from a little kid. Yeah, this was going to be a productive evening. As I sit there enjoying my beer, if that is possible with Godzilla giving you the eye constantly, Miss Diane made her return appearance. Hello, Diane, good to see you. No I didn't ask anything without your permission. I didn't want to alarm anyone. Yes, I realize that I didn't even make it past Godzilla, but I still wanted to wait.

"Beth, Joey this is Detective Spade, OPD Homicide. He is on the case of the girl murdered in the Hames Avenue alley the other evening. He wants to ask you both some questions. Detective."

"Hi. Could you guys take a look and see if any of you recognize the girl in this picture? I think she may have been in here the other night. It was Sunday. She went to the concert at the O-Rena. Doesn't look familiar. Thanks Beth. Joey? Not familiar. Damn. Diane, could I ask Godzilla?

"The name is Rock."

"Yes, you are." The monster asks to see the picture. Be my guest, I'm not stupid and I'm asking for your help here aren't I?

"Yeah, she was in here. Real pretty. She came in with two others. They were all pretty drunk when they came in; they left after a couple of hours. I don't watch the inside but I had no problems inside while they were there."

Great. That is about what I was expecting to hear, but I really could have used a little bit of guidance. Well, I know she was here. That did nothing for me as far as clues. It does however mean that my premonition was accurate. This is not a very endearing factor to me. I already talk to a dead girl on a daily basis. Now I have dreams about girls being killed. Shit. Why can't I come up with anything? I need to have a clear head to catch this psychopath. Hello. Hello? Hello? "Oh hi, Diane." I'm sorry. No I can't even begin to tell you where I was. If you only knew.

"Detective, I think you need a cup of coffee."

"That sounds like an excellent idea."

"Good. Let's go to the café and have a cup. My treat."

Done. We walk down the block past the rest of the strip mall that houses the Hurricane and cross a few more blocks before we get to the Coffee Café. I order a double espresso shot, Diane goes for the more conventional skim latte. The night air is refreshingly crisp after the usual afternoon thunderstorm cools off the early evening's muskiness. The stars are very promising but are more inclined to run and hide in the sky dominated by the luminescence of the protruding moon. The big dipper, as usual leads me to the collection of stars that form the constellation Downing, the collection of stars that lead me to the face of Elizabeth. My gaze locks upon it for a brief moment, even as Diane sits before me.

"A penny for your thoughts."

For my thoughts. I am pretty certain you don't want to share any of my thoughts. They scare me and I am used to them by now. A penny for my thoughts. Well, why can't I catch the SOB that killed that girl? Why do I see her get stalked in my dreams? Why am I so tortured by a playing card that mocks me for not solving this murder? Why did the killer leave the card there to start with? Why...

"Hello. Hello. Earth to Detective Spade."

"I'm sorry, what?"

"Are you OK detective? I don't mean to be rude, but that's twice today you totally were ignoring me. I understand you are preoccupied but it does not do a woman's ego very much homage to be put in a position of being transparent."

"Diane, I am very sorry. I don't mean to be rude. I am just trying to think of what I missed on this case. I am trying to re-trace everything in my head. I apologize. By the way, please call me Kenny."

"Well Kenny, I accept your apology. I know you are preoc-cupied but you just drifted away at the bar after you talked to Rock. That's why I invited you out for coffee. And then you did it to me once again. Am I losing it?" Or are you, she asks herself.

I look at the person before me for the first time, taking in the sight of a woman. Late thirties, long blonde hair about to the level of her shoulder blades. Fairly well endowed in the chest area with a solid build, not fat but muscular and solid. She really is in very good shape for a woman in her late thirties. I didn't see that this afternoon. I can't even think of the last time I even paid attention to the physical appearance of a wom-an. "Diane, I am very sorry. I get excessively wrapped up in my work sometimes. In fact, my boss told me the same thing as you earlier today."

"He's a smart man."

"Yes, he is." I chuckle. Diane inquires as to what is so funny. I tell her I was thinking about what she just said. Diane obviously does not follow. "You said my boss was a smart man." I continue. "It reminds me of a funny story. I had just been promoted to homicide from patrol. I was partnered up with a veteran, Detective Allaster. He was my mentor, for lack of a better word. Anyway, Allaster and I were working a domestic battery, a boyfriend who killed his girlfriend's mother." I look up at Diane who is following my story but does not have the look of someone who finds it amusing. I summon the waitress and order another coffee and ask Diane if she would care for a piece of dessert. The waitress then looks at Diane and gestures so as to see if she would like anything. Diane nods her head approvingly and orders a piece of cake, as do I. I continue with my story. "Anyway, Allaster gets a lead on this guy. Our suspect is hiding out at his cousins, off OBT. (OBT is a main road in south Orlando.) So Allaster decides to go check it out. I follow him like a good little rookie. Allaster tells me to go around the rear and then pounds on the front door and screams 'POLICE.' A second later this perp we're chasing comes barging through the back door. I draw my weapon and scream 'FREEZE.' The dude takes off like a bat out of hell running four blocks down toward a new apartment complex. So I start chasing him as Allaster radios for back up and begins to join in. The guy runs into the apartment complex, and this is my first homicide case so I'm thinking 'Oh great, a potential hostage situation.'" I look up and now see I have her interest. I continue, pleased with myself. "So I chase the guy up the stairwells of this complex. We go up six flights to the top floor, where he begins to bolt through the hallway. He blasts through an open door and runs through the living room and onto the fire escape and begins climbing. I keep chasing and radio my position to Allaster, who I find out later is still outside the complex. The people whose apartment I cut though start screaming at me but I just follow my suspect. The guy runs up to the roof and starts running across the roof of this apartment complex. It turns out the roof is full of air conditioners and skylights, so it's like a mini obstacle course up there.

We start dashing through the AC's and skylights and I chase him clear across the complex. I am in a full blown sprint when the guy reaches the end and stops and points a .38 at me. Well, I'm going so fast I can't stop so I just lunge at him and we go crashing through one of the skylights. There is a tremendous roar and thud as we land in someone's bathroom on the floor. The guy tries to get up again but I whip out my cuffs and cuff him to the pipe under the sink. He then scrambles around but I pick up the .38 and point it at him. I then secure him the right way and stand him up. Well, just then Allaster comes through the door, I guess he followed the noise or whatever, I'm not even sure. He takes the suspect away and instantaneously I have tons of back up with me, including my CO Lieutenant Murphy. So Loot, I'm sorry, Lieutenant Murphy comes in to check on me when from out of nowhere the little old grandma jumps out of the bathtub and starts wailing on me with a toilet brush, cursing me the whole time. It seems as though she was taking a bath when she was interrupted by two idiots crashing through her skylight." I begin to laugh as I continue. "So Loot grabs the brush from her and hands her a towel and apologizes. After a few minutes the scene is cleared and we walk out into the hall. When we hit the hall Loot turns to me and says, 'I guess you should have knocked.' 'You're a smart man' I replied." With that Diane busts out laughing and I soon join in. We spend a few minutes razzing over my toilet brush beating and then just talking about simple life things like cops and bars. Then Diane announces she really needs to return to her bar, when I have an idea.

"Lieutenant Murphy is a friend of mine and invited me to a barbecue Sunday. Let me make today up to you. May I take you to this barbecue? It's sort of an opportunity to reinvent myself as a human being and not a zombie. I would like the opportunity to start off on a better foot."

"You know detective, I am not really sure about you. You are a little weird. I don't know if I am interested in anything more than coffee, especially a cop party."

"Loot is one of the most down to earth people anyone ever met. He has the most amazing wife also, Kate. This is not a cop party. It is simply a barbecue with my friend. I was not intending to be too forward with you. If I offended you in any way, I assure you it was unintentional."

"OK."

"I'm sorry?"

"OK. I will go with you Sunday."

"Thank you. I will be the perfect gentleman. If you are uncomfortable at any point I will excuse myself and take you where you want to go. Please don't feel obligated to do this."

"It's OK. I like challenges. I am after all a single woman in a brutal man's world."

"Point taken. Diane, thank you. I am really looking forward to this."

"Don't get all mushy on me detective."

"It's Kenny."

"Yes, you told me." What follows is a stirring rendition of The "Sounds of Silence." Only there is no radio playing. Just a spine tingling chill of awkward and uncomfortable face time, with neither one of us knowing what we should say or do. I very coyly look into her big brown eyes to see if I can gauge her comfort level in my presence. What in the hell did I just get myself into? Stupid, stupid little man. She probably can't stand to be here with you. She was trying to be nice by taking you for coffee. Or maybe she just wanted to see how uninteresting I can be. What a jackass.

A look of confusion runs through the face of detective Kenny Spade. Wow, he's a strange one. Diane has not interacted with someone like him before. Granted, she has not been the luckiest person in the world in terms of love. That two time loser Jake is serving twenty for shooting a liquor store clerk. Don't forget Steve, who ran off with her former best friend. Yes, she is definitely not the luckiest. This Detective Spade though, he is a strange one all right. He is kind of cute in a rugged outdoor kind of way. He has long wavy shoulder length brown hair with a scruffy beard. Looks to be in fairly good shape, for a cop anyway. But man is he puzzling. Have I really lost it? I own my own bar, I could stand to shed a few pounds but I am not any pig. Did I really lose it? Damn, am I too old? Oh god, what's wrong with me. A twinge of self-doubt envelops Diane. The kind of self-doubt that only a woman could understand. The kind that eats you up inside. The need to impress. The need to feed your vanity. Where does this detective wander off too? I invited him here, didn't I? He doesn't even seem to recognize the fact I'm here. Maybe he's just an asshole. Oh damn, why did I say yes? Moron.

"Diane."

'"Yes."

"I'm sorry, I'm a little preoccupied. I think you are a very beautiful woman and I am sorry I have not given you your due props this evening. If you allow me, I will try to make it up to you Sunday, if you are still interested. Thank you very much for bringing me here. I wish I had treated you with more attention tonight. I'm sorry. I need to go back to the office. Can I walk you back to the bar, please?"

"Sure." Well at least he has manners. It figures she would find a guy with manners and he is not interested in women. Or possibly he is married to his job. Well at least this nightmare date is over. Do we dare to try this again, she asks herself.

Damn, I just blew it. I found a gorgeous single woman, my age. Single. Successful. She owns her own business. Only the great Kenny Spade could screw up something like this. Oh Elizabeth, what do I do? I will not fail you Elizabeth. I will catch this prick. Is it wrong for me to pursue some inner happiness with this maniac out there? It is my dedication to you Elizabeth, which has helped me keep this city of ours safe. I will not fail you. Is there room in me for both of you? Oh God, what do I do?

THREE

The last three days were spent in a quagmire of tumultuous crusades against my inner demons and a card that refuses to end the constant taunting of my inadequacies. The malevolence that permeated through the inner fibers of my being tortured me for the duration of the three days. I made phone calls to Diane each of the days. They were usually greeted with something akin of I'm good. How are you? See you soon. OK bye. At this point I can't honestly say that I can blame her. I guess I really don't know how to interact socially with women anymore. I did not do a lot to distinguish myself to her on our coffee date, if that is indeed the proper word to associate with our encounter. I am actually a little surprised Diane didn't attempt to cancel this barbecue. I imagine she must feel very awkward. Professionally, that goddamn ace of spades has been absolutely correct, and informing me of this. I still have no leads. Forensics has not given me one single ray of light. I cannot tell that young girl's parents a god damn thing about who killed their little girl. It is only Elizabeth that gives me any positive reinforcement. She still believes in me, if only I knew why. Anyway, the butterflies that dominate my belly tell me that I am headed for a very, very long afternoon. I pull up to the Hurricane From Hell and put the car in park. Here we go.

Oh my god, here we go. Deep down she really hoped that detective Spade would actually not show up. Well here he is, at the door to my bar. Damn, why didn't I just cancel and let this blow away? "Hey, Di, he's kind of cute." Yeah thanks, Beth. Well he is kind of cute, again. Still, he is one strange fellow.

WHAT THE HELL IS WRONG WITH ME? SHIT! WHY AM I DO-
ING THIS? He looks really good, though.

"Hello, Diane."

"Hello Detective."

Detective. Great. She is still pissed at me. Wow. This is going
to be one hell of a day. Not that I blame her. Don't get me
wrong. I know I suck at this. I don't know what the hell I was
thinking. I probably am going to ruin her day. What kind of a
jerk am I? Oh boy. She really looks great. A pink sleeveless perfectly accentuates her bust line. A simple pair of blue jeans finishes off what should promise to be some very shapely legs.
Dressy black Gucci boots complete the look. Casual with a
touch of class. Hey, when did I become such the fashion police?
Well, this I know. It works for her. I hope I don't scare her off
right away. Boy, I hope I don't make this day totally suck for
her.

More awkward silence. This becoming a staple for this guy.
He does have a little taste though. Nice and simple. Blue jeans,
a pair of slip on Sketchers and a button up the front white shirt.
He has a tattoo on his upper left arm. An ace of spades. How
clever. Why didn't he just get skull and bone saying mommy?
He does have some very nice shoulder length auburn hair and a
well maintained beard. Obviously he cares somewhat about his
appearance. The car is a late eighties Corvette. It has some paint
fade, but the interior is kept up on. It sounds pretty good. It also
moves at a very good clip. According to my very strange companion, his friend Lieutenant Dan lives in Maitland. It is a very
nice neighborhood in the northern sector of Orange County.
We get off the exit to 434 and head west approximately two and
a half miles. It is a very nice neighborhood. One of those new
subdivisions. The house is Florida peach, with professionally
landscaped grounds and a double wide driveway. Detective
Spade parks his Vette in front of the yard. He gets out and rush-
ers to the other side of the car to open the door for me. WHY
DOES THIS ALWAYS HAPPEN TO ME? Every time I meet a guy
I peg to be a jerk, there he goes and tries to reel me back in.
Why would a guy, fairly cute and yet with some serious emo-

tional and social issues, have to come across the car and play with my head after I was getting ready to lower the boom? Do you have any idea how hard it is in this day and age to find any kind of a man with manners? Most guys only care about where they can put their beer and their dick. I own a bar, remember? Trust me on that one. Manners. The one thing any guy could show me that could make me mushy. Damn you, Kenny Spade.

"Hey Loot, what's going on?"

"Spade, you made it. I wasn't sure you would."

"I told you I was coming Loot."

"And may I inquire as to who this lovely lady might be?"

"Loot, this is Diane. "

"Diane, it is very nice to meet you. You look very nice today." Lieutenant Dan looks right at Diane. "Any friend of Spade's is a friend of mine and always welcome here."

"Kate. Oh god, Kate, how good to see you." I make a beeline to Kate Murphy, who has just stepped outside the gate that leads to the backyard. "Damn Kate, it's been so long."

"Well Kenny Spade, exactly whose fault do you suppose that would be?" I finally reach the gate and give her a big bear hug, picking her a good few feet off the ground. Dan Murphy turns his attention to Diane. He extends his hand and grabs her lower arm. "Come follow me. Welcome to my home. This is my wife Kate. Kate Murphy."

"I'm sorry, how very rude of me," I interject, "Diane this is my Lieutenant, Dan Murphy, whom I call Loot. This beautiful woman over here is his wife, Kate. She is the greatest woman that I know. She would have to be to put up with Loot and me."

"Kenny, I haven't had much putting up with you recently. It's been months. Where have you been? You haven't come to see me."

"I'm sorry Kate. I've been busy at work."

"Work, hmmm?" Kate queries, "Maybe I should talk to your boss about this." She shoots Dan a mocking feign of disgust. "Maybe I should."

"Nice work Spade" Loot replies, "You just put me in hot water with the boss." We all break into laughter. Diane is reassured that they seem to be a friendly couple. She is still not confident in her companion for the afternoon, or her feelings for him. Kate, the ever gracious hostess, invites everyone to sit in the back. "Diane, what would you like to drink? I have iced tea, lemonade, Coke, Sprite and three different types of beer." A beer, sure. Regular or light. One dark beer coming up. Kenny, this is for you. Kate passes him a nice ale, one of Spade's favorites. She grabs a beer for her husband and one for herself. We sit and shoot the breeze for an hour or so, eating chips and pretzels and shading them from the sun under the deck umbrella. Dan excuses himself and invites me to go in to the house and see his new audio video room. The girls remain outside nursing their beverages.

Kate opens the conversation a little more. "So Diane, how long have you been going with Spade?"

'We are not going. This is our second event together. The first blew up like a towering inferno."

"Oh boy, I'm sorry. I hope all this mish mosh does not make you too uncomfortable. I can't say enough about Kenny. I love that guy."

"I can't really get a feel for him Kate. He seeks to be so disinterested in me and yet he can be so sweet. I was ready to throw in the towel a few times but he comes across with some very well placed charm and lures me back to him."

"Well Diane, the fact he brought you here tells me he is definitely not disinterested in you. You are gorgeous and intelligent. How could he not be interested?"

"Oh I don't know. Both times we went out together he totally zoned out and ignored me. When I finally got his attention back and questioned him on this, he said he was preoccupied with work."

"That is a factual statement, Diane. He is a workaholic."

"But he doesn't even see me, even when he looks at me. It's as if I'm transparent. It does wonders for my self confidence, you know."

"Oh Diane, it's not you. It's just how Spade is. He spends all his time at work. He works more than my Dan does."

"Why does everyone call him Spade?"

"I don't know As long as I've known him he's been called Spade. He likes it. I'll call him Kenny every now and again just to remind him that he is a human and not just a machine."

"Kate, I'm curious how long ago did you meet Kenny?"

"Gosh, it's been four or five years now. Dan brought him home after the Christmas party. He was a mess."

"Nothing has changed."

"Diane, has he told you anything about himself yet?"

"Not even a birthday."

"A little help, just between us girls. Do you remember four or five years back? There was that girl in the woods that was held for three days and repeatedly raped and mutilated. Kenny was the one who found her. He arrested the guy. He would have killed him too, except Dan came in with the backup wave. She died in his arms. He couldn't handle it. He was out of control. He went to Vegas and got himself deep in the shit. They sent him home, with an escort. It continued here for months. Until that year's Christmas party. He was certifiable. Nasty, drunk and stupid. Dan cut him off and brought him here. The next morning we talked. Ever since then Spade has just totally immersed himself in his work. He's like a man on a mission. That's how Dan and I became friends with Spade. Please don't tell him that I told you. Maybe some time he'll be ready to tell you himself. I don't want to ruin that for him. Just keep that in mind. You always have to do what's right for yourself."

"Wow, I had no idea."

"I think I'm getting hungry. Let's go get the boys to start the grill." A nod of approval from Diane starts the ladies walkabout into the house.

The video room in the house is decked out with deep mahogany. It starts with the molding and is accentuated with a beautiful cabinet that surrounds the sixty-inch TV and houses a myriad of audio surround sound equipment that I would not have the slightest idea how to use. It is accentuated with variations of white throughout the remainder of the room to enhance its beauty even further. Nice stuff is the comment I make. Thanks.

"So Spade, where did you meet this girl?"

"Diane owns the bar."

"What bar?"

"The bar from the case. The Hurricane From Hell. I went there to follow the leads."

"Spade, are you kidding me? You went to the bar? Are you getting personally involved with someone from the case?"

"Relax boss. There is no lead. There is nothing to be gained from the bar other than the fact the victim was there. Secondly, the way I'm going I doubt Diane will ever want to hear from me again. I screwed it up again. Face it, socially I'm a pariah. Professionally I'm bating .000." At this very moment the ladies surface at the doorway to the room.

"Dan, you said no shop talk today. I thought I heard shop talk. How about starting that grill? We girls are getting hungry." A quick 'Amen' from the background lets the boys know that Diane is in agreement with Kate's assessment. Some well timed scurrying from the men let the ladies know that their message has been heard. Kate gives Dan that naughty little mischievous look, the one that says if you weren't so cute you'd be in trouble. The one that says if there wasn't company present you would be in big trouble. VERY, VERY BIG TROUBLE. The twinkle is duly noted by Dan. Message received. Dan heads to the freezer to grab the meat. I tag behind. On my way out the door I give Kate's hand a quick squeeze. Thank you. It goes unspoken but it is understood. Now I have to figure out how to deal with Diane. This was a bright idea. I thought I would be able to hide in the environment. Wrong. I need to make a play or run away. Well, Romeo what's it going to be? Are you going to let her know that you are interested in her? Shit or get off the pot, isn't that the expression?

Diane catches the squeeze. A sign of appreciation from Spade to Kate. That's what attracts Diane to Spade. His appreciation and enthusiasm for what he does. For his job. For his victims justice. And now the very same thing, with his friend. A quick simple show of affection. The question is does Spade have the same appreciation and enthusiasm for her? Enthusiasm is a good thing, but if she can't tell where that enthusiasm is directed then she has a big decision ahead. Does the good detective have potential or a desperate life sucking force? She is going to have to run to this or away from this. Great.

Well Romeo, its go time. If you are serious about this attractive, elegant woman with you then you better make your play. Show her you are interested. I run in to help Loot with the food. We bring out the stakes, sausages, chicken and kielbasa. The smell that runs off the grille when the food is placed sends an aroma out that would make people hungry across three counties. Mmmmmm. It smells good. The boys banter back and forth over the grille. I make sure to get Diane another drink. Dan makes sure to rib me about being a perfect gentleman. It is actually a perfect tension breaker and the mood lightens considerably. A few smiles and laughs even crack the face of the seemingly detached me. Diane eases into her chair and relaxes. There are jokes and stories flowing freely. Maybe this could work, I say to myself. Diane senses a glimmer of potential. Perhaps attending this barbecue was a good idea after all.

The ringing of the phone breaks the jovial atmosphere. Kate runs in to the living room and grabs it. Some mumbling can be heard from in the house. Kate comes out with the phone in tow. "Work." The tone of her voice says it all. The perfect way to ruin a perfectly good barbecue.

"This is Lieutenant Murphy. Yes, yes I understand." Concurrently, my cellphone rings.

"Spade." Nice phone decorum, Diane muses. "No, I'm off today. Assign it to the detectives on duty." A pause. "What do you mean I need to be there?" Another pause. On the other phone Dan acknowledges the person on the other end and says he'll be down shortly. I am a little less happy. A few pleasantries are exchanged until I also acknowledge my presence will be granted shortly. I hang up the phone and swear under my breath. Dan runs in to the house and grabs his work stuff. I follow him in. What do you mean it has something to do with me personally? What kind of message? Loot, this isn't good. Yeah, Yeah, I know, I know.

"I'm sorry Diane, I have to go. Duty calls. Can I take you home on my way?"

"Kenny, don't worry. I'll take her home" Kate interjects. An approving nod from Diane lets him know that this is OK.

"Thanks Kate." I lean over and give her a kiss on the cheek. I go over to Diane. "Diane, I'm really sorry about this. I had a great time. I hope you will allow me to make this up to you." I then reach over and gently kiss her on the lips. "I'm sorry." I whisper again. Dan kisses Kate goodbye and with that the men, and the atmosphere of promise, are gone.

FOUR

The red Corvette sits diagonally in between a light post and a fire hydrant. The area is a stream of red and blue strobes, alternating in sequence, being dispersed for a city block. The flickering of the blue strobes gives the Corvette a purple sheen to the car. By the time Dan Murphy arrives on the scene the locale is littered with detectives, patrolmen, coroners' officials, police and press photographers and the usual swarm of curious rubberneckers attracted to the flurry of colors that saturate the Orlando sky. It is very unusual for anyone to see this much activity on a Sunday in the business district down off Westmoreland. There is a construction company warehouse and a pool cleaning company next to the Sunshine Bank. The passage of humanity streamed to the rear of the bank through the drive through and back next to the employee parking section. There is a small clump of palm and oak trees next to the corner of the lot. It borders a neighborhood house surrounded by a six foot picket fence.

Dan funnels his way through the quagmire of uniforms over to the spot of greatest activity. WHAT THE…? Where is Spade? "WHERE THE HELL IS SPADE?" Dan grabs the first flatfoot he sees and spins him around like a dradle. "WHERE THE HELL IS HE?" The officer just stands there with a stupid look on his face. SPADE!!! SPADE!!! SPADE!!!! Someone from the mass of humanity says that Spade was seen going out toward the street. Lieutenant Murphy storms toward the front of the bank. He twirls back rapidly and barks his command. "GET THEM ALL OUT OF HERE. TOUCH NOTHING! SECURE

THIS!! TEN FOOT PERIMITER! DO IT! NOW!!!!!!" Lieutenant Murphy fires back around and beelines to the front of the bank near the ATM. "WHERE THE HELL IS SPADE? SPADE?!!" The call goes out. Lieutenant, he's over here. Lieutenant Murphy walks down the walk and to the street, then in the direction of the Corvette. Next to the open drivers front door is an aromatic pile of human vomit. In the driver's seat with feet sticking out onto the pavement is Kenny Spade. He is running his hands through the sides of his hair. What the fuck. What the fuck? What the fuck? What the fuck? WHAT THE FUCK???? The theme is repetitive. It gets more and more boisterous and animated with each passing tirade. A few times Spade smashes his hands on the wheel, once hard enough to draw blood. Lieutenant Murphy makes his way over to the Corvette. "Spade, what the hell is going on?" What the fuck? What the fuck? What the fuck? "Spade? Spade?" What? WHAT! Oh, sorry Loot.

"Spade, what the hell is going on here?"

"Fuck if I know!"

"Spade?!"

"Jesus Loot, I have no idea. None. But it scares me."

"Come on Kenny."

"Loot I swear. I have no idea. I SWEAR." The look of concern on Lieutenant Dan Murphy's face is replaced by one of bewilderment. He is not sure of exactly how to read Spade. What the hell is going on here? This is totally unfathomable. WHAT THE HELL!

"Spade?"

"What?"

"Help me here."

"Jesus fucking Christ Loot. I have no fucking idea what the fuck is going on. HOW THE FUCK SHOULD I KNOW? I WAS WITH YOU, REMEMBER?"

Whoa, whoa, whoa. Calm down there cowboy. Relax. It's OK. "Spade?"

"What?"

"Listen amigo, we got some work to do. Pull yourself together. We have another case to solve. We're cool. Let's get to work."

"OK boss."

I arise from the Vette. I head toward Loot. Let's go. This plethora of looks at Loot and I would make even the most hardened of people queasy to their stomachs. Lieutenant Murphy is quick to snap at all of them and anyone who dares to acknowledge in any way shape or form the presence of the man relevant to the issue at hand would not want to be subjected to his wrath. Dan Murphy was very well respected and loved in the Orlando Police Department and there were very few who would dare tangle with him. He was a very quiet man and slight of stature, but he commanded the utmost of respect. With the exception of an arrogant prick, Lieutenant Poncher from IAD, he had no known enemies. The amount of looks the duo got was quickly silenced by the glares of Lieutenant Murphy. And along with the support of Officers Ronan and Tolliver, the first homicide detectives on the scene, I had an inner sanctum that made me feel a little more secure. Very little, but better than nothing. We meander their way through the sea of professionals and curiosity hounds and find their way toward the vision of horror that penetrates the inner being in all of them.

Lieutenant Murphy and I stand in front of the lifeless corpse of yet another woman. This one, also in her mid to late twenties, of Asian descent, lay slumped over a stanchion that prevents cars from going too far forward in the parking space. The slice across her throat was a clean symmetrical slice, most likely made with a clean effortless motion that made her death rapid and painless. She was probably dead before she even slumped to the ground. The limp pile of flesh that stood before them was once a beautiful young girl. Her jet black hair was tinged with an auburn hue. She wore a pair of navy dress slacks and a frilly white blouse. It was a familiar deep red now, eerily similar to the blouse of the first victim. Her left breast was exposed, just as this killer had done with his first victim. Leaning against her torso was another card. The ace of spades. However, this card was far more dastardly. There was a great red smudge on the corner. But this card was different. It was a giant card, the size of one of the cards you would see a clown or a musician use at a circus. Scrawled in the card was a message. It was written in red ink or blood. It read as follows. DETECTIVE SPADE. YOU DISAPPOINT ME. I EXPECT MORE OF YOU. CATCH ME IF YOU CAN. It was signed "The Ace of Spade." Lieutenant Murphy and I stood there motionless, staring at the corpse, the card, and the message for evil it promoted.

"What the fuck is this, a game?"

"Damned if I know."

By now there was a buzz around the crime scene. The whispers were growing louder. There was a serial killer. He was taunting the police. He used the death card to heckle them. The press crews gathered outside the perimeter clamoring for any morsel of information they could latch on to, correct or not. A serial killer in O-Town. What a lead in story! In time for the six o'clock Sunday news. A ratings bonanza. The race was on to see which news group could commandeer enough tidbits to piece together a story to lead in to the respective news casts. A serial killer was taunting the police. He was stalking young single girls and butchering them. He cut their heads almost totally off. He left satanic slurs behind. The stories circulating became more ridiculous and farfetched as they became more plentiful. Lieutenant Murphy had ordered a lock down as best he could, but on a glorious Sunday afternoon in Orlando it was hard not to draw some amount of attention. There was very little that could be done to control such rumors. The police could only do so much. Detectives Tolliver and Ronan had set up a second perimeter thirty feet around the body, at Lieutenant Murphy's request. No one was to get near this body.

There was no evidence left behind. There were no footprints, no fingerprints, and no knife left at the murder scene. Just a card. A card that taunted me. A card that a serial Killer left behind. A card challenging me. Inviting me, no daring me. Catch me if you can. Why me? How does this monster know me? Why has he singled me out? It has to be personal. It is the only explanation that makes any sense.

"Spade, what the hell do we do?"

"Loot, I don't know. Let's get Jane Doe to the morgue. Have a complete autopsy done. Keep these paparazzi piranha away from here. This guy has to know me. Somehow he has to know me. I'm going to process the scene with a fine tooth comb. He must have left me something. Dr. Frankenstein says it's always a game with these freaks. I have to find the clue he left me. It must be here. Then I'll go back to the office and run my previous case files. We've got to be missing something. We've got to be."

"You do have a bit of notoriety in this city, Kenny. It would not be that hard to put your name to a murder case in recent Orlando history. Check all your case logs for people coming up to trial or parole. Maybe someone is trying to distract us."

Or maybe it's a copycat. A publicity hound, just trying to call me out. Well it's personal now. I will catch this mother..."

"Calm down cowboy. You have a job to do. Let's get to work." Loot's tone is firm and poignant. Spade knows he is right.

"OK, lieutenant, I am going to the hole. I will keep you informed."

"OK Spade, run with it. I have to go deal with the press. Tolliver, Ronan keep the perimeter secure. No one gets near this body except coroners. Understood?" The pair nod their approval. Lieutenant Murphy heads off to control the damage.

I sit and look at the body. Who found her? Detective Ronan points to a male in his late teens sitting over in an unmarked car behind the bank at the edge of the perimeter. How long ago did the call come in? At two forty-five. Gee thanks. I'm a little preoccupied here. What time is it now? Four thirty-three. How long has this kid been here? The whole time? Just sitting in the car? Come on guys give me a fucking break. I grab a uniformed officer. Go get me a few Cokes. Just shut up and do it. I'll be over by the unmarked. I walk in the direction of the back of the Sunshine Bank building. On the way I intercept the coroners' people going to bring the body to the morgue. Listen I want full pictures. I DON'T FUCKING CARE IF IT'S YOUR JOB. GET ME THE FUCKING PICTURES OF EVERYTHING YOU SEE. DON'T MISS ANY OF IT. DO NOT REMOVE HER BEFORE YOU DO THIS. AND GIVE ME SOME KIND OF IDEA OF A TIME OF DEATH. SHIT. Damn argumentative people. Just do it. I then complete my journey over to the car holding the witness. Hey there. What's your name? Jack, nice to meet you. How are you doing? Good. How old are you? Seventeen. OK Jack. How did you happen across the body? At this juncture the officer arrives at the car with two cokes. Jack, I imagine you are thirsty. You have been sitting here for a while now. I hope you like Coke. Thank you, officer. I could really use this right about now, how bout you Jack?

"So Jack, how did you happen across the body?"

"I was cutting through the lot. That's my friend's house right there. I cut through the bank all the time. That's when I saw Lisa."

"Lisa. You know her?"

"It's Lisa Yeung. She's the bank president or whatever you call her. She's got a plaque hanging on the wall inside. That's how I know her name. Any piece that hot I had to know her name, you know what I'm saying?"

"Was she a friend?"

"No. she would not give us the time of day. But we knew who she was. Like I said she's hot, you know?"

"I see. Listen Jack, when you found her did you touch anything? Did you see any knife or pick up anything? Did you touch her?"

"No. I grabbed the cell and called 911. I could tell by looking at her she was dead; you know what I'm saying? I didn't do anything just called and waited. Are you the dude in the card?"

"I'm sorry?"

"The card. It was addressed to some cop. Was it you?"

"I'm not sure yet. I'll look at the card later, first I have to get her out of here. Then I'll get to work on the rest. Listen Jack, I'm going to let you go now. Here's my card. If you think of anything you think may be important call me. Did the officer take your information? Good. Jack you did a good thing today. Thank you."

Jack takes my card and runs over to his friend's house. I turn and head back to the victim, one Lisa Yeung. By the time I get to her, the bag Lisa Yeung has been reduced to is being zipped closed. The coroners' guys are loading her on to the stretcher. The forensic investigators are just wrapping up the photographs of the area. Yo guys, photograph underneath where she was. Get it all. We need all the help we can get. After the coroner gets her in the van and heads to the morgue the crowd slowly begins to dissipate. Lieutenant Murphy has held a press conference and the news vans scatter as if Paul Newman had just broken for a new game in *The Hustler*. The race is on to scoop all the other networks to headline the six o'clock newscast. It was already past five. Channel Nine stayed behind to do a remote broadcast but was kept a block away by OPD's finest. It had been a glorious Sunday afternoon with none of the common Orlando afternoon thunderstorms. In fact, it had not rained since late Friday. This aided me because anything that was left behind was not washed away yet. I squat over the parking space that was the final resting spot of Lisa Yeung. I collect blood from the ground. I was sure the forensics people had done this already, but it did not matter. This killer had made it even more personal than the rest of my cases. I stare intently, scanning the area for anything. No footprints were distinguishable. A Wrigley's gum wrapper. It could have been from anyone but let's grab it just in case. I twirl the wrapper with my hand. What happened here? Do you have a story to tell? Any dirty little secrets you can reveal to me? I concentrate on the wrapper. A cool breeze flows across my back, sending a tingly shudder through my spine. Hello Elizabeth. I know. This jerk is taunting me. No, I don't know why. But he obviously knows me. I have to be missing something, Elizabeth, I have to be. I'll get him, you can count on that. You always believe in me, more than I do. I don't understand it but you do. Even after I let you down. You always did. Thank you.

"Spade?"

"Yep."

"Who are you talking to?"

"No one."

"Spade, were you talking to Elizabeth again? I thought you were going to let her go and forgive yourself."

"Sorry Loot, don't know what you mean."

"Yeah, right. Listen Spade let's get back to the office and move on to the next thing."

"Sure. How are the piranhas?"

"In a feeding frenzy."

"Fabulous." I get up and turn toward Lieutenant Murphy, preparing to go. Just then a flicker of metal grabs my attention. "Hello there." I bend over and pick it up and place it in another evidence bag. Loot questions what I have found. "We'll see." We walk past the bank toward the street where the Corvette is parked. The vomit puddle has dried up and looks like the pizza creature from Star Trek. Channel Nine news screams questions toward the two detectives. "Is there a serial killer in Orlando preying upon women? Is he leaving secret messages for the police? Do you have any leads? Is it Detective Spade's case?" I just wave my right hand and jump into the Corvette. Loot swats the top of the car twice and I launch the Vette toward the vicinity of the interstate. Lieutenant Murphy jumps into his cruiser and takes off. I get the address from the wallet of Lisa Yeung and drives toward the southern section of town. I got to her block down near Universal Studios. I park in the street and walk toward the door. I stand out there for a few minutes and then knock on the door. A muscular African-American gentleman answers the door. "May I help you?"

"I am looking for the residence of Lisa Yeung. Does she live here?"

"Why are you asking? Who are you?"

I flash the badge and introduce myself as Detective Spade, Orlando Police. Am I in the right place?

"Yes, Lisa lives here. Is she in some kind trouble? She stayed at her girlfriend's house last night for her bachelorette party.

We're getting married next weekend. They went to Daytona. Is something wrong?"

"I'm sorry sir, but I have some horrible news. Lisa is dead. She was killed sometime between yesterday and today." What followed was the same emotional breakdown I saw every time I had to tell someone's family the tragic news. This monster of a man turned to chocolate pudding, falling to his knees sobbing uncontrollably. Then came the rage, with the questions. How did she die? Who did it? Did we arrest him already? What the hell were we waiting for? I did my best to comfort, console and reassure the man. I hated these moments. But I was good at them. The best that OPD had. Every time I left the house I went into my car and wept. It went on for a few minutes. It was always Elizabeth that came to console me. This time was no different.

I sat at my desk and looked at the gum wrapper in my left hand and the piece of metal in my right. The television in the corner of the office repeats the top news story of the day. Lieutenant Dan Murphy of OPD Homicide confirms there is a young lady that was murdered behind the Sunshine Bank off Westmoreland. He has no indication if it was linked to murder by the Arena a few days ago. No, he has no comment on a serial killer running through the town. No, he knows nothing of a note being left with the body. Lieutenant Murphy walks in to the precinct and glances toward the screen. "Damn, they shot me from my bad side. I look fat from this side."

"I told you Loot, they're piranhas." Just then the screen floats to the shot of Detective Spade waving when he left the scene and jumping into his car and zooming away. "Piranhas. I didn't realize anyone still used the word 'zooming' anymore."

"Nice Spade. So you got anything?"

"Yeah chief. I got two bodies, two cards, a lot of blood, a gum wrapper, a piece of broken metal, a 17-year-old kid that liked the second victim, a killer that has a vendetta with me, a lady I like that I have probably scared away for good, and a car that zooms."

"Wow Spade, I didn't realize you had enough room inside of you to carry all that sarcasm."

"Yeah Loot, I can do it all. What do you say we get the hell out of here and go grab a beer?"

"You know Spade, that's a damn good idea. Let's go." I lock the gum wrapper and metal chard in my desk and grab the keys. Don't worry scumbag, I'll be back. On the way to the bar I call Kate and ask if Diane is still there. It's around ten fifteen. Kate tells me she dropped Diane to work about eight. Kate says Diane is very nice. She likes her. Thanks Kate. See you. Thanks for everything today. I hang up and calls Loot. "Yeah Loot, we're going to the Hurricane From Hell. Its downtown in that strip mall by the O-Rena on SOBT. Don't worry, I know the bartenders there. They all love me. Yeah, I know that's easy to believe. I'll meet you there. And your wife said to call her. She's worried. OK Loot, I'll see you in a few." I am not a driver that can be contained. Lieutenant Murphy knows this and no longer makes an attempt to keep up.

Where was her car? Why was she behind the bank? Where was she going? Damn, there are so many things going on in my head. Why the hell am I going to the Hurricane? I hope I don't piss her off more. She has to be mad, and just when we were starting to get comfortable together. Hopefully this doesn't blow up in my face. I would like the chance to just apologize one more time and see if I can salvage this relationship, if that is indeed what you could call this. Plus, I could really use a beer. And Loot is going to be joining me. Damn, my head is filled with more junk than Sigmund Freud's. I have to start sorting through the crap in my cranium or I am never going to make any progress toward stopping this psycho.

The Corvette streams toward the O-Rena exit off Interstate 4 and glides itself down the exit ramp and makes the left that takes it to the Hurricane From Hell. The bar is not crowded but fairly active for a Sunday night. Rock is outside in his customary position making sure everyone knows that the hulk is still alive. He obviously feels my presence because my radar lock alarm goes off as soon as I exit from the car. I walk up to the stained glass doors and greet Rock with a 'what's up.' The response I get is a sneer that says if you hurt her I'll use you to floss my alligator's teeth. Sorry Hercules, but this day went shitty too fast for me to engage you in any playful banter. I rumble through the doors and sit at the far corner of the bar. Beth is the first one to approach, also with that what the heck do you want look printed all over her face.

"Diane is not here!" Obviously I did not win her over on my first visit. I hope my luck went better with Diane.

"I'm not here to cause anyone any grief."

"She's not here!"

"OK, I'm feeling you. Can I have a Sam Adams please?"

"I said she's not here."

"Look, I understand if you are not thrilled with me. I especially understand if Diane's not happy with me. A friend of mine is meeting me here. I just want to chill for a few minutes and have a few beers with my friend. Is that OK? I'm not here for trouble."

"Why can't you go someplace else?" You know I hope my beer is as chilly as the atmosphere is toward me. This Hurricane seems like it came from Antarctica, not hell.

"Beth, how about a fresh start? Let me have a Sam. When my friend arrives if you are still not happy with my presence then we will have one beer and we will both leave. I don't want to start any problems for you or gigantor outside. Is that acceptable?" Beth looks at Joey who glances over toward the mirror behind the bar as if he were waiting for a sign and nods slightly for the affirmative. She pulls out a glass from underneath and opens the tap. The head on it is bigger than that of the space aliens you see on TV. I guess I should have expected that. I utter thanks. That doesn't work. She offers me nuts. I quip that I seem to have the nuts department covered already. Beth cracks me a smile. Joey can't decide if he wants to laugh or puke. I pay more attention to the TV showing some stupid chick flick trying to keep the peace. This is the calm before the storm unless Loot shows up soon. I finish my first. Beth offers me a second. I once again say thanks. Another smile. Maybe there's hope for me yet. I sit through the sappy story about a dead mother whose ghost saves her gone astray child and await the local news. I just finish off my second when I hear a 'Kenny Spade' from the entrance. I instinctively twist toward the front and am very surprised to see Kate Murphy standing at the door. Loot strolls in behind her. Kenny Spade, what a surprise to see you in a place like this. Kate is just playing this up to the max. A little too good, because in one second Rock is sure to stick his head inside the bar to make sure that I have not created any more problems. Kate comes and sits next to me and gives me a kiss. Loot grabs the empty stool on my left.

"What are you doing here Kate?" The surprise in my voice cannot be masked.

"What you want me to leave already? Here I thought we were friends."

"Whoa, whoa, whoa. I am thrilled you are here. I think it's just what the doctor ordered. Speaking of which, Kate, Loot, the lovely lady behind the bar is Beth. That's Joey down the end. What would you like to drink?"

Beth comes over and introduces herself to both of my friends. Loot orders a lite, while his beautiful bride orders a vodka cranberry with a splash of OJ. Loot informs me that after I got off the phone with him he called Kate to tell her we were going out. Since he was already on the interstate Kate suggested she be allowed to accompany the boys out. Therefore Dan should stop home quickly and pick her up. I chip in that was a very good idea, and a truly wise decision on Loot's part. Beth comes over with their drinks. A shadowy figure emerges from a corner door behind the bar. Simultaneously, the eleven o'clock news, which was starting at eleven thirty due to a movie that ran long, leads with a picture of one detective Kenny Spade jumping into his car and taking off. The anchorwoman continues the story by adding that there was another murder of a young woman. The next clip was Lieutenant Dan Murphy confirming the death of a female but providing no comment on rumors of a note or a serial killer. The anchorwoman noted the presence of Detective Kenny Spade, OPD homicide on the scene. Detective Spade was involved in the capture of the perpetrator of the gruesome Elizabeth Downing rape and murder. He has been with homicide for around four years and has worked many of the high profile cases. Detective Spade is the best homicide has to offer, never missing a killer. The news insinuated if Detective Spade was on the case and in a hurry there was probably some validity to the theories running unchecked through the media. I summated aloud that the news was probably pissed it had to wait the extra half hour to get the news out, lost some of its flair to the other networks and decided to provide a little flair of its own.

"Well, it seems that we are in the presence of a couple of local television celebrities." The sound comes from behind Kate, Loot and me and startles me the most. Standing behind Loot at the corner of the bar is Diane. She looks as stunning as she did ten hours ago in her pink sleeveless, jeans and Gucci boots. The only difference is that she has a black knit button up the front sweater that matches the boots covering her shoulders. Kate instantly rises and gives her a kiss on the check. After regaining some color in my face, I also rise and cautiously approach Diane to give her a kiss, which I meekly accomplish. Diane orders another round for everyone, including me, and a Cosmopolitan for herself.

"So that's where you boys ran off to," Diane quips, trying to keep the mood light. "I see we always lose out to work." I am very cautious, not sure of what to say. Loot is kind enough to give us the response for us. "They always call us because we look good on TV" he retorts.

"So we have all seen." Kate is kind enough to add. I am uncharacteristically quiet. Loot gives me a nudge to bring me back. A lift of the glass and nod to Beth lets her know I am ready for another.

"We have to use all means necessary to keep up with the beautiful ladies in our presence." This is first signs of life from the famous Kenny Spade.

"Well thank you. You are far too kind." Kate's comment sets off a ring of laughter. The next hour and a half is spent with bouts of playful banter back and forth between the entire group. Around twelve thirty Rock even sat down with us and had a few drinks. I had more than a few more. Loot was actually a little worried about a return to bad habits. I turned the keys over to Loot, recognizing I was losing my ability to drive safely. I had very few binges since my infamous breakfast with Kate four plus years prior. But when I did I was very good about not driving. I loosened up a little and began to regain some comfort around Diane. Just after one Diane resigned that she had to close the bar. Beth and Joey closed all their tabs and were in shut down mode. Loot and I both threw cards on the bar to pay for the check. Diane would have none of it. The drinks for us were on the house. Both of us tried to step up and pay once again, but Diane would not be denied. I reached into my pocket and ripped out a hundred. I gave it to Beth. This is for you and Joey. You guys did a great job. Thanks. No problem was her reply.

"I'll drive you home, Spade." Loot offered.

"I'll just get a cab and leave the Vette here." I responded.

Diane would have none of it. "He can stay with me. I don't have a car here anyway. He can leave from my place in the morning. I have a nice couch he can sleep on."

"I'm not that bad off yet."

"Relax celebrity, I have it covered." Diane was asserting herself again, and I liked it. "You can stay with me. But no funny business or you'll live to regret it. Maybe."

"You better listen to the lady." Kate offers. "I would hate to cross her if I were you."

"Spade, you better listen to the ladies." Loot makes it unanimous. I guess I'm going home with Diane.

"OK, I know when I'm outnumbered… Diane, I throw myself at your mercy. Take me away."

"Cute." Diane muses over my remark. I say bye to my new friendly barkeeps, and give Kate a big hug and kiss. I shake Loot's hand and bid my two best friends adieu. I retake my seat at the bar watching some old TV reruns that play at two in the morning. Diane needs time to finish her nightly audits. It never ends when you own your own business. I sit at the bar and nurse my little buzz while watching old WKRP reruns. It's quite interesting when you watch old TV shows and compare them to what's on the tube today. The technology is all so much better. It's amazing what you realize during the wee hours of the mourning. Around a quarter of three Diane emerges and announces that we are ready to go. She has had a successful evening for a Sunday. It's time to go get some sleep. I walk over to her and offer her my hand. I then escort her to the Vette.

FIVE

Diane's house is not quite what I expected. It is very chic in an urban contemporary sort of way. It has nice Italian leather with lots of hip tables and lamps and a few of those pictures that bleed into something you could look at for hours on end and still not ascertain what you are staring at. Of course at three plus in the morning it's possible that I could be looking at a Picasso and not be able to differentiate it from a Kenny Spade doodle masterpiece. The car ride over was very civil and playful. We joked and laughed and even held hands a little. The experience was very awkward and also very exhilarating. Diane turned out to quite skilled at handling the Vette. It looks good parked out front of her house too. Of course that could be some wishful thinking on my part. Diane came out and handed me a blanket and pillow. The couch is mine for the taking. Diane sits next to me after I set the couch for myself. She is adorned in a long Orlando Magic tee shirt. Damn, she looks good! The conversation is light as it was on the way over. We giggle pretty much nonstop. We talk about everything from cars to basketball to the benefits and consequences of living in a tourism Mecca. It begins to push dawn when we finally settled on turning in for the evening. I reach across and give her a kiss. It is a simply safe first kiss. It is followed by a very passionate kiss that is a little more exploratory and frisky. We start to move a little farther with our hands. In my head the symphony and fireworks blast full thrust. An intense, sweaty and sometimes kinky encounter between us is culminated with a passionate human pretzel of love making. It was not something that I had planned, but it just happened. We wound up sleeping on the floor wrapped together in a sheet.

I awake around seven thirty to see Diane on my arm. I kiss her on her head. In my infinite quagmire of uncertainty when it comes to issues of emotional stature, I am now pressed into whether or not to wake the sleeping beauty lying next to me on the floor. What is more proper? Should I leave and call her? Should I wake her so she doesn't consider me insensitive? I so suck at this shit. Yesterday was a very long day and I need to get to work. This psycho is still prowling through my city and now HE HAS MADE IT PERSONAL. I bend down and kiss Diane on the cheek. I find a pad in the kitchen. I write a note and place it on the pillow next to her. I grab the keys to the Vette and head out.

I stop at a coffee shop and grab a double. I hit the hole in no time. I sift through the evidence once again. The small card. The ominous one calling me out. The small card found on the first victim contained no finger prints. The killer obviously had gloves. The small smear of blood was expertly placed. The photograph of the blood pool was curious. There was no track leaving the area. The body filled the center portion of the pool. It had to have taken a substantial amount of strength and effort to right the victim after he killed her. Or possibly the killer slit her and then held her up. Either way, the victim was obviously posed to show the calling card left behind. The fact is there is no indication left of the killer's identity. He had to be very cautious to do this. There must be some kind of bruising somewhere on the vic where he held her or grabbed her to place her where he wanted her to be discovered. Where is the damn autopsy file? I rummage through my desk. It is not anywhere to be found. Where is it? "WHERE'S THE GODDAMN FILE?" The voice comes out from Jenkins. Yo Spade, chill out. What file you looking for? Chill out. Chill out. Yeah I'm going to do that. Where's the damn file? Jesus, try and find something around here I dare you.

I call down to forensics. There is no one in the office yet. There is no file on my desk. Where is this fucking autopsy file?

It's infuriating! I look up. Loot is mulling around the coffee machine. I didn't hear him enter.

"Hey Loot."

"Spade, what a shock to see you here. What time to did you get here?"

"Time is all relative, don't you think?"

"What time did you get home?"

"Who the hell knows?"

"Well, I see you're well rested and in good spirits." The roar of laughter from the still increasing smattering of detectives lightens my spirit just a bit.

"What's on the agenda this morning?"

"Loot, where's the damn autopsy files? I've been looking all over for them."

"Relax Spade. The first file is in my office. Lisa Yeung's autopsy is scheduled to begin at nine, which is still a few minutes away."

Sure enough, there is the file on Lieutenant Dan Murphy's desk. Spade retreats to his desk and opens the autopsy file. It is 05-010776. It is transcribed for Dr. Parker, Coroner for the City of Orlando and County of Orange. The autopsy lists the cause of death as incised wound to the neck. The procedures are detailed in a verbose statement of paragraphs that only a professional person could comprehend. The examination reveals a twenty three year old Caucasian female, weighing 127 pounds and measuring sixty-five inches from crown to sole. There is a generic description of her hair color and pupils. There is no evidence of injury to the cheeks or chin, and all teeth and gums show no signs of trauma. The genitalia are that of an adult female with no sign of injury. There is a gaping wound to the neck measuring four inches across and one-and-a-half inches deep. The incision point is one and three-quarter inches below the victim's right earlobe. The wound to the neck is at a forty-three degree upward angle. The larynx is exposed through the visible neck wound. The edges of the wound are smooth, with subcutaneous and intramuscularly hemorrhage. The right carotid artery is severed and the right internal jugular vein is cut. The left carotid artery is severed as is the left side jugular. The spinal column is untouched the wound ends one and a half inches below the left ear lobe. The coroner's opinion is the cause of death is sharp force injury, with the injuries to right and left carotid artery and jugular veins resulting in the loss of life.

That's funny. There is no mention of any bruising. How come there is no mention of bruising? The murderer had to have prevented her from falling so he could prop her into position for display. I need to talk to the coroner. I ran to the Vette and take a short ride down to the Coroner's Office. Dr. Parker, Coroner for the City and County, is in the examination room when I arrive. His assistant Rachael shows me in. Dr. Parker is in the middle of his autopsy. He is in the middle of investigating the neck wound. "Detective Spade, I have not yet concluded anything on this one. You will just have to remain patient."

"Yes doctor, sorry to bother you. Actually, I came to ask you a question on the other victim."

"05-010776?"

"I'm sorry?"

"The young lady from last week with an eerily similar neck wound?"

"Yes, Doctor Parker, sorry."

"Yes detective, what's your question?"

"I was wondering if you had found any signs of bruising on the body."

"Bruising? Not that I recall, why do you ask?"

"I think that the killer may have held her up to position her the way she was found. I was curious if the body would support my theory."

"I see. I don't recall. I will have another look when I am done here."

"Fine doctor, I will check in with you later."

"You're welcome to observe if you are so inclined, Detective Spade."

"Thank you very much, Doctor Parker. I graciously accept your invitation."

The doctor continues with his examination of Lisa Yeung. There is a sharp force trauma to the neck. It emanates from the right side of the neck under the right ear lobe. Doctor Parker speaks with tremendous confidence and command. Rachael records the information as it is provided. The wound is continuous with smooth edges. It is three inches long and two inches deep. It intersects the right side jugular vein and carotid artery transecting both. The wound intersects skin, subcutaneous tissue and muscle. The wound enters the body at a thirty-seven degree upward angle. The wound ends contiguous to the right jugular with a small incision into the sheathing of the vein. This is the fatal injury, associated with the loss of blood pertaining to the injury to the right carotid artery and jugular vein. There is subcutaneous bruising to the right side of the torso in the rib cage region and upper right arm. There appear to be no other injuries to the person. The good doctor then plods through the remainder of physical descriptions to complete the necessary autopsy requirements.

The words the doctor enunciates do not penetrate my auditory canal. My mind is too busy processing the relevant information that I just heard. The same type of cut, entering just below the right ear. Both deaths were the result of bleeding out of the right side artery and vein. The bruising on the side of the body was a result of the fall on to the stanchion in the bank parking lot. My mind starts streaming with different possibilities and queries. What made the killer prop up the first victim but leave the second one to flop on to the ground? Why did he pose the first one so neatly and dress her up but not take the time to do that to the second? Was he interrupted? Do I have a witness out there? Why bother to make the first card so mysterious and come out so blatantly with the second one? Why has the killer specifically targeted me to taunt? Is he specific in his selection process? Did the victims know each other? Detective? Detective Spade? Hello Detective? A quick hand on my shoulder brings me back to the conscious world. "Detective Spade?" Rachel is trying to get my attention.

"I'm sorry. Yes?"

"Doctor Parker is ready to look at the other body now."
Excellent. I am looking for any signs that she was restrained. On the arms or wrists, are there any signs of an attempt to hold her still while he killed her? No. What about any attempt to keep her upright after he killed her? You see doc, she was meticulously placed down while Lisa Yeung just fell. I have to ask why.

"Well what do we have here?"

"What is it, doc?"

"There is a little bruising under the right armpit and the left armpit and a little scrape in the upper left shoulder armpit region."

"Is it from the knife?"

"Possibly, I'll have forensics check it out."

"Great. Thank you very much doctor. I appreciate the help."

"No problem."

I hit the Vette and start back to the office or as I like to call it, the Hole. I now have a lot of questions. Perhaps the autopsy will give me the starting points I crave. If I take the starting points and process them maybe I will make progress. I have a murderer to catch. And I will. "YOU HEAR ME ASSHOLE. I'M COMING FOR YOU. I WILL GET YOU, YOU SONNOFA BITCH! I WILL GET YOU!!" Yes Elizabeth, I know I am screaming at someone while I am all alone in my car. I am not alone, you are here with me. You know I have to get this monster off the streets. I owe it to this town. I owe it to you, Elizabeth. I owe it to you. I don't know why he wants to tangle with me Elizabeth, but he picked the wrong guy. I will get him.

After another trip to the coffee machine, I make my way back to the Hole. There is almost no stirring and a silently morbid aura of despair spreads through the Hole. I look around. Detectives Ronan and Tolliver are just sitting at their desks, not recognizing anything. I find this very disconcerting. They are my point men on the Yeung case.

"What's going on? Mikey?"

"One guess."

"Where's Loot?"

"Trapped in his office."

"Why?"

"One guess."

"Poncher? IAD?"

"Bingo."

"Shit. Is Loot in trouble?"

"I'm not sure it's Loot, dig? You know the history between those two. No love lost."

Detective Francis Poncher, Internal Affairs Division. Both Dan Murphy and Francis Poncher attended John Young High School in Orlando. Dan and Kate were high school sweethearts, but Francis Poncher had a very soft spot for Kate Allen. There has been some bad blood on Francis' part ever since Kate and Dan got married. Then four or so years back both Dan and Francis were up for Chief of Detectives. After Dan got the job, Poncher transferred to IAD and he has been hot to get something on Dan Murphy ever since. Loot is squeaky clean, in fact the only thing that Poncher has on him is his defense of me. Oh shit. I am so stupid. How can it get any more obvious?

Officer Frank Poncher is a massive hulking man. He stands right around six feet. He probably pushes 300 pounds. He does not possess what we would call a very athletic build. In fact, the most forgiving of souls would probably concur with the assessment that he looks like Jaba the Hut. Ironically, Officer Poncher was a very meticulous man. He was a neat freak to the point of appearing to be OCD. His suits were neatly creased and pressed and his briefcase was always painstakingly organized. It is rumored around the department that he was a master of tae kwon do. So it came as no surprise to me that there was the dapper Dr. Moriarity holding court in Lieutenant Dan Murphy's office. True to form, he smelled my presence in the Hole and summoned for me immediately. There goes the neighborhood.

"Detective Spade, how are you. Come in."

"Welcome, Officer Poncher. How are you today?"

"Very well sir, and yourself?"

"All is peaceful, thank you."

Poncher and his peace. Peace this and Zen that. They say that's all a byproduct of the teaching of his martial arts. I honestly doubt his sincerity. Something about Francis just rings phony. Loot sits behind his cheap wooden desk full of the case files and relevant evidence and paperwork. The mammoth officer Poncher stands leaning against the wall that houses the accreditations and accolades of one Lieutenant Dan Murphy, Orlando Police Department. I bet he is doing it on purpose. He can't fool me. "Yo Loot, what's going on." I clamor. "I just went and visited with the coroner. I was checking something on the case."

"Good. You can brief me in a minute. Actually Spade, Officer Poncher is here to converse briefly with you." You can just sense Poncher cringing as Loot says 'Officer' and the coy little smile on the face of Loots face as he does it.

"Yes sir, Officer" I have to interject my own little jab. I can't let Loot have all the fun after all. "What can I do for you?"

"Officer Spade…"

"Detective." A little completive one-upmanship between Loot and my adversary is always a positive thing in my book.

"Sorry." His eyes are flaming red. Score one for the Spade. "Detective Spade I need to speak to you regarding the Lisa Yeung homicide. Are you familiar with the case?"

"Sir, I believe Officers Ronan and Tolliver are primary on that."

"I understand. Your lieutenant was kind enough to inform me."

"Thanks Loot."

"No problem." You can sense the smugness in the room.

"ENOUGH OF THE BULLSHIT!" Ooh, I guess we hit a nerve. What a shame. The rant continues. "Spade, why the hell was there a card addressed to you found at the scene?"

"Officer Poncher, how should I know?" What a jackass.

"Don't play with me Spade. Why the hell is your name on the victim?"

"I don't know. How should I know?"

"Detective Spade, again I ask, why was your name found on the victim?"

"What's your problem Francis, why is IAD even here?"

"WHY WAS IT THERE? WHAT ARE YOU HIDING?"

Loot has had enough. "Calm down, both of you."

"MURPHY, HE'S HIDING SOMETHING! WHEN I FIND OUT WHAT IT IS I'LL HAVE HIS ASS. AND YOUR ASS TOO!!!!"

"That's enough officer. You can leave now."

"DON'T YOU PATRONIZE ME, MURPHY. I'LL FIX HIS ASS. HE'S HIDING SOMETHING. MARK MY WORDS. I'LL GET HIM."

"GET OUT! NOW!" Loot is fuming. "BEFORE I CONTACT YOUR C.O. GET THE FUCK OUT!"

"YOU DON'T GET OFF THAT EASY! I'LL BE BACK, BRASS IN TOW!" Poncher yells as he walks out the door and out of the Hole.

"BYE BYE!" I have to get my parting shot in. To the victor go the spoils. "Gees, can you imagine the nerve of that bastard."

"SPADE!"

"What?"

"Look Spade, there is a point here. This guy is on to you and it doesn't look good, having your name lying on the vic's body."

"Come on Loot, you know me."

"Regardless, this is something that everyone has been talking about, even if they won't admit it to your face."

"Loot, I ain't stupid. This SOB is taunting me."

"All right enough, so what did you find out with the coroner?"

"Well, the killer is probably left handed. Both victims were killed by an upward angle cut. Hmmm. That's interesting. Why didn't I think of this sooner?"

"Of what?"

"Just let me ponder this for a while. It could be nothing. I'll see you later."

"Spade, you're under the microscope. You better watch your ass."

"Yeah, I know. I'm feelin' ya."

It never ends. I weave my way through the Hole back to my desk. I pick up the phone and call a florist. I order a dozen roses, red of course, and send them to the Hurricane From Hell. A note attached to the cards was simply to read 'Thank You for a truly wonderful evening. I miss you. I hope to see you soon. Love Spade.' God, I hope that's not too mushy. I want it to sound sincere. There is a serious amount of potential in her for me. I don't want to scare her off. She needs to know I care. That is a very scary thought. The only woman I ever cared about I didn't even meet until she died. I don't know if I can share my heart with both of them. I am so not good at this. Should I call her? Maybe later in the afternoon, after the flowers. What do I say? It can't sound phony, that's for sure. All right, enough of this. Let's get the show on the road.

I call down to Forensics. I need some help. Listen, can I speak to the investigator working the slasher cases. Yes, Yeung and the other one. Justyna. Great, can I speak with her? Where is she? Can you give her my cell? I need her opinion. Yes, Detective Spade. 464-3299. Thanks. Yeah Thanks for nothing is more like it. What was the metal speck I found? What was the time of death? Come on I need to start. I cannot wait forever. My cellphone rings. "Justyna?" Oh, sorry Rachel. Yes. Lisa Yeung's body is being transferred to the funeral home tomorrow. Great, Yeah, I know that one. OK. I'll be there. Thanks Rachel. I have another wake to attend. Rachel has always been a great help to me with regards to the bodies being claimed. It is not pretty being a homicide detective. Paying my respects and catching the bad guys is my way of making the world right.

"Is there a Detective Spade here?"

I raise my hand. "Present." For the second time this morning, the Hole fills with laughter. This is not a common occurrence, especially in the homicide Hole.

"I'm Justyna. Forensics." Beautiful. A woman with some answers. I hope. "I was told you are looking for me."

"Yes. I have some questions. Hopefully you can create some answers. I need to run some things by you. Would you like to go grab a coffee?"

"OK."

We run down to the coffee shop. The clerk is amused to see me again. What's this, three or four cups today? Never enough, I quip. We grab a cup and sit by the window. What did the metal flake turn up? Nothing yet.

"Justyna, I have a question. Do you think we could figure out the killer's height from taking the angles of the insert and extrapolating them with the heights of the victims? Maybe we can get some kind of a clue as to his height. It would be a start."

"Yeah, it may work. I'll get on that. What else?"

"Do we have any idea on the type of knife?"

"Some progress. It is some type of outdoor knife. An unusual one. Not like a typical hunting knife. I can tell that by the type of cut the knife left and the unusual variance in the length and depth."

"Excellent. Keep on it. Thanks for all your help, Justyna."

With that Justyna is on her way. Well, let's see what else we have to go on. Oh yes, that's nothing. Great, thanks for reminding me. I need more coffee. Screw that. I need a beer. And I know just the place.

SIX

I make the quick jaunt back to the office and jump in the Vette. I scream down the road as the Vette glides into the horizon without knowing what destination I am going to. She will take me there herself. Elizabeth takes the seat next to me a few minutes into the jaunt. I give her the update. We may have a way to ascertain the killer's height. We believe we know that Lisa Yeung was killed Saturday night around eight. The other girl was killed between two and four in the morning. The killer has singled me out for some reason. He is left handed. He uses some sort of unusual knife and probably likes to pose his victims. He wants them to be found a certain way. Perhaps he even photographs them. Justyna is working on the knife and killers height. I have to work the personal angles. Why is he singling me out? Are there any connections between the two victims? What's that Elizabeth? I don't know if the flowers arrived yet. True. I am much better off safe than sorry. I'll stop and grab a dozen roses. Yes, I know red. The Vetted coasts into the parking lot for the florist. I stop and grab a dozen. The Hurricane From Hell is right down the street. It's just past noon so the bar is not really open yet. Rock is sitting at the bar as I push my way through the brimstone and oak doors.

"Hello Rock." I dare to address the mass of muscle, not yet confident of my status with the bars employees, or more importantly its owner. "Is Diane in yet?" I hide the flowers behind my back, which automatically puts Rock visibly on edge. I do not see any flowers on the bar, but they could be in her office.

"Yes detective, I am." Detective, oh shit am I in a lot of trouble.

"Hello."

"Hello yourself."

Damn. What am I supposed to say to that? Is she really pissed at me? One wrong move and this could all blow up in my face.

"These are for you."

"That's very thoughtful of you."

"Rock, do you have a vase in here. Perhaps I could put these in water before they die?" I wonder if there's room in that vase for me, also. I may not live too long myself. Rock takes the flowers from me and walks toward the vicinity of the storage closet. I timidly meander toward Diane. "I am very sorry about leaving you this morning. I did not want to disrupt you. You had such a peaceful look on your face and I was getting restless. I am not very good at dealing with people. I am even worse at dealing with people I care about. Diane, I care about you. A lot. Yesterday was the best day I have had, except for the work part, in such a long time I can't even remember. I wrestle with myself every minute trying to figure out what's the appropriate thing to do. Please don't take my leaving this morning as a sign of…"

"Am I interrupting something?" The gargantuan hunk of man returned with flowers in a vase.

"Actually, Rock, the detective here was just starting to dig himself into or out of a hole, I can't quite tell which." Diane retorts. This is followed by a burst of laughter from the big man that echoes through the Hurricane as if it was a cannon shot off in a cave. I sit there with a smirk on my face that is a compromise of pitiful and silly, and quite lost as if a puppy dog had lost its mamma. "Lighten up, Spade. Gees, what a worry wart." You have no idea is all I can muster under my breath. Real words escape me as I wait in awkward anticipation, not sure of what the next shoe to drop will be.

"All right detective, why don't you come with me back to my office? Then we can investigate how I can assist you." It is obvious to all that Diane is quite proud of her little investigate quip. "Please walk this way." With that Diane starts to walk, no it was more like a strut, or maybe a prance; no parade, yes she started to parade toward the southeast corner where her office is. We arrive at her office door much like Santa Claus arrives at the end of the Macy's Thanksgiving Day Parade. Diane stands off to the side and thrusts her right arm out perpendicular to her body. She then ever so gracefully swoops me up and escorts me into her office. Out of the corner of my eye I can see the most gorgeous array of roses on Diane's desk. I say out of the corner of my eye because as soon as I reached the room and the door was closed Diane had me pinned on the wall. Her tongue was exploring all of the segments of my mouth while Diane artfully manipulated my belt buckle. Both of our pants were on the floor before the clock could strike a passing minute. There was no time for anything. Diane was a woman on a mission and her mission right now was her man. The act was intense and pleasurable. There was a diploma and a dollar that was framed knocked off the wall and onto the floor. After the deed there was a slower much more passionate kiss. Diane then bent over to pick up the two frames on the ground. I fixed my pants and went to sit in the chair in front of Diane's desk. Diane glides across the floor to her office and sits on the corner of her desk. She lifts her long legs over the top of the sitting detective and places herself directly in front of me, straddling me.

"Well detective, it's good to see you again."

"Listen Diane, I just wanted to say, about this morning, I just wanted to say…"

"Would you shut up, jackass!" with that Diane leans forward and kisses me while unbuttoning her blouse. A few minutes later a big crash is heard from the office, with the most likely cause being the lamp knocked off the desk.

I spent the better part of the afternoon at the bar. After we left her office we went up front and had a few drinks and laughs with Beth, Rock and Joey. We had some chicken wings, extra spicy, for lunch. We laughed and just shot the breeze and I entertained no thoughts of the serial killer or my lack of progress related to the case. It proved to be a much more valuable way to spend my time, for back at the Hole, in front of me on my desk was the pictures of my two victims that I have been staring at incessantly for the last seventy-five minutes with no real clue or progress. Victim number one, stabbed at two in the morning. Her body was so neatly placed to be found. So meticulous was the artwork around the card. Lisa Yeung. Found in the early afternoon of Sunday but probably killed Saturday in the evening. She was not as skillfully posed. Perhaps he was scared off by some activity going on around the bank. THE BANK. YOU STUPID ASS. Where is the ATM at the Sunshine Bank? Is it in the front or the back? We could have the bastard on tape! What the hell is wrong with me?! I grab my jacket and make a dart for the back stairs out to the parking lot. I almost make it to the door handle before I am interrupted by Justyna. Yes Justyna, I am on my way out. What's up? No, I don't have a minute. Want to take a ride? To the Sunshine Bank on Westmoreland. The two of us hit the stairs and make the journey to the Vette. Once inside we hit the interstate on our way back to Westmoreland. Justyna tells me she has calculated the killer to be around five eleven. Well that's great. That narrows it down some. How many guys out there are in the vicinity of five eleven? Hell, that's how tall I am. And a few hundred thousand other men in the surrounding counties. Justyna used the angles of entry of the major wound in both victims and their respective heights to extrapolate the approximate height of the killer. It would be really useful if the killer was a woman, but the violence involved in both of these crimes suggests that it probably was not. Well, it is the first profile. Male, approximately five eleven and left handed. OK Justyna, we now have a starting point. Why are we going back to the bank? What do I mean? We have to find the ATM. Wherever the ATM is there will be a camera. We could have this guy on film and I had missed it for a day. Gees, what an ass I am. I got so flustered by the card I missed the obvious. Nice detective work, detective.

We arrive at the bank around six twenty. There is a sign on the door announcing the closing of the bank for the week due to unforeseen circumstances. The people are directed to visit the next closest Sunshine Bank a mile and a half away. The ATM is by the front entrance. There is a camera facing Westmoreland. That means that I have no murder on tape. The possibility still remains that he could have passed in front of the bank when he was arriving or leaving the bank. I'll contact the corporate office and try to find out who to contact to get access to the footage. Since we're here we may as well go take another look at the crime scene. Let's walk it. Come on Justyna; let's go have a look see.

My eyes are fixated at the ground. I scan the area like an infrared sensor built in to a military attack copter or spy plane. I notice everything on the ground. I spot a candy wrapper in the bushes to the west corner of the front of the bank. It is quickly placed in an evidence bag. Along the side of the building to the back parking lot I find a cigarette butt. Right into the bag. I walk toward the rear parking lot. Justyna is already there, examining spatter patterns. "What do you see, Justyna?"

"Nothing."

"Justyna?"

"We examined the spatter. We took all the samples. The blood belongs to the victim. No other traces were present."

"Hey Justyna, follow the spatter. Which way does it follow?"

"It flows this way, toward the west and the parking lot exit."

"Where was the body found?"

"Here. In this position. Look at the blood pool. The victim probably was approached from the west as she was facing over there, the far corner of the parking lot." Justyna tries to demonstrate where the victim was.

"Exactly. Where's the car?"

"I'm sorry?"

"Justyna, where's the car?"

"I don't follow." Appropriately annoying, my cellphone rings.

"Hello. Yeah Loot it's me. What's up? No, I'm at the bank. Yeah, I am here checking out some stuff. I needed to double check some stuff. No, I have nothing yet. I am working on it. We have a preliminary description. Male approximately five eleven, left handed. That's all we have on that. Yeah, I'll keep you updated. See you Loot. Tell Kate it was great to see her again yesterday. OK, OK, I'll tell her myself. See ya, Loot."

"Justyna, she was getting into a car. It makes sense. Why was she in the parking lot? And the perpetrator coming up from behind, from the western end. She was facing the opposite direction. Where was the body found?"

"There." Justyna points to where the body was found.

"How was she laying?"

"This way." Justyna tries to demonstrate the position the victim was found in by showing the direction the body was found in relative to the blood splatter pattern.

"This will not do. We're hot. I am not going to screw this up. Are you in a hurry?" I am very anxious.

"No."

"Good." I grab the phone and dials frantically. I am agitated and restless. I start talking. Yeah Loot. Me. Where are the pictures? Of the scene. OK grab Tolliver and Ronan. Meet me at the Bank on Westmoreland. Bring the pictures. Yeah, see you soon. I flip the phone shut. I then walks over to Justyna and update her.

I have been waiting for around forty minutes for Loot. Justyna and I are going over different aspects of everything while we wait for the photographs of the crime scene. Out of the corner of my eye I see a person sneaking around in the corner of the bank.

"Freeze. Don't move. Not even an inch." My gun is drawn. I am calm and fixated on my target. I stalk my prey not even flinching. "Step out, away from the bushes. DO IT. NOW!" My gaze is fixated on the intruder. Move. Justyna has drawn her weapon and is taking a circuitous route to cover the person's right flank.

"OK.OK. I'm out. I'm out."

"Who are you?" I am deadly serious and locked upon my mark.

"Steve Frizz. Channel Nine News."

"Keep your hands up. Step out. Justyna, check him."

Justyna walks up to the man and asks where his wallet is. The man reaches for his wallet. I forcefully remind the man not to move. Justyna goes up to the man and takes his wallet out. His license is from Florida and has the name of Steve Frizz. In his wallet is an ID from Channel Nine with the name Steven Frizz. Justyna informs me that his credentials check out.

"What do you want?"

"Well, I saw your car out front in front of a day old murder scene so I figured there was a story. Any comment?" I detest reporters. They sneak around trying to get one up on their competition like high school football players trying to get first crack at the prom queen. But they jeopardize my investigations by prematurely jumping the gun and distributing bad information. It has happened too many times before.

"You stopped here because of a car parked in front of the bank?"

"Detective, we all know you drive an old Corvette. Put a Corvette here and any genius can add one plus one."

"I see."

"So what's your young friend's name, detective? Should I give her some props?"

"There's no story. We are working."

"What about the note, detective?" Steve Frizz is very probative with his questions.

"I'm sorry, what's your name again?"

"Frizz. Steve Frizz. Channel Nine news."

"Well Steve Frizz Channel Nine, what are you talking about?" I play coy but am somewhat surprised the note has become public knowledge already.

"Knock it off, Spade. We all know the killer left a taunting note, daring the police to catch him. What about it?"

"Only my friends call me Spade, Mr. Frizz, and you are not among them. Mr. Frizz, if you have a note I suggest you surrender it to me."

"I'm not buying it detective. I know there's a story here. What about the note?"

"Mr. Frizz, if you have a note you are withholding evidence in a murder investigation. I will have you arrested."

"I'm not buying it. You are hiding it. The press always wins in the end. First Amendment. I'll get the story."

"Story, you arrogant jerk. Tell the young lady that is going to miss her wedding how important your story is. Tell her fiancée. Tell her parents." I jump on my soapbox and unleash a little tirade on the leech trying to screw up my investigation. Yes, I hate reporters.

"Touching. But you can't fool me. I know you're up to something."

"Justyna, escort the good reporter to his vehicle. And make sure he leaves. If he hassles you call a white and blue." (A white and blue is a patrol car, so named because patrol cars are white with blue and yellow stripes.)

"Spade, you can't stop the power of the press. I'll get you. I'll get the story."

Justyna grabs Steve Frizz by his elbow and walks the reporter to the front of the bank. Any time Mr. Frizz slows Justyna growls at him and ensures he keeps moving forward. The two fade from view within a minute.

Yes, I know that did not go well. I screwed up. Elizabeth I get it. I know. We're going to get him Elizabeth I promise. For you, and for the victims. I just hope we can gain something here. He will make a mistake. They all do. No, Elizabeth, I don't have enough yet. Be patient.

"Officer, who are you talking to?" In front of him is a teenage male. The one from yesterday.

"Hi. Jack isn't it?"

"Yes sir. Who are you talking to?"

"No one. Why are you here?" I am surprised to see my little information source in the same location twice.

"Cutting through to go to my friend's house."

"I see. Listen, Jack, maybe you can help me. You say Lisa was an unforgettable type, right."

"Grade A."

"Do you know if she drove to work?'

"Are you kidding? It's stupid to get on a bus, especially over here." Jack is sarcastic, but serious.

"So she drove?"

"Oh yeah, a nice Acura coupe. Sweet car. Sweet girl."

"Excellent, thanks Jack." With that Jack begins to turn and walk toward his friend's house.

"Spade why is he here?" The voice is unmistakable. Loot has finally arrived. He has Justyna in tow, as well as detectives Tolliver and Ronan.

"Hey Loot, you got the pictures?"

"Spade, why is the kid here?"

Jack speaks. "I was just cutting through. That's my friend's house right there."

"I see." Loot does not sound convinced.

"Thanks Jack. I'll see you later." With that, Jack leaves. I turn and face Loot.

"Spade, why was he here?" Loot sounds suspicious.

"He was just going to his friends."

"Spade?"

"Everything's cool Loot. Let's get to work." I instruct Justyna to fill in the voids. The spatter pattern has the victim facing the far corner of the parking lot. The spatter leads back toward the front of the bank and forward toward the parking stanchions. Where are the photographs? Tolliver breaks them out. OK. Let's find the body photo. Look at the position. She is sideways leaning on the stanchion. Her head is resting on her left arm. Look at the way she is facing. She is facing the street. It follows the spatter. But remember the profile. The killer is left-handed. So the spatter is probably more a result of follow through. The victim had no defense wounds. Where are the pictures from the autopsy? Look at her arms. No defense wounds. So she was probably not facing her attacker. If the spatter was a result of follow through the killer's left hand was probably going this way. I motion from the far corner of the parking lot toward the front of the bank. So Lisa Yeung is facing this way. I point toward the far corner of the parking lot. Why? Why is she facing that way? Loot is puzzled.

"Spade is this going somewhere?" Loot asks.

"Think about why."

"Come on, Spade."

"Why was she facing away from the street? Why? She was getting in her car. The killer came up behind her and cut her throat."

Loot is still not biting. "And?"

"Jesus, Loot, where's the damn car?"

Aha! The question of the hour has surfaced. Why was there no car? Why did it take so long for someone to find her? A serial killer is not likely to steal a car. It's not his MO. Would he do it to hide his body? Not likely a serial killer would want to hide his work. So where's the car. I talked to the kid. He said she drove an Acura. He said she never took the bus. The blood pool had no footprints and no tire tracks. It was completed close to the stanchion. What do we know? There are no marks in the pool. How does he accomplish this? Was she standing next to the car? How did she get to work that day? If she drove, would there be blood evidence on the car? Anything on the car would probably be from the victim so that will not help. But if she was killed next to the vehicle then there would be tire tracks through the blood. So was she killed next to the car? Possibly she was on the way to her car. Maybe he was stalking her. We need to look at these possibilities. Justyna, where is her purse? When we went through the purse, were there any keys? Justyna, we need fingerprints from her pants. Especially around the pockets. If she had keys, they had to be somewhere. Double check the purse and the pants. We need to run with this, gentlemen, it's the first positive we have had in these cases. Show me the pictures. How did she get here? Look at her position. The coroner says she probably bled out almost immediately. So, how did she get over to the stanchion? The autopsy says she had bruising on the upper right torso and upper right arm. Why? Was the bruising from the fall or was the killer trying to hold her until he could place her where he wanted her? Let's say it was so the killer could position the victim so he could properly place his message to us. Logic would follow with the bruise on the upper right arm because our killer is left handed. But to do this he would have to do something with the knife. Maybe he used his right hand to hold her until he could secure his knife, hence the bruise on the upper torso. Then he used the left hand to drag her over to the stanchion. Justyna, did we check the victim's shoes for excessive scratching or any kind of indication that she may have been dragged? Justyna nods affirming. What about her pants? Were there any traces of anything? Justyna shakes her head no. Thanks for working with me on this. Justyna's clever 'no problem' has us all rolling in the hills. All right gentlemen let's move it. We have to get this son of a bitch before he acts again. The city is getting nervous. We cannot allow this monster to take control of our city boys. Balls to the wall.

"What's up with the soap box antics?" Tolliver asks the question that sets the next round of belly booms through the group.

"All right, sorry." Spade says.

"Let's get cracking." Loot chimes in. "Now we have some ideas to work with."

Everyone runs to the cars. Loot calls in an inquiry and APB on Lisa Yeung's car. Justyna jumps in with Tolliver and Ronan and heads back to the office. Loot stays behind and rides with me. I spin the Vette from the parking lot and starts back toward the interstate. The reddish amber hue and purplish blend of high clouds let you know that the evening is approaching. The humidity is quite tolerable for Central Florida, a bit surprising due to the lack of rain in the afternoon today. I have the top down and seem to be oblivious to all the surroundings, including my best friend sitting in the chair to his right. Loot spends around ninety seconds trying to get the attention of the driver of the automobile with its top down. After my cellphone rings and goes unheeded, Loot decides it is time to bring our hero back to a little planet called Earth. A little quick snip of a glare lets Loot know that his compadre has returned to reality.

"Welcome back."

"Yeah, thanks Loot."

"Where were you?"

"I was just lost in the clouds, why?"

"Where you with her?" Loot inquires.

"With who?" The look at Loot says I am both unsure and a bit annoyed at the question.

"Never mind." Loot reads the signal.

"No. You initiated it? With who?" A bit of uneasiness surfaces with my words.

"Elizabeth."

"Loot, leave her out of it." It is clear I don't want to go there.

"It's just that you weren't with me. The car was driving itself. So…"

"Listen Loot, I feel ya. I was just thinking." I attempt to manage a smirk, a signal to an old friend that things are OK. A sign that my old friend is not buying. The intensity in the eyes of Loot let me know he is a little more than a little concerned. "Dan, I'm all right. Really."

"If you say so Spade. Sorry I brought her up."

The atmosphere in the vehicle is ironically stuffy if you consider the fact the car is being driven without a roof to confine it. "I'm hungry Loot. Do you want to go grab a burger?"

"I suppose you have a place in mind."

"Yeah."

"Any place I know?" Loot senses a little mischief on the horizon.

"Maybe."

Loot flips open his cellphone and calls Kate. 'Hey babe. I'm going with Spade to grab a burger and talk shop. Yeah, same place. Yeah, fine. I won't be out to late. OK babe. Love you. Bye.' I guide the Vette down the ramp off the interstate and a few blocks over to its newly familiar surroundings. The mass of humanity known as Rock opens the door and lets us in. There are around fifteen people sitting at the bar bullshitting and scanning the ESPN laden screens around the establishment. There are another set of thirty or so scattered at the tables in the remainder of the restaurant. Loot appears to be impressed with something.

"What did you do to him?" Loot inquires.

"I'm sorry?"

"Rock. He just opened the door for you. That was something I did not think I would see yesterday."

"You know me, Loot. I'm just a people person." A mass eruption of laughter from Loot soon envelops Rock and me. Loot and I walk over to a booth in the further most, darkest corner of the Hurricane. Beth comes over and greets us boys with our beer of choice from the night previous.

"Mr. Spade, I didn't expect to see you twice in one day. Is there anything I can get for you gentlemen? "

"Twice in one day?" Loot is a little baffled.

"Double bacon cheese for me please. No fries." I am on the board. Beth shoots me a wily smile. This does not go undetected by Loot.

"Spade, am I missing something?"

"Yes, a double cheese I think." Beth laughs and lightly runs her hand across my shoulder. This too is encapsulated by Loot.

"What the hell is going on here, Spade?" Loot queries.

"What do you mean?" I feign ignorance.

"Spade, I am still Chief of Homicide Detectives. Don't think I didn't pick up on those subtle little signs between you and the bartender."

"Why Loot, whatever do you mean?" I lift my glass and sip the foam off the top and giggle. Whatever do you mean, he says again, this time to himself.

"Spade...!"

"Yo."

"Why where you here in the middle of the day?"

"I was just visiting Diane, that's all." My specter of sarcasm is playful. Loot is not buying it but decides any further information will not be forthcoming. Maybe he'll try to squeeze some from the bartender a little later. I hit the glass again and break out the pictures. I lay the pictures across the table in front of me. The first one is the picture of the first girl. Her red hair is perfectly styled. The white blouse is unbuttoned five-buttons down the nine-button, frilly laden blouse. The bra is pulled away from the exposed left breast. The card leans against that breast. It has a dark red smudge in the upper right corner. She is wearing a pressed black skirt. She is propped on her side. The next picture is the side walk she was found on. The blood pool lists toward what would have been the rear of the body if the victim was still in the photograph. The crimson stain bleeds toward the dirt where the concrete ends and blends into the darkness.

The darkness that is the color of the dirt. The darkness that is the blackness of the spade that threatens me. The darkness that is the soul of the person who is destroying the lives of these girls and their families. The third picture is the ace of spades. It has a dark bloody smudge in the upper corner. The print of the killer. The invitation to attempt to capture him. The spade in the middle. Dominating the card. Taunting me. Inviting me. Daring me. The spade that wants me to stop it. To stop the murders. To stop the killer. To stop the madness. To stop the taunting. The ace. Suddenly the ace jumps out of the card. Blurs of darkness attack me. I am paralyzed. I am not overcome with fear. But I am paralyzed. The blurs of black expand exponentially. From inside the Hurricane From Hell came the hurricane from hell. The blackness emanating from the center of the card in the photograph jumped off the Kodak paper and formed a cloud of blackness that spiraled over the table. As the peak of the cloud circulated over the table it touched the ornamental red candelabra that leant the atmosphere to the Hurricane From Hell. Upon the contact of the cloud to the candelabra an opaque mass of black Smokey vision began to rain down from the lighting fixture. The rain fell into the form of a giant spade. The spade hovered over the table, dancing in front of me in such a way that it seemed to be a spitting spire from the upper boundaries of the spade. The red smudge in the picture shot off the film like a solar flare. This was followed by three other bullets in rapid succession. The first two landed at the ten and two-o'clock positions. The third landed at the base of the spade proper where the stem begins its descent. The fourth and final flare stopped and looked me right in the eyes. It did a seductive little dance reminiscent of Salma Hayek's "Goddess of the

Night" in *From Dusk Till Dawn*, seductively enticing me, drawing me into the entity of evil that was calling me out. The dancing flare then leapt into the center of the smokey spade and suddenly this smoky mass came alive with the fire from hell. The two upper flares shot through the top of the spade and took the form of the Devil's eyes. The center flare continued its seductive dance right in the middle of the spade cloud. The lowest flare spit venom from its host and began to curse at me. Spade the Meek. Spade the Failure. Spade the Stupid. Spade the Coward. What's the matter Spade? You can't catch me? You can't see me? I'm right here Spade. RIGHT IN FRONT OF YOU! WHAT ARE YOU SPADE? ARE YOU A DETECTIVE? ARE YOU THE GREAT SAVIOR OF THE CITY OF ORLANDO? DO YOU REMEMBER ELIZABETH DOWNING? YOU COULDN'T EVEN SAVE HER! SAVIOR MY ASS! YOU ARE A LOSER! DETECTIVE KENNY SPADE. NO, NO, NO THE GREAT DETECTIVE KENNY FRAUD! RUN, RUN AS FAST AS YOU CAN CAN'T CATCH ME BECAUSE YOU ARE A CLOWN OF A MAN! PUT ON YOUR COSTUME AND YOUR BIG RED NOSE. THOSE FLOPPY SHOES ARE THE BEST ASSET YOU HAVE. CATCH ME! CATCH ME! WHAT'S THE MATTER? DON'T YOU HAVE THE BALLS? CATCH ME IF YOU CAN! I DARE YOU! I DOUBLE DARE YOU!!!

Diane looks at Loot with genuine concern and then looks back at me. What is he doing, Loot? What is he staring at? How long has he been this way? What the hell is going on? Loot, come on. I'm scared. Is it normal?

"Loot, come on do something. Spade, what are you looking at? Come on you're scaring me. Spade. Spade."

"Relax Diane let's not get ahead of ourselves. He's just deep in thought with the case." Loot tries to be the calming influence. He is also very concerned. He has tried to get my attention repeatedly over the last four or five minutes. This is the longest he has seen his friend zone out. Right now all he can do is try to keep Diane calm. I was not even aware when Diane joined them at the table.

"What do we do?" Diane is becoming more agitated.

"Just leave him be." It is the only answer Loot has. He too does not know what to do with me. This is not good, Loot says to himself. It's not good. The standoff continues for around three more minutes. During the interval Loot does his best to reassure Diane that everything is OK. He does the best he can to reassure himself as well. It wasn't until Kate came in and saw him zoning out that someone knew what to do. She went over to Beth and got a large cup of pungent coffee and put it in front of him. After around forty seconds I returned to the table. I was unaware of what had transpired. I knew I was not all right. How could I be when I had just seen what I had seen? I felt flush but I looked across the table and saw an obviously distressed Diane, whom I was not even aware was there with me, sitting next to Kate, whom I really did not expect to see. I was cautious not to alarm anyone with my zone out. I knew I needed to deflect it and calm the table, much like the man who wins the big pot at the poker table but still wants to keep the table calm so he can finish his prey off. Calmness pays off.

"Hi guys, when did you guys get here?" I break the silence.

"Are you all right?" Diane has to ask just to say something. She is visibly shaken and her voice quivers and cracks with every word.

"Sure I am" is all I can muster.

"You were off on a tangent, Spade." Loot reintroduces calmness to the table.

"Nah, just looking at the pictures." Yeah right, if they ever found out what I saw I would be sent to the psych ward ASAP.

"Yeah right" Loot retorts. This brings a slight chuckle from the booth but it goes a substantial way to remove the surface tension present.

"Kate, how did you know that we were here?" I ask. Kate just throws a wink in the direction of Diane and mutters something along the lines of birds of a feather. The two lovely ladies then begin to giggle like schoolgirls. Two middle age attractive, strong-willed females. Yeah, birds of a feather indeed.

"So Kenny, another hard day at the office?" Only Kate calls him Kenny with any regularity.

"You know, the usual." was the reply. At this moment Beth brings out two double cheeses, plus chicken Caesar and a glass of pinot for the ladies. "When did you guy's order?"

"Well," Diane says, " I saw these two gentlemen out on the town and thought they were up to no good, so I called this one guys wife and decided I needed to investigate further. Well low and behold if I wasn't right. These two guys thought they could get away with no good without their ladies and I could not allow that. So I call my friend here and invited her to dinner." Birds of a feather indeed.

"Well then, I guess as policemen, Loot, we are bound to seek out these two *alleged* men who are up to no good and stop it before someone gets hurt, don't you think?" Loot responds in kind and breaks out the badge and handcuffs. Loot makes some kind of retort about people who are up to no good being unable to escape the long arm of the law. This coincides with Loot extending his arm, handcuffs in tow. The gesture is met with a smirk by Diane and a roll of the eyes by the lovely Miss Kate. I remark that in the presence of dangerous company there may be a better use of such devices, and Kate quips right back with a 'promise, promise.' The banter eases the tension that was present at the table. The remainder of the evening is spent in the dark little corner of the bar with a little party that even Joey, Beth and Rock join. After that the couples all left, and as for the handcuffs, well that's for your imagination.

SEVEN

The pressure for the three weeks has been unfathomable. The press has been brutal, led by the Sentinel and my old friend Steve Frizz of Channel Nine News. The paper and TV station have been insinuating all kinds of things about homicide and Lieutenant Dan Murphy in general and Detective Kenny Spade in particular. Frizz went as far as to suggest that maybe Detective Kenneth Spade was responsible for the killings himself. Channel Nine quickly retracted the statement and reprimanded Frizz for unsubstantiated allegations. Steve Frizz continued to blast me through the Sentinel and signed on as a special correspondent for the paper to investigate the murders himself. The excessive publicity and ill will between the homicide department and press led to OPD brass getting a lot of heat from the mayor's office. This in turn led to a substantial increase in the amount of time that IAD spent visiting Lieutenant Dan Murphy's precinct. Francis Poncher ensured that he was the point man for IAD. Officer Poncher was in Loot's office and his face daily for a minimum of six hours daily and one day eighteen. I was kept on a tight leash, and anything I had to do was done with Detective's Tolliver and Ronan in tow. Poncher had tried rather vigorously to put himself as the sidekick but Loot's protesting had led to the Chiefs implementing the current arrangement. My personal life was suffering as well. Steve Frizz had reported that Kenny Spade had been seen during day hours at a local watering hole called The Hurricane From Hell. The owner of the establishment, a woman named Diane, had acknowledged she was a friend of Detective Kenny Spade. Steve

Frizz had a field day with this and ran off all kind of stories and tangents that had brought a lot of people to The Hurricane, some to gawk, some to drink, some to support and others to protest. It was taking its toll on Diane, Loot and I. Officer Poncher even went as far as to confirm IAD's interest in the investigation of the murders. The allegations got more far-fetched and brazen as the weeks went, and the standard no comment from Loot and I as per departmental policy just fueled the whirlwinds swirling around the case.

The table in the kitchen was quiet. The coffee in front of both Diane and I was steaming. There was no conversation. We just stood staring at the copy of the Sentinel on the table in front of them. THE HEART OF SPADES. Underneath the caption was a picture of a red convertible Corvette sitting in front of a house. The byline of the article was credited to one Steve Frizz. Mr. Frizz went on to inform everyone that the house belonged to a Miss Diane Ellisin, owner of The Hurricane From Hell, a pub down by the arena district. Mr. Frizz then quoted anonymous neighborhood sources who said they had seen this particular car had been seen in front of Ms. Ellisin's house frequently over the last month. Mr. Frizz then rekindled the fact that Mr. Spade had been seen in the past visiting The Hurricane From Hell during the daytime hours. It never mentioned any type of alcohol intake but merely pondered the facts over why a detective involved in a high profile murder case would be spending his hours in such a manor. The reporter then touched upon the proximity of the bar to the first murder scene, never stating anything but insinuating maybe there was a connection to the proximity aspect of the crime. Mr. Frizz then over sensationalized the lack of progress on the case and began dumping more and more onto the case, the personal and professionally relevant connections between Ms. Ellisin and Detective Kenny Spade, Orlando Homicide. As the article became more abusive and verbose the couple sitting over coffee became more disgusted and finally had no more interest in reading it.

We sat at the table, saying nothing. For moments this went. Both with plenty to say, but never speaking in words. The words were evident. Diane was devastated. Her whole life was violated. Her ethics were questioned. Everything she had worked for was now being called into question. What would this do to her? It could ruin her. What was she going to do? My words were much angrier. The color of my face had migrated from pink to red to purple. The hairs on my arms were standing on end and I could see how much pain Diane was in. A fleeting thought through my head came of Elizabeth. Ironic, for I had not thought of her over the past few weeks. I felt I had just let Diane down, much as I had let Elizabeth Downing down all those years ago. We just sat in silence for an awkward eternity. The coffee had gone from steaming to lukewarm, and had gone untouched since being poured. The quiet was finally shattered when Diane cracked. She began sobbing uncontrollably and buried her hands in her face. I ran over to her and wrapped her in my arms. The crying continued, with Diane moving her head from her hands to the safety of my strong shoulders. She began to cling to me with all her might. I tried to reassure her by holding her as tightly as possibly. Still no words were spoken. The silence was only broken by the melodic ring of Van Halen's "Jump" on my cellphone. I released Diane and went to grab the phone. 'Spade.' I answered. Yes I had seen it. Yes I knew. Couldn't talk, be right there. I violently slammed the phone on the coffee table and went back to Diane, who was disheveled but no longer crying.

"Baby, I am so sorry." was the best that I could do.

"What the hell was that?" Diane sputtered, the disbelief apparent.

"Are you OK?"

"OK! OK! YOU ASSHOLE, DID YOU JUST READ THAT! ARE YOU OK! WHAT'S THE MATTER WITH YOU?!" The anger was beginning to surface.

"Calm down." was my reply.

"CALM DOWN! CALM DOWN! CALM DOWN!" the emotions were beginning to overwhelm Diane again and she started uncontrollably sobbing. I ran over to her and tried to pacify her but Diane was inconsolable. I wrapped her up and then grabbed both sides of her face.

"Listen to me. I Love You." The words were both sweet and sincere, and judging from Diane's reaction was very, very unexpected. "Please listen. I Love You." I had the look of a mother dog that had just given birth to her first litter, compassionate and longing. I hung my head slightly and muttered again I Love You breaking eye contact. The look of shock that had occupied Diane was replaced by one of guarded enthusiasm, if but briefly. She put her hand under my chin and lifted my head.

"What did you just say?" The anger that had been so obvious in her voice before was replaced with a quiet, curious confidence.

"I Love You. I knew it weeks ago when I had to say goodbye to you at the barbecue at Loot's house. I am so in love with you Diane, it scares me." My face was flushed and my voice was trembling. Diane lifts herself and gave me a passionate kiss and melted away to my arms. I held on for a minute or two and then looked at my love.

"Diane, we have a big problem. Huge. We need to talk. But I have to go. That was Loot. Well, you can imagine the rest." I retreated to the living room and grabbed my cell. I dial and begin talking. "Yeah, it's Spade. I need a favor. Grab a copy of the Sentinel. Front Page. You already saw it. Do you know where she lives? Excellent. Yeah she'll be here. I owe you one. Big time. I mean it. Thanks man. See ya." I again turn my attention to Diane.

"Diane, you have just been thrust into the maelstrom know as the public eye. Hopefully it's just an unwanted fifteen minutes of fame. Rock is coming over here to pick you up…"

"Rock? You know his number."

"I have learned to be prepared for anything. Listen to me, there will be even more people around The Hurricane than usual after this. Also, I would expect our friend Steve Frizz to come calling. He will be looking to instigate something with you. Please be prepared. I am so sorry I got you involved in all of this. He wants to hurt me. He will try to hurt you to do that.

The Hurricane can't keep getting all this bad press. Some press is OK. This is too much. I should have known better than this."

"Would you shut up? I have survived a divorce and as a single woman in this town for many years. I know how to protect myself and my bar. But thank you."

I get up and give her kiss. A real kiss. Then I grabbed the keys to the most famous car in Orlando today and heads out the front door. As I reach for the handle Diane calls out.

"Kenny, I Love You, too." I look at her, smile and walk out the door. As I approach the car a portly, middle aged woman approaches the car. 'Is it you?' the question is asked. 'Have a nice day.' is my reply. 'You get that son of a bitch.' the woman answers. I nod my head affirmatively, start the Vette and take off.

The ride to the Hole is quick, but in reality it seems to have taken hours. I play the scenes over and over in his head. Poncher sitting there with his little smug look on his face, musing over his little kangaroo court. The whole time he was giving Loot his stupid little looks like 'I got the better of you. I got the better of you.' By the time the Vette parks itself I am livid. This is evident as I ascend the stairs to the Hole. I am met by Ronan and Tolliver, who try to calm me down. They confirm what I already know, it's Officer Poncher, in all his grandeur, just waiting to sink his teeth into my carcass. I enter the hole and head right to Loot's office. There in his shiny GQ suit is the mammoth Francis Poncher, IAD.

"Well, Detective Spade, nice of you come to work this morning." Poncher is definitely in the house. I dismiss Poncher's presence and turn to Lieutenant Murphy, nod and shout 'Loot.' I then cross in front of Poncher and sits in the leather chair next to Loot's desk, still refusing to acknowledge IAD's presence.

"Well, Detective Spade, as I said, it's nice to see you this morning." Poncher has thrown the first jab.

"*Officer* Poncher, how are you this morning?" I am jumping out of my skin, just wanting to get my hands on the fat pig and stuff him with an apple.

"Well detective you are certainly popular this morning. What do you have to say for yourself?"

I can't resist the opening. "I need a cup of coffee. Can I get you one, *officer?*" Loot gives me a little left right head nod, as if to tell me not to antagonize the animal in their presence. Too late, the fuse has already been lit.

"NO I DON'T NEED A FUCKING CUP OF COFFEE! SIT DOWN!! THIS IS AN OFFICIAL IAD INQUIRY INTO YOUR CONDUCT, DETECTIVE SPADE!" Poncher takes a breath and appears pleased with himself, as his face loses the rosy color it just had and returns to its more normal appearance. I wear a scowl and glance like a lion ready to stalk a gazelle. The look is short lived as it is interrupted by a pouncing. However the response does not come from me.

"INQUIRY INTO WHAT CONDUCT, PONCHER? WHAT KIND OF A GAME ARE YOU PLAYING?" Loot has blown his stack, and everyone in the Hole knows it. The locked door or the drawn blinds can't contain the melt down in Lieutenant Dan Murphy's office. Now the look of slyness is coming from Poncher.

"*Detective* Spade, what do you have to say about the article this morning?"

"What article would that be?" I play it cool but lose the sarcastic tone. Again Loot gives me the nod advising me not to antagonize Poncher. Poncher seems content to stick with the chess match, for now.

"The Heart of Spades I believe it was called. It was quite informative. Well written, too. Are you familiar with said article?"

"Yes."

"So what do you have to say for yourself?"

"Nothing why. It is just more propaganda by a man who dislikes me."

"And what of Miss Ellisin?"

"I'm sorry?" I try to seem clueless but grow increasingly more agitated.

"Is this going somewhere?" Loot is also becoming increasingly annoyed.

"Detective Spade, are you involved with the bartender? Compromising a material witness is grounds for discipline, including suspension or termination."

"WHAT?!!!" I am furious.

"Shut up!" Loot turns to me. "Not another word." Loot picks up the phone and instructs the person on the other end to call Captain Cutler at IAD. Loot is informed that Captain Cutler was aware of the questioning. Good enough, we'll be right down. Damn right, Loot screams, we're coming down town. Loot then slams the phone down and dials frantically. Yes, could I please speak to Ashley? Dan Murphy. Yes, I'll hold. He turns to Poncher and points.

"We'll talk to you downtown." Poncher tries to say something but Loot has him rushed out of the office so rapidly even Poncher himself is not aware of what had happened. Loot then returns back to the phone. After a few minutes Loot starts speaking again. Hi Ash, it's Dan. Yes, I need some help. Downtown. In an hour. Yeah, thanks.

"What's that all about?" I sense Loot is getting uneasy.

"I know a rotten fish when I smell one. This is a head hunt not an inquiry. I am not going to let them put one over on us. You know as well as I Poncher was probably feeding that prick Frizz. So I have a little insurance policy to ensure a level playing field. Are you all right?"

"Yeah Loot, I'm good."

"And how's Diane?"

"Not to good, as you would expect."

"I figured as much. I'm sorry this happened to both of you. You know, Kate said to me yesterday she has never seen you this happy."

"Thanks Loot, I'll be happy when we catch this son of a bitch and put the whole mess to rest."

"Let's go. You know Poncher won't be patient very long." I nod in agreement. We walk out of the Hole. Loot mumbles something in the direction of Poncher notifying him that we will be going downtown together in Loot's unmarked. Poncher is clearly unhappy with that and yells something back at Loot.

This is completely ignored as Loot motions Detectives Ronan and Tolliver to accompany both of us. We make our way down the stairs out of the Hole and through the lot and scurry into Loot's car. Poncher scampers after them, impressing everyone with how well he moves for a man his size. That martial arts rumor might just be accurate. Loot doesn't even acknowledge Poncher as he peels out of the yard.

Loot, Ronan, Tolliver and I all walk into police headquarters and meander to Internal Affairs. I am the recipient of some uneasy glances from some of the patrons of the building and the beneficiary of some back slaps from others. It is definitely a divisive opinion, much like the taste great, less filling argument of years gone by. Captain Cutler is waiting for them Tolliver, Loot, Ronan, and I make our way into the frosted glass door that read INTERNAL AFFAIRS. All four of us are sure to be polite and recognize the secretary as they enter. It is likely to be the only friendly encounter they have for the foreseeable future.

As the group finds their way toward Captain Cutler's office the unmistakable presence of Officer Francis Poncher cannot be mistaken. Judging from the indifference shown when the animated Poncher enters, the fellows IAD employees are aware of and unimpressed by the entrance. Loot, the others and I find Captain Cutler, who simultaneously dismisses Ronan and Tolliver and ushers me into an interrogation room. Loot follows but is directed to follow an assistant into the viewing room. Loot's vehement protests upset Cutler, who screams an obscenity at Loot. Loot screams back to me to hold my ground and wait for what I know is coming. This really pisses Cutler off. Cutler runs out of interrogation and into the viewing room and right into Loot's face. Cutler turns bright reddish purple, spitting all the time. Over and over he asks what have you done, what surprise do you have? You are not going to pull any surprises on me. Cutlers tone increasingly becomes more violent, rage filled and oppressive. Concurrent to Cutlers outburst, Poncher strolls into the room where I am being held and turns on the charm. He offers me a cup of coffee that is accepted. Poncher dispatches someone to get me a cup of coffee. Poncher waits patiently for the lackey to return with my beverage, leaning against the wall with a clever, sly shit eating grin on his face. He never takes his eyes off me and never utters a word. I return the glances, stone faced and passive, but serious. My cup of coffee arrives and is placed on the table. I pick it up and sip it and return the coffee to the table. Cutler's tirade must have concluded because he has joined the party in the interrogation room. I glance to the two-way mirror and gives a nod to Loot. Loot is a little restless, pacing around the viewing room. Cutler runs over to Poncher and whispers something to him. Cutler then retreats to a corner of the room and Poncher walks toward the table and sits on the opposite side of me.

"Hello again, Detective Spade." Poncher's tone is smug and powerful. He projects an image of being content that the proceedings have been brought to his home turf. I turn toward Cutler, who is still camped in the corner.

"What's with the muscle?" I ask, motioning with my head to the police officer manning the door. He is a large man dressed in slacks, a pressed white shirt and tie and armed with a 9 mm and shoulder harness. "Is there something I should know?"

Poncher slams his hands on the desk. "I AM THE ONE ASKING THE QUESTIONS HERE, DO YOU UNDERSTAND?!" He is forceful but not angry. I turn toward the corner and shrugs at Cutler as if to say 'What gives?'

"You were the ones to ask to come down to me, or were you unaware of this?" Cutler is pleased with his little dig. He shoots a wry smile in the direction of Poncher and waves his hands in a circular motion that seem to be both a sign of encouragement and an invitation to get the proceedings moving forward again. Poncher starts up with the questions again.

"Detective Spade, are you currently working the serial killer cases?" Poncher enjoys being in command. I look at the window as if to reassure the friend and commanding officer I know is stuck in that box on the other side of the mirror.

"I am currently investigating a couple of murders. At this time we have not determined that this is the work of a serial killer."

"I'm sorry?" Poncher is stunned.

"Apology accepted." This time it is me in control. Loot is sure to have a smile on his face right now. Poncher starts to slowly boil. The next words come from Cutler.

"Answer the question." His tone is firm and arrogant.

"I believe that I just did." Knight to Rook four. Check.

"Detective Spade, is it not true that you are working the cases of the two young women who had their throats slashed in the past few months? And is it not true that as a result of the course of that investigation you have come to become in contact with the bar The Hurricane From Hell? And is it not true the owner of the Hurricane From Hell is a Miss Diane Ellisin? And is it not true that there is a picture of your car in front of the house of one Miss Diane Ellisin on the front page of this morning's Sentinel."

"I am not sure I understand your question, Officer Poncher." I remain calm and collected, showing no signs of being frazzled by Poncher's questions.

"WHAT?!"

"I don't understand the question." I retain control of the room right now.

"Are you sleeping with her?"

"With whom, the victims? No, Officer I had never met either of the victims before." I am sly but not overtly abrasive.

"NOT THE VICTIMS YOU IDIOT! DIANE ELLISIN! ARE YOU SLEEPING WITH DIANE ELLISIN?"

"DO NOT ANSWER THAT QUESTION!" With that the door to the interrogation room gets thrown open and a stunning, five-foot eight-inch blonde bombshell walks in. She is immediately grabbed on the wrist by the muscle working the door. "IF YOU PLAN ON GOING HOME WITH A JOB TODAY, LET ALONE BEING ARRESTED FOR ASSAULT AND HARASSMENT I SUGGEST YOU GET YOUR HANDS OFF OF ME, SIR!" Her arm is released.

"Who the hell are you?" Captain Cutler is livid.

"I am Ashley White. I am Mr. Spade's attorney and as such I am advising my client not to answer your question." It seems a new force has entered the room. Ashley walks around the table and sits next to me. "Now gentlemen, may I inquire as to why my client is seated before you?"

Poncher jumps out, trying to regain control of *his* interrogation. "This meeting is being held at his behest. He wanted this."

"I see," is Ashley's reply. "Is that true Detective Spade?"

"No, not at all. I came in to work this morning and I had these fine gentlemen waiting for me. They left me with an impression that something was not quite kosher, so I decided I had better bring it to the proper channels to find out if I was in some kind of trouble."

"I see. OK then. Officer ... I'm sorry I didn't catch your name. Nor yours." Ashley turns in the direction of Cutler. "Or that of the gentlemen who was kind enough to put his hands on me."

I am Captain Paul Cutler, Orlando Internal Affairs. That is Officer Poncher, head of this investigation." The muscle at the door remains tight lipped.

"I see. So are you informing me of an official investigation of my client, Detective Kenny Spade?"

"We are simply trying to get some answers." Now it is Cutler who is trying to regain the room.

"So there is no investigation?" Ashley is meticulous.

"There were insinuations in the press today that Detective Spade may be compromising a witness in an ongoing murder investigation."

"Really. Well that is quite serious. Is it really possible that the Orlando Police Department is being guided in their investigations by the local tabloids?" There is no longer any doubt of who is in control of the room.

"I RESENT THE IMPLICATION!" Cutler is becoming unnerved.

"I'm sorry if you misunderstood. I made no implication. You stated you were reacting to an article in the paper. It was a logical progression for me to ask the question that I did."

"Spade, you know you are sleeping with the girl." Poncher has opened his mouth again, trying to make his presence known.

"What girl would that be, officer?"

"The owner of a bar Diane Ellisin. She is a material witness to the investigation."

"I see. So Detective Spade has informed you of her relevance to the case?" Ashley continually throws daggers at the people in her presence.

Cutler is pissed. "He has not told us anything. That's why we are investigating."

"So there is a formal investigation being conducted here?" This woman is on a mission.

"We are simply trying to get to the truth. Isn't that what we all seek?" Poncher is trying to throw an olive branch but would be more successful with a piece of driftwood.

"I see. And what truth would that be?"

"You're client may be compromising a relevant witness in an ongoing murder investigation." Poncher presses forward.

"Have we ascertained her status as a witness yet? Did I miss something?"

Poncher is stewing to a point of boil. "Listen Spade, we know you are sleeping with her. We have multiple reports of your car being spotted at her residence overnight over the last few weeks. We know. Do you hear me? It's in the paper for Christ sake. Are you sleeping with her?"

"Where did you spend last evening, Officer?"

"I resent that. Who the hell were you sleeping with last night?" Cutler has blown his top.

"Captain, I asked where you spent last night, not with whom. And for the record, I spent last night at home, with my husband, Deputy District Attorney White." The silver bullet just pierced the heart of the werewolf. "Would you like to know anything else about my private life, captain?"

"No, ma'am."

"OK then." The onslaught continues. "Have we determined if there is an official inquiry of my client yet?" Ashley mows through the IAD boys.

"No Ma'am. We are trying to determine if an inappropriate act of conduct was occurring between Detective Spade and a witness." Cutler is in major league damage control.

"I see. Have we ascertained if this person, a Miss Ellisin, is indeed a witness to anything?"

"She owns a bar involved in the investigation." Poncher is now trying to focus on issue.

"And, officer, how is the bar relevant to the investigation?"

"Well counselor, the first victim went there the night she died." Poncher appears pleased with himself.

"Was she killed there?" Ashley will not let this go.

"Not that we know."

"I see. Officer … I'm sorry what was it again?"

"Poncher."

"Right. My apologies Officer Poncher. Have you ever been to a bar before?"

"Yes but that has no bearing on anything here." Poncher is again defensive.

"I agree Officer Poncher. Neither does the fact that Detective Spade may or may not have a personal relationship with a woman who owns a bar that people go to but do not get killed in, if I understand you correctly. A woman that, again if I understand you correctly, did not witness any portion of the crimes that Detective Spade is currently working on. Do I understand you correctly?"

"Yes." Poncher is looking for a place to crawl into a fetal position and suck his thumb.

"Captain Cutler, it is Cutler, correct? I am sorry I am really not very good with names." Cutler nods. "I really see no basis for an investigation of my client's personal life if there is no merit based on fact. And for the record, I am contacting the newspaper responsible for today's article and notifying them of my clients intention of prosecuting the entire paper and the author of the article for liable. I believe that my client is no longer needed here. Are we free to depart?"

Cutler nods up and down as Poncher looks at his shoe laces, too defeated to raise his head. Counselor White utters a 'Thank You' and a 'Goodbye.' I get up with my best poker face on and nod at the muscle at the door. He does not crack a smile as he had the same nondescript look throughout the entire conquest. The guy at the door utters an 'I'm sorry' to Ashley who shoots him a subtle smile. With that The Massacre at Internal Affairs is concluded.

Ashley and I are met at the door by Loot, Tolliver and Ronan. Tolliver and Ronan appear agitated. Loot is calm, but not excited. He gives Ashley a hug. I know something is awry.

"What's up, Loot?" Loot says nothing but motions everyone to go outside. There are no words of congratulations of celebration. It is so quiet that anyone of the bunch could have heard the ghost of Elizabeth Downing speak if she were present. No words were spoken in the elevator or the lobby. It is not until they get all the way to Loots patrol car that the myriad of silence is broken.

"He struck again."

"Shit."

"It's bad Kenny." It must be bad. Loot never calls him Kenny. Loot then hugs Ashley and introduces all of the Detectives to Kate Murphy's sister, Ashley. He gives her a kiss and promises to call her later. Ashley knows there is work to be done. Spade gives her a hug and says thank you. He makes a note to self to send her something. Then the four men jump in Loot's car and speed off.

EIGHT

The midday sun glistens off the tinted glass panes of the downtown skyscrapers. The large rectangular metallic sheen sheets of glass give off the appearance of a disco ball being spun by a hip DJ at a teen laden sweet sixteen. The usually ominous afternoon thunderclouds have not yet materialized in the early afternoon heat. The temperature approaches the lower nineties and the pre-storm humidity is settling in over the greater Orlando area. The stickiness of the atmosphere sits on my face. I muse over the simile as the air I breathe hangs over me much like my own desperation to end the madness that is gripping my city, and my life. The deflating ride in the afternoon muck is very unnerving to me. This was the last thing I needed after a particularly brutal morning, not to mention the turmoil of the past few weeks. What I really needed was a good spiritual cleansing of the soul. A cleansing to clear my thoughts and my belief in myself, my abilities, and my imposed determination to protect the citizens of his city. I had to. I owed it to Elizabeth. Oh Elizabeth, where have you been? I have needed your guidance. I am sorry I have been ignoring you. I have been so busy trying to fight the allegations of the ridiculous Steve Frizz that I have forgotten my place. In fact if not for the great friendship of Lieutenant Dan Murphy, I could be in even more desperate circumstances then I care to imagine. Forgive me please, Elizabeth.

Tolliver, Ronan, and Loot tried to speak with me on the way to the newest crime scene but were not being acknowledged by me. Loot told them this was to be expected given the stress of recent events. Both men agreed. Now if only Loot could convince himself. The police cruiser glides off the interstate toward downtown. It rumbles past Church Street Station and off in the direction of the Casa de Zaidi, a new trendy, chic hotel open the previous year right on the skirts of Orlando proper. The building itself was not massive like the tourist havens of International Drive, but rather it stylishly blended into the neighboring architecture to fit the block. The contemporary architecture that is new Orlando was awash in the brilliance of red, blue, white, yellow and orange strobes. There was a gathering mass of paparazzi and curiosity hounds as the police cruiser carrying the homicide team of Murphy, Tolliver, Ronan and I found a channel through the sea of people and pulled in line with the rest of the official vehicles littering the street in front of Casa de Zaidi. The quartet exited the car and walked toward the crystal revolving door that leads to the Casa de Zaidi's lobby. Someone shouted disparaging remarks in the direction of the detectives as they walked toward the entrance. Then came a barrage of insults in particular questioning the ability of Detective Spade to stop the murders that were threatening the city. I knew the voice, but ignored it. Not now, Steve Frizz. Not today. I will deal with you another day.

The situation inside the lobby was one of a mass of chaos. The sergeant in charge came to greet us as we entered the building. He introduced himself as Pedro Vallez. The introductions were passed as the situation became increasingly more hostile. Three men were screaming at a policeman in some foreign language. They were becoming louder and more animated as the situation unfolded. Vallez informed Loot and us that the men were from the Russian Champions on Ice. That group was in the middle of a run of five shows at the TD Waterhouse Center. So why are they in my lobby, I queried? Vallez informed us that it appears initially that the victim was a part of the group, although Vallez was unsure of exactly what she did. Great, said Loot. He told Ronan to call headquarters and get the Chief down here. He needed some higher up to deal with the potential political fallout of this situation. I recommended calling Disney, they usually had access to someone who spoke foreign languages and may be able to help communicate. Who was running the coordination on the arena's end with the skaters? They also may be able to help communicate. Ronan took off to facilitate these issues. Where is the victim? Vallez escorted Loot, Tolliver and me down the hall and up the stairs. The hallways are of a classic, elegant yet contemporary décor that validates the external facade of the hotel. The carpet that runs the hallway and staircase is a curious mosaic of purple and brown geometric shapes that somehow manages to manipulate itself into a palatable pattern. People penetrate all nooks and crannies trying to catch a clue as to what had transpired. There are heads popping from every doorway like the moles from the bash 'em on the head game you see at the arcade. Vallez escorts the detectives up two flights to the third floor. The whole third floor was overrun by flatfoots trying to escort the third floor occupants from their rooms. The odd number rooms on the western wing numbered between 309 and 317 were emptied. The occupants of these rooms were currently being pacified by the proprietors of the Casa de Zaidi at the house restaurant. Fortunately, it was currently lunch time so the timing was convenient. Convenient, but a temporary reprieve. The bright yellow police line tape sectioned off the wing of the hotel that housed the now vacant rooms of the third floor of the Casa de Zaidi. There were two uniforms monitoring the hallway that led to said rooms. Vallez escorted Tolliver, Loot and me through the tape. There was an opening twenty feet down the hall on the left, across from 311.

The body was that of a female, approximately five three and 110 to 120 pounds. She was leaning against a wall on the left side of the third floor ice machine. Her throat was slit from right to left. There was no blood visible on the carpet in front of the hallway. There was a substantial amount of blood staining the ice cubes in the bucket on the ice dispenser tray. The victim was wearing a pair of gray sweatpants and a red and white Russian skating sweatshirt. The shirt had been sliced between the drawstrings that tighten the hood. The cut ran all the way through the letters of the word Russia in the native language. The victim had nothing at all under the sweatshirt. Loot has seen enough. He sent Tolliver to cordon of a larger section of the third floor, which he did without question.

The victims left breast was exposed, and leaning against the barren flesh was a playing card. A now all too familiar card. An all too familiar card with an all too familiar red smudge in the upper front corner. This particular card also had something left to say. A single word, and for me an all too familiar one. SPADE. It was written in blood. It ran from the lower left to the upper right corner, directly across the center of the ace of spades. Loot and I survey the scene. There are no words spoken. The peripheral noise coming from the uniformed officer cannot penetrate the silence that envelopes the two men. The box of a room that houses the ice machine engulfs Loot and I in a cloud of ignorance to all that surrounds us. There is focus and intensity on our faces. Still there are no words to be heard. There is no movement between them.

Two giants stand motionless, as a totem pole at a great Indian festival. Silence and tension are the only prevalent detectable emotions. We don't acknowledge any inquiries made toward us. The stalemate between victim and investigator is pierced by Officer Vallez, who tried to pick the card up off this once beautiful young woman. A death grip second to none applied to Vallez right arm by me announced the stupidity of Vallez's decision. I dismissed Vallez by simply flicking the officers throbbing arm back from where it came. A nod of my head and Vallez was off, heading back to the lower lobby. I mentioned to Loot he had better get Justyna down here to process the scene thoroughly. Loot lifts his head in agreement and breaks out the cellphone and dials quickly. A short conversation confirms the request and with a quick glance I know that she is on the way.

I reach into my pocket and grab a pair of gloves. I put them on and pause. Loot queries as to what's up. I comment on how these are probably similar to what the killer wears. The irony as to how a piece of form fitted rubber or nylon based product can do so much to hide evidence as it can to preserve it is inescapable to both of us. I reach down and pick up the card calling me out. I place it in an evidence bag and seal it. I then return to the girl's shirt and starts examining the fraying caused by the instrument of death at the hands of a killer. The cut appears to have given the instrument of death a bit of a hard time. The cut is not straight. It pulls down toward the left as it gets just below the victims breast. The cut is jagged. It appeared to have given the killer quite a little tussle. There are little red fibers spouting off both sides of the cut. I start to look under the sweatshirt for evidence of any kind when I am interrupted by swearing in some foreign tongue at a volume that would wake the dead. I turn back behind me to the unfriendly site of the three gentlemen from the lobby being escorted by Detectives Ronan and Tolliver and a tall, skinny nerdish looking fellow.

When asked to identify himself, the man answered Timothy Terrence Thomas. When questioned further he informed Loot that he was the interpreter working for the TD Waterhouse Arena to facilitate the Russian Champions on Ice performances in Orlando. The three foreigners are still screaming at the top of their lungs. I rise from the body and hold my hands up and speak not a word with my mouth. The fury in my eyes speaks volumes enough for the three to shut up. I then turn toward Timothy.

"Tim, who is she?"

"It's Timothy." I sigh. Yes, he's one of them.

"Sorry, Timothy, Who is she?" I continue.

"Svetlana Ihavtokysa, three time World Champion, Olympic Gold Medalist and current reigning World Silver Medalist, behind an Ethiopian."

I am aghast. It's my worst nightmare. This is going to be a press spectacular. Worldwide media attention. The preverbal poop and fan would soon being flying directly at me. A world champion. The last thing Orlando Homicide in general, and me in particular, needed was an incident that would bring throws of national and international reporters, photographers, paparazzi and just good old gawkers down on my great city. Yes, the worst day in my life just got exponentially worse. The son of a bitch hell bent on ruining my life had just played his trump card. And right now the killer was playing the master hand. I needed a little bit of luck before the final card was played. Without Lady Luck, I may be in serious trouble of losing this hand. And this city. I know this. I turn to my left and steal a glance in the direction of Loot. I can read his body language. I know the game has just taken a serious turn for the worse. The killer has raised the stakes and now I have to save my city, my friend, my new love and my career. Indeed, I have just been introduced to the worst day in my life.

"Timothy, please take your associates and return to the lobby. We need to collect the evidence. Thank you." I dismiss the Russians, and they are not happy. When Timothy reiterates what I have told him already said they starts flailing their arms violently to and fro and speaking unknown words in a very animated fashion. The trio of foreigners tries very hard to protest their dismissal but my evil glance convinces Timothy Terrence Thomas to persuade the Russians to leave the third floor. The Russian are not convinced and continue to try to push their agenda. One of the Russians breaks out a cellphone and starts dialing frantically. The Russian starts screaming in the phone and the other two gentlemen with him begin to smile wryly. Timothy Terrence Thomas grabs one of the men and tries to lead him back in the direction of the stairs that lead to the lobby. The man that Mr. Thomas grabbed would have none of it and broke away, instead choosing to lunge at me. Detective Ronan pounced on the situation with catlike reflexes and pinned the man to the wall. The other two Russians start to help their comrade but are detained by Tolliver and Loot. The Russians again start screaming something undecipherable to the collection of detectives. The standoff increases in intensity. There is a lot of tussling going on back and forth that is only interrupted by a "What the hell is going on here?" It is emanating from the mouth of an attractive blond lady in a business suit. One of the Russians starts speaking to her and the lady replies back to him in a similar sounding language. I am next to talk.

"Are you the person from Disney?"

"Excuse me?" was the ladies reply.

I am confused. "Are you the translator from Disney?"

"No, officer, I am the hotel manager." was the response.

I am really confused. "Do you speak Russian?"

"Yes officer, I do."

I introduce myself and the rest of the officers present. The hotel manager introduces herself as Emilia Ignolia.

"Emilia, nice to meet you. Could you ask these three gentlemen to calm down and then could you please ask them what their concerns are? I don't want anyone else here to get hurt."

Emilia turns to the men and starts speaking. The words make no sense to us but they seem to have the desired effect. The three calm down and then begin to speak back to her. After a minute or so Emilia turns to me. "They do not want you touching her. To them it is considered shameful to be looking at a woman's body in such a matter."

"I understand. I don't want to upset them any more than necessary. Would it be possible in your opinion to get these gentlemen to return to the lobby?"

Emilia pauses for a second and then says that she thinks the Russians feel the need to protect their fallen comrade. I nod my head in an understanding manner. Then I ask Emilia to see if she could convince them to go down stairs and try to comfort the other members of the ice show. Everyone's job would be easier if we could all calm down. Emilia nods her head and begins to speak to the three Russian men. Her words seem to have a comforting effect on the gentlemen who say something back to her. Emilia turns back toward me.

"They ask me that you give them your word you will not disgrace or dishonor their countryman."

I take my middle and index finger and put them together. I then make an x over my chest. "You have my word. All I want is to find the person responsible for taking her away from them. Please tell them I am very sorry for their loss."

Emilia translates these words back to the men. They appear to be content with what she has just told them. The man who ripped out the cellphone gives a gentle nod in my direction and utters something. He then turns and starts to walk in the direction of the staircase. Loot gives a gentle nod to Tolliver and Ronan who accompany the men. As the men start walking down the hall I turn to Emilia and asks, "What did he say?"

"Politely translated, 'Get the bastard.'" she replies.

"I will. I will." I pause for a second. I am curious. "How is it that you speak Russian?"

"Her grandmother is Russian." These words are spoken by another female voice. Finishing her journey down the hall is forensic specialist Justyna, who walks over to Emilia and gives her a big hug. "Hey sis. Sorry this had to happen to you."

"Thanks. Just help this guy catch the asshole soon. The owners are not going to like all the press this is going to get them."

"No doubt. Don't worry. One thing I know about this case is Detective Spade is very determined to get the killer. He is very passionate about that."

Emilia nods her head approvingly.

"You guys are sisters?" I am in disbelief but Loot is the one who asks the question. The two ladies just crack a smile. I am next to talk.

"This must be Orlando. Talk about a small world. Who would have thought that? Emilia thanks for all your help."

"No problem. Now, when can I get my hotel back?"

I look at Justyna. She is going to need a little while to process the scene. Then we can get the body out of here. I look at Loot. I ask Loot if he thinks they can release the rooms back to the hotel. Loot suggests doing a thorough interview with everyone. I ask him to go with Tolliver and Ronan and begin so I can stay with Justyna and assist her with processing. Loot agrees and accompanies Emilia back toward the stairs. I abruptly stands and shouts, "Emilia thanks for everything." She waves back in his direction as she continues to head toward the stairs. I just chuckle. It's a small world indeed. Now where were we?

Justyna begins by taking out her camera and photographing the ice room and floor and the victims position. Then she breaks out her investigation kit and begins to process the scene. She dusts the sweatshirt for fingerprints. She collects the fibers from the slice put in the shirt by the knife and puts them in an evidence bag. The blood spatter runs from the letter E in the word ice where it is a small sample, perhaps on the order of one millimeter, to the letters C and I where there is a much more prominent concentration of blood. The size of the droplets is about twice those of the droplets at the letter E. There is a substantial blood pool underneath the C right before the cutout that holds the ice buckets.

The ice was dispensed before the girl was killed. The top of the cubes as well as the side of the bucket were all filled with blood. There is a rain band pattern of blood running down the brownish tan metal base of the ice machine that made little droplets dry at the base of the large metal machine. There was evidently a large pool of blood on the floor in the center of the machine, probably from the initial bleed out of the victim. This pool was disturbed by the killer when he placed the victim against the wall, as the blood is not displaced by what you could call drag marks that are only evident when Justyna lifts the victims right leg up. There is present a small pool of blood approximately three-forth of an inch by two inches in this center area of the white tile that is the flooring to the ice room. To the left side of the ice machine is the major area of bleed off that measure almost twenty inches and run four- to five-tiles long and possibly more, as the blood runs under the ice machine as well. I surmise that the killer must have acted quickly to get the victim against the wall, as most of the blood appears to have left her body in this position. Justyna finds that conclusion to be logical. The sweatshirt was red to begin with, but the moisture content was greater on the victims left side and her sweatpants had substantially more staining on the left side, as well as on the back of the legs, which no doubt was from the fact that she had been sitting in blood for a little while. I can only guess from the thickness of the remaining blood pools and spatter and the amount of drying of the blood on the victims clothes that the crime has taken place at least a little while ago. The external edges of the blood pool where already dry and the tackiness but yet not truly stickiness would indicate that. Blood dries from the outside in and the last parts to dry are the very center. This is also where the blood pool is usually thickest. I look at my watch. One forty five. My guess is the killer struck between midnight and dawn. I will let Dr. Parker and the coroner's office decide the exact time. Let the professionals do their job. I rip out a little flip memo book. Was there an ice show last night? Did she attend? What time was the performance over? What time did the group return to the hotel? Did they stop at any local establishments where she could have encountered someone? I can check with Emilia later and see and if she could provide him with any of the answers to these questions.

"What's this?" Justyna has found something.

"What do you have?" I jump up, my curiosity at a fever pitch.

"Look." Justyna pulls back the ice skaters long curly brown bangs and reveals a large contusion or bruise about three inches above and two inches outside of the victims left eye just at the hairline so that only the outer most portion is visible. Justyna manipulates the long brown hair side to side and reveals the rest of the bruise. It is about the size of a baseball. She must have hit her head on the ice machine. "It must be from her hitting the ice machine when he attacked her." I nod in agreement.

"Take her clothes off. Let's see if she has any other bruising." Justyna complies and begins removing the sweatshirt carefully. She gives it to me and I place it in a big evidence bag and seal it. Next she removes the sweatpants. They drip spots of blood, probably picked up from disturbing the blood on the floor when the pants were dragged across them. Again the process is repeated and we remove and bag the victims clothing. We carefully lift the victim and rest her in the middle of the floor. Justyna takes out the camera again and begins photographing the evidence. She begins with the ice machine again. Next she photographs the blood pools in the center of the floor. There is a big void in the pool on the left from where the body actually rested and prevented the blood from spreading out. She photographs it and the drag pattern we noticed first before when we determined he had dragged her. I have a very pained look on my face. Justyna questions me as to what's wrong. I reply nothing, but I know she is right. Something is eating at me. I just can't finger what it is. We next turn our attention to the body. It is a very muscular athletic build, as you would assume from someone with the accolades of an international champion. Justyna photographs the bruise and the death wound. She then turns her attention to the upper torso. I break out my cellphone and call Loot. I tell Loot to send the coroners up. I know this will be a very bad scene if the Russians came back up and see their prize attraction lying naked in the middle of the floor. Justyna points out another small bruise on the victim's upper left shoulder, just in front of the collar bone. I comment on how it is not as big as I would have expected. Why isn't the bruise bigger? If she hit the ice machine hard enough to have such a large bruise on her head, then why is the bruise on the shoulder so small. It does not make sense. Or does it? That's it! "He caught her!" Justyna is puzzled by my outburst and questions me. What do you mean? Oh no, he caught her all right. Caught her indeed. Then he threw her against the wall.

"SHIT!"

"What is it?" Justyna does not follow his train of thought.

"STUPID, STUPID, STUPID! SHIT!"

"WHAT?"

"HE CAUGHT HER!"

"AND?" Justyna is not catching on.

"WHERE'S THE KNIFE? THE GODDAMN KNIFE! WHERE IS IT?" Aha! Finally a question to be asked.

"The knife?"

"THE KNIFE. HOW DID HE CATCH HER WITH A KNIFE IN HIS HAND?" I have finally found that little itch I could not scratch. "How did he catch her with a knife in his hand? Answer; he didn't. He dropped the knife. But where? Roll her over. Photograph every inch of her. I want to see something else. Don't ask me what, I don't know. Make it quick, too, the coroners on the way up. Take them. Then we'll do the ice machine floor. Hurry." Justyna grabs the camera and photographs Svetlana up close. She does the whole upper body. Then she does the legs. She carefully rolls her and photographs the upper back, shoulder blades and rear legs. She then photographs the back of the victims head. The coroner's team has made its way up to the third floor and is coming down the hall. They make their way to the deceased.

"Why was she moved? The coroner's office moves the victim. You know that."

"Sorry. We thought we found a secondary wound." I glance at Justyna and raise an eyebrow as if to say 'What the hell' and the return to the coroner's guys. "Listen, can we get her out of here before the rest of her ice show comes back? She deserves better."

"Yeah, we'll get her out of here, but Dr. Parker will hear of this."

"OK, OK." I step aside as the coroner's office bags the victim and puts her on the stretcher. They then cover the black bag with the ever clichéd white sheet. The white sheet presents a less offensive signature of the fate of yet another victim of the maniac who so enjoys taunting the great detective Kenny Spade. The stretcher is then rolled down the hallway and on to the elevator.

Now that the body is gone I once again turn my attention to the floor of the ice machine on the third floor of the Casa de Zaidi. It is made of ceramic tile, white with an almond marble pattern. The twelve-inch squares run five deep and nine across. I take out a pen and proceed to scour through the blood splatter. Justyna prompts me to stop so she can photograph the area without the body present and also so she can get some good shots of the drag pattern. I comply and allow myself to step off for a second. Justyna takes photographs of the pool and drag pattern. I postulate from the length of the drag pattern and its varying widths that he only dragged her two feet. The killer must have just caught her just before she hit the ground. Could it be that she was almost all the way down? Maybe when she hit her head it startled the killer, so the killer panicked and grabbed her thus forcing him to drop his knife. That may explain why she blocked most of the blood from reaching the hallway. My cellphone rings. I pick it up with a heartless "Spade."

"Hi. It's Diane. The press is reporting the killer has struck again."

"Yeah."

"Spade, listen, this is not just the local press. CNN is reporting some international star has been killed in Orlando. They just put the breaking news out."

"Excellent." The life has just been sucked from my soul.

"Spade, are you all right?"

"No. This fucking guy is ruining my life. Di, the only good thing in my life is you. I meant what I said this morning. I love you. No matter what else happens from now on, please remember that, even if I get distant and stupid and forget to tell you. Please know I mean it. I love you. I haven't ever felt this strongly before and I mean it. I do love you. I gotta go." With that I hang up. I dial Loot. Yeah, it's me. It's on CNN. Yeah, I know. Yeah, I'll be down. Justyna finishes photographing the ice room.

"I'm all done here."

"OK" I reply, "Thanks a lot. Let me know if you get anything else."

"Yeah, I will." With that Justyna starts to gather her materials. She walks down the hall and off to the elevator. I break out my pen again and starts to meander through the volume of dried burgundy stain that has made the white marble tile look like a great cranberry sauce accident from a Thanksgiving gone awry. I gently poke and prod around the scene, stirring and scraping the dry bloody mixture. I break out a flashlight and peer under the ice machine. I cannot see much. I try to budge the ice machine but it only moves an inch or two. I cannot detect any signs of the knife blade striking the floor of the ice room. Did the killer really drop it? Maybe I should come back after the area has been cleaned. There has to be something. There has to be. Damn. Why can't I find it? I throw my hands up in disgust and run them through my thick, wavy hair. Then I slump back against the wall.

Clarity in times of frustration. That's what Elizabeth always says. So why can't I see clearly? Yes, Elizabeth, I know. There has to be something I am missing. This killer knows me, or at the very least knows of me. He has made this a very personal battle, a battle of which I am in jeopardy of losing the whole war. What's that, Elizabeth? Yes, I know I can't allow that to happen. I know I have to focus on his motives for using me as the focal point. I think he must be using me because of my stature as a known homicide investigator. What if I'm wrong? What else could it possibly be? I don't know. What else can I do? The evidence takes me nowhere. So what does that tell me? I don't know, what does that tell me? It tells me that the killer knows what he is doing. It tells you he is very meticulous. And more importantly, it tells you that he is very familiar with your investigative techniques. OK, Elizabeth. That seems to be a logical conclusion. But what does that tell me? Yes, I know that is the question I have to answer. That and many others. I need your help Elizabeth. Please don't let me down.

"Spade?"

"Detective?" Loot and Emilia have returned to the third floor and are inquiring about my status. I grunt as if to subconsciously be aware of their presence. After another thirty seconds reality sets in and I recognize that I have once again been caught in a space not of this earth but rather deep in my soul. When I am questioned by Loot, I just ignore him and move on to another thought. Emilia enquires about when her hotel can be released back to her. I look to Loot for the answer. Loot says he has no issues preventing the turnover from occurring. Emilia wants it as soon as possible because her guests are becoming antsy. I suggest we turn the crime scene back to the hotel, but asks that the ice room be cordoned off. Emilia says she can make that happen. I request another trip to discreetly return to the scene after it has been cleaned. Loot is inquisitive but decides not to press the issue. Emilia concurs and the issue is resolved. We then leave the last known resting place of one of the most known and decorated women athletes in the world.

NINE

Hello, gorgeous. Well, aren't you quite the little looker. You know I have a real soft spot for Asian girls. So young lady, why are you here all alone. It is going to be another beautiful Saturday in Orlando. Don't you have some man to go home to? Some devilish need that you need to satisfy. Oh, yes you do. And satisfy that need you will. Don't look back. No, no, no, don't do that. You can't see me. Na, Na, Na, Na, Na, Na. Hey, nice car. It's an Acura, right. Oh yeah, I bet all the boys check you out in this thing. Oh yes, and you love every minute of it. Where's the fire? You think there's someone following you. Oh, but you don't have to worry about me. I am here to save you. To free you, and to free this city from that damn asshole cop. But don't you worry. It won't hurt a bit. HI THERE. Oh, don't be scared. It's OK. It's OK. The hand reaches out across the neck and the blade it carries slices very neatly across the throat of my pretty little Asian princess. It's all better now my dear. Just sleep. Get your rest. It's all better now. Watch your step. Don't want to give super cop any footprints. The killer puts the knife in the pocket of his sweatshirt. I'm sorry beautiful, could you do me a little favor. Let's just move over here, could you? Oh, you are such a good little girl. Yes, your man friend must be very lucky to have you in his life. You are just the most beautiful thing. Yes, indeed. But something is missing. What could it be? Oh yes. We need to show a little more cleavage. That always gets their attention! We'll just undo this and undo this and this. Well, that is beautiful. You are gorgeous. Can I call you sometime? No, oh well. There is still just something missing. What could it be? A business card. Of course! What was I thinking! Stay here for just a second will you. I have something right over here on the side. Wow! Now that's what I call a business card. Let me leave my number. Where's my pen. Oh yes. Here it is. DETECTIVE SPADE. YOU DISSAPPOINT ME. I EXPECT MORE OF YOU. CATCH ME IF YOU CAN. *The Ace of Spade.* Now I just have to sign it. Sorry dear, mind if I borrow a little bit of your blood. You are so kind. Here we go. A big ol' smudge just for you. THE GREAT DETECTIVE KENNY SPADE! SLEEP WELL ORLANDO! SPADES ON THE JOB! Don't let the bedbugs bite. Mind if I borrow these keys. I just have to run a small errand. That's OK, right? Thank you very much. Enjoy your evening. With that the killer enters the Acura and speeds away. The car drives as a blur until it hit's a certain neighborhood. A certain, eerily very familiar neighborhood. Now let's all wave to the pretty red car. A pretty little red Corvette. Prince would like that.

I jump from the bed. My head is pounding. I sweat profusely like a junky coming off the worst fix of his life. The chills ripple through my body like a stone that skips across the surface of a river or stream striking the surface seven or eight times. I sit upright for two or three minutes, hands covering my ears. He is stalking me. HE IS STALKING ME. THAT WAS MY CAR. HE KNOWS WHERE DIANE LIVES. HE IS STALKING ME. I know full well this won't keep these voices out of my head. This is just simply a reflex action. Diane lies next to him, sleeping quietly. I get up and bolt into the living room. This guy is after me. I was prepared for that. But what if my visions are true? Suppose that the killer really did drive by her house. What does that mean? I have to protect her. But how? I can't tell her that I am seeing visions of the killer in my head. Visions of the killings themselves. That would scare Diane off, no doubt. I sit in the worn down recliner and stare at the beautiful three foot framed spade that sits on the wall to my house. I muse over how much cleaner the apartment is now that I have someone in my life. Someone I now have to worry about simply because I got involved in her life. I sit there quietly and stare. Sitting quietly for what seems to be an hour. Just staring. Hello Elizabeth. I was waiting for you. I KNEW YOU WOULD COME. You are the only one who can help me. I know you would never let me down. That was my department, remember. I let you down. I know, I know, we won't go there. It's not helpful to either of us. No, No. I'm sorry. Please don't go. I need you. I'm sorry. Please Elizabeth, don't give up on me. Please. This guy is in my head again. Why am I seeing this? Why? Elizabeth, what am I missing? It has to be right in front of me. It has to. Yes, I should calm down. I need to think clearly. I know. Thanks Elizabeth.

"Spade?" Oh shit. I'm busted. I woke Diane up.

"Hey babe. Why are you awake?"

"Spade, who were you talking too?" Diane's voice quivers ever so slightly with a twinge of concern.

"No one babe. I was just talking out loud." I am trying really hard to sell this. If she found out whom I was talking to and what I am seeing I just might scare her away. Play it cool, Jack.

"Spade, it sounded like you were having a conversation."

"Nah, babe, I was just talking out loud, trying to verbalize the case. Thought maybe it would give me a clue, you know. Someplace to start, that sort of thing. I'm sorry I woke you." Diane's face leads me to believe she is not buying it totally but she seems to let it slide, at least for now. Diane strolls across the living room and sits on my lap. I rap my arms around her as she buries her head in my shoulder. I try to reassure her as I embrace her tightly. This is as much to reassure myself that I can hold on to her as it is to reassure Diane that I'm OK. We sit in a ratty old recliner just sitting there. A feeling of relief envelops the chair and for a few minutes the problems that engulf our lives are nonexistent. For a few minutes. Until the power button was pressed.

The TV screen blazes the big black letters on the yellow back drop. The message is inescapable. The bright letters in the corner announce the coming of the firestorm. CNN is running the story. "Death of an Olympic Champion." The subscript underneath it finishes the remainder of the horror. "Former Olympic Women's Ice Skating Gold Medalist Svetlana Ihavtakysa Brutally Murdered In Orlando, Fla." The backdrop of the scene is the lit up TD Waterhouse Arena sign that sits outside the multipurpose venue. The reporter is an attractive thirty something who I remember having seen covering a few of the local interest stories for CNN in the past. She worked the last hurricane that crossed southern Florida but spared a substantial amount of the state from serious devastation. Here she stands in the middle of the early morning hours in casual attire reporting what little is known. Some local officials confirmed to CNN on the condition of anonymity that Svetlana Ihavtakysa has indeed been killed. They would not confirm the cause of death but would confirm to her that the circumstances did not appear to be of natural causes. She went on to report that there was not much other information available at this time but that Orlando Police Officials were planning on a news conference tentatively scheduled for 10:30 a.m. There is little else known at this juncture and the reporter very eloquently throws the program back to the host. As the television reverted back to the CNN anchor station the host of the program was joined by a member of the Russian Skating Federation and Interior Minister of Athletics from Russia. The woman from the Skating Federation, a middle aged portly thick necked woman named Nina Shakalova, stated that the Skating Federation was deeply troubled at the loss of their most prominent and recognizable talent. Miss Shakalova went on to say the ice show had been traveling the United States for three and a half months. The Russian Champions on Ice still had another month and a half left on their current North American Tour. Miss Shakalova was unsure at this time what the tour was currently planning to do for its remaining shows. Next the Interior Minister for Athletics got on the air. A well dressed man named Nikolai Savin informed the CNN anchor that he had already requested from the Russian Consulate in Washington that the body of Miss Ihavtokysa be returned to Russia as soon as possible so her family could have a traditional Russian burial. Mr. Savin further stated that the Russian Ministry wanted every effort by the American Police to catch the people responsible for this act of evil. The CNN anchor went on to remind Mr. Savin that there had been no official confirmation of the cause of death of Miss Ihavtakysa. Mr. Savin replied that he had it on good sources from his own people that the death of Miss Ihavtakysa was not an accident at all and he then reiterated his call for justice from the Americans. Both of the guests on the program were then thanked by the host. I picked up the remote and clicked the TV off. I then threw the remote across the room, which scared Diane. I try to console her, immediately recognizing my mistake. Diane quivers, and I back off.

"I'm sorry, babe. This guy just gets under my skin and I feel so helpless. He is daring me to try and stop him, but he is good. The clues all lead me nowhere. I need to catch a break." I try to be honest and reassuring. I realize Diane has not been fully aware of what her relationship to me would mean; but I can see the doubt starting to creep in on her. 'I love you, Diane Ellisin. I did not know that I was capable of that. But I love you. I can never repay you for that. You reminded me of that. No matter what else happens in my life or between me and you, I will always thank you for reminding me what love is. Always. Thank you." I raise my left arm over the tattered recliner and stick it out straight at Diane. There are tears apparent from my eyes, but I make a concerted effort not to cry.

Diane looks at me and stands as if she has met Dr. Freeze of Batman fame. She does not move. She is not in shock as if a deer in the headlights. It is more a question of amazement that this man, whom she has grown so close to over the last few months, had just opened Pandora's Box. The emotion and honesty were not what she had expected. She had been coached by Spades friends, such as Loot and Kate, that he was not capable of such actions. But right in front of her was a man. Not the man she was expecting. Not the man who was trying to capture his arch nemesis. Not the man who was trying to save every person in the city of Orlando, the city this man loved so. This was a man who was solely interested in her. A man who was capable of actual human emotions? A man capable of such honesty that Diane had never seen before, even in her prior marriage. Standing right in front of Diane Ellisin was Diane's soul mate. The perfect person she had wished for while she was a 12-year-old little girl at Western Hills Middle School. Standing in front of her, with his arms stretched out and a look in his eyes. This was not a look of sadness. It was not a look of desire. This was not the look of a man scamming to get a sense of satisfaction. No. This was the look of a man who pouring his feelings out to the one person he thought could understand what he was saying. This was the look of a man in love. And Diane knew it. And it scared her, what had changed? Spade was never like this with her before. Even the afternoon at the bar after the evening they had first made love, Spade was not like this. This was a different Kenny Spade. Not better. Not worse. Just different. And a lot more scary. And a lot more sexy.

Diane dropped the straps on her night gown and jumped on to the top of the recliner, which was not quite prepared and abruptly rolled over to its back. I tried to regain my bearings but Diane did not miss a beat. She was overcome with a need to be with a man so completely in sync with her and she worked her magic. I was a bit surprised but Diane was not allowing any doubt to be present in this moment. The moments that followed were legendary. They were equivalent to Cleopatra and Marc Anthony, Prince Rainier and Grace Kelly, or Pamela and Tommy Lee. This was love pure, spiritual and physical. The festival continued for the better part of an hour, causing the end of the coffee table as we knew it. The aftermath was ruined by my cellphone. The familiar Van Halen "Jump" rings through the living room. Who could this be, I ponder. Who the hell is calling me at five ten in the morning? This can't be good. I wander over to the phone and answer it.

"Spade."

"Detective Spade? Rachael from Coroner Parkers office."

"Good morning. What's up?"

"Well Detective, I just wanted to give you a heads up. Dr. Parker has decided to hit the Ihavtakysa autopsy early so as to avoid the intense scrutiny it is sure to promote so that he can dedicate all of himself to the task to be completed. He is planning on beginning at seven thirty. Out of respect to the OPD and you in particular he asked me to call and wake you. Since

Dr. Parker felt compelled to wake me I felt it was probably wise for me to wake you as well. Sorry for that."

"No problem." I retort. "I was already awake anyway. I think Dr. Parker probably called this one correctly. I know the kitchen has been getting really hot lately." A quick moan on the other end lets me know that Rachael agrees with him. Rachael apologizes again and excuses herself, saying that she'll see me in a few hours. I mutter a 'see ya' and hang up from her. I look around the living room but cannot find Diane. I walk past the recently remodeled coffee table and past the now sideways beat to hell recliner. The living room had been remodeled into primitive caveman after the encounter the two soul mates had just shared. I make it to the kitchen entrance and lean against the doorway. Diane had heard the conversation and knew that I had to work. She stood by the counter back facing me. She was reaching in to the cupboard to grab a cup. The coffee pot was already half full of joe. I stood in the doorway musing over what stood before him. Diane would make the perfect cop's wife I think to myself. This very thought made me very scared and very angry. These emotions surprised me as the thought of something more permanent had been invading my thoughts for the last week or so. It surprised me for as much I was excited to see that Diane could cope with the profession that I had endeavored upon, I was angry. Angry that I was forcing Diane to change from the independent free willed high spirited person who almost turned me down to the introductory barbecue that Loot had thrown all those months ago. That last thought brought a smile to my face as I remembered. It was actually only two or three months prior that I had met the lovely Miss Diane Ellisin. And yet it seemed like so much longer. Yes, I knew she was a keeper. It was this very thought that I was wrestling with. I did not want Diane to change from the successful strong-willed person I fell for, and yet I was ecstatic to see Diane in the kitchen preparing to accept me for what I was and what I believed in.

Diane turned around and caught the smirk that was on my face and questioned me as to its origin. I just shrugged and shook my head. Diane turned and replaced her attention to the coffee pot and the counter. I slithered up behind her and ran my hand up the side of her now replaced nightgown. I then proceeded to fondle her breasts, working in a slow circular motion. Diane giggled. Then my fingers did the walking as they explored the rest of her gorgeous body. Diane's squirmed a few times but actually began to shiver as I worked the side of her neck and left earlobe with his kisses. Within as few seconds the kitchen floor had been occupied with excess clothing that was no longer required to cover its owners. Once the circus of love had ended we hugged silently in a moment as romantic as any that had happened in the last few hours. Then we proceeded to make our way to the table and drink the coffee. Nary was a word spoken as we just looked into the eyes of our counterpart on the other side of the table. Both of us were peering affectionately and yet we both were aware of the inner turmoil that was being masked by their blissful story our eyes tried to sell. We sat in silence for fifteen minutes just gazing through each other until Diane broke the gaze to check on the time. It was approaching six thirty and the dawn was starting to announce her presence. I looked at Diane. I spoke first.

"I'm sorry babe. I have to go."

"I know. It's OK." Diane gave no hint of angst and tries to encourage her man to get on with it. I got up and walked over to her. I gave her a deep, passionate kiss. This was very reassuring to Diane as I went to prepare myself to go tackle my visit with Dr. Parker. I knew better. I knew that Diane was just playing the good role. I knew deep down Diane was terrified. I also knew I had to play coy to keep the façade up, even though they both knew exactly what had just transpired. So I rambled into the bedroom and threw on a green button shirt and a pair of navy khakis. Can they be khakis if their navy? Anyway, that's what I was wearing. I slipped on my black Nike's and rolled over to Diane and gave her one last kiss. I repeated 'I love you,' then I slipped out the front door. The clock was starting to push seven and I was going to have to motivate the Vette for a little magic if I was going to see Dr. Parker before he began the most famous autopsy in America today. I hit the front stoop and turned to lock the door. The spider sense starts kicking into overdrive. Or the Spade sense if you will. Anyway, something was awry and I knew it. I spun and started to make my way down the walkway to my trusty little car. With every step I took my right hand inched ever so slowly, ever so subtly toward the gun sitting on my right side hip. I was within a second and a half of winning the fastest draw in the west when the spider sense caught the picture out of the corner of my eye, just in the edge of his periphery. Hello. Gotcha. I knew. I should have figured. OK slick lets deal with this. I made my way to the front door of the Vette and unlock it. Seconds later a rustling sound, very faint, emanates from the yard of my neighbor to the right. This guy is good. I know Karl does not leave for work until nine thirty. Man, this guy is good. But I gotcha. I open the door. As I duck into the Vette, I pirouette and scream, "Hey Frizz, can I buy you a cup of coffee? I'll be at Louie's for the next ten minutes." I then shut the door and hole shot from the street in front of the house. Diane is alarmed at the way he left. She peeks out the redecorated living room and sees a suspicious man on Spade's neighbor's lawn. Diane ducks and calls 911 to report the suspicious person. The shadowy figure melts his way three houses down and into a small four door car.

I check the rearview and whip out the cell and dial Diane frantically. She does not pick up. It goes right to voice mail. I swear a little and throw the phone on to the passenger seat. WO,WO, WO, WO, WO . SHIT! I spin the Vette two hundred and seventy degrees in a move that Michael Andretti would envy. Louie's is six blocks down on the right. I dial Diane again. This time she answers.

"Hey beautiful. Listen, that reporter out front."

"I know. I saw someone out there when you left and called 911."

"Good job. Be careful. They're after you now as well. I love you Diane."

"I can take care of myself." Diane retorts. No argument here, I think to myself. "I'll go out the back."

"Be careful. I love you."

"Relax, I am fine. Bye Spade." With that Diane hangs up the phone. Oh yes, she'll be a perfect cops wife I say to myself as I hang up the phone. Louie's is just coming into view. The Vette coasts into the parking lot and shuts her down. One final look into my rearview mirror lets me know some maniac is gunning for me. And I eagerly await this visit.

Louie's is a little mom and pop diner set just off the main drag. It has the look of an old Streamliner but it has the ambiance of grandma's kitchen when we were growing up. Louie and Edna have run Louie's for thirty-seven years. I have graced them for the past five or so years four to seven times a week. As I stroll in Edna seats me and Louie shouts "Mornin' Spade" from the kitchen area. Edna seats me and asks if I want coffee. I inform her that I will be joined very shortly by someone, I think. She pushes for more information and I say it probably will not be friendly. She leaves it at that and returns to the counter. Ninety seconds later the oppressive Steve Frizz bounds through the door. He huffs over and across from me at the table. Edna comes over and offers to take their order. I start with a coffee. Edna turns her attention to the stranger seated across from me. I introduce them.

"Edna, this is Steve Frizz."

"The reporter?" This is followed by a humph and a scowl that a grandma would give to scold a misbehaving young one. "Would you like some coffee?"

I chime in. "I highly recommend the bacon and eggs. The best in O-Town."

Steve Frizz bullies up. "Coffee. Black." Edna turns and asks me if I'm eating. The usual was the reply. Edna turns here and asks Steve Frizz if he would like anything else. He snarls back "Just Coffee." Edna takes her leave and the DMZ across the table stands as tense as always. I fire the first foray. "So Steve, why were you at my place? I figured you'd be at Diane's."

"Oh, I had Jungha Pongre covering Diane's. I just happened to get lucky today."

"Well, lucky me I guess. It's been awhile since anyone agreed to have coffee with me."

Frizz fires back. "It's my honor, detective."

I am equal to the task. "You know, I really do recommend the bacon and eggs. They're awesome."

"No thanks. So detective how's that case of yours coming along?"

"Which case would that be Steve?" I am content to throw the jab.

"Let me fill you in detective. There is someone killing people in Orlando. Someone who has a thing for you. In fact, some people speculate it is you."

"Well, Mr. Frizz, allow me to reply. Would you like my opinions on or off the record?"

"Spade, there is no off the record with me." Steve Frizz's tone is abrasive and sarcastic.

"Well that's good to know." My tone oozes its own venomous sarcasm. Anyone who was familiar with his reporting for the last few months know that Mr. Frizz is very hot on rhetoric and very low on content or reliability. I can only chuckle inside. "Well Mr. Frizz, for the record, I am aware of the fact that there are some cases involving some very gruesome murders in Orlando. In fact, I am investigating some of them. That's my job. Detective Kenny Spade, Orlando Homicide." I extend my hand across the table. "Do you know anything about these crimes? Maybe you can offer me some clues." Frizz begins to spew some more vicious insinuations at Detective Spade but he is interrupted by a cup of cold Black coffee. My coffee is hot and the bacon and eggs smell divine. Frizz gets a growling in his gut but is unwilling to give me my due. He looks unfavorably at his coffee and returns to his adversary.

"Spade, my best clue is to look in the mirror. You know who did it. You should. You guys are real close. Real close."

"The only one close to me right now is you, Mr. Frizz. Should I investigate you?"

"Cute. But you aren't that smart Spade. I'll get to the truth."

I, as always, have an answer. "Mr. Frizz as a reporter you should know not to use the word aren't in an official capacity. It is grammatically incorrect." Frizz has had enough of the cuteness and rises from his seat. He turns to leave and then pirouettes and slams his fist on the table, spilling his full cup of cold coffee around the glass. "You are not rid of me yet." He then spins away and heads for the door. I holler after him. "I will keep reading your articles. Hopefully you will get the truth. Then I will arrest that person. Happy hunting." Frizz turns and glances at his breakfast buddy, shoots him a look and throws the doors open and leaves. I just turn my attention to my eggs. Edna comes over with a big smile and asks if everything is OK. I answers with my standard, 'Excellent, as always.'

I glance down at my watch and look at the time. Seven twenty-five. Fabulous. I throw some money on the table and runs and gives Edna a kiss on the check and take off. I run out to the Vette and rub my hand across the roof. "Well girl, we're going to have to fly." I jump in and fire her up. Seven thirty. Fabulous. The good doctor will have already begun his investigation of the most famous dead Olympic Champion in the world today. I slam down the interstate to get to the Orlando Coroner's Office. The trip takes me seventeen minutes. I roll in and find Rachael at the doors. Dr. Parker is indeed half way through his examination of Svetlana Ihavtakysa. I question Rachael regarding any unusual or alarming issues that Dr. Parker has noticed so far. Rachael states that Dr. Parker actually started his autopsy early and has not given her any indication of anything unusual during his investigation.

Rachael has had many different opportunities to witness Dr. Parker work over her three plus years in the Orange County Coroner's Office. She had come to admire her mentor tremendously during her tenure there. Rachael was mesmerized by Dr. Parker's meticulousness. Dr. Parker always had his diagram chart set on the end of his work table. He would always indicate the wounds or injuries on his chart as soon as he hit the cold stainless table that supported his newest subject. After he was finished with his markings he would go through the hair very finely looking for any signs that would assist him with the diagnosis. Next Dr Parker checked the eyes ears nose throat any body cavities. He had a mind as sharp as the scalpel he used to dissect his topic and would step off, so as to take in mentally all of his discoveries. Dr. Parker never wrote anything down until after he had completely finished his examination. After his exploration of the orifices the next thing to be done would be the internal search. The good doctor would be looking for any signs or clues to whatever happened to be the usual suspect, depending on the specific case at hand. Dr. Parker was exceptionally meticulous treating every search. As a spiritual man, Dr. Parker treated each and every person he had to autopsy as someone's mother, father, daughter or sister; with the utmost dignity and care. After he concluded his business, Dr. Parker would leave the examination room and discard his green scrub type doctor's jacket in the laundry basket on the other side of the thick white rubber and plastic door that separates the examination room from the scrub down room. At this point in time Rachael jumps into motion. She is responsible first for the collection and processing and securing/labeling of any biological samples Dr. Parker may have collected during his process. After she makes all of those arrangements, Rachael next cleans up the instruments of Dr. Parker's art. Then Rachael would arrange the return of the body to its holding place until it gets transported or released to families or funeral home personnel. The entire process took around a half-hour after which Rachael would retreat to Dr. Parker's office. She would find Dr. Parker writing the findings on his official Office of the Coroner letterhead. On cue, he would begin discussing the case at length with Rachael. He would go into great detail about his findings or suppositions ask her what she thought and then explain his conclusions. They would speak for long periods of time, professor and apprentice just discussing the science of death.

I stood in amazement at the passion portrayed by Rachael as she discussed Dr. Parker's procedures. I had never expected to be given such a zealous dissertation while waiting for Dr. Parker's conclusion. Rachael beamed as she talked about her mentor, and it was obvious she felt more than just admiration. I just chuckled inside, surmising that Rachael never went any further where her feelings were concerned. All of her musings had surprisingly made time fly by, for when I looked up from Rachael I saw Dr. Parker finishing up with the most renowned autopsy being done on the planet today. Rachael too was surprised, and a little embarrassed, for when she realized the doctor was done she blushed a little and ran into the room to jump into action. I now understood why I had gotten a phone call from an assistant to the coroner at a quarter to six in the morning. These two were a very tight team, and I now understood why she would be aware of middle of the night decision made by the coroner.

Dr. Parker gave a shove to the great plastic white door and made his way into the scrub down room. Rachael was already in the examination area securing all of the blood for processing. Dr. Parker discarded his lab coat and began cleaning himself up. Rachael finished up her mission and went into the scrub room. She put her hand gently on the good doctor's shoulder. He finished washing his hands and she handed him a towel to dry them off. The two of them then came down the small, dimly lit hallway and joined me in the observation room. Rachael blushed.

Dr. Parker extended his hand out to me. "Sorry to drag you out of bed so early in the morning. I thought this would probably be a little more prudent, to escape the media onslaught."

"I was awake anyway doc, but I thank you for the heads up."

"Yeah, I kind of figured that. I'm afraid I can't be of that much help." The room fills with the sounds of Van Halen's "Jump" as my cellphone goes off. I look at the caller ID and sees it Loot. I slam the silencer and shove it back into my pocket.

"Sorry doc, you were saying?"

"Do you need to answer that?"

"No. So?"

"Well, as I was saying, I am not going to tell you much you don't already know. She was killed by a wound to the neck. It was a substantial neck wound, running right to left. Fairly deep. Sliced her jugular and carotid. Victim bled out. The knife wound looked similar to the others. It was probably the same guy. I did see some subcutaneous bruising on the upper left shoulder. There was also some less traumatic bruising running under her right breast and across her chest and a small bruise on her right wrist..."

"Where he grabbed her to break the fall."

"Probably. Other than that she looked to be in perfect health. I should have the bloods in a week, maybe a little less. Rachael has everyone putting a rush on all your victims. Whatever you need."

"Thanks doc. Rachael, thanks for calling and thanks for all your help."

Rachael blushes once more. "No problem detective. Call me if Dr. Parker or I can be of any further assistance."

I shoot her a sly smile. "Thank you. I hope it doesn't come to that." I extend a hand to Dr. Parker. "Thanks again, doctor. I appreciate you keeping me informed."

"No problem." Dr. Parker extends his hand and we shake. I am impressed by how strong a hand he has to do such delicate operations. "I will have Rachael send you a copy of the final autopsy report when the final blood work analysis comes in."

"Thanks." I extend my hand out to Rachael. "I appreciate everything. Good luck." Then I return to Dr. Parker. "You have quite the little assistant here. A true professional. You are very lucky."

Now it is Dr. Parker who is blushing "Thanks, detective. This I know." Rachael shoots me a little smile and wink. She receives a quick hand squeeze from Dr. Parker that startles her, but her smile grows. Curious, is all I can muster. Very curious, these two. I exit stage left and head down the dreary hall toward the rear exit of the building that houses the coroner's office. I make it all the way to the lobby and peak outside through the sun glare reflecting off the full-length glass windows and doors that encase the lobby. Already massed outside is the unsightly image of 10,000 antenna littering the parking lot like the screen segments of a cartoon fly's eye. It seems there would be no waiting for the ten thirty news conference at city hall. No, everyone was going to get answers at, I glance down at my watch, 8:33 a.m. At least that's what the army of worker ants whom were masquerading as reporters, all dressed up with the husky camera men and women would like to have you believe. I doubted very seriously that any of these little brown insects I had grown so fond of despising over the last few months was going to get answers at 8:34 a.m.

I circle back through the dreary hallways and went to the front lobby. There I found an even more populous smattering of news trucks, including all major US networks, CNN and BBC, lining the street that passes in front of the antique brick building that has suddenly become the hippest place in greater Orlando and probably the entire U.S. The Corvette was left by the side entrance closest to the exit near the rear lobby. It was currently being staked out by a few of the locals whom had become very familiar with the Vette over the recent press blitz one Detective Spade had received. I had to decide how to run out to the car. I stood in the hall adjacent to the rear lobby attempting to avoid being spotted. There was a pair of uniformed OPD officers checking all identifications of all persons attempting to enter the building under employee credentials. Standing just outside the glass confines of the rear lobby was one local reporter that I had become very familiar with. In fact, we had just shared a less than lovely cup of coffee. I decided to try and make a stealth exit back out the locked side door that I entered through and turned to go find the key master, aka Rachael.

The very familiar riff of Van Halen emanated from my pocket and virtually the whole lobby turns and looks at the newly exposed whereabouts of the owner of the red Corvette. Busted. Damn. So much for the quiet exit. Steve Frizz has also heard the guitar laden ring tones of Detective Kenny Spade's cellphone and was now thrashing at the security checkpoint to get my attention. The overbearing egomaniac was now trying to play himself off as my long lost brother. Probably everyone in the quarter mile vicinity heard the man scream my name and the rear lobby entrance became a screaming mass of humanity. It became so encased that the pair of OPD officers checking ID's were unable to control the influx. The familiar "Jump" begins to permeate the chaos that is the back entrance to the building housing the coroner. I hit silence. The phone rings again. A mob mentality is now running supreme, and the two officers are doing a masterful job, but like the Alamo the fort can only be held so long. "Jump" fills the air again. I grab the cell and scream WHAT! "Loot, I am at the coroners get me some help down here! NOW! … No I am trapped down here, Can't even get to me damn car! Yeah I'm trying. I KNOW! I'll be right there." With that I decide to confront the beast head on. I walk over to try and rescue the officers and again take control. I make it through.

"Why are you here? The news conference is at City Hall!"

"Spade, why are you here, what did the coroner say?" Frizz is barking, grandstanding and demanding an answer.

"The coroner told Detective Spade the following; there will be an autopsy performed within the next twenty-four hours. It will be as dictated by the coroners guidelines issued by the state. All appropriate testing will be done and the results will be available in seven to ten days. The coroner will be asking for the results to be expedited. When we have those results we will notify the appropriate authorities and the media will be informed of its release, allowing the authorities to make their decision on its release to the public. This is a place where we have more than one case we are responsible for. There is no information here and no statement will be released today. Please go away so we can start our workday. We have a lot of families that need our help and we ask your respect to them in their time of grief. Please leave. That is the only statement the coroner's office will be issuing today." The voice is booming and commanding. The chaos that was rampant has been replaced by a stunned silence. A silence only broken by a platoon of flashing strobes and ear piercing shrills that enforce that my message was received and the reinforcements have arrived.

Steve Frizz tries to fire a parting shot, "Who are you, what is your name? Who are you and what authority do you have to make that statement?" Rachael shoots Frizz a devilish smile and starts to walk back to the coroner's office. I take a few steps and whisper 'You're Amazing' in her ear. A much more devilish smile a squeeze of my hand lets me know it's all in a day's work. Rachael then struts as if in a victory lap down the hall and back to her assigned spot next to the most amazing man in pathology today.

I pirouette so as not to draw attention to Rachael and make my way to the recently stunned back lobby. I navigate through the myriad of press. As I scoot by Steve Frizz I can't resist. "You should have had the bacon and eggs. I told you they were delicious." The comment does not go unnoticed and all of the fellow story hounds begin grilling Frizz as to why I would say that. Did they have breakfast? Is Frizz getting an inside scoop on the murders? What kind of deal did Frizz have set? As the emphasis changes from one person to the other I make my way to the Vette and fire her up. Some of the newly present reinforcements clear a path for me as the rest of them try to detangle the back and front lobbies of the media bog down. I navigate the masses and hits the open road then starts to fly toward the Hole, and a pissed off Lieutenant Murphy.

I make my way through the Hole across the sea of lifeless desks that clutter the floor. I made my way to Loot's door, knock, and then enter. Inside the office stands an attractive looking Latino and a bevy of suits that number three. I look at Loot trying to gauge the magnitude of the situation. I address the group with a nod and go over to Loot's desk and sit in the chair to the left side of the desk. The three suits are huddled in the corner by the American flag. The leggy lady in the short black business suit is sitting in the chair closest to the suit huddle. Loot is perched leaning against the back of his high back desk chair.

"Spade, these are special agents Smith, Johnson and Thomas. The young lady is special agent Lopez."

"Of course." I reply.

Loot continues. "These special agents are from the FBI. They are here to assist with the Ihavtakysa case."

"Loot, why are they here?"

Legs is next to reply. "I am special agent Lopez from the FBI. I am a profiler. I am here to assist you by trying to help you see what the killers thought pattern could be."

"I'm all ears." I can't masquerade the sarcasm in my voice.

"Spade, please." is Loots reply.

"Feds? WHY?" I am upset at the presence of my new found allies.

"An International superstar has been murdered, detective." One of the suits has proven to have knowledge of the English language. "This is a very important international situation. We need to show the international community that we are capable of handling this. The Russian embassy has practically demanded it."

"I'm sorry did I miss something. I thought this was a murder case." I am not the least bit intimidated.

Loot is becoming agitated. "Spade, we have our orders from the Chief. Hand in hand with the FBI."

"Loot come on. How can I do my job while I'm baby-sitting?"

"Spade this is now a political situation. We need to appease everyone."

"Bullshit Loot. This is a goddamn murder investigation. I need to find out who is killing girls in Orlando. I don't care about politics."

"Come on Spade. There is a right way and a wrong one,"

"Come on Loot, don't feed me that crap."

"Damnit Spade, that's an order. We will graciously accept their help."

"Loot come on."

"Spade. That's an order."

"Shit." The rage in my eyes is second to none and the venom from my lips rivals that of the king cobra.

"SHIT!" There is nothing more to be said.

"Detective Spade, as I said I am special Agent Lopez. I am here to give you a profile."

"Left side or right?" My venom has now liberated itself from its cobra basket and is hissing away wildly. That draws another bit of venom, which of that his best friend and boss. "Spade, sit down and shut up. THAT'S AN ORDER! Go on, Agent Lopez."

"Thanks. Well, let's start with the basics. From your forensics we can assume he's male." I look at Agent Lopez with a contemptuous look of amazement at what Agent Lopez had just determined. *Well thank God for your insight, that was most helpful.* Loot tries to reel me back in and focus on the agent. I shoot Loot a look of disgust and become restless, fidgeting in the chair. Special Agent Lopez pushes forward. "Do you think he is disturbed?"

"What?!"

"Do you think the killer is deranged?"

"Hello! He is cutting off young women's heads!" I am jumping out of his skin and screaming at this point. Loot tries to calm me and get him to sit down, but meets with little success.

Agent Lopez is not fazed. "Do you think the killer is mentally unstable?" I try to be serious and answer her. "He knows perfectly well what he is doing." Lopez presses on.

"What can you tell me about the cards?"

"The first had a smudge. It was blood. The second had a smudge. It had a hand written note addressed to me. It was written in red ink. The third had my name on it. Written in blood, the letters probably shaped with the tip of the murder weapon."

"Do you think he knows you?"

"I think he is probably familiar with me. He probably followed my cases over the past few years through the news and decided to test me with a battle of wits."

"So you think he's intelligent?"

"No, I think he's a killer."

Agent Lopez is not amused. Her pretty little Latin blood begins to boil. "Listen detective I am here to help *you.*"

"Bullshit! You are here because some suit in DC is trying to soothe some politician who is trying to appease some pissed off comrade in Moscow because this asshole you want to *Go Fish* with is killing girls in my town. You aren't here to help."

With that outburst Special Agents, Thomas, Jones and Smith have heard enough and get up to go intervene for their associate. Loot tries to intercept and pacify the situation but the king cobra is out of his snake pit. He is in full colors and will strike at anything moving.

"Help me? Help me how? Listen, what are you going to tell me about him? What do you want to know? He is most likely male based on the size, force and angles of the cuts. He is obviously familiar with me, which means he knows me or is able to follow the news. He is excessively meticulous, every act he commits he has perfectly planned. The prior two indicate at least a decent amount of intelligence. He studies his victims, is very careful about when to act, for there is never an indication of the act he has committed until someone finds the body. Think about that. He has killed a woman in a lobby who is a very famous athlete. She was killed in a hallway of a well populated hotel. Victim number two. Killed in the parking lot of a bank less than fifty feet from someone's backyard at eight o'clock on a Saturday night. This guy kills them and doesn't even give them a chance to scream. He is psychotic but not deranged. He is OCD based on how he even manipulates the massing of the blood pools. He chose a world famous athlete, a successful attractive professional woman and a young rich girl with little else distinguishing her. He stole a car no one realized was missing for twenty-four to forty-eight hours. He does not distinguish based on race and the only thing that all these victims have in common is that this maniac used them to get to me. He is probably well groomed but not GQ, for he distinguishes himself from no one, either in a hotel lobby or in an industrial/residential district. A loner? I don't think so. This guy is an everyday Joe. Maybe someone his co-workers pick on behind his back for being too neat. A nerd. All his pencils in his pocket protector. He always has neatly pressed suits and newly buffed shoes. He has an active if not exceptional social life. Is there anything you can add to that, Agent Lopez?"

"I don't mean to insult you, detective. I am just trying to help." Agent Lopez is slightly embarrassed.

"I don't mean to be mean, agent. I have analyzed this bastard for the last three months. You guys are here simply to be suits. I know all about this ass. I just need to catch him."

Agent Johnson, the shortest of the generically named FBI agents decides he must get his two cents to make his presence official. "Regardless, detective, of your opinions we are here to stay. We are here to help. But with one snap of my fingers this will all go away and the FBI will be in control and you will be writing parking tickets. Don't mess with us."

"Listen to me you disgusting little jumping bean, you couldn't catch a mouse with peanut butter. Don't you threaten me, you son of a bitch. I know more about this shit then you'll ever know about your own mother. Trust me, there will be no more. I promise you on the life of Elizabeth Downing there will be no more!!" I have the fire of brimstone glowing in my stare and I am ready to take mighty mouse and make him the final stake of the transcontinental railroad. The little jumping bean fires up as if he is going to take a smack at me, who sits glaring as if to invite the deed to occur. Agents Smith and Thomas restrain Agent Johnson, probably to save him from a serious beat down. Loot fires over to intercede between the two men and Agent Lopez quietly backs herself against the wall. Johnson still has a head of steam and the shouting between us creates a cavernous echo in The Hole that leads everybody in the vicinity to be drawn to the vicinity of Lieutenant Murphy's office. The tension is so thick the iceberg that sank the Titanic would just bounce off it. As order begins to be restored, that all too familiar guitar riff from a certain detective's cellphone begins to saturate the testosterone filled cubicle. I pick it up with a 'Yeah' and after a couple of nods and uh-huhs say 'I understand' and hang up. I shoot up from the chair and extend my right hand to Agent Lopez. "It was very nice to meet you. I am sure you're very good at what you do. Good luck." With that I turn and drift to the door. I grab the handle and spin it. The door begins to creek open and allow fresh air to infiltrate the tense atmosphere, Agent Johnson yells at me to get in here and sit down. I just smile. The other two begin to chime in telling me to stop, to which I reply, "Go back to DC and shine someone's shoes." I then rip the door open and begin to walk across The Hole. Loot jumps up from his spot and rips the door, chasing after me.

"Spade, where the hell do you think you're going?"

"Church."

"Spade, get your ass back here now."

"Sorry, Loot, got to purify my soul."

"SPADE!!!" The last bellow falls upon deaf ears as I navigate the Hole and find the back stairway. The door slams shut with Loot still screaming. All eyes in the Hole are now fixated on Loot and his office full of mouth wide-open suits. Detective Ronan spoke up and asked if he should go chase after me but Loot knew better. It would do no good at this point. He would read me the riot act later. It will do no good anyway.

I jump in the Vette and let the rock blare. The ever so needed interruption was provided by Rachael, my favorite new county employee. She had called to inform me that the body of Svetlana Ihavtakysa had been released to the people from the ice show. Rachael had heard through the grapevine that they were going to have a small mass for her at an Orthodox church on the Southside. I glance down at his watch. 9:45. The mayor's news conference begins in approximately forty-five minutes. But I had another place to be. I never missed one. And I knew of a certain little orthodox church on the Southside. And I knew where my presence was needed. As I began to approach the area where the church lay, I turned the radio down and slow the car so as not to draw attention or intend disrespect toward Ihavtakysa's colleagues and friends. As I reached the church the coffin has just been escorted into the church. There is a contingent of around seventy-five to one-hundred persons who have come to pay their respects to this champion, their countryman, who has truly shown the world what a great individual effort can do and what a true champion is and what they can do.

I do not exit my car until after the simple wooden box holding a nation on its shoulders is escorted in to the elegantly simple little house of worship to honor their fallen hero. I allow the entrance of people who have a more personal interest than I and then I made my way to the rear of the church so as not to bother them. After a couple of minutes to allow everyone to settle in, I made my way back to the last pew of the church. I sit very quietly in the last row of the church paying my respects to the very last victim of the psycho that was terrorizing his city. I had made this promise to Elizabeth. I made it after leaving the coroner a few hours ago and I made it again on the way over to the church. I sat quietly and listened as a beautiful aura of music words and loved filled the main hall of the sanctuary. Although I understood nothing of the proceedings, I was still moved by the genuine passion and affection the congregation gave its fallen comrade. After the ceremony was completed, the three Russians that were at the hotel on the third floor asked why I was here. I informed them that I was here simply to pay my respects and for no other reason. It was important for me to tell Svetlana that I was sorry and sincere to do my absolute best to find the monster responsible for this gathering. The Russians muttered something indecipherable and then thanked me for showing up. I shook their hands and made his way out the back door.

I waited back by the Vette as the congregation escorted the coffin out to the hearse that awaited its precious cargo. Once again the silence of the day is disrupted by the familiar ring of Orlando's most famous detective's cellphone. I pick it up with the customary 'Spade.' It's Loot. He wants to know where I am. I tell him I went to church, just like I said I was going to do. Loot is at the mayor news conference which is about ten minutes underway and expects me to be there. This has become a highly charged situation and I need to be a part of the team, not the lone wolf. I tell Loot I'll be there but I have unfinished business first. Loot will have none of it and orders me to show in ten minutes or I will be reprimanded. I say I'll sign the paper. The conversation is terminated as I will listen to no more. I lean against the car with this rugged look and just wait for the finishing of the service in front of me. The coffin gets loaded into the hearse and the car leaves. There is a mini tour bus behind the rear of the ice-show participants, along with a few miscellaneous cars. I quietly absorb the proceedings, allowing it all to unfold in front of me.

As the Russians gather themselves an attractive short female approaches me, unaccompanied by anyone. She walks straight up to me and stops right in front of me. She has streams of mascara covering her brightly red painted cheeks, evidence of her recent crying. The black streaks streaming down her pale, rosy cheeks make her look like a painting of a sad clown. The girl cannot be more than sixteen or seventeen. She musters all her strength to speak to the strange rugged looking man in front of her. The English is broken and not very fluent, but I admire the considerable strength the girl is showing. She stares directly into my eyes and begins to speak. Her voice is quivering and wrought with distress. Her words are weak and her accent is thick. The words are simple and the message is clear. A tear drops across her lips as she speaks. "Mister, she was my friend. She teach me. She teach me a lot. You get this bad man. You get him and you kill him. You kill him mister." She starts to cry as the last words fall. I reach out and hug the young Russian skater. Just then the loudest of the three gentlemen I had first seen on the third floor of the Casa de Zaidi comes and interrupts. "We will take her now." His voice is thick but surprisingly lacks any compassion. The gentleman grabs the young skater by the arm and escorts her to the bus. I shout out, "I will catch him." The girl looks back and attempts to throw me a smile. I mutter again under my breath. 'I will catch him. I have to.'

TEN

The Vette hides behind the dumpster that sits in the back of the strip mall that houses The Hurricane From Hell. I sit at the bar with Beth and Diane behind it. I tell Diane that the Vette is better not being out in plain sight. Diane is worried about vandals. It is a strip mall, after all. I don't care and I just work on my draught. The TV above the bar is set to the local CBS affiliate. It is showing coverage of the Mayor of Orlando's news conference. The coverage is national and it shows clips of the mayor reviewing and confirming the facts of the case. The mayor does verify the fact that the Olympic Gold Medalist Svetlana Ihavtakysa was killed sometime late Monday or early Tuesday. Miss Ihavtakysa was in Orlando as part of the Russians Champions on Ice tour that was in Orlando for a six day run. According to the mayor the cause of death was unknown pending the results of an autopsy. The mayor stated the autopsy was scheduled for sometime in the next twenty-four hours. I just chuckle and say 'yeah right.' Diane and Beth queried on my little comment but I just let it slide. If anyone wanted to know that I had just watched an Airbus take off headed for Moscow about ninety minutes ago holding the body of the most famous dead Olympian in the world today, I was not going to kiss and tell. Rachael and Dr. Parker had obviously done as good job and the Mayor had either sold or been misinformed as to the current status of the situation as it truly is. As always the press was simply too slow or too speculative or subjective to provide accurate information to the masses. The fact that I know what they do not seemed appropriate yet sad. Truly sad that the masses bought into this conspiracy that the freedom of the press provided for true and accurate information being provided to the masses. I took another sip of my beer and chuckled inside as to what I had just seen. Beth takes a run from behind to go tend to the patrons on the floor. I seized the opportunity and stole a kiss from Diane. I asked Diane how the morning went since it started at such a ludicrous hour. She is more interested in the little chuckle she had heard a few minutes prior. I tell her it's nothing and again try to see how my love survived the morning. Diane tells me that after the officers left following her report she went down to see Edna and have a little breakfast. It was not yet nine but Diane didn't want to go home so just she came to the Hurricane. She came in and buttoned some paperwork up and inventoried her supplies. She then perused the schedules and such and prepared for the early lunch crowd. After the bar opened everything was pretty quiet until this cop walked in thinking he was 'all that' and Diane has had nothing but grief ever since. I just laughed, and Diane soon joined me. Beth returned to the bar and asked what she had missed. Both Diane and I just shrugged their shoulders and chuckled. Beth gave them a look of disbelief and just rolled her eyes and went back to washing the glasses. The phone behind the bar rings and Beth answers it. She gives an inquisitive look at me. I shake my head no. Beth conveys that message to the person on the other end of the phone.

Diane looks at me and asks what that was about. I recount the incident with the Feds that were called in and tell her I am in a spot of trouble with Loot. Diane is flabbergasted. Loot? Loot and you are always on the same page, she says. I concur but at this point in time I cannot agree with Loot. I know the killer is out there and I have to stop him. Diane is puzzled. Why would I not want help? I remain defiant. The Feds are not there to help. The feds are there to put a bow on the new gift. It's all window dressing. I tell Diane that the Feds will slow down what is an already slow investigation. But what about Loot, Diane inquires? I will deal with Loot later. Speak of the devil. Van Halen fills the air as I ignore the fact his phone is ringing. Diane reminds him of that very fact. I acknowledge her but ignore the phone. Diane is concerned. This is the most stubborn she has seen me so far. Why don't you answer the phone? I already know who it is. I don't need to talk with them. Diane really wants to know what's going on. She hasn't seen me this stand-offish, even the first time they met. Something is really wrong here, and Diane is concerned because I will not tell her what it is. I down my beer and motion Beth to pour another, which she does. My attention returns back to the TV.

The mayor and the Chief of Police are fielding questions from the media. I catch Loot hidden in the corner of the screen, hidden off toward the back of the mass of politicians. I sneer at the vision I see. The question is asked of his honor if the FBI will be able to help the homicide detectives investigating the Ihavtakysa murder. The mayor reminds the reporter who asked the question that the conclusion of homicide in the death of Svetlana Ihavtakysa had not yet been ascertained. I mutter something akin to 'yeah right.' The question is then repeated as to the value of having the FBI on the team. The mayor responds by deflecting to the Chief of Police who answers that the FBI can only assist the police's response to attempt to find a positive conclusion to the Ihavtakysa case. I start screaming at the TV calling the Mayor and the Chief incompetent assholes. Diane tells me to stop, reminding me of her customers. I roll my eyes but bite my tongue and say nothing more. Diane starts pleading with me, expressing her concern over my lack of concern for the current situation. I jump down her throat, saying that my only concern is the current situation, for Diane, for the investigation and for my city. *My city.* It was my sworn obligation to protect this city and to find out who was responsible for these crimes. Diane again tells me that I am being unreasonable that every-one was there to help and support me. I was becoming increas-ingly agitated and began to foster my attention on my beer. Di-ane becomes increasingly emotional and begins to question me on whom I was speaking to this morning. I remain ever intent on my beverage. Diane becomes insistent, expressing her con-cern for her love. I fondle the beer and ignore her. After a few more minutes of berating, I turn and say that I didn't know what Diane was speaking of. Diane refuses to relent and tries more subtle approaches. I stick around until the news cast ends, then proceeds to finish my beer. I throw a fifty over to Beth and head to the bathroom. Diane looks pale but does nothing further. I return a few minutes later. I run over to Diane and apologize, but say I have to go to work. I pull her over to a corner and give a sweet, sensual kiss. Then I sneak out the back door and spin the Vette out from behind the mall. Diane closes the door to her office and cries softly.

The red blur that is the Corvette of Detective Kenny Spade streaks through the streets of Orlando. Its destination seems undetermined as it circumnavigates the town that I have sworn to protect. I am not alone as the passenger seat has been occupied once again by Elizabeth Downing. I am aware of her presence but I am not very talkative. As always, Elizabeth is quiet and a commanding presence. Ironic, considering a quiet ghostly figure can be such a commanding presence. She sits quietly and supports her guardian while he figures out what his next move is. The Vette passes a plethora of night clubs and tattoo parlors. I continue my destinationless journey through my town and come to rest at a lake in northern Orlando. I idle the car in the parking lot and stare out across the ripples on the water's surface. Elizabeth floats out to the surface of the lake and sits down at the water's edge. I stare at her. I am mesmerized by the image before me, all decked out in white looking every bit the angel she is. I am stuck on the contrast with the image of Elizabeth that I always see: the broken and swollen face, amputated ankles and maggot infested wounds. And yet there she is, the beautiful vision, just sitting on the sand in glowing white. The day turns to dusk turns to night and still I sit in the driver's seat, just staring. And still the angelic presence of Elizabeth Downing sits on the edge of the lake.

I gaze across the lake. The moonlight reflects off it and gives off a shimmering glow. After about ten minutes or so I look at my watch. Eleven fifty-three. Already? Damn. I look back at the lake and I am caught by a sudden burst of white light reflecting off the moonlights glow. Inside the light a door slings open and a thin attractive, girl walks down the hall. She is maybe thirty feet ahead. She is clad in gray sweats and a red and white sweatshirt with some sort of logo on it. Oh yes, you too are quite a looker. I have been waiting for almost two hours for you to emerge. I thought I almost had you a while ago but you were just teasing me, bringing out the room service tray. Shame on you, torturing a poor soul like that. What's the matter, are you AFRAID OF SOMETHING? This is a safe haven, a downtown motel in the most beautiful city in Florida. There is nothing to fear here. Where are you going? Why did you go in that room? That's OK; I am a very patient person. Very patient indeed. I will just settle in right here.

Well that was a quick little visit. What's in your hand little lady? Some kind of round thing. That's OK; I'll help you carry that. Where are we going now, to an elevator? Nope, we crossed that entrance way. Ahhh, I see. We need a little ice, do we? Well, hold on for just a second will you? Hello there! The blade slides out of its holster with the grace of a gazelle and skillfully manipulates its way across the throat of the young lady clad in sweats. The wound is precise and effective. HEY! WHERE THE HELL DO YOU THINK YOU ARE GOING? The young ladies body sloughs to the floor. No, No, No, Not yet. I need you to be perfect when they find you. SHIT. The knife falls to the floor as the hand holding it reaches down to stop the lifeless body's descent. It's too late; her head hits the ice machine. The left hand then reaches down and prevents her from collapsing on to the floor. Hold on, there's no rush. We need to look just right. Here now baby, this will work. The hand puts the body on the floor. My, my you are a messy one. Look at the mess on this ice cube tray. Tsk, tsk. Here we go, lets rest against this wall right here. Very good. You are such a cooperative young lady. And beautiful, too. You should not try to hide yourself. You are so beautiful. Let it go, flaunt it a little bit. Let's see what you got. Where's my knife? Oh here you are. The knife is grabbed from under the ice machine and begins to cut through the red and white sweatshirt, down two thirds. Say baby, what does that word mean?

139

Hmmm. It probably means beautiful. No matter. Damn, the tip is broken. I'll have to get another knife. Maybe I'll ask Spade to chip in. Or maybe his hot little girlfriend. Don't worry darling, she has nothing on you. One more minor adjustment. Let's liberate that beautiful little breast right there. You should not try to hide these. You are perfect. No. Something is missing. What could it be? What could it be? Ahhh, yes. That's it. An ace of spades emerges from a pocket and is placed leaning against the exposed breast. Beautiful, but not quite perfect. The piece de resistance. The hand extends the tip of the knife and dips it in the deceased girl's blood. He then started on the lower left corner and made its way up to the lower right. The word it spelled was simple and single. SPADE. The image is finite and unmistakable. A deafening laugh echoes through the air. The knife is picked up and starts to walk away. The wailing ring chimes of a certain Van Halen song begin to funnel through, permeating away the now waning echoes of laughter. The familiar tones get louder and louder.

A sudden wave of consciousness strikes out at me and smack me to wake up. I begin to open up my eyes. I am paralyzed by the fear that stares back at me. In front of my eyes is an over sized skull, probably twice the size of an average human skull. The eyes are a burning mixture of opaque blue and red flames dancing a salsa in their sockets. Looking deeper into the flames I see the knife continuing on its voyage away from the last vicious act. Suddenly the flaming skull shoots backward into the sky and settles in orbit in the sky, eye burning bright, approximately fifty feet away. This event is followed by a luminous white flash with the same proximity equivalent of everybody's supposition of a supernova implosion. Descending from the white flash is an angelic figure that reels down to the shore and shoots me the all too familiar smile. Instinctively, and subconsciously, I make the familiar ringing stop.

"Hello." There is a voice on the other end.

"Elizabeth!"

"Hello, Hello, Spade, are you there. Hello. Spade? Are you there?" The voice penetrates the cloud of consciousness or unconsciousness that envelopes me long enough for me to press the talk button on my phone.

"Hello?" My tone is uncertain and shaky.

"Spade, is that you?" The voice is unmistakable, but my lack of cognitive clarity adds a slight delay for any ability to process it.

"Diane. Hi." I try to gather my wits as I speak. "What's new?"

"Where are you?" The concern in Diane's voice is evident.

"Hey. I am the office."

"I called the office. You're not there." Diane is growing increasingly more concerned and angry.

"Nah, I just told them to hold my calls. I am just mesmerized by the day's events. So I told the guys no calls."

"Spade, I called Dan. (Loot) He told me he had not seen you since this morning."

"I know baby. I told him to do that. Sorry."

Diane is hesitant to believe me. "Don't lie to me. Where are you?"

"I'm at the office. Everything is fine."

"Who is Elizabeth?"

"I don't know any Elizabeth. Why do you ask?"

"Spade, when I called you said 'Elizabeth.' Who is she? Is it the girl from the case years ago?"

"I haven't been there in years, babe. I don't know any Elizabeth, like I said. So what's new?"

"So what's new? Nobody has been seen you since lunch. It's now midnight. What the hell have you been doing?" Diane's tone grows increasingly more agitated.

"I am at work babe. All is fine. No worries. I'll be leaving in about ten minutes. I'll see you in a little while." I try very hard to sell it. There is no response on the other end. "Hello?" I go fishing.

"Yes, I'm here." Diane's voice is very soft.

"Babe, I'm going to go. I'll be over in a few minutes. I love you. Bye." I wait for a reply on the other line but receive on silence, followed by a click twenty seconds later. Well that went well, I say to myself. Damn, did I say Elizabeth out loud? Really? How am I going to get out of this one? She'll never let this go.

I look through the windshield. Elizabeth is no longer sitting on the shore line. I look around, but see nothing. I look down at my watch. Two minutes after twelve. Great. I've been AWOL for twelve hours. I fire up the Vette and spin her around effortlessly. I take off down the interstate, heading back toward Diane's house. I begin cursing at myself. Damn, how could I not have known! I should have known all along it was you. You have never let me down, Elizabeth. You always come through. How could I not have known? Oh shit, did I really say your name to Diane? Jesus, can this possibly get any worse? Elizabeth settles in the passenger seat next to me. The angelic white figure shoots me a little smile to reassure me. She always did bring an air of ease when she comes to sit with me. I begin to reticulate the vision I just had. The killer slit her throat and then dropped the knife under the ice machine but picked it up. Why was their no tip found? It was time for a return trip back to the Casa de Zaidi, in the morning, after I dealt with the upcoming Diane backlash. I make my way to the neighborhood where Diane lives, and instantly my thoughts flash to the vision or dream I had, the one where the killer drove Lisa Yeung's car past Diane's house.

I glide the red car to a stop and make my way toward the door. I get all the way to the door and take a deep breath. 'Here we go' I say to myself. I knock, unsure if Diane will answer. A slight chill in the nighttime air sends a shiver up my spine. Either that or maybe the uneasiness as to how to deal with the damage this day from hell hath caused. My stomach growls and I get a queasy feeling. So far Diane is not inclined to answer. I fumble with my keys, anticipating that there is no one coming to answer the door. I stand there nervously shaking my feet, playing through what to say to her if Diane does indeed answer the door. After three minutes I throw in the towel and begin to meander back to the car. Let's go sleep this one off and deal with it another day. I made it all the way down to the side walk when I heard the creek of the front door opening. I stand still for a moment but do not turn around. I take a deep breath and slowly spin. Standing at the door is Diane, clad in a white sweatsuit, holding a glass of wine. I finish my spin and stand stationary, not moving toward the door at all. "Are you coming in? It's cold out there." Her tone is unsympathetic but not quite angry. That little shiver returns to me as I slowly retrace my steps and return to the front door. I offer a small peck on the cheek, an offering that is not returned. I walk through the entrance hallway clad with pictures of Diane's little nieces and sit at the table in the kitchen. I feel the glare of her eyes piercing through him. She walks into the kitchen and unleashes a fury of where have you been and what the hell is wrong with you that would have the angels of Satan shaking in their shoes. It is kind of appropriate that she owns a bar called The Hurricane From Hell, I think to myself. I do little to defend the onslaught, instead deciding to allow her to vent before trying to offer any lame excuses. I know I cannot explain my way out of this one. After a few minutes she smacks me in the head. "Are you listening to me? What the hell is the matter with you?!"

"I'm sorry" is all I can muster with the whimper of a dog just beaten down.

"Sorry. I've been worried sick about you. I have called Dan and Kate five times. They have called me three. Don't you try and tell me Dan was covering for you. I know better. Where the hell were you?"

"Nowhere."

"NOWHERE. WHERE THE HELL IS NOWHERE? IT ISN'T ANY CITY I'VE EVER HEARD OF. IS IT IN FLORIDA?"

"I just went for a ride to clear my head."

"TO CLEAR YOUR HEAD? FOR TWELVE HOURS? NO ONE, INCLUDING DAN, HAS SEEN OR HEARD FROM YOU SINCE ONE O'CLOCK. EXCEPT FOR YOUR FRIEND ELIZABETH. WHO IS SHE? IS IT THE DEAD GIRL? IS IT? ANSWER ME! IS IT THE DEAD GIRL?" I sit diligently but won't break my silence. I stoically face the wrath of demons without responding, setting Diane off into a more furious state. Diane then abruptly shuts down and walks to the window in the kitchen and takes a deep breath. Then she walks over to the coffee pot and fills it with water. She fills the chamber with coffee grinds and turns the pot on. Then she turns and walks over to me. The eyes that were filled with rage just a few minutes ago are now welled up in tears. Her voice is uneven and broken as she tries to speak. "I love you. But I can't do this. You tell me what you did this afternoon. You tell me everything that has happened in the last twelve hours. Everything. If you don't I will walk out that door and that will be the end of us. I am not kidding." With that she sits down and tries to maintain her composure. Tears begin to trickle down her face but she won't allow herself to fall apart.

I get up and grab two mugs. I pour us both coffees. I put a mug down in front of Diane then return to my chair. "Listen. I was at a lake just thinking. It's this case. This son of a bitch for some reason unknown to me has singled me out to solve these crimes. Singled *me* out. I don't know what to do. I don't mean to scare you but I am going to because you want the truth. I love you but you may rethink your feelings after you hear what I have to say. I have had visions or dreams, whatever you want to call them. It's like when you play a video game. You see the outstretched hand and you try to shoot whatever it is that's in the game. I have had a vision for each one of this psycho's three killings. All three. I don't know why. I just have. And it scares me. But I am trying to use this information. Hell, I'm not even sure it's real or not. This morning I was with Loot. The suits are making him turn my investigation over to the Feds. This guy is not taunting the Feds. He's taunting me. ME. I can't catch this freak with Feds crawling up my ass. It's been hard enough to get any leads at all, the last thing I need is some unhelpful people slowing me down. I have to stop this guy. It's personal. He made it personal. That's why I wasn't myself at lunch. Then I went to the memorial service and watched the Russian girl get on the plane. I need to clear my head. I need to figure this out. Now, before it is too late. I'm sorry if I am distant, it's just a lot." I look like a whipped dog as I finish my sentence and sip my coffee.

"What about this, Elizabeth?"

"Baby, I don't know anyone named Elizabeth. I was just trying to figure this out. I have too."

"Spade, I heard you call out Elizabeth."

"I have no explanation." I am remorseful and sincere. I take another sip of coffee. Diane nurses her cup as well, sitting there for a few minutes digesting it all. I stare aimlessly out the window. Diane finishes up her coffee and sits there, looking at Spade's face. I continue to look into space. Diane muses over how much different he looks from the first gung-ho officer that crashed into her bar the first time she met him. He looks beat up and tired. He has not been sleeping much but today was the first time she had really seen how consumed he really was. He has lost some weight and Diane has only seen him drink coffee and beer for the last week. After about ten minutes of silence broken only by the occasional lifting and dropping of my coffee cup, Diane reaches out and gently squeezes my hand. "I believe you" she whispers, very much trying to convince herself as well as me. I return the gesture and whisper back 'thank you.' Diane rises and turns to the counter that houses the coffee pot.

"Spade, I don't know what to make of this. You scared the shit out of me today. And your explanation is that you have dreams of you being the killer? That is not reassuring."

"They are not dreams of me being the killer. I just see what he sees. I know it doesn't make any sense. It doesn't make any sense to me either. I just needed some time to try and think clearly."

"I understand. I love you, Spade."

"I love you too. I just need to rest." I take Diane's hand and we walk into the living room where I find some old Gilligan's Island reruns on. We sit quietly. After about twenty-five minutes Diane falls asleep in my arms. I gently kiss her on the head. I watch Gilligan and then sit through F-troop. Then I surf through ESPN and CNN. When I look over at the clock on the wall I realize its quarter to four. I click the TV off and close my eyes. But I can't sleep. All I do is replay the day's events and the vision of what I saw at the lake.

ELEVEN

The first rays of dawn streak through the blinds in the living room. One of the bright yellowish orange bursts strikes me in the face. After a few minutes I am unable to escape the annoyance and open my eyes. I look down on my arm where Diane still lies, covered in a blanket. The tingling sensation in this arm lets me know she slept in the same spot all evening. I try to slide out without awakening her. I arise and stretch. A quick glance at the clock tells me its six fifteen. It seems like we just went to sleep. No matter now, there was no more sleeping here and I knew it. I amble past the bookshelves and into the kitchen. On my way I glance down. *War and Peace, A Tale of Two Cities* and *The Selective Works of Edgar Allan Poe* jump out at me as I cross the threshold into the kitchen. Classics and Poe, I would have never guessed. I make my way over to the coffee pot and stir up a fresh brew. After a brief trip to the bathroom to wash my face, I return to the kitchen and pour myself a large cup to go. Then I take a piece of paper, scribble something grab my keys and gently close the door. Steve Frizz is leaning on the Vette waiting for me. I rip out my keys and keep approaching the car. "Morning Steve. I though Jungha Pongre covered this house. How did I become honored with you again?"

"You can't escape me Spade. You should know that by now." The smugness of this piranha is evident but Spade just brushes it off. "So listen Spade, I hear they brought the Feds in. I guess they finally realize you need help."

"Only my friends call me Spade, and you are not among them. As far as the Feds are concerned you would have to ask the Mayor and Chief, and City Hall's about twenty minutes away from here. I am just a detective and I am trying to find a killer. You would have to ask the suits what they are planning, I can't speak for them."

"Very funny, Spade. But you can't stifle the power of the press. I will get my story, even if that story is you."

I am amused as I open the door to the car. "Good luck Frizz. I'm going to have breakfast now. You know the place. I'll see you later." I pull out from Diane's house and slowly make my way down the street watching to make sure Frizz leaves also. I do not need Frizz harassing Diane, especially the way things are now.

After a quick breakfast at Louie's I head downtown, past Church Street and back to the Casa De Zaidi. The Vette occupies the unloading zone in front of the hotel. I flash my badge to the valets and tell them to leave the wheels where they are. I look down at my watch. Seven minutes after seven. I hope that Emilia, the GM is an early riser. I walk through the front door and go over to the check in area. A nice tan young Spanish lady named Maria (at least that's what the name tag says) greets me and asks to be of assistance. I ask her if Emilia is in. Maria inquires as to which Emilia he wants. The General Manager is my reply. Emilia Ignolia, just one minute while she checks. After a brief phone conversation Maria asks what I need. I tell Maria who I am. She quickly relays the information on the phone and comes back to the desk.

"Miss Ignolia will be right up to see you," Maria asserts.

I nod his head approvingly and make my way over to the coffee machine. I am in the middle of the second cup when she appears about four minutes later.

"Hello detective, what can I do for you today?" Emilia is quite chipper given the hour of the morning, I think to myself. I extend my right hand and greet her.

"I was wondering if I may have another look upstairs. I wanted to check with you before I went so as not to cause you anymore unnecessary grief."

"Certainly," Emilia says. "I'll walk with you."

The two make their way over to the elevators where Emilia pushes the button with the number three that subsequently lights up. "You know, we have become quite the little tourist spectacle ever since you were last here. The Russians come and lay roses on the ground. It got so bad I had to close the third floor off."

The elevator doors open and a hotel employee stands guard at the doorway. He is just about to shoo me away when he sees Emilia and lets us pass. "From here they went down to the lobby, where they were wreaking havoc. So I made a deal with them and they have a little memorial out front." I nod my head. "Ever since the news broke my reservation calls have gone up 200 percent. But everybody wants to stay on the third floor. It was overwhelming. So I finally had to close it. OK detective, let me know if you need anything else." With that she turns and starts back to the elevator. I look back and utter a 'thanks' and turn down the hall to the ice machine. I get to the ice machine and look underneath. Then I break out my little pen light and begin looking for something. Anything. Emilia's crew did a fine job of cleaning up. You couldn't even tell what had transpired. The tile once again appeared to be white and the blood is a distant memory. The letters in the front of the machine and the catch basin and the tan metal base are all as they were prior to the heinous crime, if not better. It appears Emilia was very serious when she said she wanted to get life back to normal. I probe with the flashlight further under the machine to see if there are any further clues. Nothing is visible to me with the naked eye. Damn, I need to find the knife chip. If the killer broke the knife and he is going to continue his murderous spree he will have to get another. It could lead us to him. Where the hell is that chip? I start fumbling through my pockets. Wallet, keys, penlight. I need something just a little heavier. Think, what can I use? I sit in wonderment for a few minutes. It must be a little heavier than his penlight. I get an idea, and run down the hall to the Casa De Zaidi employee guarding the elevator. "Do you have a restaurant here?" I ask panting from the run.

"Yeah, it serves Italian" he replies.

"Do you have a radio?" I ask.

"Like am/fm?" the boy is puzzled.

"No, like one to call downstairs to the lobby."

"Yes, I have one" the boy replies.

"Good." I push the button to bring the elevator up to the third floor. "Call downstairs and asks Emilia the General Manager to meet me at the restaurant. Where is it?" In all the excitement of my thoughts I chuckle inside that I am on a mission and don't even know where the target is.

"Go down to the lobby past the concierge and turn right when the hallway ends. It'll be right in front of you."

I jump in the newly arrived elevator and screams 'thanks.' I then hastily push the L button and starts toward the lobby. When I arrive I follow the directions given by the elevator watcher, pass the concierge, hit the end of the hall, and turn right. Staring me in the face about thirty feet down is a bright red and green neon sign announcing my arrival at *Pompeii and Lava*. An interesting name for a restaurant indeed. I wait for a few minutes and then hear someone approaching down the hall I just came through. Twenty seconds later Emilia is at my side asking what she can do.

"Can I borrow a knife from the kitchen?"

"I don't think it'll be a problem. Let's go ask the chef." Emilia responds. The two enter the restaurant where Emilia is given a nod by the hostess. We keep walking toward the back of the dimly lit dining room. The walls are covered with pictures and paintings of Rome and Florence. There are all kinds of antique and ornamental figurines and sculptures laid around the wall. We go down the back hallway past the sign that announces the restrooms and in through the swinging white plastic door. Emilia and I walk through the kitchen over to one of the preparation tables. Chef Julian is prepping for his afternoon lunches, still some three hours off. In front of him are an array of sliced and diced tomatoes, red peppers, potatoes and various other cheeses and vegetables. Emilia introduces us to each other.

"Chef, this is Detective Spade. He is here investigating the murder." There is no need to detail it any further, for it is all the hotel has whispered about since the incident. "Detective, this is Chef Julian." I extend out my right hand to Chef Julian, who wipes his own hand on his apron and shakes mine. I am impressed with how a man with such strong hands can perform such a delicate profession. I am first to speak.

"Chef, I need to test a theory and I was wondering if I may impose upon you to borrow a knife."

The chef nods his head. "Anything I can do to help. This guy is bad for business, you know." His accent is not quite Italian and I cannot place it. The chef continues, "What kind of a knife do you need. I have paring, cutting, slicing, meat, long, short, serrated. Tell me what you want."

"Well chef, I cannot pretend to know what all those mean. I could use something about four-inches long with a little bit more of a blade than the typical steak knife." The chef nods his head approvingly. He then turns and walks a few feet away where he has a station of his tools of the trade. He rummages through a few and then grabs one. "Here, I think this will do the trick." He hands me the knife. I flip it over and jostle the knife up and down, so as to get a feel for the weight of it.

"Thanks chef, I think this will be good. May I borrow it for about ten minutes?"

"Sure," chef replies, "I have plenty of time until the lunch crowd. This guy he hurts our business, you know."

"Among other things" I mutter under his breath. "Great, I'll get it back to you as soon as I am done." I next turn to Emilia. "May I borrow you for a few minutes?"

"Sure." Emilia and I excuse themselves from the chef's presence and walk back toward the lobby. I am in a hurry suddenly and rabbit toward the elevators. I frantically push the button without realizing it and then I am forced to stick my foot in the elevator door to hold it for Emilia, who has lagged behind. The doors open and Emilia skips in. I then push the door close button and utter an 'I'm sorry' to Emilia. The doors open and the same doorman is there to greet us, unaware it was a return engagement. I lift my head slightly and Emilia and I begin the journey down the hall to the ice room. I surmise that Miss

Ihavtakysa probably hit the machine somewhere around the I and the C about a foot and a half higher. I ask Emilia to bend over and put her head in that approximate position. Then I grab her around her neck. "OK" I think out loud, "That would put the knife around here." He tries to note the spot. "Emilia, how tall are you?"

"Around five one I guess."

"Great. So Miss Ihavtakysa would be around two inches taller. But since she would be bent over, the position of the knife in his hand would only be a little bit higher. I elevate my hands position a touch. "Emilia, can you sneak out of my little head lock?"

"Sure." With a graceful little wiggle Emilia frees herself from me.

"Great. Now I am going to drop the knife. See if you can determine where it falls."

"Sure thing." Emilia is quite the little helper. Emilia signals she is ready and I give her a nod. Be careful I tell her. Then I drop the knife. Emilia stands back and tries to note the position. I hand her a penny and instructs her to put it on the spot. Next we try the experiment again. It lands about two inches away and bounces in the direction of the hallway. Hmmm. I was not really expecting that. One last try, I think to myself. I raise my hand and drop the knife. It lands pretty much in between the first two pennies but also bounces toward the hallway, except this time over toward the left hand corner. Emilia marks the last spot with a penny. I then pick up the knife and hand it to Emilia and mark its final resting spot with a penny. "Thank you. Can I ask one more favor of you? Will you return this knife to Chef Julian for me? I am going to look around, but I should be gone within a half-hour so I don't cause you any extra advertising." Emilia nods her head approvingly and takes the knife and walks back toward the elevators. I begin to study the penny party on the floor. I take out my handy dandy pen light and inspect the white tile closely. I am once again impressed, or depressed as it turns out, at what an excellent job the cleanup crew of Casa de Zaidi did. I inspect the tile closely, and although I see a few indentations, I cannot positively identify the landing point of the knife due to the texture of the tile. I examine the positioning of the pennies. They all seem to be toward the front left corner of the ice dispensing cubicle. I kneel at the corner of the carpet, pondering what this tells me. The knife fell toward the carpet. Or does it? What if the knife was blocked by something? Perhaps it was blocked by the victim's body, or maybe even the killer, maybe by his leg? Shit, that piece could have fallen anywhere. I look around in disgust. Why does that always happen when you have a good idea? I stare aimlessly at the ice machine. Why is every bright spot covered by a thick black thundercloud? My apparent lack of focus inadvertently causes me to drop the penlight that I was fiddling in my fingers. It rolls under the center of the ice machine. I lie horizontally on the floor and stretch my left hand under to retrieve the light. I accidentally push the light while it is under the ice machine which causes the light to roll in an elliptical orbit. A sudden reflective glimmer of something leaning up against the light beige walls of the room that houses the ice machine on the third floor of the Casa de Zaidi catches my eye. I grab a pair of tweezers and try to pick at the item that caught my attention. I squeeze the tweezers together and slide the piece away from the molding. I then make a second attempt to try and squeeze the item. I fumble through the small space and gently squeeze the forks together. Success. I retract my arm and try to pull the item out. I bring the piece out and hold it up.

A smile begins to slowly crawl across the sullen look that had become tattooed upon the face of one Detective Kenny Spade. It is not a prominent smile, but it is slowly making its way transversely across my face. The grin expands and I whispers an 'it's about friggin' time' to myself. I reach down into my jacket pocket and pull out a small manila envelope. I drop the particle into the little satchel and seal the lid. I then put the small packet that holds what I hopes will turn into Pandora's Box into the pocket from where it came. I collect my penlight and tweezers and gather everything up then snap toward the elevator. I dish the uniformed employee watching the door a feigned salute and scamper inside the sliding door.

Inside the elevator my mind starts to process this. I need to get back to the lab. Then I'll give Justyna the knife tip. She'll run the serration. That will give us a manufacturer and hopefully a model number. Then I can work backward to see where the knife is sold. The hope that had brought his cheeks flush wanes momentarily. What happens if it is a common Wal-Mart type knife? Then what? No, no must be positive. This is the first thing that has gone right during this whole case. Well, with the exception of Diane, that is. Anyway, this has to be a good thing. It has to be. I need to see Justyna. What the hell is taking this elevator so long? As the though finishes enveloping my brain the familiar ding informs me of its arrival at the lobby. The door slowly spreads open and I jump out of them so excitedly I almost wipe out, stumbling across the decorated Persian Carpet after an unfortunate run in with the retracting piece of steel in turn two. I gather my composure and begin a brisk pace toward the lobby doors. "You know you'll never get style points for a landing like that." The voice echoes from behind the front desk and when I whip my head in that direction I see Emilia standing behind the desk. I slam on the brakes and almost repeat my award winning form when my feet slide on the stylish, short carpet. With the grace of an elephant and the style of a walrus performing "Swan Lake," I shimmy my way over to the desk. Here I offer Emilia a 'thank you' along with the promise of keeping her informed of any potential progress of the investigation. I then bolt out the front door and into the Vette and take off.

I wield my way through the streets and past the Sun Bank, Church Street Station and onto the interstate. The rush hour traffic is fairly thick at this time of the morning, mainly from the north where the Seminole County residents come from for the daily grind in O town. I am fortunate the crime lab where I hopes to find Justyna leaves me going north against the flow of traffic. The sun's early morning bursts color the highway a deep golden orange and I curse myself for leaving my sunglasses at home. I cruise down the highway and get all revved up when a vintage Iron Maiden song hits the radio. Ah, the good old days I say to myself. I slide off the exit ramp and navigate the few blocks until I get to the forensics lab. I maneuver the car into a spot in a fashion that would make the best of Hollywood's stunt drivers take notice. The oblivion that engulfs me prevents me from acknowledging the woman in the stroller on the sidewalk in front of the building that houses forensics. It also quells the stream of profanity that she unleashed at me for almost crashing into her and her child. I ram through the door and almost gallop through the halls. I am a man on a mission. I fly through the door to the forensics department with such force that it almost buckles and scares almost everyone in the immediate vicinity with a horrific thud. Someone from one of the cubicles shouts a 'take it easy' of which I am only partially cognizant. "Can anyone tell me where to find Justyna?" The commanding bellow is not missed by a single soul, primarily because its creator would not allow it to be. A slender African-American man who reminds me of Richard Pryor introduces himself and inquires as to who the obnoxious tart that just entered his department was. I recognize my error and apologize slightly. He is then introduced when the same voice that reprimanded his entrance announces that the man in front of the Richard Pryor clone is 'the great detective Kenny Spade.' Oh, of course, the great detective Kenny Spade. I was used to such ribbing but still did not understand the need for it. After all, all I did was try to find the truth. I wished they would all just shut up and tell me where to find Justyna. I sat there awkwardly and take the abuse for a few minutes before I try to get things back on track. "Excuse me, I'm sorry, could you tell me where I could find Justyna." The questions then turn to 'is it the Ihavtakysa case?' All of the obvious follow ups about suspects and leads are included in the next barrage of curiosity. If you would all shut up and tell me where to find Justyna then maybe I could answer these questions. Oh god, I hope I didn't say that out loud, I say to myself. The answer comes from the cubicle with a voice but no face. 'Nine o'clock.' "Thank you," I retort to my invisible conversation partner. I glance at my watch. Eight forty-seven. Great, I think. The aura of optimism has been replaced by an uneasy anxiousness and I become increasingly fidgety. When in the hell is she going to get here? Patience has never been an especially strong point of mine and I know it. I look down again. Eight forty-eight. Great, this will be the longest ten minutes in history. I run up to the nearest human I can find and blurt out, "Excuse me, where can I get some coffee?" I receives a look of uneasy disgust and gets generic instructions to go down the hall past to corridors and the cafeteria will be on the left.

I turn and head out the door of forensics, but I can still hear and feel the room salivating over the celebrity in their mist. As the door clicks back into a closed position my anxiety grows. Probably the last thing I need is coffee, I tell myself. I go down the hall and peak at the other doors he passes. DNA grabs my attention. I wish I had something to give you I whisper. I continue to make my way down the hall and after a few hundred yards encounter the sign. CAFETERIA. The awful stench of burnt toast almost renders the sign insignificant. I go into the door and get in line. The line is about four deep, the first two young ladies discussing how the first ones boyfriend called the second because she didn't reply in a timely enough fashion to the text message the boyfriend sent. I wish that was the extent of my problems. I get up and order coffee. I throw two dollars down and go to hide in the corner.

The local news is on the TV in the corner. The top story is, to no one's surprise, the murder of an Olympic Gold Medalist. There is an anonymous report out of Washington this morning that the FBI had been called in to assist. The report went on to say the Mayor had asked for the assistance and the FBI's Orlando branch had sent a small delegation to offer any help possible to apprehend the perpetrator of the crime against Miss Ihavtakysa. I just play with my coffee, taking in all the information but never looking at the screen. I actually chuckled out loud with the alleged information of the FBI, a move that caught me a look or two. I sat through a set of commercials and looked back at my watch. Eight fifty-six. If I walk slowly enough

I should get there at just the right time. All of the enthusiasm and swagger I had just twenty minutes ago were draining from me, but I was hoping to rekindle the fire through my favorite CID forensic. I walked slowly through the hallways without purpose, paying attention only to my half full cup of coffee. I made my way back to the forensics department and opened the door. This entrance is far less dramatic than its predecessor fifteen minutes prior. As the door opened the silence became deafening as everyone stared at the person whom had just entered. Justyna was waiting for me, with two cups of coffee in her hand. She hands me one and overstates the obvious. "I heard you were looking for me." I grin. Justyna continues, "What's up?"

"I have to show you something."

"OK."

"Where can we go?"

"Follow me" Justyna states. "We can go to any evidence room down the hall." I follow my companion and go into the room. It is an almond shade with a big examination table in the center. There are spotlights hanging from the ceiling and a big lighting box similar to those doctors use to view x-rays running the length of the room, probably a good eighteen feet. I close the door and Justyna sips her coffee. "What's up?" she asks again.

"I need you to follow up on this." I pull the tiny evidence bag out and slide it on the table. "This case got way out of hand yesterday and I want our conversation to focus on work, which is why I needed to leave forensics. It got a little weird."

"Take no offense. You have to be part weird, part geek and part lots other things to be in forensics. The ability to see something for what it is and what it is not at the same time is not a very common trait." Justyna slides the package open and a piece of metal slides on the table. "This looks like a …"

"The tip of a knife?" My tone is optimistic but I am fishing for just the slightest hint of confirmation.

"Where in the hell did you find that?" Justyna is more than a little shocked.

"The scene of the crime. Underneath the ice machine."

"But we went through that."

I shrug my shoulders. "I know we did. I went back to play a hunch that the knife was dropped and inadvertently, and fortunately I hope, I dropped my pen light. When I was picking it up I saw this flickering. I saved it and hot tailed it over here to see you."

"Yeah, I heard about that part." Justyna smiles slightly.

"So..." The impatience is evident in my voice. Justyna will have none of it.

"Hold on there cowboy. Rome wasn't built in a day."

"OK. Well is it workable?"

"Oh yeah, it's workable. I'll check it for serration, thickness and incision angles. I'll also check for metallic composition and the presence of any casting numbers. It'll take a little while."

"How long?" Spades impatience surfaces again.

"Hours at least. I'll get right on it." Justyna smiles.

Spades enthusiasm is revving up again. "Justyna, this could be our big break. Our first true clue, other than the taunting of a maniac. Please let me know."

"Where do you want me to reach you?" Justyna asks. I throw a card down on the table.

"Do your thing then call that number. Keep in touch. Happy hunting." I then swagger out the door, my hope once again restored.

TWELVE

The ride over to the Hole had been a very uncomfortable one for Diane. She had been awake since Spade wrestled her arm away so he could get up. She could smell the coffee as Spade made it. It was quite good actually. He left in a few minutes and did not even give her a kiss. Maybe he was afraid to wake her, she kept telling herself. The note Spade left was on the kitchen table. It was very simple. *I'm sorry. I love you.* Diane believed the note. But she did not know what to do with that information. She had heard Spade talking to someone and went over to the window. Diane pulled back the corner of the white frilly curtains and saw Spade and that pain in the ass reporter having a short conversation. Probably just another attempt to get under his skin, Diane thought to herself. Spade left in a hurry and Diane saw the reporter look up exactly at the window where she was spying. Diane ducked down quickly, afraid she had been caught. She stayed motionless for about three or four minutes before crawling to the next room over where she again spied through the window. The reporter had waited for about forty-five minutes before cashing in the cause and leaving. Diane waited until around seven and then called Spade's office. No, he had not checked in yet. After another cup of coffee, which was surprisingly good yet again, she called Kate Murphy. She had informed her of everything that had passed since they spoke the night before. She did not go into excessive details about Elizabeth, but Diane did tell Kate that Kenny was dreaming about the murders. Kate said that should be normal, that Kenny was preoccupied. But Diane felt no better. Kate told Diane that Dan was on his way into work, but that Kate would have Dan call her. Diane said that was not necessary and bid her friend goodbye.

Diane waited around restlessly for the next half-hour. She took a nice hot shower, but could deal with her worries no more. She blew her hair and did a quick makeup job and flew down to the office of homicide detectives. Diane made record time, obeying no speed laws and nearly wrecking twice. She got to the building and made her way toward the homicide office. Her walk down the dimly lit hallways made her realize why Spade and Dan called this place the Hole. It was like a shit hole and a hole in the wall all wrapped up into one. There were precious few other rooms on the floor that housed the office. The walkway stank of muskiness and the pale green and brown bricks and dampness made you feel like you were walking through a cave. Yes, to her the Hole seemed rather fitting. Diane made her way to the door and went inside. There was a desk on the left that housed a telephone and a two dollar sign that said reception. Diane went to the desk and waited to be acknowledged by the heavy set white woman who manned its contents. A man in a JC Penney quality suit walked past and released a 'morning' Peggy.' Mystery number one solved for the day Diane thought to herself. After a few minutes of playing with paper and tending to her fingernails Peggy finally looked up and asked Diane what she could do for her. The same JC Penney suit cop walked past her and Diane recognized him as the one she saw with Kenny one day on the news. It was Detective Tolliver. Diane asked Peggy if Detective Spade was in this morning. Peggy said that he was not and asked what her inquiry was pertaining to. Diane said it was personal and asked if Lieutenant Murphy was in. Again Peggy asked what it was pertaining to.

Dan Murphy left his office on the far corner of the Hole with the file of Lisa Yeung in hand. The FBI already had all of the reports pertaining to the Ihavtakysa case in their hands almost immediately after showing up yesterday morning. Murphy had sent over the case file to victim number one late yesterday afternoon, but he had to retrieve the Yeung file. He had found it on Spade's desk but in all the franticness of Diane's phone calls last evening he had not gotten it over to the FBI guys. Murphy wasn't really concerned, for to him it was known that Spade would often disappear for hours on end. It was just the way he thought things out. Murphy left his office and turned toward the front of the homicide department. What he saw then surprised him. The woman in her late thirties with long blond hair could only be one person. Lieutenant Murphy walked over to a middle aged man and handed him the file that was in his hand. "This is Yeung. Get it over to the FBI. Now." The gentleman nodded and left for the door. Murphy then walked over to Peggy. When he came within fifteen feet Diane saw him. "Dan" she screamed, maybe a bit too loud for a few heads popped out of their cubicles like the bash a mole game you find in game rooms or carnivals. Lieutenant Murphy reached over and gave her a hug. "What are you doing here?" was his reply.

"Can we talk?"

"Sure," Dan answers, "Come on we'll go to my office." Diane follows Dan through the hole. The partitions separating the cubicles all stand about five feet high. They are organized in five rows of five, all covered in a dark tan fabric. The walls are mustard yellow. At the end of the last row there is a counter with a coffee pot, a small refrigerator underneath and a cheap long table that probably tries to pass as a conference table. The chairs are more of the computer desk variety and not metal folding that would seem to be more fitting for the décor in the office. Diane trips at the last row and Dan catches her under her arm. "Are you OK?"

"Yeah, I'm fine. Thanks." she replies. Dan takes her past the conference table where they make a right and go to Dan's office in the corner. Peggy is no longer visible, and given her size that is no small feat. Dan and Diane walk in and Diane slides the door behind her.

Dan goes over to her and grabs her hand. "Are you all right? Did Kenny finally show?" Diane begins to break down sobbing hysterically. Dan pulls her closer and gives her a hug. "What's the matter? It's OK. You can tell me."

"Oh Dan, I don't know what to do. It's Kenny. I don't know what to do. What do I do?"

"Tell me what happened." Dan tries to console her. Diane takes a deep breath and begins.

"I tried to reach him last night. All night long."

"We all did."

"I know. Well, I finally got hold of him around midnight. He answered the phone. When he did he said the name Elizabeth. Dan, who's Elizabeth? Is it the girl from all those years ago?" Dan gets a look of concern but very quickly masks it and tries to control the situation.

"Diane, I'm sure you heard something else. In all the years I've known Spade he has never had anyone even close to how much he is in love with you. I know the man and you have nothing to fear. What else did he say?"

"He said first he was at the office. You know that was bullshit. Then he said you were covering for him. That too was bullshit. And then when I confronted him about why he said the name Elizabeth he said he didn't."

"Is it possible that he didn't?"

"I know what I heard." Diane is growing more emotional and tears begin to well up in her eyes. Dan walks her over to his desk and sits her down in one of the subpar chairs. He walks over to the door and screams to someone to bring him two cups of coffee. He then walks over and sits behind the desk. Dan then presses on.

"Did he ever come over?"

"Yes, around one."

"Where was he all day?"

Diane begins to cry. Not sobbing, but the tears begin to stream down her checks making her rapidly applied blush run. Her voice quivers as she continues. "He said he was at a lake all day thinking." Dan replies that that sounds like the Spade he knows. Diane continues, still crying but trying very mightily to control it. "When I confronted him about Elizabeth he said he had no explanation and didn't remember saying it. Then he told me that he is having dreams." She stutters at this point and Dan asks the obvious follow up question.

"What kind of dreams?"

"He said he had dreams of the murders. All three. He compared them to a video game, like when he could see what the knife was doing."

"WHAT!" The outburst was sudden and vehement. The fear of it broke Diane's barrier and she began to cry uncontrollably. Dan realizes his mistake and goes over to comfort her. Dan is holding her when he hears something outside his office. The door is open ever so slightly. Dan gets up and goes over to the door. Diane sits in the chair and tries to compose herself. Dan opens the door and sees Francis Poncher perched outside his door. Also there is Detective Ronan who informs Lieutenant Murphy that he brought the file to the FBI.

Dan is angry and spits out, "Officer Poncher, how may I help you this lovely morning?" Dan's voice oozes sarcasm and he is very anxious to hear exactly why this jackass is outside his office door.

"I am looking for you, lieutenant." Poncher tries his best to put forth his own fear of God image, but it is not quite working. "You and Detective Spade." Poncher bullies up to his surroundings. Dan is quick to reply.

"I have not seen Detective Spade yet this morning myself, but what can I help you with?"

"May we go in your office?"

"I'm sorry officer but I am in the middle of an investigation in my office and I cannot have my materials disturbed. So again, what can I do for you?"

"I want to know why Detective Spade was insubordinate yesterday and what you are doing to make him comply with the requests of the Chief and Mayor to assist the FBI in the Ihavtakysa case." Poncher is devoid of all composure and is almost yelling at Dan Murphy.

"Well, officer, Detective Spade has been officially reprimanded for disobeying a direct order from a superior officer. He has also been informed that if he does so again he will be suspended. Since I am fairly certain that Detective Spades number one goal is to catch the killer of Miss Ihavtakysa as well as his other open cases I don't think we will have any other problems, because he will not be able to catch anyone else if he is suspended." Dan is soft-spoken and forceful and Poncher takes a step back. Poncher then regains his composure and shoots back.

"Is it true that there was another card at the Ihavtakysa murder scene, one with his name on it?" He has a smug look on his face. Dan is quick to counterstrike.

"Officer Poncher, The Ihavtakysa case is not mine. I am simply trying to monitor it as I do with all my detectives' cases. I am not familiar with the specifics unfortunately."

"Lieutenant Murphy, I suggest you cooperate with Internal Affairs or I will have to look at you for obstruction." Poncher tries to connect with a jab. Murphy blocks it.

"Officer I am cooperating. I told you my responsibility. I told you I haven't seen Detective Spade and I told you what I did in response to yesterday's actions. Now, how else may I help you?" Poncher stews as he often does after an encounter with Lieutenant Murphy. He blurts out 'that will be all' but throws in an 'I'll be back.' Dan says he can't wait until the next time they get to converse. The room begins to buzz around as Poncher spins and leaves. He truly is a graceful man for someone of his size. Poncher wafts past Peggy and slithers out the door. Lieutenant Murphy then twirls his hand and motions for everyone to get back to work. He returns to his office where he finds Diane crouching behind the door. Murphy closes the door. Diane is upset.

"Is Kenny really in trouble with Internal Affairs? And did the killer right his name on the cards at the murder scene? Did he? Tell me!" Diane is now very hysterical and is not even trying to be calm. Dan sits there and answers her quietly.

"Yes, to both questions."

"Are you really going to suspend him?"

"I hope not, but if he pulls the same stunt he pulled yesterday he may leave me with no choice." Dan is somber.

164

"What the hell are we going to do?"

Dan speaks very quietly and very poignantly as he answers her. "Nothing. We are going to do nothing. Right now only Spade can do something..."

I ran the Vette hard to get to the Hole in near record time. I was still buzzed by the hope that Justyna had given me. I was very anxious and flew through the halls that lead to the Hole. I was motoring when I stopped dead in his tracks. Poncher. Here? That can't be good news I thought to myself. I proceed cautiously past Poncher waiting to be stopped. Poncher ignores me and dials a cellphone shooting me a smile out the side of his mouth. I look uneasily but continue and enter the Hole. When I hit the door Peggy tells me there was a woman looking for me and she is now over with Lieutenant Murphy in his office. I look quizzically and make my way past the conference table and over toward Loot's office. I open the door to Loots office and hear "Only Spade can do something..."

"What can I do, boss?" A startled Loot shoots his eyes toward me and the person in the chair spins around. I stop dead in my tracks for the second time in just less than two minutes. Fifteen seconds of awkward silence follow before Loot stands. "I have to go check on something. I'll be back in a few minutes." Loot walks over and leans next to Diane and whispers something in her ear. Then he puts his hand on her shoulder gives a little rub and walks out, closing the door behind him. Diane rises as the awkwardness continues. I stand silently for a few seconds before Diane walks over to me and gives me a hug and a big kiss. I have now gained enough sense to speak.

"Hey babe, what are you doing here?" my tone is positive, yet uncertain.

Diane stands in silence, unsure of how to play it. She waits for about twenty seconds and then grins slightly. "I came to tell you that I love you and that everything's OK. I am not going anywhere." Her smile grows to be genuine.

"What were you and Loot talking about? What is it that only I can do?" What were you talking about?"

"We are planning a birthday surprise for Kate."

I am not buying it. "Kate's birthday is in March." My tone is rather emphatic.

"It *is* March." I sit dumfounded for a few seconds as I reflect over the chaos of the past few months. Everything passed without even a thought. I am now stuck with an answer I wish to dispute but have no grounds to do so. Diane is looking around the room trying to avoid the remainder of the conversation so she will not get trapped in a lie. She is next to speak, formulating a grand escape. "I wanted you to know no matter how hard last night was for me I am still dedicated to us. I love you. It has been a long time for me to feel this. I love you." She pauses to allow this to settle. Then she swings for the quick getaway, "I have to go open the bar. Will I see you tonight?"

"Yeah, I'll call you later." I am dumbfounded and not sure what to say. Diane walks over to me and gives me a big hug and a kiss. She squeezes me strongly and then leaves Loot's office. As she is escaping Diane runs to Loot and quietly cries on his shoulder. She then gathers herself and takes off, never crying again until she leaves the Hole.

Loot makes his way back to his office. I am sitting in the chair previously occupied by my girlfriend. I sit at the desk looking like a puppy just taken from his mother. I look up at Loot, who has just sat down at his desk. I am full of things to say but can't find the starting point. "What do I need to do? When I came in you said to her it's something only I can do. What is it?"

"Play ball. IAD was here."

"Yeah I know. Poncher passed me as I entered."

"You saw him? What did he say?"

"Nothing. He just gave me a dumb ass grin."

"He didn't say anything? That can't be good. He came here looking for you to blast you about the Fed incident yesterday. It's all over the department."

"Great."

"Listen, Spade, your going to have to get on board and play ball. They're gunning for you now."

"I know. Listen Loot, about yesterday. I know."

"Relax. I understand. But it can't happen again. I already told Poncher I issued you an official reprimand, which I didn't, but if you screw up again you'll give me no choice." I nod my head understandingly. "The next thing you have to do is make it up to Diane. You scared the shit out of her last night."

"I know. I was just… I don't know seeking clarity."

"Well, it better be clear now."

"Yeah, I know."

"Listen, Loot, I may have a lead. I found a piece of metal back at the hotel where the skater died, under the ice machine. I think it could be from the knife. I have forensics working on it."

"Good, you could use a break. What's next?"

"Well, Justyna is working on my metal now. Hopefully by this afternoon she can tell me who made the knife. Then I work backward for counts, suppliers and possible receipts. It's a long shot but it's a start."

"OK. Let me know what you find out. And Spade, no more theatrics like yesterday."

"Yeah Loot, I feel ya."

"Pull that crap again and you will." Loot shoots him a smile. I then get up and walk out. Loot picks up the phone and calls Kate. Yes she just left. No, she's not all right. Went to work. I think that would be a good idea. Yeah, love you too. Loot hangs up the phone and wonders what will happen next. He wouldn't have to wait long.

THIRTEEN

The call came into to my cell about one thirty. I was driving over to the Hurricane to see Diane when Justyna got the news. I spun the Vette around and made a beeline to the building I visited this morning. The midday sun left me cursing for the second time today that I had left my sun glasses behind. The temperature was fairly warm and I had the top down. The wind whipped through my long mane of hair but my mood was tempered by the lack of a decent song on the radio. I wondered what kind of results I would be able to find through Justyna's work. I had all my cards in the one hand and was hoping to win the big pot. I had not had anything good to play within the last few months and was hoping to end the losing streak. I made my way to the building where forensics was. Little did I know it was beginning of the worst few days of my life.

I hit the forensic department with a little less drama than I did five hours earlier. I walked through the door quietly and waited for the Richard Prior look alike to show his face. When he did I asked to be directly shown to where I could find Justyna. The cubicle with the voice but no face again made its presence felt by announcing that Justyna was down in the criminalist exam room. I ushered a 'thanks' to my unknown assistant and made my way through the halls I first met this very morning. I arrive at the door where I left Justyna this morning and walked in. To my surprise I find that the room is empty. I look over at the lighted boxes on the wall and see a few photographs of the piece of metal I had found at the ice machine. There were seven photos in total. Two had close-ups of the serration at the end of the blade. Two had been of the severance point where the tip had separated itself from the blade. One was a close-up of a scratch in the middle of the metal. One was of the tip of the knife with a small ruler measuring the thickness of the knife. The last and most interesting was of two small numbers embossed on the blade adjacent to the point where it snapped from its sheath. I walked up to this picture and began to pay significant attention to it. I squinted over the picture and almost jump out of my skin when I feel something touch me on my shoulder. Justyna just smiles and says 'hi.' I swallowed hard and muster a 'hi' of my own.

"So are you ready for some interesting information." Justyna's question is obvious and understated.

"Please." I am cautious but hopeful.

"Well, I don't know if it's helpful but here we go. It is indeed the tip of a knife that you found under the ice machine. More precisely, it is the tip of a Jackson Barrett model 715 Hunter special. It measures six and a half inches from tip to shaft. The handle is grooved wood slightly under three-inches long. The whole knife is nine and a half inches. They call it the hunter's special because of its ability to easily slice through the underside of large animals so they can be cleaned. If you notice the serration pattern the staggered serration on one side is one-sixteenth of an inch behind the starting point of the other side. The offset of the serrations is supposed to make it easier to slice or cut. Now here's the interesting thing. You can't buy the knife in a store. It is available only through the mail or online. You get it from *The Outdoorsman* via the magazine or their website. Herein lays your dilemma. I contacted them and asked them to check for recent shipments to the central Florida area. They do not have the appropriate software to just type in an area or ZIP code. So they have to do a manual search. I had them start back around four months back. I hoped that the killer would have purchased the knife new with the intention of starting with a new implement of destruction to his liking. I examined the tip closely and saw no other noticeable marks other than the numbers. The scratch in picture four is very ordinary and tells us nothing. The two numbers are filed through in picture seven. They appear to be a three and five, my best guess. I used metal shavings to make that determination. Unfortunately they are no further use because they are specific to all Jackson Barrett 715 series. The numbers that follow may have been slightly more helpful but again they are not available to us. So as of this minute we are at the mercy of *The Outdoorsman's* shipping department."

"That leaves us where?" I inquire.

"Well, *The Outdoorsman* has a bimonthly circulation of just fewer than 93,000 across the U.S. and Canada. They sell everything from vests to knives to guns, etc. They estimate they sell about $1.2 million worth of merchandise annually. Break that down to one-hundred grand per month so they have quite a few minutes of paperwork to siphon through. Add in a two or three month range and, well, it could take a little while."

"Great, where are they located?"

"Savannah."

"Really? Road trip?"

"You would have to ask the boss. That's not my call."

"Richard Pryor?"

"Actually his name is George Overdunn. I don't think you'll get too far by calling him Richard."

"Noted. I'll go ask."

"Good luck." With that I take my leave from Justyna and head back to the main forensics office. As I walks my mind starts to wander. A hundred-thousand dollars a month. Let's assume the average price of this kind of specialty stuff is fifty to three-hundred dollars. So we divide a hundred grand by an average of, say, one-hundred fifty dollars. OK, do the math carry the one, drop the zero divide the five that's, what, 660 or so invoices per month. Spread that out over a three month period that's 1,800 invoices. And that's only if my guy bought the stuff right before he started his spree. Suppose he planned a year out. Great. Plus we don't know how much time the shipping department has to dedicate to looking for us. They could be swamped. It seems my great break is turning to the preverbal needle in the haystack. Why can't I catch a goddamn break? A swelling of frustration begins to manifest itself in me. As I grows increasingly agitated I find that I have reached the forensics door.

I walk in the door and ask to speak with Mr. Overdunn. A small person with a bunch of papers in his hand runs through some aisles and becomes invisible. A few minutes later George Overdunn surfaces and asks how he may help. I explain the situation to him and ask if I could have someone sent to Savannah to assist with the search through paperwork. Mr. Overdunn not so politely informs me that he has forty criminalists working more than 2,000 cases. He simply does not have the man power to send someone and suggests to me that I send a request to the Savannah police to send someone there. Interdepartmental cooperation is always a good thing, he adds smugly. I throw an unpleasant but not excessively sarcastic 'thank you' back at Mr. Overdunn. I then turn and start to head back toward the front lobby. Justyna runs up behind and asks how it went. I tell her that she and her colleagues are overworked to which Justyna remarks that she is surprised that Overdunn was aware of that. I tell Justyna that I will call Savannah PD to see if they can lend any assistance. I then bid her thanks and head out toward the lobby. I don't make it to the door before the familiar cellphone ring chimes through again.

"Spade."

"Spade, it's me."

"Yeah Loot."

"Listen, we found the car."

"Car?" I am uncertain of what Loot has said.

"Lisa Yeung's Acura. We found it."

"Great. Where? I'll be right there."

"Go home, Spade." Loot's voice is wavering.

"WHAT! NO FUCKING WAY! DON'T DO THIS TO ME LOOT!" The venom in my voice is nothing that Loot has ever heard directed at him before. But Loot moves on.

"Go home Spade. I'll meet you there. And Spade, hurry." With that I hear a click on the other end. What the hell is going on? He'll meet me there? I cannot figure what exactly the hell is going on. Why do I have to go home? I told him I would play ball. Why tell me they found the car and then send me home? I would expect that from Poncher but not from Loot. It makes no sense. And why would he meet me at my house? He can't possibly fire me. He needs me. I may be a pain in the ass but I get results. What gives? And why hurry? Where's the car? I dash to the Vette while entertaining all these questions. The Vette screams as I drive like a bat out of hell barreling down the side street and on to the interstate. The speedometer easily hits one thirty as I pass everything on the highway, gliding along like a master of the road race at Watkins Glen.

I make it home in seven minutes flat. The mid afternoon skies grow ominously threatening, an appropriate metaphor for the pending storm about to rage in the Orlando serial killer case. When I reach my block I am greeted by a kaleidoscope of neon strobes that light the street up like a forest of Christmas Trees strung with Christmas lights from top to bottom. The mass of white and blue patrol cars clog the entrance to the street to the degree that I curb the Vette and ride the sidewalk, leaving the car on my front lawn. I jettison from the vehicle to see what the commotion is all about. I make it two houses down before I am intercepted by Loot. I look over Loot's shoulder. Three houses down on the other side of the street. There it sits. Lisa Yeung's silver Acura coupe. Now I have a complete moment of clarity. It makes sense. It makes sense why he had to come home so quickly. It makes sense why Loot was so flustered. It makes sensed why I saw the car in my dream. I was being stalked. If he knows where Diane lives then he surely knows where I live. What kind of a detective am I when I don't even know when I am being followed? Goddamn freedom of information act. I always said too much information is not necessarily a good thing. I begin to wander as my thoughts consume my mind. I have no focus, instead dealing with the fact that I am once again one step behind. I curse under my breath at that very fact. Loot is trying to talk to his friend and subordinate, whom Loot realizes is on his own personal mission to Mars. He accidentally on purpose steps on my right foot hard enough to bring his detective to the planet known as Earth.

"Spade. Spade… Spade?" A look of confusion on my face is replaced by one of smugness. The look is puzzling to Loot. "Spade?"

"Yeah."

"Spade, did you hear me? We found the car."

The look on my face tells Loot I am not listening at all but I already know what is coming. "Spade we found the car."

"Good." I am apathetic toward Loot's announcement.

"You parked on someone's front lawn." Loot is trying to be sarcastic, knowing damn well whose lawn it was. I will have none of it.

"I'll be sure to get a signed waiver granting me permission." My tone tells Loot not to wrestle with the master. "Let's go see the car." We begin to walk over toward the vehicle. The Acura is already swarming with people as if it were a beehive that was under attack by Winnie the Pooh and the queen bee (Aren't they all) sent forth the entire colony to thwart off the advancing intruder. I rip out my phone and dial. Loot questions exactly whom I am calling. Again I ignore my friend and boss. I tell the person on the other end to come to this address ASAP. I then tell them that protocol and procedure are crap and they need to get their ass here now. Then I hang up. Loot questions the call. I say it's a person of interest.

We cross the street and approach the vehicle. The car is cordoned off by the clichéd yellow caution tape that is wrapped around the trees in front of the house where the car stands and on the street side is bordered by two white and blues. Loot reaches into his pockets and pulls out a pair of synthetic rubber gloves. I follow suit. A couple of the neighborhood kids that I play hockey with on occasion ask me what the big deal is. I tell them I am thinking of trading in the Vette and I wanted to check out this car. The kids tell me it's a bad idea, that I should keep the Vette. JP, the kid in all the goalie gear reminds me the Vette is a chick magnet. The flatfoots guarding the perimeter all break out laughing. I just smile and give JP a nod.

Loot goes up to the car and opens the passenger door. "It's clean" I mutter. Loot looks very suspiciously at me. I just repeat the phrase. Loot opens up the right front door and sneaks in. I go around to the driver's side. Loot is shining a flashlight on the floor of the passenger side. He currently has the floor mat up and is scouring the carpet. "Nice touch" I mutter as I enter the driver's side. Loot looks at him in wonderment. I just point up. There in front of them hanging from the rear view mirror is an Ace of Spades air freshener that you can find at any of a dozen car washes throughout metro Orlando. Loot stares at the item. I just grin and begin my own search. I investigate the front driver's side. I find nothing, as expected. Next I rummage through the ashtray. I find roughly a dollar seventy in assorted coins. I fold the seat forward and investigate the rear seat area. It looks fairly unremarkable. Loot screams back from the passenger front that forensics will be here shortly. "No need" I say. Loot looks suspiciously at me, who am just as inclined to ignore it. Loot continues to dig through the papers in the glove box. He finds nothing of value. I continue to dissect the rear seat, again to no avail. From down by the intersection, a patrolman yells out to tell Lieutenant Murphy that forensics is here. I tell Loot to send them back. Loot is becoming angry with my indifference. I just blow it off. Loot begins to walk over toward the intersection and away from me.

Across the street from me I see an attractive girl holding a big briefcase. He motions her over. As she approaches I tell the beat cop to let her in. It's clean I'm sure. You know what to do. Justyna just smiles and breaks open her kit. 'Thanks for coming' I utter as Justyna begins her tedious inspection. After about two minutes Justyna screams "Detective" and hands me a small rectangular envelope. It is about the size of a three by four postcard. I very carefully examine it. On the front of the envelope is one word, typed. SPADE. I carefully open the envelope and read. It is a Valentine's Day card. The front side of the card has a big red heart. On the back side of the card is a note; short, succinct and typed.

OH DETECTIVE SPADE, COME CATCH ME

THE DEVIL MADE ME DO IT, AND YOU ARE HE

I stare at the note in front of me. The killer is continuing to taunt me and is still that one step ahead. Loot makes his way back and introduces Gregory Kerpow, the forensic specialist. Justyna sticks her head out and smiles. 'Hey Greg' resonates from her lips. Loot looks at Justyna funny. I tell Loot to dismiss Mr. Kerpow. Loot is bewildered about the current state of events, I again issue the request. Loot is a little pissed by his lack of control. I tell Kerpow to leave and thanks him for his time. Justyna sticks her head out and tells her co-worker it is evidence pertinent to an ongoing investigation of hers. Gregory looks at Loot, shoots him an evil eye, then turns and walks away. Loot screams at me asking what the hell that was all about. I thrust the card in Loot's face. Justyna asks me what the card says. I tell her it is just one more taunt. Loot reads the card and looks at me. What is this, Loot queries.

"Where was it?" I ask.

"Tucked next to the driver seat between the chair and center console."

"That tells you what kind of world class detective I am. That just jumped at me when I searched the vehicle."

"Let's see what else we can find." Justyna is a bit optimistic.

"It's clean."

"How can you be so sure?" Justyna asks the question but Loot would like to know the answer as well.

"Because he wants it that way. He is taunting me. He wants me to know who is in control, running the show. This monster wanted me to find the card. Thanks Justyna." Justyna is not sure how to react and offers a half smile. "He has placed this card. He has placed a card on everybody. He put the air freshener in this car. He placed the car here, right next to my house. He is telling me that he knows my every move and I know none of his. It's so obvious it's brilliant."

"So what do we do now?" Loot is the adventurous one to throw the question out there. I am ready for that one, too.

"What's the matter, Loot? Don't you watch all those cop shows on TV? Game plan. Justyna, finish the car, then have it impounded and go over it again. It's definitely clean, but just in case. After the car is impounded Justyna, take the letter to trace. Trace. What the hell is that anyway? Are we working for some kind of art convention? That crap on TV always pissed me off. Trace. What BS. Anyway, go to *trace* and analyze the note. Check the font. Look for distinguishing printer marks on the card. See what you can find. What else can we do at this point, right? Go." I wave Justyna off like a drill sergeant with a new recruiting class. Justyna is so impressed or possibly afraid, that she complies. "Loot, grab these flat feet and go door to door. Ask everyone when they first saw the car. Was it last night? This morning? Did they see anything or anyone suspicious? Try and get a time frame. Unless he has an accomplice, which I doubt because he is too articulate, he would have had to walk away from the car right here. Check with the cab services. Check the last twenty-four hours. Six square block radius. He had to get back to his safe house somehow. After we strike out with all of these possibilities, then we reassess."

Loot is dumbfounded. A man who is so soundly defeated by his own admission has structured in two minutes a possible scenario for counterattack while fully believing in his own heart that all of his efforts will have zero net result. Loot stands in admiration for a minute. That's my Spade, Loot tells himself. The great Detective Kenny Spade. Loot follows the directions to the tee. He calls Ronan and has him get on the cabs angle. Twenty-four-hour window and call them all. Loot grabs the first patrol officers he can find and goes instructs them to go door to door. He gives him very explicit instructions what to ask and what, if anything, they saw. He sends them out in waves to cover all of the surrounding streets. Loot sets things in motion and then goes and turns back toward me, who am nowhere to be seen. Loot looks around but can't find me. Loot then sees me playing hockey with the kids from before over on the driveway next to my house. Loot is not sure what to make of this. He slowly makes his way over toward my house as the wrecker impounding the Acura pulls up and begins its task. As Loot walks over I start running around in circles in the driveway. "He shoots. He scores!" is heard as all the neighborhood kids jump in on the group hug except for J.P. in the goalie gear who shadow boxes his nemesis in a mock show of disgust. The kids and I all break out laughing.

"Spade can I see you for a minute, please?" I run over to Loot, and the posse straggles behind him. "What's going on?"

"Ah, nothing Loot. Me and the guys were just talking about the Lightning game. They beat Philly last night four to one. Looks like they'll make the playoffs, right guys." The chorus of kids break out into a 'let's go Lightning' chant. All except for J.P., who reminds me my favorite hockey team is the Anaheim Ducks. What can I say, I'm a night owl. I like the late night games. And their cool uniforms. The boys all pick on me and the Ducks. Loot's patience is growing thin and he pulls me off to the side.

"What the hell are you doing? We just found a murder victims car two doors down from your house and you're outside playing with kids. What's the matter with you?"

"Relax. Did you do what I said?"

"Who's the CO here?" Loot is getting angry.

"Chill, Loot, I feel ya. I always feel ya. You see J.P. over there in the goalie gear? He watched the Lightning game last night. It started at seven thirty. Around seven fifteen his mommy and he came back with some KFC. They brought it home so he wouldn't miss the game."

Loot interrupts, "Is this going somewhere?"

"Just listen. J.P. knows there was no car right there when he came home from KFC. Your time frame is now seven fifteen last night to…" I look down at his watch to 4:43 p.m. today. You see the little red head wearing number thirty four? He said he saw the car there this morning at eight o'clock when he went to the bus stop. You are now down to a thirteen-hour search. Furthermore, Adam, the really skinny one, has garbage duty this week. His big brother Ben got out of it by spraining his knee playing baseball in school. So, Adam is out at nineish last night putting out the garbage because his mother wouldn't leave him in peace. So Adam is putting out the garbage and as he brings the pails to the curb he sees this car stopped in front of my house. Just stopped. He can't see inside the car or what they were doing but Adam paid attention because he knew it wasn't my Vette. He said he thought maybe it was my girlfriends. He can't even be sure it was the Acura. But he is sure the car stayed there for a good two to three minutes because he went in and watched from the window in his kitchen. So, who is working the cabs?"

"Ronan."

"Cool." I rip out my cell and flashes through some numbers then put the phone to my ear. "Yeah, Mike, Spade. Listen, you working the cabs? Cool. Try cutting your search from seven thirty last night to eight this morning. Also, ask all of them to pay particular attention to let's say eight thirty to eleven thirty last night. Let me know what you come up with. Thanks. Peace bro." The click of the phone being shut tells Loot that the cab search is now more defined. "I told you, Loot. I feel ya."

Loot is impressed but still concerned. "Spade, this is not good. The victim's car was found after two months across the street from *your* house. Poncher is going to have a field day with this."

"Yeah, I said I feel ya." I have now returned to a sullen state.

"So" Loot asks, "What's next?"

"Well, I have to go see someone. The stuff's getting a little too real for my liking."

"All right. I'll go check with the flatfoots and see how the door to door is going."

"Cool. Keep me informed." With that I go over to the kids and gives them all a high-five. When one of them makes a passing comment to Justyna, who is leaving now that the Acura is leaving, I smack him lightly and say, "Dude, she's a cop. She'll mess you up." J.P., always my protagonist, has to reply. "She's a cop? I didn't know they had any hot cops."

"Like I said boys, it ain't easy being a cop. Go Bolts!" I raise my right fist in the air and race it down diagonally like a lightning strike. This gets a rise out of the boys who repeat the phrase and gesture. I then fire up the Vette and back off my front lawn and proceed down the road, using the flat bed carrying the Acura to clear my way. Then I turn off the block, slide around the impound vehicle and scream away, leaving screeching rubber behind him.

I bolt through the local streets and ease my way on to the interstate. A familiar angelic figure sits next to me as I glide down the highway on my way to my destination. "Hello Elizabeth" echoes through the car. I feel the presence of my guardian angel as I drive. What am I supposed to do now? This creep is attacking me. He is drawing me in. What do I do, Elizabeth? I do all the basic things. I need to do the extraordinary things. Am I too slow, too old to keep up with him? He is not one step ahead, he is several. He has planned his assault from start to finish. But where does it end? What is the ultimate ending for this maniac? And how do I facilitate its undoing. Elizabeth, I can't thank you enough for what you have done for me. It is what I did not do for you. You have given me clarity. You have helped me try to understand, to show me. I will not let you down. You will see, Elizabeth, I will get this creep. I will get him. I slow the car and exit off the interstate. I pass the O-rena and make my way toward the Hurricane From Hell. In the few minutes it takes me to hit the beautiful blown glass door, I play over and over in my head what I am going to say to Diane after the debacle that was yesterday. One thing for sure, Elizabeth's name will not be among the issues I want discussed.

I make my way to the strip mall and navigate the parking area. It appears to be fairly well populated for a weeknight. The Magic are at home for a basketball game so maybe that could account for some of the people. I opt for the front entrance today and settle into a spot in front of the Laundromat. I walk the two stores over to the front door and shake my new friend Rock's hand. "How goes it today?" I ask. Rock just nods his head. "Not so good." he mutters. Not so good at all. I just put my hand on Rocks shoulder, take a deep breath, and open the door. Here we go I say to myself.

I enter the Hurricane From Hell and looks around. The bar is pretty full, given the day. The basketball game is on four of the six TV's in the bar. I scan the floor. Both Beth and Joey are working on the floor with Diane sitting behind the bar. I feather my way through the bar and sits on the far end closest to the back of the bar. Diane walks the bar taking care of all of her patrons. After a few seconds she makes her way to me.

"Hi." Diane is the first to speak. She reaches over and gives me a quick kiss.

"Hey." I can say nothing. I have regressed to the awkwardness from the first time I met Diane. I feel the need to say something but I don't want to be a dufus. Diane again takes the first poke and asks me if I want a beer. Sure, the usual. Diane goes and pours me a perfect beer, very little foam. She brings it over and puts it in front of me on a very pretty Irish beer coaster. "I'm sorry." I mutter the words. My voice is cracked and unsteady. Diane tries to dismiss it as nothing. I just stare at my beer. I don't pick up my drink, I just twirl it. Diane runs down and serves some others at the end of the bar. Beth returns from the floor and gives me a hug on the way in. I say hi and ask how things are going. Busy, Beth says and goes down to tend to more customers. Diane makes her way back to me. She tries to keep the conversation simple and non engaging. I am distant but not totally shut off. A familiar lady comes from the back of the bar. She sees the situation unfolding and runs back to the area by the bathrooms. I look up at Diane again. "I need to tell you something." I try to muster confidence that is not free to come to me. "It is kind of important." I am not commanding. Diane stays waiting for the rest to follow. Joey comes from the floor and comes behind the bar. Diane asks him to stay back. He complies. I continue. I take my first sip of beer and begin. My eyes are swollen with water and my lips quiver as I attempt to move them with words. I am unsteady and shaken. I take a more substantial swig. "First, I am sorry about yesterday. About everything. But all of that is secondary right now. Something happened at work today. Something important. I…" I turn the palest of white as I feel an unfamiliar and unwitting hand on my shoulder. I choke as I try to prepare for this action. I stand abruptly and turn in a defensive posture. I stand with a ghostly white face and stare into a face I was not expecting to see. My heart jumps all up in his throat but he manages to push out an 'Oh Hi.'

"Hi yourself, stranger." I can still not believe I am looking at Kate.

"What are you doing here?" My tone is still uneven.

"I beg your pardon. I am visiting my friend" Kate mocks being offended.

"Sorry." I am not sure she was kidding. "It's good to see you." I am laboring over exactly what I should say. Diane watches the entire exchange and stands quietly by monitoring the situation. Diane can feel my uneasiness. This troubles her for the only people that Diane had ever seen me at ease with during their entire relationship was Kate and Dan. Diane wonders if Spade's uneasiness was a byproduct of the episode last evening or something more. Diane was very grateful that Kate had come to see her this morning.

It was perfect timing this morning when Kate arrived at the Hurricane. After Diane had left Spade this morning she came to the bar. She was totally hysterical when Rock had found her just before eleven. Diane would not say anything. She just tried to put on the ferocious independent working woman front and shrugged it off. When Rock asked her about deliveries she didn't even comprehend that someone was speaking with her. It was around eleven fifteen when Kate showed up. Diane was oblivious to everything. As soon as Kate came over and gave her a hug Diane began to cry uncontrollably. It took Kate thirty-five minutes to calm Diane down in her office. Diane told her the same story about Spade's dream and her suspicion about this Elizabeth, although Diane did admit she was not sure of who or what this Elizabeth was. Kate worked very hard to ease her friend's worries and convince Diane that there was no one else for Spade. Kate even surmised the dreams could be a byproduct of the amount of stress that Kenny was under trying to catch the killer. Kate told Diane that Spade takes everything personally, especially his work. Spade, Kate told her, felt he was the great protector of Orlando. So whenever there was a killer in Orlando, Spade made it his mission to make sure he was caught, directly or indirectly. That's how Spade had gotten the reputation of being the best homicide detective in Orlando. And with Dan's guidance and friendship, Orlando had grown to be a pretty safe place. Diane smiled after Kate told her this and she began to refocus on her day. Kate had stayed and spent the afternoon, with a chef salad and a few glasses of white zinfandel the two had actually had a good time. Diane was pleased that she had a good turnout for a weekday, and she was glad that her friend was here to share it with her. But right now she wished Kate were not here. Spade had something to say and he just froze when he saw Kate. Diane was very edgy, expecting the worse. Could he, in his excessively convoluted mind, be planning to dump her for the sake of what Spade may consider protecting her? Diane was not prepared to grapple with this concept and seemed very nervous.

I surveyed the situation and had to decide. What do I tell Diane, now that I let the cat out of the bag? And what of Kate? Should I tell Kate about what had transpired today? I needed guidance and had no one to call upon for help. I nervously twitched as I fought with all my options. Then I fumbled around with my glass. Screw it, I said to myself. I then announced again that I had to tell them something important. I said I felt they both had the right to know. I then began to recount the events of the day. I started off on the positives of the early morning as they pertained to the piece of the potential murder weapon. I did not want to compromise my police requirements but I said I was happy they finally had a potential clue. Next I went on to discuss the fact that the second victims car was found essentially across the street from where I live. I told the girls I figured the killer did it on purpose to send me a message. A message that I told them both that I received loud and clear. I told Kate and Diane that the killer's message was that he was in control and he could reach out and get to me whenever the monster deemed necessary. I then got to the punch line.

"Babe, I am worried. If he can get to me he can get to you. I have no reason not to believe that this sick SOB already knows where you live. And by letting me know today that he can get to me, it seems reasonable to assume that he can or will get to you. Kate, you are around Diane quite a bit. Therefore I think you should also be aware of this. If…"

"I couldn't agree more, Spade." I spin and see my best friend and boss right behind him, Rock in tow.

"Babe, can I get my friend here a drink? Beer?"

"Scotch straight." Kate is surprised. Diane motions Joey over and tells him to get the lieutenant a scotch. Kate and Diane then ask for a pair of white zinfandels. Lieutenant Dan Murphy then begins a brief synopsis of the situations of the day and it sounds like an abbreviate version of the story that I just told. I down my beer and order another. I offer Rock a drink. On me. Rock politely informs everyone he does not mix business and pleasure. I laud his ethics. Diane tells Rock it's OK. Rock still stands his ground. Rock takes his leave and mans his position. Loot and I go on to tell our women that everything has changed in the case. Loot agrees that the killer is telling them he can get to everyone. I am worried about this. I suggest that maybe Diane could possibly go stay in the Murphy guest room. Diane vehemently objects stating she will not let any monster dictate the way she lives her life. I acknowledge this and tell her it is her *life* that I am concerned with. I put forth my argument and we go back and forth for quite a long time. Every now and then Dan and Kate interject, usually along party (gender) lines. After about an hour and a half the issue is brushed to the side. The conversation turns to small talk and an air of relief settles over the group. There is a little more alcohol involved. Around eleven thirty I get up to answer the call of Mother Nature. When I return I take in the scenario. Then I make my way back to the bar. When I sit down I order another. Joey complies. I then decide the time to go for the jugular is now.

I put forth a proposition to the group. I ask Diane if it would be possible to include Rock in the conversation for the time being. At first Diane protests, but then relents and asks

Rock to come join them. The bar is dimly lit and populated only by a couple of mid- fifties types who are either afraid to go home or have no home to go to. I get up and offer Rock my chair. The massive man refuses but after a few seconds of continual prodding and a push by the boss he relents and takes my seat. Beth and Joey are behind the bar simply following the proceedings. Diane sends them both home. Joey agrees but Beth wants to stay. I then begin on a torrid rant that would consume the session and be broken only by the phone call that would change my life forever.

I begin my soap box dissertation by ordering a round for everyone. Again Rock protests but I counter by saying that we should be able to handle the door, given the day, the time, the presence of a mass of humanity such as Rock and the presence of two of Orlando's finest. Rock is forced to concede and orders a Johnny Walker Black. I also invite Beth to grab a drink. Beth goes with a Cosmo that Diane makes for her. I then go through an excessively abbreviated version of the day's events for the benefit of Beth and Rock. At the end of the recap I order another round for all except myself. Need to stay clear, I say. Loot also excuses himself but the others comply with the request. After the recap I then begin to prepare for the fallout. I reason that it's fairly obvious that the killer has some sort of a personal issue. Loot nods in agreement. This being the case I feel that while not predetermined it is also reasonable to conclude that Diane would be in danger as a way to hurt me. Everyone around the bar nods their head to this one. I then admit out loud that I love Diane more than I ever had loved a woman in my life. This startles both Beth and Rock, and even Loot and Kate seem surprised, for although they both had known this they never expected this kind of statement from me. I then continue after the bombshell that I agree with Diane, that we should not put our life on hold for the sake of appeasing a monster. But, I continue, it is wise to be prudent with regard to this situation.

I then outline my master plan. First, I ask Rock if he has an associate that could work the door with him. I want to keep the bar open, just to be a little extra cautious. Rock says he may have someone who can help out short term. Perfect. Next I ask Loot and Kate if they would mind having a guest for a little while. Diane protests vehemently, saying she will have none of it. I offer a counter that she will stay with me whenever I am available. I only want Diane to stay with the Murphy's whenever I am not around. Diane still protests but Kate rescues me by first agreeing and then saying it would be fun while the guys are out playing cops and robbers. Diane slowly relents and I have my referendum passed. I also inform Beth to be extra careful when coming or going from work and have either Joey or Rock get her to or from the car. I remind Diane that the Sweet Sixteen and Final Four of March Madness are right around the corner and that means that she will be working late and be very busy. I tell Diane, Rock and Beth all that they have to be very cautious. Kate chimes in and offers to help whenever she can during these times. Diane smiles and offers her thanks. I also offer to be present at the bar during my down times Diane nods and says thanks, but Kate tells me to leave that to her. Kate tells me to get the son of a bitch. I nod and say 'I will.' I begin to mellow after accomplishing this two point process to protect Diane and everyone else. Beth runs from behind the bar and rousts the two patrons still remaining. I then 'volunteer' to take the first shift and offer to take Diane home. Your place or mine was the response. Everyone chuckles as Rock and Beth escort the last two out the door. As Beth and Rock return I reach out and grab my cash.

"The evening's entertainment is on the house." Diane declares. I continue to flip through and throw fifty at Beth.

"This is for your outstanding hospitality and service. Please take care of your coworkers as well." Beth nods and takes the money. I then offer my arm to the very attractive proprietor of the bar and ask if I may escort her home. "I guess I can allow that." Diane says with dramatic flair and starts to reach for my arm. Just as she touches me the familiar sounds of Van Halen's "Jump" echo through the bar as my cellphone rings.

"Spade." There is a momentary pause followed by a "WHAT!" I then mutter something and slam my phone closed. Everyone is shaken by my tone. Diane is first to speak.

"What happened?"

"I have to go to work. Kate can you take this lovely lady home with you?" My tone was forceful and direct but sympathetic. Diane begins to protest but I will have none of it. Kate nods her head and tells me she'd be happy to. Loot asks me what is going on.

"There is some kind of disturbance on the third floor of the Casa de Zaidi."

"What kind of disturbance?" Loot is inquisitive but not concerned.

'I don't have any idea. But it's the third floor. And that floor has been shut by Emilia."

Loot is confused. "Who is Emilia?"

"The GM. She helped me this morning." Loot does not appear overly concerned by my words. I run over and give Diane a kiss then tell her I will see her in a little while. I then run over and gives Kate a kiss and head to the door. Loot looks at Kate and gives her a hug, then leans over and kisses her as well. "Hold on. I'm coming." Loot screams to me, who has already reached the door. I stick my right arm out behind me and wave as if to say message received. Then I bolt out through the beautiful stained glass doors. Loot reaches over and gives Diane a kiss and asks Rock to escort the three lovely ladies to their cars when they are done shutting down the bar. Rock nods and says 'No problem.' Loot then walks through the front door and out to the outside. I have the Vette in front and am gunning the engine. Calm down, Loot thinks to himself. He walks down the path and over to my car. Loot gets in. I take off like a rocket. His window is down and Loot can't help but notice how chilly the late night air is this evening. I run everything I see. I am on the freeway in ninety seconds. I hit the open road and open up the Vette. Loot looks over. One twenty-five. Loot says a quick Hail Mary and clenches his door handle so hard his knuckles turn white and his fingernails dig in to the leather of the handle. I

186

pass Church Street and fly off the interstate. The buildings look like they have a frosting on them because of the way the moon reflects off the dark architecture of the area. I turn the corner and reach the Casa de Zaidi. There is a white and blue in stealth mode sitting out front. I zip in right behind it. Total distance from door to door seven-point-three miles. Total time elapsed four minutes forty-eight seconds. Little did I know that events that would change my life forever would be moving around me just as fast.

FOURTEEN

The car had barely begun to stop by the time I burst out of it and through the doors of the most infamous hotel on the planet today. I shot in through the lobby where I proceeded to repeat my wacky dance step, much as I did that morning. I then scurried up to the front desk and ask what happened.

"Some guy got off three. The Man with the Hat tried to stop him as he wanted to go down the hall. The guy sucker punched the Man with the Hat and shut his eye. The guy then started to run and the Man with the Hat tripped him. The guy hit the wall pretty hard. The Man with the Hat jumped him when the guy hit him again in the same eye. The guy then bolted and got back in the elevator. He came running through the lobby and took off out the door. Then the Man with the Hat called down on his walkie talkie telling us he had been attacked."

I looked at the employee, not quite grasping what I had just been told. "Who in the hell is the man with the hat?"

"I'm sorry?" The girl behind the desk was now intimidated.

"Who is this 'the man with the hat?'"

"Bill."

"Excuse me?" The girl is now really frightened. She attempts to answer, obviously nervous.

"Bill Pikal. He is our bellman assigned to watch the third floor tonight?"

I now begin to understand a little more clearly. "So this man with the hat, he works here?"

The girl now feels much better. "Oh yes I'm sorry. We all call him the man with the hat because every time he's at work he wears that silly bellman's cap. He is the only one to do so."

"I see. And where is this gentleman now?"

"He's in the back. Dave got him some ice after he called for help."

"I'm sorry, who's Dave."

"Dave's the doorman who is working the doors tonight."

I am now enlightened, but more curious. I lean over the desk to read the shiny name tag on her left lapel. "So, Nancy from Rhode Island, whom else is on duty here tonight."

"It's the midnight crew. Night Auditor. We only have me, one bellman the bellman watching the third floor these days and the two hospitality guys in the basement."

"What, pray tell, is a hospitality guy?"

"They are the guys who make the sandwiches on the room service menu at night, or cut the pies, you know the simple things. They also bring amenities like razors or towels if someone asks for them."

"Great." I say, "Get them up here. You don't have anyone else working here right now?"

"No sir."

"Excellent." I move forward. "Where is this man with the hat guy now?"

Nancy points. "He is behind there in back. He is icing his eye." I turn to Loot, who joined me in the middle of the conversation, and motions with his head. The two men are then let into the back executive area by Nancy. There we find an older gentleman holding a big ice pack over his left eye. A uniformed police officer is standing next to him, as is Dave the bellman. Loot and I furnish our badges and ask the policeman what he has. Not too much is the reply. White male six foot very heavy. Dark blue Magic sweatshirt and blue sweatpants. Nike basketball sneakers. That's it. Dave then chimes in the guy was clean shaven. I nod. Not much at all I say to myself. I turn to Loot, who still believes he is wasting his time here. Little did he know the truth.

The front desk bell rings and Nancy goes to the desk. Loot and I can hear her talking and then she opens the door to the back area where everyone is. Two guys enter dressed in black pants and white polo's embossed with the Casa de Zaidi insignia on them.

"Yo, Hatman, what happened to your face?" I turn and look at them.

"What is your name?" I ask.

"Nikki, and this is Omar." Nikki points to his friend. "Who are you?" I flash the badge and both men pipe down. I continue.

"Have you had any calls in the last half-hour?"

Omar answers. "No boss, we had nothing since we started at eleven."

I continue. "Have you heard anything out of the ordinary since you came on shift?"

This time Nikki replies. "The only thing we heard all night was Hatman asking about something on the handheld."

I nod. "All right thanks. You can return to work now."

The two turn and begin to leave. As they walk out the door. Nikki turns back and says, "Damn Hatman that looks like it hurts." Then they depart. Loot is annoyed at the triviality and asks me why we are here. I hear him but pay no attention. My spider sense is tingling. I know something is wrong. My gut tells me. Loot's phone rings and he picks it up. It's the girls wanting to make sure everything is all right. Loot tells them everything is fine. I spin and roll out the door. I hit the lobby and rush to the elevator. I head up to the third floor. I am anxious. I remove the strap from my sidearm but do not brandish it right away. The third floor stop is currently unmanned. I exit the elevator cautiously. I check the first door but finds it still locked. The elevator doors shut behind me and I hear the elevator begin to move. I walk cautiously down the hall looking around closely with every step. I make my way down to room 311 then stop, horrified. I approach the cut out across from 311 and look, stunned. Then I rip out my cell and dials. "IT'S SPADE. CASA DE ZAIDI. NOW. HOW LONG? MAKE IT QUICKER!" I then shut the phone off. Loot has just exited the elevator and has heard all the commotion. He screams down the hall, "What's wrong?" I do not answer, I just begin looking. I reach into my pocket and pull another pair of rubber gloves out. Again I begin to approach the offset hole in the wall. Loot now begins to jog to where I am. When he arrives Loot finds me poking around at the top of the ice machine. "What's wrong?" Loot asks. I step back and point. Then I tell Loot "get me three more uniforms. Keep it quiet. I don't want any lights. No attention. Have them park on the corners and walk their way down. Get them here ASAP." Loot just looks at me and again asks me what's wrong.

"That gash was not there when I was at the ice machine this morning."

"So?" Loot is beginning to worry that his friend was overreacting to everything. I wasn't.

"Lift the top and look inside." My words strike Loot very surprisingly. My tone was not as authoritative as it had been all day. It was more anxious. Loot walked over and stuck his hand out. "STOP!!" I screamed at the top of my lungs. Loot turned to protest but I already have my hand outstretched with limp pieces of powdered yellow rubber in them. "GLOVES." I handed the gloves to Loot who then put them on. Then Loot continued to the ice machine and looked at the gash. It was at the top one-third of the way across from the left hand edge. It was an inch to an inch-and-a-half long Loot guessed, and deep enough only to track a pen. Loot rubbed his finger over it and he could catch his nail on the groove. It may have been deep enough to guide a pen rolling along it. "LOOK INSIDE" I tell Loot again. Loot reaches over and lifts the top to the ice machine. He looks down and stares. "Is that what I think it is?"

"That's my guess." is my reply. "Now, please sir, can I get those three uniforms and can we request them on the QT? I don't want any media attention back here."

Loot questions me. "What about forensics?'

"On the way. Should be here soon."

Loot is puzzled. "How the hell did you do that?"

"I made a call to someone who cares."

Loot rips out his cell and calls command. He asks for three patrol cars to be dispersed to the Case de Zaidi location. Loot asks for them to leave the cars on the corner and approach by foot. Loot tells command to keep it as quiet as possible. He then hangs up. I suggest to Loot to go and tell the officer down stairs what is going on. I then stare at the machine as I wait and wonders how all this could be.

I stare and wonder. How could this be? I was sure I did not remember seeing the scar in the machine at all this morning. It never even dawned on me to check the inside where the ice gets filled. The ice machines in these hotels get filled by five gallon buckets. There is usually some kind of larger scale ice maker on the facility floor where the washer and drier and housekeeping supplies are kept. The hotel staff then uses the five gallon bucket to fill the machines whenever mandated. Why did I not check the machine? The thought never even occurred to me. That fact alone infuriated me mightily. That was simply careless and sloppy detective work as far as I was concerned. And since I took pride on being the great Orlando protector that fact sat all the worse with me. I was sure the scratch was not there in the morning. So when did it get here? And how? The Hatman said the guy did not get past him. He said he knocked the intruder off his feet. After a brief scuffle, the Hatman said the guy ran out the lobby where the other two employees remember seeing him fly through the revolving doors and out to the street. What if he was a diversion? Maybe he was working with the killer to help the killer hide the knife. Maybe he was trying to get the knife back. Yes, that could be it. Maybe the killer knew I came back this morning and was afraid I would find the knife so he came back to remove it but was scared away. I am such a jerk. I should have checked that right away. Why would he put the scratch there? Could he have been that sloppy? Maybe when he came back he had difficulty getting the top off the lid. That makes no sense. Why would he have problems with that? I stand there staring blankly at the ice machine when I hear the familiar ding and the elevator doors begin to open. I look back and see my two favorite people right now, Justyna and Loot, exit the elevator and make their way down to the spot where I am standing. Justyna walks up suitcase in hand and says, "Hey detective, long time no see." I give her a smile and a "likewise."

Justyna inquires about why she is here again. Apparently Loot felt it was better that she get the information directly from me. Loot tells me the three officers have arrived. Loot tells me he has one at the front and rear doors. The original officer on scene is on his way up to man the third floor. The third officer is manning the lobby. I nod my head approvingly. I do not want to have any other issues right now. I show Justyna the scar and asks her if she remembered seeing it at any point during their initial visit. Justyna does not but she takes out her camera. She photographs the ice machine. She will compare them against the original crime scene photos. Justyna asks me what happened and why she got called back. She said that Loot told her of the disturbance but Justyna did not yet see the sense of urgency. "Do you want me to compare the grove to the tip we found? I can take a casting of it and see what we can find."

"No, I want you to compare it to the knife."

"What?!" Justyna is confused.

"Look inside." I tell her.

"NO! DON'T TELL ME!"

"Look inside." I am very calm as I issue my direction. Loot just stands by and watches. Justyna walks over and lifts the ice machine's fill top. She stares inside and says "I DON'T BELIEVE IT. I JUST DON'T BELIEVE IT!" She steps down and pauses. "How did I not check there the first time?"

"I've been asking myself the same question for the last half-hour." My tone carries a hint of disappointment.

"I'm taking the machine." Justyna takes out her cell and calls someone. She identifies herself and asks for 'the truck.' She whispers a chorus of uh-huh and mmmh-hmm's and hangs up. "I'm taking this ice machine out of here down to my lab. I can study it there. I need to see if there are any tiny hidden pieces of evidence left."

"Are you going to leave the knife in it?" Loot asks.

"I'm debating it. It'll only take fifteen minutes to get to my lab from here but it will probably take at least that long to get it into the truck from here. If I leave it would probably be better. Less chance of disturbing anything. But if any ice melts, I don't want to compromise any evidence left on the knife. I've got about ten minutes left to decide."

I shrug my shoulders. "You are the expert. I'll put my faith in your judgment."

"Good idea…" Justyna says mockingly. The three of us all share a little laugh.

The merits of the issue are debated back and forth as we try to plan the best way we can to protect the potential evidence. The discussion takes up the whole time as the policeman in the lobby radios up that the guys from forensics are here. Justyna decides that she will remove the knife now, before the ice machine gets unplugged. She asks Loot, who is the tallest, to reach in with her forceps and remove the knife. Loot complies and carefully removes the knife and places it in the bag that Justyna is holding. Justyna looks at the tip. "It could be our boy," she says. The tip is missing and the numbers just past the tip of the knife have been filed off. Justyna seals the bag and puts a marking on it with some kind of case number. Then she places the bag and its contents in her suitcase in an empty carrying compartment. The elevator rings and two gentlemen come out and walk down the hall. Justyna greets them as they reach her vicinity. "OK Boys, I need this to be brought to the shop. Set it up in room five. The guys place the machine on a small homemade roller dolly. After Justyna unplugs the ice machine the guys start to roll it off. "Slow" she yells at them. "I need to preserve as much evidence as possible." The two guys give her a look and then continue slowly down the hall toward the elevator.

Justyna, Loot and I all look at the room that was just vacated. I show Justyna and Loot where I found the tip and I show Loot where the knives fell in my little experiment this morning. I look at my watch. It's almost one. You had better make that yesterday morning, I say to myself. Justyna gets on her hands and knees and takes out a light that shoots all kinds of pretty purplish colors that would have some kind of funky off the wall name if that color were in a box of Crayolas. It shows up some kind of shadow on the floor which I recognize by the drag marks as the blood pool. Justyna explains that is the light shows where blood was even after the floor was cleaned. She then takes a regular flashlight and scours the tile. I ask her what she's looking for. Justyna tells me she's just looking. She then rises and grabs her suitcase. "I have to go to work." Justyna starts to walk toward the elevator. Loot and I follow behind her.

We exit the elevator where the ice machine is waiting. I walk over to the desk and hand Nancy from Rhode Island a card. "Tell Emilia to call me in the morning." Nancy nods her head and asks what's going on with the ice machine. Good question, I think to myself. I go over to the ice machine and ask what the delay is. I am told there is no delay; the bellman at the door is showing the cops how to get to the service entrance. It seems the ice machine will not fit through a rotating door. I nod.

After ten-minute struggle and a lot of verbal reinforcement from Justyna, the ice machine is loaded and the truck takes off. Justyna grabs her suitcase and turns to me.

"I have to go process the knife. I'll call you when I know." I shake my head and Justyna's hand and says thanks. With that Justyna leaves. Loot and I then begin to walk out. I turn to Nancy from Rhode Island and say thanks. Then we leave the hotel.

The ride back to the Hole was especially painstaking for me. The frustration of the days and months events were beginning to take their toll. I had dropped Loot at The Hurricane From Hell where he picked up his car and agreed to go check on the girls. The bar was deserted, a far cry from the bustling scene when I arrived earlier in the evening. The little lizard pool was breaking over the parking lot as it often did at this hour and I actually laughed as the lizards all scattered when Loot drove away. It reminded me of Moses and the Red Sea. Now I was all alone to wrestle with my thoughts and anxieties. Patience was never something I was good at, I thought to myself. If Justyna was able to find anything on the knife I would be ready to pounce, that much I was certain of. Elizabeth accompanied me down a long stretch of the trip. I was grateful for her company, given my inability to think clearly. I could not wait. My town needed me. I was closing in. Just one viable print. Just one. I decided against going down to the forensics lab and waiting there. I knew I hated being watched and felt I would be a distraction. So I decided to go back to the office. When daytime broke I would call up *The Outdoorsman* and see if they had made any progress. I also had not yet seen if there was any report back from the processing of the Acura that belonged to Lisa Yeung. I was hoping that would be on my desk when I arrived at the Hole. Elizabeth remains next to me. Stay calm. This is coming to a close. You know he will be caught. Remain vigilant. I always had confidence when Elizabeth was around. She brought me a sense of reassurance, of not being alone. I continued the drive. I was in no hurry this time, knowing I was dependent on someone else before I could move forward. It was not a feeling I liked.

The early morning passed over quickly. I had spent the greater portion of the morning sifting through the files and photographs of each of the scenes. I started with the statements from the friend of victim number one. The friend had left her at the bar they went to after the Barenaked Ladies concert. There was no further contact after that. No one had seen or heard from Lisa Yeung since the bank closed at four that Saturday. Lisa had decided to stay and finish some administrative functions, which according to the bank employees was fairly normal for her to do. I sat there pondering. The Hole was empty except for me and the smell of the coffee pot which I rejuvenated when I returned. What made this monster pick these girls? How could anybody know that Lisa Yeung would be alone at the bank on a Saturday night? And that no one would see anything? Did he stalk them? I could see how the killer would randomly strike at a girl after a concert at a bar nearby the TD Waterhouse Center. It's logical. A bar on a busy night after a concert, she was probably just a random target. The witness testimony I reread gave me no indication the girls felt threatened. But Lisa Yeung? What made the killer feel confident he would be successful? There must be a reason. And the ice skater was certainly a pick. He wanted the attention. Whoever he is he undoubtedly knew who he was targeting. I sat there pondering in the Hole, trying to understand the killer. They always say you need to think like your adversary. But who possibly can think like a killer? No one, no matter how intelligent, can think like a killer? The infamous mass murderers of time were always asked that question, and after you heard the explanation most people were unable to comprehend the explanation they were told. Why? Because it is not something a rational person would think of. So how can I possibly rationalize it? Simple. I can't. Don't think like him, I tell myself. Think of it as a hostile business takeover. The last victim was definitely chosen to attract international attention to his deeds. It makes perfect sense. So, what makes him kill in the first place? That again is something I realize I cannot probably understand. That in itself makes it the wrong question. The correct question, I surmise, is why me? Why me, Detective Kenny Spade? Yes, that is finally the correct question, I decide. Why me? I look back down at my pictures. Why me? The answer has to be here somewhere. I keep looking at the pictures. The killer has obviously taken the time to plan everything meticulously. Therefore, would it be wrong to conclude that he wanted me to find the knife? I keep looking at the pictures. Victim number one. A victim of chance. Victim number two. A victim of opportunity. Victim number three. A victim of means. A victim of chance, the chance to expose himself. A victim of opportunity. The opportunity to show seriousness, diligence and opportunity. A victim of means. The means to bring unfathomable amounts of attention and pressure upon this person, to show the world that there is someone who is capable of doing anything and that the United States and Orlando in particular are not exempt from unspeakable violence. My heart skips a beat and I break out in a cold sweat. Was I just thinking like a monster? What is wrong with me? I look at the pictures again. I see nothing. I stop and stare. Of course. What a dummy. Where are the pictures? I start funneling furiously through the pictures until I find what I want. The cards. What do the cards tell him?

The first one is an introduction. A spade calling me out. A dark red smudge introducing me to its sinister origin. The second one is massive. The monster calls me out. A whole story calling me out. The third one is daring, inviting and evil. Taunting. Bringing my weakness to the forefront. Each card is perfectly complimentary to its owner. (victim) Together they make up a perfect trinity of bedlam left to torment me and instill terror in my city. *My city.* All of this is my fault. These girls died so he could get to *me*. What is his issue with me? That is the key. He has issues with me. I start racking my brain. Who would have issues with me?

I think back over my homicide career. I am guessing the last four years since I became a homicide detective would be most relevant. I do not think it goes all the way back to my patrolman days. So I start to rekindle all my prior cases. The Lester Jester case was the first one I remembered. Lester was a father of three who sodomized and killed a 13-year-old friend of his daughter. He was a local legend, Boy Scout leader and former Colonial High School and University of Central Florida stud. No one, including his wife, had any clue at all about his diabolical alter ego. He attempted to plead an abusive childhood defense and insanity, but no one bought it. He was sent up for twenty to life for murder two. I could not think of why anyone related to this case would have it in for me. I remembered that Lester's youngest son was reconciliatory toward Lester but the other family members had disavowed being related to him. I did not think that the youngest Lester would be the type to go after me. The next case that stuck out to me was the homeless man, Joe Huff, who killed a pretty young Disney girl for not giving him any money. That one took the better part of a year to solve, due to the lack of evidence. Joe Huff was only captured because he kept a scarf of the victim that was not the most common. A fellow Disney employee recognized the scarf and when it was tested we found the victims DNA on the scarf. The most likely suspect, I surmised, was the case of Lewis Caster and Nicole Jacks. Lewis and Nicole were found executed in an apartment in northern Orlando off Route 436. This is the case that created the legend of Kenny Spade.

Lewis Caster was the owner of an auto mall in central Orlando. He had a Chevy, Cadillac and GMC truck dealership situated in central Orlando. Mr. Caster was in his late forties with a family. He was short and heavy set. And loud. Local Orlando competitors used to mock him as Loud Louie. The running joke was if you wanted to buy you would go to (insert name here) but if you wanted to beg, steal, or scam you would go to Loud Louie's. Anyway, I recalled, it seemed that Loud Louie was aware of these tauntings and became determined to dispel his inadequacies. So Loud Louie began a public and expensive affair with his receptionist, a buxom twenty three year old blonde named Nicole Jacks. Louie caught her drunk one day and weaseled his way into her pants. After that he was in he was in. Nicole was quite the looker and Louie used a combination of oppression and lavish gift giving to keep Nicole around. Nicole was once rumored to have said that whatever Lewis lacked in physical appearance he compensated for in other fields. Most people dismissed that as the three carrot earrings talking. Anyway to keep his young filly in tow Louie began to present her with coke and pot. Louie became quite a fan of his mood enhancers. He also became quite indebted to his benefactor and suppliers, The Latin Conquistadors.

The Conquistadors were known in Orlando as a powerful gang. They had a membership about four-hundred deep and were known to be responsible for a number of rapes and robberies in the area. Anyone who dared to testify against any Conquistador would soon end up with a visit to a loved one with a not so veiled threat, or worse. The entire town was running scared from them. After Nicole and Lewis were found executed in Nicole's apartment a young Detective Kenny Spade was assigned the case. It was only a few months after the Joe Huff case and I was still learning my way. I brought the heat after I found the drug connection and I applied constant pressure to the Latin Conquistadors. No one would dare testify against any of the gang so I could never formally charge anybody. But I pushed. I fought like a ravaged lion being dropped in a gazelle field after not eating for a month.

One Friday in August, in the middle of lunch hour at the intersection of 436 and 50, one of Orlando biggest intersections, I found myself sitting at a stop light in my police issue brown Chevy Caprice. It also happened to be the only car I had. Coming from behind me an SUV pulled up and a myriad of Conquistadors, including their leader Raul Nieves, jumped out of the truck and began to shoot. The first set of shots sent all the locals fleeing. The first white and blue on the scene took an onslaught of automatic weapons fire. Its pilot, a young man named William Tudor, took a shot in the leg and one in the torso. I was hiding on the side of my cruiser after the assault began, but I ran out from my safe haven and kept firing my nine millimeter to provide cover for the downed officer. I pulled the officer behind the police car and continued firing. One of my shots hit Raul Nieves in the head and brought him to the ground. As he went down, Raul's two top lieutenants went to his aid. I took them down as well. Within four minutes the intersection was awash in police reinforcements, ambulances and a coroners van. Raul Nieves, his top two lieutenants and another member of the gang were dead. The three remaining in the hit squad were in the hospital with gunshot wounds. The officer I saved was brought to the hospital. While in surgery it was discovered that he was hit in one of the major blood vessels in his leg. He had bled out and died on the table. I myself was hit twice but was unaware of it. I was treated and released, but I was readmitted three days later with an infection that almost killed me.

The backlash in Orlando was intense. There was overnight a threefold increase in arrests as well as a willingness of the populous of Orlando to stand up to the goons that had caused the death of a cop. The face that people had put with it was Detective Kenny Spade. The news that August night had a home video shot by some tourist from Nebraska showing Orlando Police Detective Kenny Spade pulling the injured officer to safety. Lewis Motors had offered me a new Cadillac for my heroic efforts, but I instead bought a used 1987 red Corvette which I financed and was still currently paying for. That was the time that Orlando became Detective Kenny Spade's town and I its official protector. I sat and thought. For the last eighteen to twenty-four months the Latin Conquistadors had been silent or small time. There had been no buzz about a sudden resurrection of the Conquistadors that I knew of. Besides, I surmised, if the Conquistadors were going to go after me they would do something a lot more dramatic and violent. No, I didn't know who was mocking me. The more I thought the more confused I got. I kept looking at the cards. The cards mirrored the crimes. The first was an introduction. The second was the message, and the third declared the winner. The trinity of terror. I continued my analysis.

After two pots of coffee and three hours of no progress I had enough. I went out of the Hole to get some fresh air. I looked down at my watch. Just about eight. The early morning March sun had begun to peak but it was still quite chilly. I figured it was around fifty, but I was counting my blessings. After all, they were expecting twelve inches of snow in New York. I sat down and looked at the ground around me. I watched an army of ants march across the ground in front of the Hole and devour a piece of banana that someone had left behind. I watched the ants and marveled at their structure. Methodical and dedicated to their craft. I pondered their mission carefully. Elizabeth joined me. She also saw the ants. Elizabeth noticed how their diligence reminded her of the job the killer was doing. He was following his plan like one ant was following the other. She also noticed that the killer was moving from one murder to another, each meticulously planned and executed, and each thoroughly efficient like the ants retrieving the food and bringing it to their colony. I just turned toward her and smiled. Elizabeth always thought so clearly. I marveled at how fortunate I was that Elizabeth had not abandoned me. She had every reason to but did not. I kept looking at the ants and thinking. And Elizabeth just sat by my side, reassuring me that the answers I sought was right in front of me. Be clear and focus, she told me. Soon enough the truth will be revealed. The truth to come was not what I would be expecting.

It was fairly warm in the sunny Orlando air when I felt the touch of a hand on my shoulder. I looked to my right fully expecting to see Elizabeth and I spoke accordingly. It took me a few minutes before I was able to see the hand on my shoulder was that of my best friend and superior, Lieutenant Dan Murphy. I had to shake some more cobwebs off before I was able to string together some diction.

"Hey Loot, what's up?"

"Elizabeth!?"

"What?"

"Elizabeth," Loot struggles.

"I told Diane there is no Elizabeth, why can't she let it go?" I am concerned about the potential problem this causes me. I will never be rid of Elizabeth, and do not want to be. But I do need to keep her to myself.

"Spade, *you* can't let her go." Loot voice is concerned but firm. "You just called to her."

"I did not!" I am becoming hostile. Loot tries to counter with some compassion.

"Spade, when I just touched your shoulder you called to Elizabeth. I have heard from four different people you have been out here for hours staring at the ground and talking to yourself. Or Elizabeth." I shoot Loot a look, who dismisses it without a second thought. Loot continues. "Tolliver tells me he had to chase off a couple of kids because they were tying your shoelaces together. He says you wouldn't even respond to him."

"Maybe I was sleeping."

"Outside. With your eyes open? Don't give me that!" Loot is now taking command of the conversation.

"Loot, it's no big deal. I was just thinking about the case."

"Don't feed me more of your crap, Spade. I am not stupid. But I am concerned."

"Relax Loot. What time is it?" I don't want to look at his watch.

"Time for you to stop feeding me crap."

"On the clock." There is a lack of patience in my tone this time.

"Eleven thirty."

I look at his watch. Holy shit! It really is eleven thirty. I had been commiserating with Elizabeth for hours. Damn, that can't look good. I decide I had better counterstrike soon before I get buried. I decide to go with the obvious out, trying to get caught up on the ladies. I ask how the evening went and the like. Loot plays along but is familiar with the game and will not give me the out I so desperately seek. I then turn my attention to the case but again Loot is not buying. I jab back that we can sit out here for the rest of the morning like a bunch of dummy heads or we can go back to work. Loot again is not biting but decides a return to work is the correct thing to do. We go up to the Hole and rehash the morning's events. I tell him all of the thoughts I had about the evidence trail and the Conquistadors. Loot agrees it's too smart for them. The next two hours are spent in a round table on the conference table in the hole. Loot, Ronan, Tolliver and I all went back and forth with the evidence. There was none. Tolliver had called *The Outdoorsman* in the morning and they had nothing to report. Ronan had called about the Acura. The person in forensics said they found no prints in the car. The quartet had examined all of the photographs of the crime scene and the Aces found on the victims. All of us had no discernible guesses as to anything that could be conceived as a clue.

The phone in the Hole rang at one eleven. Peggy picked up and then paged Loot. This is a good sign, I thought. Three of a kind. Good enough to win a lot of cash in poker. A minute later the familiar Van Halen ring penetrated from my beltline. Loot was embroiled in a conversation. I put my attention to my phone with my familiar "Spade." It was Justyna on the other end. They were able to get a partial print off the knife. Could I come over to forensics right away? I have been waiting for you all damn morning, I thought to myself. I will be right over. I left the group and went to my cube to grab the keys. When I returned to the table Loot was just getting off the phone. They have a print, Loot said.

"Yeah, I know. Justyna called me. I'm going down there right now."

"Hold on, I'll go with you."

"Are you ready? I want to get moving on this right away." I was jumping again.

"Yeah let's go." Loot told Ronan and Tolliver to clean the table up and meet them at forensics. He also told Ronan to tell the FBI they had a print. Loot wanted to be ready to move as soon as they had the positive ID, so he told the pair to hurry. I was already down the hall trying to exit the building.

I strode out to the car and fired my lady up. Loot ran down the stairs and jumped in with me. Loot had been down this road before and knew it was pointless to try and tell me anything. Loot always tried to get me to drive a police issue vehicle. He even tried to coerce me with a police issue chase Camaro once. I told Loot it was pointless, the Vette was my car, period. Loot knew better than to argue. I manipulated the red Corvette through the streets as if he were a proud member of the Andretti family. Loot found himself at the door to forensics before he could finish his first Hail Mary. It would be the first of many prayers before the day was done.

I strode through the halls with much vigor and walked right up to forensics, leaving Loot in the dust. I calmly opened the door, remembering my entrance of yesterday morning. I politely asked Richard Pryor where I could find Justyna. When I spoke everyone in forensics was quiet. Even the cubicle with a voice but no face had nothing to say. That's odd, I thought. George Overdunn, the Richard Pryor clone, told Loot and me that Justyna was down the hall in Forensics Five. I said I knew the place. Loot and I left the office and began to walk toward Forensics Five.

"Did that strike you as weird?" I asked.

"Extremely." Loot answered.

We walked down to Forensics Five and enter the room. Justyna is waiting. "Hello" I say as I enter the room. Justyna and Loot exchange pleasantries as well. My manners and patience escape him again. "So what do you have for us?"

"Well," Justyna begins, "This was a very difficult print to identify."

Loot interrupts. "You have a positive match?" He sounds like he is looking for reassurance more than anything else.

"Yes," Justyna continues. "As I was saying, this was not an easy print to match. I ran it through our system and came up blank. So next I ran it through state. Again I got no hits. By this time I was no longer sure that I had a viable print. So I rescanned the print and ran it through DOJ." Department of Justice is a national database of law enforcement agencies that helps all the different groups share information. "As I ran it through DOJ I got a hit. A ninety-seven point two six three percent match."

I am concerned. "Ninety-seven point two six three? Is that good enough?"

"Well, it seems that some of the identifiable ridges are not perfectly concise. But the software said the likelihood of a positive match was one in 118,934. The number would have been much higher except for the fact that the print was simply a partial and not complete and due to the fact that most of the edges were distorted."

Loot sits trying to grasp what he is being told. "Do we think we have the killer's identity?"

Justyna pauses and tries to steady herself. "Like I said the probability factor is ninety-seven point two six three percent."

I chime in. "I'll take my chances with those odds on a spelling test. So, who's our mystery monster?" Justyna points to the television screen that sits on the wall behind her. On it I see a photo ID of a white male, long hair, mid thirties. I look again. This ID is familiar to me. I turn and look at Loot who is staring, aghast.

"You." Justyna's voice is weak and beaten.

"Excuse me?" I am confused by her response.

"The print comes back to Detective Kenneth Spade. Orlando Police Department. You see when cops are hired they are finger printed and given identification badges. Both of these pieces of information are then recorded in the DOJ computer. According to the finger print, you are the killer." The words leave Justyna's lips and her eyes begin to well up. She stands there as do we all in awkward silence, each waiting for someone else to speak. I break the silence. My tone becomes hostile as if I do not find the joke funny. "Funny, now tell me the truth." Outside the room there is a commotion. The door to Forensics Five is thrown open and in walks Officer Poncher, as well as Captain Cutler and Officer John Cage, the mammoth man I remember from the downtown IAD interrogation room. Poncher is next to speak.

"The truth, Detective Kenneth Spade, is that you are under arrest for the murder of Svetlana Ihavtakysa. You have the right to remain silent. If you give up that right anything you say can and will be used against you. You have the right to an attorney. If you cannot afford an attorney one will be appointed for you. Please place your hands behind your back." Poncher grabs my hand. I try to resist but find the massive Cage there to help Poncher. Loot blows his cool.

"What the hell is going on here?"

"What's going on here, Lieutenant, is that we have caught the killer of Svetlana Ihavtakysa. Soon we will have evidence to link him to the other two murders too, and then your crown prince who can do no wrong will get his just desserts." Poncher glows with smugness with every word that comes out of his mouth. Poncher then turns to Captain Cutler, who nods. "Lieutenant Murphy, you are hereby removed from any involvement in any of the three murder cases your subordinate, Detective Kenneth Spade was working on. Additionally, any supporting officers, including Detectives Ronan and Tolliver are forbidden from working on anything involving any of these cases as well. A detective from Internal Affairs will be along to debrief all of you and take possession of any relevant evidence forthwith." I stop, despite the best efforts of Officer Cage.

"I didn't do it. Damnit Loot, I didn't do it." Loot nods and says "I know." I am now forcibly escorted from the room. I try to stammer. "Wait, let me give him my keys."

Poncher stops and takes the keys from me. "Sorry, these are material evidence in a murder investigation." I am then led from the room. I am escorted down the hall and past the forensics office. As I pass everyone from inside forensics looks at me. Some appear to be genuinely shocked, but the majority wears a look of disgust as I am marched past them. Poncher, Cutler and Cage then march right through the lobby and out the front door. I am placed in a brown Crown Victoria and the door is closed.

Loot looks at Justyna and asks what the hell is going on. Justyna tells him that the print came back to match Detective Spade. Justyna was stunned by this and unsure of what to do, so she went to her supervisor, George Underdunn. Mr. Underdunn said anytime a police officer was alleged to have committed a crime Internal Affairs was to be notified. After Underdunn notified IAD they asked Justyna to call Detective Spade and bring him down here under the guise of identifying the killer, which she did as required by protocol. Loot screams an obscenity and runs out the door. Loot runs down the hall and out the front door. As he exits, the brown Crown Victoria begins to pull away with its precious cargo in back. Loot shouts at the top of his lungs "KEEP YOUR MOUTH SHUT!" As the car leaves Loot dials his cellphone frantically and starts screaming at the person on the other end. "CALL ASHLEY. GET HER DOWN TO POLICE HEADQUARTERS. AND TELL HER NOW!"

FIFTEEN

The ride to Police headquarters takes what seems to me to be hours. How can it be? How can it possibly be? How the hell did they get my print off the knife? It makes no sense to me at all. I sit there and wonder over how this can possibly be. Officer Poncher, who is sitting in the front passenger seat, asks me how I am enjoying the ride. I do not even acknowledge the remark with a glance. Besides the mammoth Cage, who is seated right next to me, probably would have put a stop to any shenanigans that I could have mustered. Coconut. The cruiser has a horrifying odor of coconut. I hate coconuts. I always have. I realized just then how much trouble I was in. My collective thought process changed. Throughout the investigation I had been playing a cat and mouse game of who is the hunter and who is the hunted. I now had to change my philosophy. I actually felt that the best way to exonerate myself would be to catch the actual killer. But I was not able to do that given my current status. I now had to focus on how to find a way to exonerate myself.

Oh Elizabeth, what have I done? For the second time in my life I have let you down. I remembered the last time we had communicated. Be clear and focus, she had told me. The answers I had sought were directly in front of me. I tried to head her words. Be clear and focus. I tried to think but I was distracted. As the brown Crown Victoria turned down the street running to the front of Police Headquarters, I saw a mass of humanity awaiting my transport. The car stopped directly in front of the building. The car was instantly besieged with photographers and reporters all trying to get a glimpse of the man in the vehicle. It seems that someone in the police department had leaked some information to a couple of noisy members of the press that there had been a break in the Ihavtakysa case. There were satellite trucks and reporters from all local news networks, as well as some national venues and even CNN International. Cage slowly opened his door as the reporters snapped away. Cage then went around and opened the rear passenger door. Officer Poncher stepped out and went to the rear of the car. A deafening silence overtook any of the local press who were familiar with who I was. There was an uneasy silence as murmurs and buzz started to radiate through the mass. My great antagonist Steve Frizz was at the forefront. As I exited the vehicle Steve Frizz is instantly in my face. "I told you I would get the truth. I knew it was you, you son of a bitch. It was you. Wait until you see what I do to you now. Your sexy little girlfriend will be out of business in a week." Poncher does nothing as Frizz gets up next to me and throws a shoulder in to me. I, whose hands are still cuffed behind me, begin to fall toward the rear of the car. A massive push forward by the media aids in my lack of balance. Poncher reaches and grabs the handcuffs by the metal and pulls violently. I feel a shooting pain run through my right wrist and feel a pop. Poncher rips again and pulls me up next to him. Poncher had the smugness of the guy who just bedded the Prom Queen as he strolled down the walkway that lead up to the main doors to police headquarters. Captain Cutler walked triumphantly behind and Cage walked out front, clearing the path for the procession behind him.

I sat in the interrogation room all alone. I look at the big glass mirror. I am sure that there is no one on the other side supporting me. I feel a sense of aloneness that I have never felt before. An irony when you consider for the longest time I considered myself a loner. I look around the room. The desk, or more accurately table, is a very nice oak. The walls are solid white. The chair that I sit in is hard plastic, while the chairs on the other side are a nice leather computer type chair. I begin to feel the pain again from my right hand but ignore it. I am more concerned with what is going to happen next. I anticipate a pleasant session with Poncher and probably some more kind words from Captain Cutler. My cellphone begins to ring again but of course I cannot answer it. I am surprised they have not taken my gun from me yet, if they truly view me as a suspect. All of the questions again begin pouring into my mind. There is only one thing that I want to figure out. How did I end up here? To me that question encompasses all the rest. I sit and ponder that question. Where did I go wrong? If I knew the killer was targeting me, then why not see this coming? Simple. The killer was smarter. I always guessed it was some kind of chess game. A maniac trying to play against the most visible opponent in Orlando today. I was dead wrong. He wasn't playing against Detective Kenny Spade. He was playing against me. Me! I go off kicking myself, metaphorically speaking, angry at my carelessness. The door opens, and so do the flood gates. I can do nothing to stop the tide flowing all around him. Along with Poncher and Cutler, Cage, FBI Agents Smith, Johnson, Thomas, and Lopez and the Chief of Police enter the room. I sit there stone faced as the procession scuttles about, trying to find a suitable position. The Feds stand along the back wall straight in front of me. Cutler, as he did the first time I visited this room, sits over in the corner by the window. Cage again guards the door. The Chief stands just inside the door and Poncher sits in the chair in front of him. Poncher begins his interrogation.

"Detective Spade, how did your fingerprint get on the knife that killed the Russian, Ihavtakysa?"

"I would like to speak to my lawyer."

"Damnit Spade, where you're going your lawyer can't help you. Tell me how the print got there." Poncher is pressing the attack. I remain calm.

"I wish to speak with my attorney."

Poncher is unrelenting. "Detective Spade, your print is on the weapon used to kill an Olympic Champion and International superstar. How did it get there?" I sit back and listen to his words. So, I think to myself, they know that is the weapon that killed her. I wonder if it has been linked to the other two cases. I sit there thinking, ignoring all around me. The Chief of

Police comes over with a mean scowl and demands that I answer the question. I look at the Feds. They just sit there all smug, especially the little one Agent Johnson, with whom I had the run in with when I was in Loot's office a few days ago. I just sit there and say nothing. Poncher again begins to badger me demanding answers or explanations and threatening me. I sit their stoically. After twenty minutes of berating, Agent Lopez with the legs can take no more and leaves the room. She always was weak; Agent Thomas told the other two. It has been over and hour and a half, I guessed, since I was arrested. Why hadn't I seen or heard from Ashley? I really wanted to lash out with my smart ass comments. No one in this room is smarter than me, I told myself. That is why I refrained from making any such comments, realizing my troubles this time were much more severe. Captain Cutler came over to get in my face once and demand I say something. I asked for a cup of coffee. This enraged Cutler to the point that The Chief had to remind the captain to be professional, or the Chief would ask him to leave. Poncher continued the assault for another fifteen minutes during which I said nothing. Poncher turned to the Chief and said that this guy was famous for his zoning out moments. Infamous in the department. Poncher went as far as to accuse me of zoning out when I killed these girls. Again the Chief had to warn him. I sat there statuesque. But I wasn't zoned out. I was working. They think I killed all three. What has the evidence turned up? How can I get a look at the evidence. I knew. I knew right away. I needed to be charged with the murders. Then I would be allowed to see everything. But I knew I needed to have Ashley. One mistake, even the tiniest of slip ups would cost me the rest of my life. I knew I had to find the killer. It was the only way to prove my innocence. But I also knew the same thing I had known for the past five or six months. I was running second in a two horse race. I did not have a clue in the first five months, why would my desperation change that fact now? Captain Cutler suggested to the Chief that maybe everyone should leave the room and give me a chance to think about his situation. The Chief agreed and all left. I sat in the room all alone.

Once again I felt some discomfort in my right hand. Arrogant prick, I thought to myself.

On the other side of the door the Chief had to excuse himself, telling everyone the evening news was about to start a frenzy that he had to manage so as not to endanger the department. He took his leave. As he did there arrived a second commotion. Out in the hall there was a frenzy of activity trying to be handled by a short supply of police officers. The media were popping questions at the police and as they tried to get a comment for the Chief someone recognized the long blond hair of the lady trying to squeeze through the mass along the wall.

"Miss Ellisin, Miss Ellisin, is it true that your boyfriend murdered those girls. Miss Ellisin." The well planted puppet of Steve Frizz had done his job. The mass of press simultaneously turned and became to swarm upon Diane like flies on poop. Steve Frizz the master then slithers past everyone and walks into the Internal Affairs door. He went right over to the congregation of IAD and FBI agents and tries to butt in. "Is it true you arrested Detective Kenny Spade for the murder of Svetlana Ihavtakysa?" Captain Cutler and the feds try to reign in Steve Frizz. Steve happens to be very determined though, and spins in past the door. He gets into the doorway of the interrogation room and snaps a quick picture on his pocket digital camera. Officer Cage then intercepts Steve Frizz and throws him out. As he goes back toward the door, escort in hand, Frizz gives a thumbs-up sign to no one in particular. At the same time Frizz is shown the door Loot pushes in with Kate and Diane in tow. Captain Cutler heads right for him.

"You were dismissed from this case. You are not wanted or needed here."

Loot tries to bull his way in. "Where is Spade?"

"That is not your concern."

Diane is miffed. "I want to see Detective Spade."

"Miss Ellisin, isn't it?" Cutler is pleased with himself. "Yes, I believe it may be. Miss Ellisin, I may have some questions for you." Cutler is giving her a thorough once over with his eyes. "Questions related to your possible involvement as a material witness in a murder investigation." Cutler is looking forward to taking a shot at Diane. Kate tries to intervene but Poncher intersects and stands right in her way.

"Hi Kate. How have you been." Poncher does little to hide the disdain in his voice.

"Hello Francis" is her reply. Loot has had enough and tries to get some control. "I want to see Spade."

Poncher is obviously thrilled that his biggest adversary and the girl that scorned him are sitting at his behest. "I'm sorry," Poncher begins, "Officer Spade is in interrogation. If you wish to wait for him to will have to do so down in the visitors area. You cannot stay here." Loot turns to the ladies and motions them to follow him, right now they can't do much else. Captain Cutler intercedes, restating his desire to question Diane about her relevance to certain murders being investigated.

"I don't think so Captain Cutler. You have already told me the last time we met that Miss Ellisin was not a relevant material witness to anything that you could definitely ascertain. There will be no questioning of my client." The tall, gorgeous attorney that represented Kenny Spade was now in the house and like last time, had taken charge. Ashley White had arrived and announced her representation of Diane Ellisin as well. Captain Cutler felt sick to his stomach and announced the presence of a derogatory word usually associated with female dogs. Ashley responded with a thank you and instructed Loot, Kate and Diane to wait in the visitors' room. Then Ashley turns to officer Poncher and asks to see her client, Detective Spade.

I sat in wonderment of the commotion I hear outside. I am sure there is some kind of circus. The door cracks open a little but I can't see from where I am seated who has come in. This is followed by a closing of the door right away. I try to turn all the way around but it is difficult to do this with my hands cuffed behind me. I hear some more commotion and can only imagine what is happening out there. A few more minutes pass and I am still left to sweat it all alone. I try to look at my watch but am unsuccessful. I guess the time is around six. I am sure that the local news is probably going ape right now over my arrest. I close my eyes and try to clear my mind. Be clear and focus. Just like Elizabeth said. I realize for the first time how tired I really am. It has been a few days since I had any sleep of significance. The door to the interrogation room begins to squeak slowly and I hear some people talking behind him.

"Why is he cuffed behind his back?" I hear the voice and become aware that the talented lawyer that chooses to help me is back for round two. Ashley walks around the table and sits next to me. "Hi" is all I can muster.

"Why are you handcuffed behind your back?"

"I am under arrest for the murder of Svetlana Ihavtakysa." I make the statement without fear or pride. It is cold, calculating and, in my mind, accurate.

"What?" Ashley cannot believe what she is hearing. Ashley turns to Officer Cage and asks if this is true. Officer Cage says nothing. Typical, she thinks. Ashley then rises and asks Officer Cage to retrieve Captain Cutler. Officer Cage opens the door and motions, never leaving his post and never uttering a word. Captain Cutler enters attitude in tow.

"How may I help you?"

Ashley wants clarification. "Why is my client in handcuffs, behind his back?"

"He is a suspect in the murder of Svetlana Ihavtakysa." Cutler is brief not wishing to spar with her.

"Is he under arrest?" Ashley's questions are poignant.

"Yes."

"I need a room to meet with my client in private. A room that does not have a viewing room so I may have complete confidentiality."

"I will provide you with one." Ashley is impressed with his directness, not something she expected from Cutler.

"Can I have his handcuffs removed?" Ashley is reaching. Cutler remains direct.

"No ma'am. He is under arrest for murder. I cannot allow him to be uncuffed."

Ashley asks if she can have the handcuffs moved to the front of me then, promising that I will remain cuffed. Cutler agrees to reposition the cuffs when they are in the private room, although he is not pleased. Cutler then leaves the room. Ashley brings her finger up to her lips so as to show me not to speak. I nod my head indicating I understand. Cage stays in the room with the two. After a few minutes Cutler announces he has found a suitable room for their conversation. Cage rambles over to me and helps me up. I wince after a sharp pain shoots through my hand when Cage lifts me. During the walk across IAD Ashley asks if it would be OK for them to have a cup of coffee when they get to the room. Captain Cutler appears annoyed with the request but agrees. It's only coffee, he says to himself.

The room is an eight by eight. Its walls are covered in peeling dirty beige paint that look like they haven't been maintained since the seventies. There is a small desk similar to what a high school student would use in the middle of the room with two hard plastic chairs on opposite sides of it. I sit down and utter a "Thanks for coming." Ashley tells me she would have been here sooner, but that she got stuck in court. When she tells me she tried to call I remind her that I am handcuffed and can't readily pick up my phone. Cage comes over and removes the hand cuffs. I rub my right wrist and put my hands together so that Cage can re-secure the cuffs. Cage nods his appreciation. A floozy that neither of them had ever seen before brings in two IAD mugs full of semi hot black java, along with a couple of sugars and some creamer. We express our appreciation to the lackey. After the delivery boy leaves Ashley asks me what was going on. I inform her of the events of the past few days. I tell her about how I found the tip of the knife and how it led me to *The Outdoorsman*. Then they found the Acura three houses down from where I live and a little message was found next to the driver's seat. Then I tell of the phone call in the middle of the evening and going to Casa de Zaidi, the scratch in the ice machine and finding the knife inside the machine. After I got the phone call we went to forensics where I was arrested by Poncher. Ashley is shocked by the calmness with which I tell the stories. Then I tell her what Steve Frizz said about Diane. When Ashley tells me Diane is here I become visibly more upset. I pick up the coffee cup and scream. The cup goes crashing to the floor spilling coffee all over. Ashley gets up with great concern as Cage comes rushing into the room gun drawn. "What the hell did you do to him?" Ashley has a fire in her eyes as she screams at Cage, who again stands in the doorway and motions for support. Captain Cutler comes running in asking what happened. Ashley starts screaming at him.

"What did you do to him? Who touched my client?" There is much anger in her voice. Captain Cutler tells Ashley that no one has been physical with me since I was arrested. Ashley is still angry. "Look at his hand. It is all swollen. It is twice the size of his other hand. Look at them. Look!" Cutler looks at the hand and, although he appears very annoyed, he cannot argue with the visible evidence. Ashley vehemently insists that her client be taken to a hospital. Cutler fervently protests. Cutler offers to have a doctor come in, reminding her that Ashley's client is under arrest in a high volatile international murder scenario. Ashley mutters that Cutler should have thought of it before putting his hands on her client. Cutler barks back that I was never touched. There is a horrific exchange of vulgarity and accusation that goes on for three to four minutes before I stand. Cage is on me in a second and puts his hand on my shoulder. I snap my head around so fast it startles Cage. I tells him it's OK and to please take his hand off. Oddly, Cage complies and nods. I then tell the two adversaries to stop. I tell Ashley it's OK and I will accept the doctor. I then ask Cutler if he could leave us alone. Cutler does not like the direction of the issue and refuses, instead offering to have Poncher in the room. I say no way, trusting Poncher as far as I could reach him. Instead, I counter with Cage. "Let Officer Cage stay in the room with us." I could sense Cage was a good honest cop, following orders and doing the job by the book. Ashley protests. She needs to talk to me in utmost confidence. Cutler becomes irritated again and insists on someone in the room, especially after Ashley just accused IAD of police brutality. I again, oddly enough, become the facilitator. Officer Cage will not testify to anything he hears in this room, agreed. Officer Cage agrees. That's not good enough for Ashley. Cutler tells her that's it, take it or leave it. He is becoming less patient. Ashley counteroffers. "Give me a legal document, notarized, stating that Officer Cage will not testify or provide any remarks about what is going to be discussed in this room and I will agree." Cutler tells her that we have no notary on staff. Ashley tells him there is a notary in the building. She then leaves and runs out into the hall. I sit motionless so as not to disturb the progress being made.

After three minutes, Ashley comes back, Kate in tow. She announces her presence to Cutler. "I am a notary." Poncher, who has been making his congratulatory rounds through the Internal Affairs division, comes over to see why Kate is here. "Why are *you* in here?" Kate is excessively uncomfortable around Poncher and I rise to come to her aid. Officer Cage also rises, putting an end to my chivalry. Kate just looks at Poncher, remembering why he creeped her out all the way back in high school. Kate says nothing to him. Cutler looks at Poncher and says nothing. His eyes do all the talking and his message is not congratulatory. Cutler agrees to the notary and tells Poncher to type it. I object. "Captain Cutler with all due respect, please type it yourself. Officer Poncher may stay in here with me. I would much rather you type it, please." Cutler is sick that he is considering taking orders from a suspected killer but he needs to get this issue expedited so he agrees. Poncher just stares glaring at both Kate and me, but for much different reasons. Kate tries to come over to me, but both Cage and Poncher will have none of it. Ashley just nods and Kate stops where she is. Cutler comes in a few minutes later with a letter that Ashley reads and nods her head affirming to. She signs the paper and hands it to Captain Cutler, who does the same. Kate then takes the paper and scribbles something on it and pulls a stamp from her pocketbook and stamps the paper. Cutler tells Poncher to escort Kate back the Visitor Room. I ask for Cage to escort her. This time Cutler says no. He is done taking orders from murderers. Kate and Poncher leave the room. Ashley asks Cutler for a copy of the paper which he sends Cage to get. Cage is back in three minutes, copy in hand. Ashley thanks Cutler for his cooperation and asks for the doctor to be sent in.

Ashley and I then sit in the room with Officer Cage. I look at Cage and back at Ashley. "I know of Officer Cage. He has a great reputation for being professional in a division that no one likes. He is a good cop." Ashley then stops. "You are accused of murder. They have your fingerprint on the weapon. These are very serious charges."

I am conciliatory. "What are our options?"

"Well, not to many. Are you going to be charged?"

"I hope so."

"What?" Ashley is stunned by my answer.

"Look, they think I killed her. I didn't. I know that. I hope you know that. I hope the three people in the other room believe that. If none of what I just said is correct then the only person who could save me is dead…"

"What the hell are you talking about?"

"Never mind." I continue. "They think I killed the skater. They have my print. How? I have no idea. And I won't know unless they charge me." Ashley looks at him funny. I keep talking. "Look, I am off the case. My two colleagues, Ronan and Tolliver, are off the case. Loot is certainly going to get nowhere, given the bad blood between him and IAD. So, the only way I have access to anything is to be charged. Then the prosecution must provide everything it has to the defense to ensure a fair trial. It is the only way I have to trying and find out who is framing me." Ashley is impressed with my thoroughness of thought. He would make a good lawyer someday, she thought. I turn to her. "Can I ask to be charged?"

"You don't ask to be charged, you ask if they will charge you. You will probably spend the night in jail. We will ask for bail, but depending in the judge you will probably not get it. But you will have access to your evidence." I nod. I knew I could do no better. I ask if I can see Diane. Ashley says that it's not likely given the charges and my public face. I then ask Ashley to do something about Frizz, that he is trying to hurt Diane. Ashley says she will take care of it. A restraining order and the threat of liable should mean he only has eyes for you. I chuckle and even Cage cracks a smile.

Captain Cutler returns with a doctor from the police EMT division. The doctor looks at my arm. I wince every once in a while during the brief examination. The doctor comes out and talks to Cutler, who screams. Ashley runs out the door to hear the word X-ray. The doctor then tells Ashley, much to Cutlers chagrin that my arm is most likely broken at the wrist. Ashley scours at Cutler and demands to go to the hospital.

"Is he going to be charged?"

"I am working on that very thing right now as we speak. I am waiting to hear from the district attorney as to what he decides. I expect an indictment within the hour, followed by an arraignment tomorrow."

"Excellent, we are going to the hospital. If you get your indictment we will be back."

Cutler has had enough of this overbearing female. "You are not going anywhere."

"If you refuse my client medical care I will have the whole world listen to me scream police brutality and then you can try and prosecute this case." Captain Cutler is livid and shoots a look at Poncher. "The hospital it is. Detective Spade is still under arrest. He will be accompanied by my officers."

"And me. I don't want anything else to happen to him." Cutler is more furious but knows he has no argument.

SIXTEEN

There was quite a commotion when I returned from the hospital. My arm was in a sling courtesy of a break in two of the small bones in my wrist. The indictment had been signed by the DA's office while I was at the hospital. Poncher, who along with Cutler, Ashley and Cage had accompanied me to the hospital, was quite pleased. Although I made great outward signs not to show it, I also was very pleased with the indictment. It allowed me to move forward to seek what I needed. The commotion was back at Central Booking, at police headquarters. I was forced upon indictment to turn in my badge and gun. I relinquished my weapon without incident but refused to turn in my badge to anyone but Lieutenant Dan Murphy. This was not acceptable for a newly charged man to dictate terms, but I did not care. I would not cooperate in any other way. Officer Poncher was as vehement, insisting the badge be turned over immediately. Captain Cutler for once tried to be sympathetic and take the badge which led me to blurt out the commonly known but little spoken fact that Cutler was Poncher's uncle. This burst infuriated both men and Poncher went up to the handcuffed and newly casted me and tried to forcibly remove the badge. That got both Ashley and I screaming brutality and led to quite the tense standoff. The issue was resolved when someone called the Chief of Police, who ordered Lieutenant Murphy to come seize the badge and personally deliver it to the Chief immediately. Murphy, who was still in the building with Kate and Diane, was summoned and reported to the hostilities where he asked me for my badge. I took my good hand and took my badge and surrendered it to Loot. Loot was obviously angry and concerned over the presence of a cast that was not on his friend the last time he had seen me. I said not a word but thanked my friend through my eyes. Loot returned the acknowledgement, making no visible gestures so as not to set off any further hostilities.

Loot then walked out, with an escort. Poncher followed as Loot took the badge directly up to the office of the Chief of Police. The two ladies traveled behind, and Poncher shot Kate the most hostile of looks as he left. It actually scared her. Loot then updated the girls on what had transpired, both in shock when they found out about the cast. Diane actually broke down when she had heard I was indicted.

Ashley escorted me to central booking, where I was processed. I surrendered my wallet, cellphone and cash to the receiving agent. I was then fingerprinted. My cast covered my wrist and very lower arm. There was a support piece between my thumb and pointing finger common in these types of casts, so my fingers were still free to move. Central Booking processed all ten of my fingerprints. I was then given a lime green jump suit that said ORLANDO across it in black with a number on its back that read 7294365. I was then escorted away. Ashley had arranged, through her husband the deputy DA, to have me put in solitary. It seemed to be the only safe thing to do, they had agreed. Ashley told me she would see me tomorrow and left. I was all alone now with the honor guard of Officer Francis Poncher, who cherished every minute of it. I received more threats walking to get to solitary than the prettiest of girls would get invites to the prom. When I entered my home for one and the door was closed, Poncher was smiling from ear to ear. The smugness was oozing from every pore. "Gotcha" he said as he turned and left me to myself.

The cell was concrete. There was no window, except in the door for the guards. It was six-feet wide and had a bed and a bowl for natures calling. There was no sink. The bowl was nasty and filled with little bugs that would make anyone not have to go. The bed was ancient and rusty, with a wooden base and mattress that was thinner than the Bible. I looked over my new found accommodations and mused over how much this was what my apartment felt like before Diane entered my life. I was angry now. What had I done to Diane? I entered her life and turned it up-side-down. I cursed the day that I ruined her life. What must she be going through now? I sat on my piece of material attempting to pass as a mattress. I looked around the room. There were green and brown streaks running down the grungy cement wall, obvi-ous signs of how well the jail liked all of the midday thunder-storms. The musk held over my cell like a cloud around Pigpen, and I was finding everything hard to believe.

As the night grew long the pain started to return to my hand. The pills they gave me had obviously been wearing off. And since I was allowed to have nothing else where I was I knew I was going to have to deal with my discomfort. I sat on the floor in my cell pondering the next step. And cursing myself for hurting Diane. For hours I pondered back and forth some-times debating the evidence and sometimes debating the Diane factor. It was very late in the evening or very early in the morn-ing, I could not be sure which, when I got the visit I needed most. Elizabeth came and sat with me for a while. Be clear and focus, she told me. Do not worry, you will figure this out. I sat there listening to her. Then I did something I had never done. I spoke to her about personal relations between us. I never had really gotten that part of our relationship settled. I looked at her and began to cry. "Elizabeth, I need your help. You are my soul and my conscience. I feed everyday off the guilt I have for let-ting you down. It is a source of strength for me and I love you. You are a part of me that I can never let go. But I am torn. I feel like I am cheating on you by being with Diane. But I love her as well. She has been the only positive to come from my past few months of hell. She is wonderful and I want to make her happy. But I can't talk to her about this and I can't make peace with it myself. Please tell me what I do. How do I keep both of you in my life?" My emotional breakdown caused a guard to come over and investigate the noise. He yelled some obscenity about being quiet and left. Elizabeth then turned to me.

For the first time she spoke to him. Physical words leaving the mouth of the angel, not by touching my soul like she always did but by providing an actual auditory sound. "My darling Kenny, you have never disappointed me. I am now and forever dedicated to you much as you are dedicated to me. You treated me with humanity and respect when all I had known was violence. You took your anger and had to face it. You found a man who helped you and gave you purpose. Right now it will be up to you to put your friendship to the test again. Know I will always be with you. I will never leave you and I will always guide you. But you cannot live in the past. Diane loves you more than you know. And she is doing and will do for you more than you can imagine. Have faith and trust in her and live in her love, as you do in mine. For it is not necessary for you to share us. You live for her and that is as it should be. I am here to be with you when you need it. It is you who summon me. I like Diane and I will watch over her as well. There is much to come ahead. All the answers you seek are coming to you. I told you to be clear and focus. That is what you must do. Focus on what you do know. It will be the answer to what you seek. Put your trust in your friends, for they will come through for you, and you will for them. Fear not my love, for all will work out. Just believe in yourself." With that the ghostly presence of Elizabeth Downing was gone. The guard who had come by earlier retuned again to investigate the noise and started to say something, but when he looked into the cell he saw me asleep in the corner on the floor. "Ah, screw it" he said to himself.

Kate rose from bed to sounds that she did not expect. She looked over to Dan, who was still sleeping. The three of them had been up until way into the night trying to figure out how to help Kenny Spade. Diane was becoming emotionally unglued, and Dan and Kate tried to provide the reassurance. Kate looked at the clock. It was just after six. She would be rising soon to get ready for court. Spade's arraignment hearing was at ten thirty. Kate again heard the noise and became unnerved. She walked through the house tracing its origin. She found it when she reached the bathroom in the back. Diane was sitting there kneeling over the bowl and gagging after her last expulsion. "I'm sorry I woke you." Diane tried to say between tears and spit. Kate went over and put her hand on her shoulder. She asked Diane if she was all right. Diane said she was OK, that it was just nerves. Kate told her not to worry, that Kenny and Dan would fix it. They are a dominant team, and they always get their guy in the end. She asked Diane if she slept at all. Diane wasn't sure but didn't think so. Kate walked Diane back to the couch and laid her down. Kate just sat there and tried to comfort her. Close your eyes and rest she said. Diane softly began to cry.

It was just after six when the guards came through. Jail policy lights on at six. I found myself on the floor in the corner where I last remembered being. I rose and went to my bunk. There was no real other place for me to go. Breakfast came through about a half-hour later. It got fed on a tray through a slit on the door, just below the window. There was some kind of white mushy substance in a paper bowl with a plastic spoon and a small container of orange juice. I guessed it was trying to pass for grits or oatmeal. I tried a spoonful. It was lukewarm and had no taste. Now I know what to expect from prison food. The guards came calling about fifteen minutes after the food. "Shower time convict. You got three minutes." I knew better than to do anything but comply. I got in the shower and did my best to finish in three minutes, but I was unprepared for not having the use of my right hand. I had gotten half way through when I was ordered out. I was given a brush and deodorant and a hand towel. "Welcome to jail convict." I did what was asked of me and did my best to try and appear clean. I was back in my cell by ten past seven. I sat there reflecting on what Elizabeth had said to me last night and that I had to make things right. I knew I had nothing but time on my hands right now. I played over and over in my head what I would say to Diane when I saw her. I knew the most important thing was for me to show how much I loved her. At eight o'clock the door opened to the cell and two burly prison guards came calling. "Let's go convict. Time to face the man." I knew they were telling me that I was going to face a judge. The guards did not appear to know who I was. There was a lot of noise and catcalls though, when I was walked through general population to be lead over to transport. By the time they reached the transportation dock, everyone in the vicinity knew who was going 'to face the man.'

The ride from lockup took roughly twenty minutes. Two uniformed Sheriffs deputies sat in the back of a large brown Dodge van. There were bench seats three deep, with no windows in the side of the van. I had a mammoth man on my right and a hulk in the seat behind me. There were two more uniforms in the front. The passenger front housed the mouthy one.

"So you Spade, huh. Yeah, that was a good trick trying to investigate yourself. Yeah, but they got you didn't they. You guys all think you are so good out there, huh. What happened, you take your work too serious and decide to try the other side? Yeah, well they got you. Now the man going to give it to you. You'll see." I said nothing but looked straight ahead. As the guy tried to continue the conversation the driver said, "Shut up Stan." After Stan protested the driver said it again. The rest of the ride went in perfect silence.

Dan got up about seven fifteen. Looked over his shoulder but Kate's side of the bed was empty. He got up and walked toward the kitchen. There in the living room he saw Kate sleeping on the couch, holding Diane's hand. Diane was on the couch, covered in an afghan. He walked into the kitchen and started a pot of coffee. Then he went and took a shower quickly. When he was finished he went over and woke Kate. "Hey…" Kate was groggy but opened her eyes. "Is everything OK? How is she?"

"Not good. I woke about an hour ago she was on the bowl, throwing up. She's taking it real hard."

"I know." Dan said. "We still have to be real careful. The real maniac is still out there."

"I know." Kate said. "I'll go get ready. Let her sleep."

"I'm not asleep" said the voice from the couch. "I can't sleep. I just need to see Kenny."

Kate squeezed her hand. "I know honey. You will, you will." Kate got up and went to shower. Dan went to the kitchen and poured two cups of coffee. Diane took a sip as Dan tried to prep her for what she would see today. After a second sip Diane shot like a bat from hell right to the bathroom. She just made it to the bowl before it all came out. Kate shut the water then grabbed her bathrobe and leaned over trying to comfort Diane. After the event was finished Kate tossed Diane in the shower. They found her twenty minutes later crying and curled up in the tub. Dan and Kate worked furiously to get Diane calmed down and ready. They needed to be to court on time.

The transportation hub of the Orlando Court House was in the basement parking garage. It was not really a hub, but it was a loading dock with long brown corridor attached. As the four men walked down the hall one was heard saying that there was a real media circus out there. I figured that would be the case and Stan referred to me as 'The Star.' The taunting continued all the way until we reached the service elevator that led to the second floor, where my arraignment courtroom was apparently located. At the service elevator I encountered two new guards. One stood with me while the second pushed the button. The elevator stopped on one. As the door opened the guard who pushed the button informed the people waiting to get in they would have to wait for the next elevator. Someone from the mass of humanity said "There he is" and the whole mob of press tried to make it to the elevator. The courthouse officers working that day did everything in their power to keep organization. They were only partially successful at best. The doors were starting to close as the mass reached the elevators. One photographer threw his camera in to get a picture of the prison garbed Spade but I jumped back accidentally hitting my guard, and my broken wrist. I flinched as I said "Sorry." "No problem" was the response. When the elevator arrived I walked down some corridors to a little room. I marveled at how much brighter and cleaner the halls were up here than down where I came in. There were all kinds of plaques and accolades on the hallway walls. I got to the waiting room. It was beginning to push nine. The room was marked Conference Three. It was twelve by fourteen with a six-chair conference table and dark wood paneling.

It was a very nice room but a little dark, I thought. Ashley was already seated at the conference table when I arrived. She showed me the paper. JADED SPADE. The article in the Sentinel was authored by Steve Frizz. The picture next to it showed a man in handcuffs wearing blue jeans and a brown suede jacket with long brown hair. The picture was taken from behind and showed no facial features at all. Steve Frizz had quoted Officer Francis Poncher as announcing the police department had arrested Detective Kenny Spade of Orlando Homicide in the murder of Russian figure skater Svetlana Ihavtakysa. Officer Poncher could comment on nothing further because the investigation was still ongoing. Steve Frizz then went on to blast Detective Spade for misleading the citizens of Orlando and using his position to cover his tracks. Steve Frizz called on the Chief of Police to fire Detective Spade, noting that currently he was only suspended without pay. Steve Frizz demanded an open trial saying everyone had a right to hear what this monster had done. Frizz then went off on a two column rant about what a rat I was and told everyone to boycott The Hurricane From Hell. He then went about bad mouthing Diane Ellisin and various other people who know me. I read the first part of the article and threw the paper away in disgust. Ashley told me she just wanted me to be prepared for the worst. Ashley told me it would get no better and probably a whole lot worse. She had no idea how right she was.

Ashley told me they had been given a tough judge, Shannon McCale. Ashley told me that she had known of Judge McCale from Cornell Law School, where they had both gone. Ashley told me her reputation was to take no nonsense. McCale was known for having thrown everyone from rock stars to pro athletes in jail for contempt because they tried to disrupt her proceedings. Ashley told me to answer all questions clearly and concisely and to follow the judge's word to the letter. I nodded in agreement. Ashley then asked me what the strategy was. I told her I had no strategy, but that I needed to know exactly what they had against me. Once I knew that we could plan a defense. I had asked if there would be bail. She didn't think so given the nature and publicity of the crime, but she said she would try. I then asked if I would be able to see Diane. Her response was the same. Ashley then said we had an hour until the hearing opened and started walking me through the process.

Kate and Dan worked furiously to get Diane together. Every five minutes she would break down hysterically. They finally got her dressed, conservatively and tastefully. Diane helped her with her hair. It was almost ten by the time they hit the road. Diane had eaten only some toast with breakfast but it had stayed down. She was much more composed as the three of them made their way to the car. Be strong, something told her. For a minute Diane felt the presence of a guardian angel, giving her strength. Be strong for Kenny and be strong for yourself. As they arrived at the courthouse Dan parked in the basement garage. It was a trick he had used many times before, just as Spade had followed it up earlier this morning, he guessed. Dan parked the car and escorted the girls in. "Can you walk?" He asked them. "There is much less chance of being attacked by the paparazzi if we go up the stairs." Kate looked at Diane who nodded and they walked up the two flights of stairs. They made it all the way up to the second floor without being discovered. Dan looked down the corridor. It was full of press. He told the girls they would have to make a break for it, so follow him. Judge McCale's courtroom was third on the left he told them. Dan opened the door quietly and they sneaked along the wall alongside the press. They made it two court rooms before they were spotted. Dan covered Diane and grabbed Kate's hand and squeezed it hard. Dan's hand was very sweaty. This made Kate very nervous, for she knew that Dan was not easily shaken. Dan pulled the girls in the door as the press descended on them with every question imaginable. Dan then got them to the inside of the door where the court bailiffs held the rest of the masses out.

Kate, Dan and Diane walked all the way down the courtroom and sat in the front row behind the bench where the defendants usually sit. Diane marveled and shook at how full the courtroom was. There were spectators and reporters all around. Diane was glad that Kate had suggested on the ride over that

Diane should close the bar today, because Diane was in no position to do any work related thinking at all. There was a massive presence of at least six bailiffs to keep order during the hearing. Diane could feel her stomach get anxious again. Hold on she said, hold on.

At exactly ten thirty the court officers sitting in the room with Ashley White and Detective Kenny Spade announced it was time. Ashley and I rose and began to follow the officers. The conference room was in an inaccessible portion of the courthouse so there would be no episodes exactly like what would have happened if they walked me in the front door. They brought me in through the side door. Once the doorway opened I looked around. I marveled at the grandiose marble statues and the massive oak bench that the judge sat behind. The giant eagle crest was golden bronze set off against a light tan wall. It was truly beautiful.

I was snapped back to reality by a sudden stinging sensation to my right cheek. The mother of the girl from Winter Park had walked right up the side uncontested and smacked me across the face then went of on a tirade about how any monster could sit at a wake for a person he killed. I stood there and took it as the two embarrassed bailiffs restrained the woman. Just then the door to the left side of the judge's seat opened and a very attractive but serious looking woman in a black robe came out. The words came out from her mouth and echoed through the chamber. "Remove that woman from my courtroom." The lead bailiff then followed the comedy of errors with an "All Rise. The Honorable Judge Shannon McCale presiding." Judge Shannon then walked up to behind her bench and announced that court was in session. She then ordered me to sit down. The bailiffs escorted me over to the defendants table where Ashley and I sat. I shot Diane a smile, telling her all is well. Judge Shannon McCale remained standing as she laid down the law of the courtroom.

"Ladies and Gentlemen, I understand this is a highly sensational public case. I will tolerate absolutely no outburst of any kind. I will have no photography in my courtroom. If I see any disruptions of any kind I will immediately hold the offender in contempt and put them in jail. I will additionally close off the courtroom to any and all observers and allow only the lawyers and defendant in the courtroom. Is that understood?" Ashley nods her head yes. The judge looks over at the prosecution table. District Attorney Eddie DeSantos was prosecuting the case himself. Ashley was afraid of that. He was very thorough and articulate, and it was very difficult to argue a case against him. DA DeSantos also acknowledged the judge's request and the judge then turned her attention to the defendant. The bailiff asked the defendant to rise.

I stood up in my lime green jump suit. I stood out like a green jelly been in a bag full of black ones. The 7294365 stared Diane directly in the face and she began to cry. The judge issued her a warning and Kate tried to console Diane. Judge Shannon McCale was next to speak.

"Mr. Spade, what happened to your hand? I saw your picture in the news paper today and there was no cast on it."

"I broke some bones on my wrist." I was direct and simple, as Ashley had directed.

"Did this happen after you were in police custody?"

"Yes, Your Honor."

The judge was getting angry. She turned and looked at District Attorney DeSantos. "District Attorney DeSantos, what is your explanation for this?"

"I do not have one, Your Honor." He is direct.

"Excuse me?" It is obvious from her answer that Judge Shannon does not like surprises and does not like unprepared people.

"Your Honor, I was unaware of the presence of an injury until the defendant just mentioned it." De Santos is trying hard to stand his ground without ruffling the judge. Judge Shannon is not pleased.

"Very well, Mr. DeSantos. I will give you until three pm to investigate this matter. I will expect a full report on my desk at that time." Judge Shannon's message has been received.

"Yes, Your Honor."

Judge Shannon then returns her attention to me. "You are Detective Kenneth Spade, Orlando Police Homicide Division?"

"Yes, Your Honor."

"Detective Kenneth Spade has been charged with the murder of Svetlana Ihavtakysa. Is that correct, Mr. DeSantos?"

"It is, Your Honor." DeSantos replies.

"Mr. Spade, how do you plead against said charge?"

"Not guilty, Your Honor."

"Mr. Spade do you wish to press any charges against the individual who smacked you earlier this morning." Judge Shannon is forthright and stern, and this catches me off guard.

"I believe she has been through enough." I say sympathetically.

"Mr. Spade, unless you are on the stand, I expect you to simply answer 'Yes, Your Honor' or 'No, Your Honor.' Is that clear?" She is one tough judge.

"Yes, Your Honor. I mean no, Your Honor." I am stammering and Ashley touches me on the arm to calm me down. Judge Shannon is not amused. There is more than a hint of scorn in her voice.

"Mr. Spade!"

"Yes, Your Honor, I am clear on your direction. No, Your Honor, I do not wish to pursue charges for the slap." I am shaking. Loot has not seen his friend rattled that bad since the day he found Elizabeth Downing barely alive.

"Very well then." Judge Shannon continues, "Mr. DeSantos, Let's hear what evidence you have against Detective Spade."

"Yes, Your Honor. We have a knife that was used in the murder of Svetlana Ihavtakysa. On it we found a finger print that belongs to the defendant, Detective Kenneth Spade."

"Can you produce this fingerprint, Mr. DeSantos?"

"Yes, Your Honor."

"Very well then. What else Mr. DeSantos?"

"We will produce a witness who has direct knowledge of Detective Spade admitting to seeing the murders in his dreams. This will be a hostile witness." The whole courtroom goes abuzz when this is let out and Diane lets out a gasp that startles everyone. I turn and look at her, confused. Judge Shannon then throws a look at Diane that pierces her soul. Diane's urge to vomit is once again in overdrive.

"There will be order in the court! Do you have anything else, Mr. DeSantos?"

"Yes, Your Honor. We believe the same knife was used to kill two other victims. We are currently matching evidence at this time and will introduce charges against Detective Spade once they have been linked to said knife. Then we will introduce the presence of one of the murdered girls cars across the street from Detective Spade's residence as well as the presence of taunting messages we believe were left with the murder victims to throw us off."

"MR. DESANTOS! I do not like grandstanding in my courtroom. Are you prepared to charge Mr. Spade right now with additional crimes?" Judge Shannon always remains in charge of her courtrooms.

"No, Your Honor."

"Very well then. Let's stay to the matter at hand. If you are prepared to deliver more charges against Mr. Spade, we will rejoin the issue at that time."

"Yes, Your Honor."

"Ms. White, does your client have anything he wishes to put before the court?"

Ashley rises and speaks clearly and concisely. "Your Honor, my client proclaims his innocence and looks forward to defending himself in your court."

"Very well, Ms. White, the record will reflect your client's position. I find that the presence of a fingerprint on the murder weapon and statements he may have made with relevance to the case at hand are sufficient to hold the defendant over for trial. Anything else Mr. DeSantos?"

"No, Your Honor."

"Ms. White?"

"Your Honor, my client would like to request bail."

Mr. DeSantos was expecting this and immediately objected.

Judge Shannon will consider the opinions. "Mr. DeSantos. What says the state?"

"Your Honor, the state says that this man has murdered one person and probably more and did so while violating the public trust. We request bail be denied."

"Thank you Mr. DeSantos. Ms. White?"

"Your Honor, my client maintains he did not commit these atrocities. He has worked for years to defend this great city. He has given many years of loyal service and caught a significant number of criminals and made sure they were off the streets of this great city. We humbly request bail."

"Ms. White, I strongly recommend you save the election speeches for November. I will consider this motion for bail. Anything else, Ms. White?"

"Only one more thing, Your Honor. We would like to move for discovery so we may analyze the evidence."

DA DeSantos was not prepared for that one. "Your Honor, I object. Detective Spade was the only one with access to evidence for the past five months. Evidence that he probably fabricated to try and execute a cover-up to his crimes."

"Mr. DeSantos, you are surely familiar with the point of law. The defense will be granted discovery. I will take fifteen minutes to consider bail. This court is in recess until eleven fifteen."

The bailiff announces the retreat of Her Honor to chambers. "All Rise." With that everyone stands and Judge Shannon McCale retires to her chambers behind her court. I turn and look toward Diane, who has run out into the hall. She makes it as far as the door before the masses converge on her. Diane turns and runs back up to the front. Kate pushes her way out of the aisle. "Garbage pail. I need a garbage pail." The bailiff standing by the door where I entered picks one up and runs over to where Kate is. The pail and Diane arrive at the same time. The violent eruption that Diane was fighting is contained no longer and the courtroom is filled with the foul stench of puke. Diane relieves herself for about ninety seconds. The bailiff takes the garbage can down and throws it outside the door. After a minute of trying to regain her composure Diane apologizes and says she was blocked from the bathroom outside because of all the press. The bailiff tells her to use the one in the restricted hall, down on the right. Diane says thank you. Kate follows her out to the bathroom.

I turn to Ashley and ask what just happened. Ashley asks about the dreams. Loot answers that question. "They're going to put Diane on the stand."

"What!" I am pissed.

"She is the only person you told about the dreams, right?" Loot is formulating his thoughts as he goes along.

"How do you know?" I am confused.

"She told me. The morning she was in my office when you found her there. She told me when you came home you told her about the dreams. She was scared. She does not want to lose you. Anyway, right after she told me there was commotion out in the hall. I went out and there was Poncher with Ronan. Poncher must have heard us talking. He was under the guise to see what I was doing with you about the Feds incident. That's why I was so shocked when he passed you without an encounter. It makes sense now."

I grow a soft frown on my face. What have I done again to this poor girl? I have turned her life upside down. Ashley is totally lost. I begin to zone out again. Ashley asks for clarification on the dreams. Loot smacks me, who returns. We begin an abbreviated version of the dream sequence.

Out in the hall Diane is falling to pieces. She vomited again once she made it to the bathroom. Kate went in to calm her. She washed her face good and tried to regain her composure. As soon as she hit the hall Diane broke down. "I am responsible. He only told me. How did they find out?" She keeps muttering to herself. Kate tries to settle her down. Diane tells Kate how Spade told her about the dreams. She knows Kenny didn't tell anyone else. Now she is going to be responsible for him going to jail. What is she going to do? Kate stands her up and brushes her off. "None of this is your fault. You are going to be strong and go in there and support your man. After that we will all walk together and sort this out." Kate grabs her by the arm and brings Diane back to the courtroom. The bailiff opens the door when he hears the knock.

Kate and Diane walk in and return to the seats. Diane reaches over and kisses me deeply. Then she turns her attention to my injured hand, asking how it happened. I tell her it happened by the handcuffs somehow. Loot mutters something about having a little help. I just shoot him a look and the issue is left. I apologize and ask Diane how she is feeling. She begins to answer me when the bailiff returns and announces that court will reconvene in two minutes. The group of Kate, Loot, Diane, Ashley and I all plot strategy as the people filter back into the court. I survey the audience as they reseat themselves. I see the woman that hit him along with her husband. I also sees Lisa Yeung's fiancé. Steve Frizz filters into the very back row. There are a plethora of others, some looking like reporters and a few who look like they have no reason to be there at all. I feel all alone and responsible for the pain that I am putting a whole lot of people through. The bailiff returns with the "All Rise." Everyone in the courtroom stands and Judge Shannon McCale returns to the bench.

"I have made my decision regarding bail. The crimes the defendant is accused of are great and horrific. However, the defendant's years of loyal service to rid the streets of criminals must be considered. Mr. Spade, on a personal note, there is nothing more vile than a person who is sworn to defend and protect society that abuses the privilege and becomes that which he is supposed to stop. God have mercy on your soul if you have crossed that line, for I will not. Taking everything into account, I am granting bail. It is set at $1.5 million. This court is adjourned until April 1, when we will begin to hear criminal proceedings in this case. Court dismissed."

"All Rise." the Honorable Shannon McCale then retreats to her chambers. My eyes fill with tears. I know another night in jail waits. Many nights do. The courtroom erupts as the doors are opened. I am sure that everyone is rushing to get their information on the twelve-o'clock news. Kate turns and clutches

Diane, who to her surprise is excessively calm and defiant. Loot comes over and grabs my shoulder. "We'll catch this guy some-how. Just hang in there." The words are encouraging but hol-low. I know right now more than my hands are cuffed. The bail-iffs come over to take me away. Ashley asks that I go back to conference room briefly. They agree, but it must be quick. I am lead away by my left hand. I turn to Diane and say "I'm sorry." Diane steps out to the aisle. "One question. Do you love me?"

Tears begin to stream down my face. "More than anything." Before anyone can move Diane lunges forward and gives me a kiss. "Don't worry" she says as the bailiffs take me away. Loot asks Ashley what the next step is. Diane shoots over and grabs Kate. "I need your help." She does not stop, just grabs Kate and brings her to the back of the courtroom. As I am led away I hear an 'Oh my God' from somewhere and I am then hustled out the door.

I sit at the conference table in his room as I wait for Ashley to return. Above the door to the room I see a sign I did not no-tice before.

In God We Trust
Through Justice We Rule
Be True To Both

I read the sign. I never considered myself to be a person of faith. I am a person of fact. It is facts that get killers caught, I always told myself. I hate televangelists, always trying to milk people from their hard earned money. Yet here I am finding the need for a little prayer. I sit at the table and throw my hands in my face. One-and-a-half million. I know no one with that type of money. What the hell am I going to do? After a few minutes Ashley returns. She sits down and lays it out. "Well, that dream thing is going to be a problem. Did you really have dreams about the killer?"

"Yes."

"Who knew?"

"Only Diane. She told Loot."

"Dan?"

"Yeah, Dan is Loot. Only I call him that. Loot thinks Poncher of IAD overheard Diane telling him about my dreams."

"I don't know how to fight that." Ashley is concerned.

"Don't worry. We have until April 1 to catch the real killer. But I can't do that. Obviously I'll be in the big house. So who do we use?"

"For what?" Ashley is not following. I lay out the plan for her. We can't use Dan because he has been banned from the case. Obviously the police are not going to help us. So who do we use? I tell Ashley there is a receipt for the purchaser of the knife. The company that sold the knife was digging through paperwork. It wasn't on the stuff they said they had on me. I ask when we get discovery. Ashley tells me the prosecution is allowed twenty-four hours to turn it over. I tell her that I can't make bail so Ashley is going to have to get a legman, someone to do the work. Also, who can lift a print? Somebody obviously had access to my print, through my car or whatever. But how do you transpose it? Only someone with skill could do that. We have to find out whom. Ashley has to remind herself her client is a detective. She asks me what else. I say "We have to find a killer."

SEVENTEEN

Six o'clock rolls around early. The night was especially chilly, even for Orlando. The chill, in combination with the current accommodations, allowed me to awake wondering if I had ever indeed actually gone to sleep. I spent the evening tossing and turning, reviewing the day's events in my head. Once I flipped so violently I hit the cast on my hand and woke up seeing stars. I had just found a comfortable spot, or more honestly no longer been able to fight off physical and mental exhaustion, when I was awoken by the guards. The routine was the same. Gruel just after six followed in about ten minutes or so with the fastest three minute shower on earth. I was much more successful this time around as I was able to wash just about my whole body and get a quick hair rinse in too. By ten past seven I was back in my lime green jumpsuit sitting on my bunk pondering the next move. Until I get out I am at the mercy of those helping me, I thought to myself. I knew my best bet was a smoking gun from *The Outdoorsman*. I guessed that by the time *The Outdoorsman* found any paperwork I would already be planning my appeal. Plus I knew there would be nobody from OPD sitting on their case to sift through everything. I knew my other best chance was to catch the killer. That's not going to happen from in here, I thought. I took my pencil and paper and began to scribble all the facts I could think of. I tried to remember the messages on the cards. I wrote them down. I closed my eyes and tried to replay the vision that I had of the killings, the very thing that would probably ensure my staying in my new home environment for a long time to come. I spent the morning deliberating everything, drawing outlines, time frames and trying to connect the dots. The product of my work was a piece of paper that had so many squiggles only a 3-year-old could be proud. I would need a miracle. And I would need to get out of jail. No problem, I told myself.

It was early afternoon when the guard came to my cell. Lunch had been at high noon and consisted of peanut butter and jelly, and a glass of milk. The jail had regular 'free time' right after where inmates could go congregate outside before the rains came. It was decided that I would forgo this privilege for my own safety. I didn't mind. With my wounded limb I would have been easy carnage for someone in my vast fan club at the facility. "Convict, visitor, move it…" the guard said. I got up and made my way to the door where the guard cuffed him. Due to the cast the cuff rode way up my right arm and was very painful. I followed the guard as I was ushered into the waiting room. I was left there for a few minutes. A burly middle aged woman came in and said 'follow me.' She escorted me to a smaller grimy room with a chair and no windows. "Put these on" she said as she threw some clothes at me. I looked at them. These were my clothes from the day I was arrested. "I don't understand" I said to the lady, who grunted and slammed the door shut. In ten minutes the lady was back. "Follow me." Her tone was commanding and I did as I was told. After we navigated a maze of trails, I was shoved. "Wait here." In a few minutes the door opened and in walked Ashley. I was shocked. "What are you doing here?"

"I have to be here to execute your release on bail."

"I made bail?"

"Yep," Ashley smirked. "Some good Samaritans paved the way and your bail was posted."

"Who?" I was suspicious.

"Don't know. You'd have to ask them." Ashley was not giving any information.

Ashley and I were escorted back to Central Booking, where my personal belongings were returned, minus my badge and gun. Ashley and I were then escorted by the same friendly woman to Ashley's car. When we reached the car our escort left us and we sped off. "Where are we going?" I asked. "My house" was the reply. I said nothing more, satisfied enough that I was on the outside.

Waiting for me at Ashley's was a note and a set of keys. 'Take the car and meet me at The Hurricane. Drive around back and park behind the dumpster. Come in through the back.' The note was unsigned. I looked at Ashley in a state of confusion. Ashley told me to do what the note said. She then handed me the keys and pointed to a red Impala parked in front of her house. I gave Ashley a hug, took the keys and drove off. I made his way toward the interstate to go to the Hurricane. I made a pit stop along the way driving onto West Colonial. I pulled into an Eckerd pharmacy on Hiawassee and parked the car. I then walked down two blocks and went down the side street. When I got to the pink house with the Blessed Mother statue out front I cut along the shrubs and through the backyard. Then I jumped the fence again, putting far too much weight on my right hand. After I cleared the fence, which I had done quite a few times before, I snuck around the back and in through a basement window. It was just as well, I thought. Poncher had stolen my keys. I rummaged around in my living room until I found my small metal lock box. It was beaten like the lunchbox of a kindergartener, but I didn't care. I grabbed the box and whatever files I had and exited through the window that had allowed my entrance. I also grabbed my Tampa Bay Lightning cap, in a bad attempt to disguise myself. I then went back over the fence. That was a true fiasco with the hand considering I was now trying to hold a box and files and climb, all with only one good hand. I counted my blessings that my neighbor behind me owned a doughnut shop and was usually not home sixteen hours a day. I followed my way over the fence and found my way back to the Impala. I threw my stuff on the seat and went to The Hurricane From Hell. As I reached the Hurricane I was surprised to see two cars out front, blocking the way. There was also a big wrought iron bar gate in front of the door. I followed the instructions from the note and went in the bar. I was surprised to see the bar was empty. Diane was sitting at the bar with Joey and Rock. I came over and joined them. Beth slid me a beer and a burger. I devoured both instantaneously. I asked Diane how I got out. No one was forthcoming with any information. Diane asked if I was OK, but my reply was to question the Iron Gate and cars out front. The answer was obvious and no one bothered to reply. I was upset at the bar being closed, but the others didn't seem to care. Beth poured me another and told me to relax. Rock told me to enjoy myself, tonight was a celebration. Diane was especially quiet but carried a big smile. She was watching the clock with an unequivocal amount of attention. I picked up on this after my return from the restroom. There was an aura of secrecy, as if I was on the bottom of a totem pole of mystery, a Jack looking up at his beanstalk and his friends who knew what lie on the other side of the clouds. I, being the Jack, looked up at my queen pondering her motive. It was a uniquely ironic moment for me, who was used to being the ace. I quickly decided to be discreet and wait for the slip. Something was definitely up. I kind of secretly enjoyed the cat and mouse and for a little while forgot about the personal difficulties I was having.

The ring echoed through the empty bar with a heavy cavernous riff. Van Halen had never sounded so good from a cellphone, I thought to myself. I looked at my caller ID and saw a familiar name on it. "Spade." I answered, as always. My friend Loot told me that there were some papers that I needed to go through, and it needed to be tonight. I protested and invited Loot and Kate down to the bar. Loot stood steadfast and said it was urgent, and that he would meet me at Ashley's. "Ashley's?" I asked, the concern rolling back in and not very hidden. Before I can finish my sentence Loot has hung up. I look around at my cohorts and frown. "I have to go to the lawyer's house. Loot said it was important." I sulked around and got myself together. No one else in the bar appeared overly concerned about my apparently pressing issues. I fidgeted in my seat and began to pace. Diane had seen enough and offered some consolation. "Listen, I'll go with you." I smiled and said thanks. Diane threw her keys and instructed the guys to move her car around back and lock up. As Diane and I walked out to my rental, Diane turned back at the door, whispered a 'see you soon' and winked.

I was very nervous on the ride over to Ashley's. I thought I knew how to get there but I was so uptight about the reason for my sudden beckoning that I missed the exit to her house. Twice. Diane was beginning to sense my fear because for the first time since she had known me I was driving the speed limit. Maybe, she thought to herself, this is the first time he wasn't in a hurry to get somewhere. Diane wondered if that would be the case if he knew the truth. Diane grabbed my fingers and gave them a squeeze. I winced and recoiled slightly. That one must have hurt. I finally righted the ship and found my way to Ashley's house.

I parked out front and swung around to open Diane's door. I was very nervous, Diane could tell. We walked up to the house and rang the bell. A man answered. I knew him right away. Deputy DA Jason White looked much more common dressed in jeans and a green pleated front button shirt. The house was a magnificent four bedroom Florida special, complete with vaulted ceilings screened pool, Jacuzzi and sunroom. Deputy DA White escorted Diane and I back to the backyard. There we found Ashley, Kate and Loot sitting at a glass table with a bright blue umbrella canvassing it. The White's backyard was massive, with palm trees and small reddish brown fern trees lining a path lit by stainless steel solar lights. The path ran back a few hundred yards up to a gazebo that fed down to a lake. Loot got up and flipped the grill open and began to attend to the steak and ribs. There was a cooler full of beer and a bottle of Dom P chilling in the ice bucket. There also was a Strawbrooke Vineyards Chardonnay and a Widler Pinot icing in the cooler with the beer. "What's this all about?" I asked. Loot worked on the grill and told me there were some important papers that I needed to read and sign. Loot told me to relax, after they ate that Ashley would go over them with him. I was very nervous but had no problem postponing the inevitable dread. Diane pulled me aside to tell me that this was the surprise party for Kate. The real party was supposed to be next week on the twenty-seventh, but since I was out Diane and Loot decided to have it today. Diane told me the guise was my paperwork and please not to spoil the surprise for Kate. I appeared relieved, and almost as if on cue Kate came over to see what the secret was we were keeping from her. I, in one of the better lies of the night, said that we were discussing plans for an outdoor bar in the affluent Metro West area of Orlando. I was so impressed with the White's backyard I thought it could be a good beginning blue print. Kate pondered what I said and liked the idea.

"What would you call it?' Kate asked.

"Why, hell on Earth of course." Diane choked on her drink and spit a little on my clothes. Kate started to laugh and shook her head. I wiped myself off as Diane began to gather herself. "Hell on Earth" she said, trying to hide her sarcasm.

"Do you like Stairway to Heaven better?" I asked as I walked over to Loot, and safety. Loot worked over the steaks and ribs and out from the house walked Joey, Beth and Rock. Jason White came out and the boys talked a little baseball, basketball and hockey. There was no mention at all of anything at all related to legal or political on goings in Orlando or any personal situations of people occupying the backyard at the current moment in time. Dinner was delicious and everybody had a fair share of their choice of beer and wine except for Diane, who was still feeling a little under the weather. Around nine Ashley's cellphone rang. There was someone waiting at her door but the party was so loud no one heard the bell. Jason went into the house and answered the door. After a few minutes I stood up, white as a ghost. Kate grabbed my good hand. Strolling through the house was Judge Shannon McCale. I couldn't believe it. "Hi everybody" Shannon said as she made her way to join everyone in the backyard. Judge Shannon walked over to Ashley and gave her a hug. "I brought you those papers you asked for."

"Thank you. Perfect timing." Ashley replied. Shannon turns her attention to me.

"Well detective I see you made bail. I would like to know how you pulled that off."

Me too, I thought to myself, but I was still too terrified to do anything more than politely bow of my head and stammer out a "Your Honor." I was now terrified that this was not a surprise party for Kate and that I really did need to be here for some relevant paperwork. Loot looked concerned by the presence of Judge Shannon in Ashley's backyard. Jason came in and gave Ashley a kiss, then commented he had to go out and take care of something. Ashley carefully read the document that she was given and nodded her head approvingly. Beth asked Kate who this was. Ashley apologized for her rudeness and introduced Rock, Joey and Beth to her old friend Shannon McCale from Cornell Law. "Friend?" Loot said, too loud and got himself busted. Shannon, her demeanor much different outside her courtroom, explained how she met Ashley while pledging the Alpha Beta Beta sorority. "Alpha Beta Never Betta" both girls chuckled as they said their signature phrases. Shannon turned to the group and announced her exit. "It was very nice seeing all of you but my presence here raises serious conflict of interest potential so I must bid you adieu." Ashley turned and offered to walk her to the door, the paper still in her hand. I rose and offered Judge Shannon a hand and said goodbye, but nothing more. I still remembered being undressed by the judge during the morning hearing the day prior. Loot turned to Diane, who had a small little smile beginning to crack her face. "I thought we were here for a surprise party." Loot was not at all sure what was happening, and even less sure he liked it.

"You are" Kate jumped in. "I was just surprised." Loot did not find the joke funny, but Kate had that same small little smile that Diane did. "Am I missing something?" Loot asked.

"I am." I added. The two girls continued to look at each other trying really hard to display their poker face. Joey, Beth and Rock stood around like opera fans in a heavy metal concert not grasping anything happening around them. Ashley walked back through the house, paper still in hand. Then, in a move that shocked almost everyone she handed the paper over to Diane, who examined it carefully and returned it. Ashley then took the paper over to Kate, who read it very thoroughly.

"Looks good" Kate said. I sat in bewilderment as all of this information sharing was going on. Loot was a little disturbed.

"What the hell is going on? I thought the paperwork story was just an excuse to get Spade here for the surprise party." Kate comes over and gives him a kiss.

"It was. Moreover, it was an excuse to get *you* over here for the surprise party."

"Huh?" Loot is totally confused. Diane is next to try to explain. She turns to me and grabs my hand, gently.

"Do you remember what I asked you before you were taken away yesterday?" Diane's voice starts to shake a little and her hand begins to tremble.

"Do I love you?"

"And do you remember your answer?' Diane is getting very emotional.

"More than anything."

"Did you mean it?" Diane's voice is very sincere.

"More than anything." Diane takes my hand and places it on her heart. She asks me if I can feel it beating. Then, in a most unexpected of moves, Diane gets up from her chair and gets down on one knee. "Kenny Spade, Will you marry me?" The love that penetrated from her voice could have lit a big city in the middle of a blackout. Loot just about fell over as I sat there dumbfounded. I stared at her not saying a word. I looked at her and my eyes began to tear.

"How can I marry you? I have one and a half feet to a life sentence. I can't let you throw your life away because of me." My answer deflated everyone present. You could see the disappointment begin to creep into Ashley's face. Oddly, it seemed that Diane expected that answer.

"You said you love me more than anything. I believe you. So put up or shut up. Will you marry me, Kenny Spade?" in such an emotional moment the expected look of nervous duress was absent from Diane's face and replaced with one of absolute determination.

"Yes." My voice was soft and my heart was pure and audible through my words. Diane shot up and gave him a big kiss. She then turned to her coconspirators and nodded her head. "Ready ladies." The girls all indicated they were. Kate took me by the hand and began to walk down the path lit by the palm trees and solar lights down toward the gazebo. I tried to inquire as to exactly what was transpiring, but every time I asked Kate would just stall and make small talk about the beauty of the trees and lights. Kate took me to the gazebo and told me to wait right here. I asked why and was told I would find out soon enough. As Kate walked back to the house I watched as Ashley and Diane were very intently doing something on the deck.

What a difference twenty-four hours makes, I thought to myself. Yesterday at this time I was attempting to stay warm, today I was standing looking up at a beautiful, pleasant March sky. "What are you looking at?" Loot had come to join me on the structure. "Just pondering the universe," I told my friend. The pair of brothers in arms then had a colorful little discussion over what the girls were planning. Whatever it was it was a secret. Both of us were amazed at how well Ashley had taken to Diane. They were behaving like to old school girls. After a little while the girls reappeared on the deck. They were certainly up to something. They began to walk down the path but Diane stopped half way. Kate and Ashley kept walking but Ashley suddenly stopped half way between Diane and the gazebo. Kate continued all the way up to meet the boys.

"Welcome gentlemen. The ladies have a surprise for you today. Dan, would you please hold this box." Kate hands the box to her husband and chuckles. Her presentation continues. "You fine sirs are now required to go escort your ladies up here. Honey, since I am already here you may grab your sister-in-law. As for you, Kenny, your fiancée has one more surprise for you tonight." I looked at Loot and begged for help with my eyes. Loot just shrugged it off. "We better do what we are told." Loot then walked down and met up with Ashley and offered her his left arm. I walked past Loot and Ashley and over to Diane and stopped. I gave her a kiss and whispered 'what's going on?' in her ear. "You'll see." she said. "It's a surprise." I just nodded. There was little doubt of that.

After Diane and I triumphantly marched down the path and up to the gazebo, we stood there in awkward silence. Loot and I looked at each other, feeling like the ugly ducklings at the high school dance. After an excruciating three or four minutes of silence during which the girls kept tormenting the boys with their giggles and smiles, one of the girls finally spoke. "Gentlemen, how did you like the rehearsal dinner?" We nodded approvingly, not totally understanding the true meaning of the question. "Very well then. Let's get on with it." It was Kate who was the commander, the Bobby Fisher with her chessboard. Kate whirled around and strategically placed in spots her knight, rook, king and queen. She very much enjoyed being chess master. When Kate was done with her props, I was standing next to Loot, while Ashley was closest to the stairs and Diane was between the two. Kate appeared to be very pleased with her progress and content to let the play drag on a little longer. There was a small amount of small talk and banter between the groups. Kate went along with it until she felt it was time. She put a stop to it as she began to reassert her control. "Dearly beloved we are gathered here today to unite…" Goddamn, I thought to myself, how freaking stupid am I? A rehearsal dinner I said to myself. A rehearsal dinner. This is the rehearsal. Diane obviously wants to have the weeding in an outdoor area with a gazebo or tent. Joey, Beth and Rock waiting on the grass are meant to symbolize the audience. I always thought the concept of rehearsals was silly. You pick a spot; you say what you have to say and it's over. The whole thing is orchestrated anyway. I sat there and paid little attention to what was being said. Kate pulled out all the stops and would make a good minister, I said to myself. I wondered where Kate had gotten the script for the ceremony from. It didn't matter. I would marry Diane and it would be a beautiful ceremony. I looked over to my newly anointed fiancée. She had a strange look on her face. It was a look that could only be described as a combination of love, fear, excitement and nausea. I was surprised at how serious Diane was taking everything. Kate was continuing on with her dissertation and had just arrived at the part where it was my turn to say his vows. I began to repeat after Kate. "I Kenneth take you Diane to be my lawful wedded wife." I continued following her lead and was performing flawlessly. Diane's look had remained as before except she was a little more restless as I continued my monologue. When I got to the 'til death do us part' I had an exceptionally unnerving epiphany. It was a sudden burst of clarity that gave me this epiphany. Kate is a notary. This was not his rehearsal dinner. This *is* my wedding ceremony! I stopped after I recited the word part. It was an abrupt and unnerving finish to a seemingly flawless dissertation. Everyone looked at me and wondered. Kate worried. As Kate decided to keep things moving she turned to Diane. When Kate began to say "Do you…" she was interrupted by me.

"I have more to say." I told her. Diane instantly assumed that she was overly presumptuous and was about to get her heart shattered… 'What was I thinking?' she told herself. 'I should have known.' With that last thought I began to open my mouth. And more.

I reached out with my hands, cast and all, and grabbed Diane's. I began to speak. With every word I spoke my lips trembled and my voice quivered. My words were very genuine and heartfelt. This is what I said. "Diane. I told you I love you more than anything. That is true. This is what I didn't say to you. Thank you. Thank you so much for believing in me. Thank you for giving me that chance all those months ago. I get very involved with whatever I do, and that is usually my work. You had every chance to free yourself from my burden, but instead you decided to stick it out. I know I have brought a lot of weight upon your shoulders. Weights that should have been only mine to bear. I will not say I am sorry because I am not sorry at all. I wish that many of these things I did not have to bring upon you, but I can think of no one else I would rather share them with. Sorry is not a word I choose to use in any way when it comes to you, my love. I say to you I love you so much. Now I can only say to you two more words. You ask if I love you more than anything. I DO!" I grab her hands strongly and feel her grip tighten. There is not a dry eye on or next to the gazebo. Even the manly men, Loot and Rock, have to wipe away tears from their face. It was a truly stunning moment after a whirlwind few days.

Kate tries to regroup herself and push forward. She begins with the repeat after me. "I Diane take you Kenny to be my lawful wedded husband…" Kate runs through the entire gamut and after a few minutes Kate gets to Diane's I Do. Diane has a simply little finisher "I love you." I am not crying but rather stand there looking very proud and confident.

Kate keeps the ceremony on target and asks the best man, Loot, for the rings. Loot looks at her oddly and begins to protest that he was not included in the surprise but Ashley politely asks him to look in his pockets. Loot reaches into his pockets and pulls out a small red felt jewelry box. He opens it up and inside is a set of matching gold rings. Kate gives Loot a sly thank you and instructs Diane and me to remove the appropriate ring from the box. As I reach for a ring Diane has to tell me I am taking the wrong one. That gets a big laugh from the contingency. Diane and I each have the correct rings and Kate continues. She starts with me. "Please take her hand and repeat after me. I offer this ring as a sign of my love and commitment to you and to us. Through good times and bad, I will be there sharing my life with you." I repeat the words exactly as instructed and gently slide the ring up Diane's finger. Upon completion of my task Kate turns to Diane and repeats the exact same procedure. When Diane is finished Kate takes and puts their hands together. "With God as our witness, we have watched as Diane and Kenny have committed themselves to a life together. I am now exceptionally happy and honored to announce by the power given to me by the State of Florida as a Notary Public to introduce to you Mr. & Mrs. Kenny Spade." Loot then reaches over and taps me on the shoulder. "This is where you kiss your *wife*." I nod and says 'I know.' and Diane and I engage in a deep and passionate kiss. Everyone present begins to clap. Kate then invites everyone to return to the deck for a toast.

The Dom P is poured and the glasses are raised. Loot, who was a little slow to come around to his role, his wife informed him, stepped up to the podium and proposed the toast. "To the Spade's. May the next flush be that of all their problems down the drain." A loud raucous applause follows. Loot then continues. "No, in all seriousness, to the lovely Mrs. Spade…" Diane squeezes my hand and makes me wince. She immediately releases. Loot goes on, "Diane, I also thank you. This man is my brother from a different mother and although the last few months have been difficult for both of you, I can tell you I have never seen him this happy. And I have seen Spade at all of his extremes, believe me. The way he looks at you I have never seen from him before in all of the years that I have known him. So I thank you. And to my brother Spade I can only say one thing. Don't screw this up! I love you." Loot raises his glass and everyone else follows his lead. They raise their glass and everyone drinks their champagne. Diane takes only a small sip and puts hers down. I ask my wife if she is OK. Kate comes over and tells me that Diane just feels a little under the weather. Ashley then chimes in with a note of praise to the weather gods, who gave them a beautiful starry night and one quite a bit warmer than the previous few nights. I go up to Loot and gives him a big hug. "I love you too, my brother from another mother."

The party goes on for a while. There is a cake acquired by the lovely Ashley White that congratulates Kenny and Diane. As the clock pushes eleven, Ashley's husband Jason returns home. Ashley goes and gives him a big hug and kiss and whispers a thank you in his ear. He is then invited to join in the celebration. The evening begins to get late and people begin to show signs of tiredness. Kate catches this and makes one more announcement. "Before we come to the end of our night, I must make this ceremony official. Kenny and Diane, would you please come over here?" The Spades then walk over to the table where she is. "Kenny, I need you to sign right here." I look at the document. An Orange County, Florida Wedding License. It was signed by Judge Shannon McCale. So that's what she brought over earlier. I sign the best I can with this cast covered right hand and give the pen to the former Diane Ellisin, who does in kind. Beth and Joey say goodbye and take their leave.

Rock follows shortly after. On his way out Rock asks Ashley if her judge friend Shannon is single. Rock seems to be a little smitten with her. Ashley says she is unattached and she will throw in a good word for him. Rock thanks her then turns and bear hugs the newlyweds. Then Rock takes off. Loot also thinks that Kate and he should go. I agree and go up to my lawyer and friend and give her a big hug and a kiss. "You never told me how you got me out."

"You'll have to ask your family" Ashley says pointing to Kate, Loot and his now blushing bride. I thank her again and tell Ashley that I too am leaving and that I will call her in the morning and get back to work on my defense. I then shakes Jason's hand and says 'nice too meet you' and walk over to my family and says "Let's go."

Diane and I went in my rental while Kate and Loot traveled in Kate's car. We four had decided that we were going to stay the night all together at the Murphy's. Loot thought that maybe Diane and I should have their honeymoon night alone, but Kate said they had a guest bedroom. Besides, she wryly smiled, he would be too busy to hear anything anyway. I then said that I really wanted to share this night with Loot and Kate and Diane said she wouldn't have it any other way. They are family. As Diane and I drove back to the Murphy house in Maitland, Diane clutching my hand told him she had to give me her wedding present. I objected vehemently, stating that I was not aware of the day's events and had no opportunity to get her anything. Diane spoke passionate and firmly. "I already have my gift from you. I do not need anything else. My gift for you is not physical anyway. Upon consultation with *my* lawyer, Ashley White, whom you may have heard of, I have been advised that legally I cannot be forced to testify against my husband in any criminal proceedings he may be involved in. Therefore I will not discuss with anyone anything you and I may have talked about with regards to anything. Anything at all. I don't have to speak about whatever you told me. Additionally, *your* lawyer told me that if a certain friend and supervisor were called to testify about what he may have been told about whatever you saw, it would be easily refuted as hearsay third party testimony and probably carry very little weight. She doubted if the DA would even call him. Now all you have to do is your job and find out who the real killer is. This is my present to you." I looked at my new bride, amazed at how much forethought she had done about this. I whispered a little too loud "I am so lucky." It was heard by Diane who echoed back "You better believe it."

At the Murphy house I again brought up the issue of my freedom. "Ashley said I should ask you guys how I got out."

"We're family." Loot said. Kate and Diane nodded their approval. "It was a no brainer." I look suspiciously at them and press the issue. Kate went inside and started a pot of coffee. Diane told her to put on hot water for tea. I again asked how. Diane tried this time. "We did what we had to do." I am not sold.

"Which was?"

"Get you out."

"Again, I ask, how?"

"By any means necessary." Diane is getting nervous and looks to Loot for help. Loot nods to her as if to say it will be all right. Kate comes back from the kitchen and tells Diane I have a right to know. Diane tries to fend me off. "We posted your bail."

I stare at them, stupefied. "How did you get $1.5 million?"

Diane shifts in her seat and Loot also gets a little squeamish. "I put up the bar and Kate and Dan put up their house."

"WHAT! NO!" My voice is filled wither anger and pain. "You guys, you can't. What happens if something goes wrong?" I begin to cry and bury my face in my hands. "You can't" I say over and over and over. All three of them went over to me and hugged me. I was still inconsolable, realizing how much I cost them. Kate picked up my face from my hands. "You do have to pay us back." she told me sternly. Loot looked at her funny.

"How can I ever do that?" I asked, knowing it was not possible.

"You catch the son of a bitch!" Kate said with much determination. I would get my chance sooner than I thought.

EIGHTEEN

The hole in the Internal Affairs office wall told the story. The Chief of Police was embarrassed and was feeling a lot of heat over the pictures of one of his most decorated officers in a cast in handcuffs. There had been no rhyme or reason for the stunning arrest of his star homicide detective. When Judge Shannon McCale ordered District Attorney DeSantos to find out how the suspects arm was broken, the DA did his job. Ironically, it was Steve Frizz' picture that was the unveiling. Frizz had a picture of Officer Francis Poncher yanking Detective Kenny Spade by the handcuffs after Spade arrived at the Internal Affairs building. Lieutenant Stein, head of IAD ordered an immediate inquiry after hearing from the District Attorney. There was a report back to Judge Shannon McCale as to that fact from Mr. DeSantos on the day of Judge McCale's order. Lieutenant Stein had a formal investigation started. It had gone on the entire day. Steve Frizz' photo was the straw that broke the camel's back. While Officer Poncher was cooperating, the picture presented some damning evidence. Lieutenant Stein ordered the investigation to be concluded quickly. Lieutenant Stein spoke with Dr. Parker of the Coroner's office, who said that it was very possible that the pulling of the handcuffs was responsible for the detective's broken wrist. Dr. Parker also professed his belief Detective Spade was innocent, and told Lieutenant Stein he would be a character witness. Lieutenant Stein told him the investigation was still ongoing and recommended the good doctor should contact the defense.

His information now in hand, Lieutenant Stein went and sought Captain Cutler. Since Cutler was Officer Poncher's immediate supervisor, Stein left it up to Cutler as to how to proceed. Stein made it clear he wanted a formal documentation of the infraction. Lieutenant Stein said the Chief and DA demanded it. Captain Cutler reviewed the evidence and realized he had no choice. When Officer Poncher showed up for work the next morning, Cutler called him in and informed Poncher of what had transpired. Poncher strenuously protested and pleaded his case. Cutler said his hands were tied. "We're family." Poncher screamed. Cutler could only issue back an 'I'm sorry.' Poncher was livid. "You know I'll never get my promotion if this is on my record. " Again, Cutler could only apologize. Poncher picked up a big desk chair and flung it directly into the wall, leaving a three foot triangular hole and knocking down some pictures. Poncher was screaming as he promptly left the office. "That murdering son of a bitch isn't going to cost me my promotion. I'll get him. I'll have the last laugh." Poncher was screaming the whole way as he left the building.

The honeymoon night could not have been more passionate, both couples had very private intimate moments as they finished up a long day and retired to their individual rooms. I had awoken around six when I heard someone getting sick. I went over to the bathroom and saw Kate throwing up. I went in to see if she was all right. Kate thought she might have gotten the same virus that Diane had been fighting for the past two days. Kate stopped and cleaned herself off, only to be blown past by Diane as she shot past both of them, barely making it to the bowl. I suggested my wife go see a doctor. Diane said she would think about it. Since everyone was up anyway, I went into the kitchen and turned on the TV. The big story of the local Orlando morning news program was the release of Detective Kenny Spade on bail. The reports gave no details and said the detective had not been seen or heard from since his release, which was confirmed by DA DeSantos. I started some coffee and went out to grab the paper. *THE FREE OF SPADES*. The headline jumped across the top of the paper, with Steve Frizz reporting the murderer Kenny Spade had been released on bail. Frizz blasted Judge Shannon McCale for allowing bail and blasted DA DeSantos for allowing it to happen. Frizz' story was offset again by the picture of me in handcuffs being escorted by Officer Poncher from Internal Affairs. Frizz praised Poncher for being so steadfast anti -Spade and not being fooled by the good guy heroics. I brought the paper in and placed it in the table. Kate looked at it disgustingly. Diane did not look at it at all. I asked the ladies if they wanted breakfast. Both of them said no. I was relentless and coaxed both into a cup of tea and a piece of toast. "You know they're in bed together." Kate said.

"Who?" asks Diane.

"Frizz and Poncher." Kate answers the question but I ponder its significance. In all actuality it makes perfect sense to me. Curious for a little more opinion, I have to ask her "Why do you think so?"

"It makes perfect sense to me." Kate continues. "They are both your biggest two adversaries. Poncher is always after you, even tried to get you a month or two back, remember? Then everyday Frizz would write articles about you, about Diane and about how incompetent you were. Then he would quote anonymous sources. Then Poncher would be back after you trying to prove Frizz' accusations. It's like a piranha feeding a shark." I contemplate what Kate has just said. It makes perfect sense to me. Sometimes you need a clear perspective to figure stuff out. Of course, it does nothing to help me figure out who the killer is; it just helps me understand why Frizz is always on my case. I give the ladies their toast and tea and sit down.

The next portion of the morning is spent discussing the events of yesterday. There was certainly a lot happening and again I find myself apologizing that they had to put up as much as they did to bail me out. Each of the girls had another bathroom run, the last of which awoke Loot from his slumber. We then talked a little strategy as we tried to figure out where the next step was from. It was just before eleven when the familiar Van Halen ring tones began to flow through the living room. I answer and follow the conversation. I take the information on the other end and then hang up. I look down after I end my phone call and see I have two voice messages. I dial in to my voice mail as everyone queries who the call was. I tell them as I try to connect to voice mail it was Tolliver. Tolliver said it was all over the department that Poncher was on the warpath. Poncher was reprimanded for breaking my wrist so he lost his promotion. Threw a chair through a wall. Poncher was out for my blood. Tolliver just wanted me to be warned.

I push a button on my phone. I start to motion frantically for a pen as I keep listening to the message. I push some more buttons. Loot brings over a pen and a pad and I thank him. I keep pushing something on the phone and putting it back to my ear. I begin to scribble something on the pad. I push something else and listen to its message. After a few minutes I hang up. I begin frantically talking in riddles. Why didn't I check my messages yesterday? Loot has to go over and calm me down. I am making no sense. I pause and gather myself. I wasted a day, I keep saying. Loot finally gets me to focus. I tell Loot that *The Outdoorsman* has a name and address on the knife. I also say I got a call from Emilia, the GM at the Casa de Zaidi. This could be the break we needed. I recognize that I am now persona non grata thanks to the press and my good friend Steve Frizz. Anything I try to accomplish will be tainted with the use of my name. I realize that I myself cannot take care of these issues, for people do not go out of their way to help famous accused murders. No, I knew I had to try something else. Loot, Kate and Diane just looked at me as I worked. I picked up my phone and dialed frantically. The voice on the other end of the line answered *The Outdoorsman*. I spoke into the phone with great clarity.

"Yes hi, is this *The Outdoorsman* magazine?"

"Yes." The voice on the other end was male.

"Good morning. This is Lieutenant Murphy from Orlando Homicide. You were doing some research on the knife for a detective of ours."

"Yeah, I saw they arrested that guy the other day." The man sounded pleased with that fact.

I continued. "Yes sir. We were wondering if you had turned up any leads yet." I gave no indication that I knew that the magazine had called me indicating they had found the receipt for the murderer's knife.

"Yes, we had found the receipt for the knife. But you already got your guy." Bite your tongue, I thought.

"Yes," Spade continued, "But we would like to get the receipt. We don't want to have any loose ends. We wanted to have every piece of evidence so that we can close the door for good on this case. Can I get whatever you had on the receipt?"

"Yeah, sure hold on." The man on the other end puts the phone down and comes back a few minutes later. I start scribbling as frantically as I can trying to keep up with the information I was receiving. When I was done I thanked the gentlemen from *The Outdoorsman* for all his help and hung up. Loot, Kate and Diane all pressed as to what I had found out. I looked at the paper in front of me.

K.S.
P.O. BOX 4892
Orlando FL
Cop

I looked at the paper in front of me. A P.O. box. A box that had my initials on it. Or at least my initials were used to order the knife. Plus the person who ordered the knife said they were a cop. This guy sure went all-out to put this off on me. I'll send Loot to the post office. I sure know I can't go. I pick up the cell and dial frantically. When the voice in the other end answers I ask for Emilia. Yes, the GM. After a minute or two Emilia picks up the phone.

"Hello, Emilia, this is Lieutenant Murphy, Orlando PD. I am calling to follow up after the ice machine incident."

"Yes, lieutenant, how are you?"

"Very well, thank you. Do you have any further information on the man who broke in? We have not found anything. We will need to keep your ice machine for a little longer, we are still processing it."

"It's OK. I have a new ice machine. I do not want that one back. I, for one, hope Detective Spade is innocent. He seemed to care much more than the other guy."

"Other guy?" I was not expecting that for an answer.

"The officer that came after Detective Spade did the knife experiment."

"There was another officer there?"

"Yes, a very rude one." Emilia leaves little doubt with her tone. I know I have to see her. I decide it's better not to set her off right now.

"I am very sorry about that. I thank you for all your help. We'll be in touch." I sign off and hang up the phone. Everyone is sitting at the table in the living room. The barrage of questions that came after I hung the phone was constant and loud. Who, what, when, where, why. I think I got the entire spectrum. I recognize the situation and dictate a game plan. I tell Loot to tackle the post office, seeing as it would be very difficult for me to get around without drawing a crowd. I give Loot the information. I am going to see Emilia at the Casa de Zaidi. She had a visit from someone else four days ago. I needed to see if she can shed any light on who that was; maybe they were responsible for planting the knife. I told both ladies to stay together, whatever they do. Take the day off and stay here, but if you are going to go to work, go together. I know it's silly, but it's the safe thing to do. If anyone runs into any problems, call immediately. Everyone agrees to the plan. I grab my Lightning cap and shades and head out. Loot is right on my heels. The ladies decide they'll wait and decide what they are going to do.

Yes, that's right, look at the little chickens run away. You silly little boy. You thought that I would not be able to find you once you got out. A ball cap, what a good disguise. Yes, my little chickens, let's see how you run when I cut off your head. Maybe I'll even find your little girlfriend inside. You have underestimated me, Spade. You won't make that mistake again. I guarantee you that. As two cars leave the house in Maitland, a door opens from a car three houses away. Silly little boys.

Loot takes a run down and within twenty minutes finds himself at the main Orlando post office. He walks through a corridor filled with numbered golden lock boxes and walls pasted with government information and propaganda. When he gets to the pods where the tellers are he flashes his badge and asks for help. The line of patrons, six or so deep begin their grumbling. Loot pays them no attention. The small female clerk goes to the back to retrieve a supervisor. In a little bit, an elderly African-American man named Willie shows up. Willie inquires as to how he may help the police. Loot asks if there is another place they may speak, for the benefit of his customers so as not to be a distraction. Willie brings Loot back to the cafeteria room in the back of the postal facility. When they get to the room Willie graciously offers Loot a cup of coffee. Loot is very thankful. Orlando is not widely known for its southern hospitality. It is more known to cater to visitors. Loot then goes on to inquire about a P.O. Box, Box 4892. Loot tells Willie the police believe that some criminal has been using the box for criminally related activities. Loot would like to know if Willie would be able to help him. Willie tells Loot that he will have to check with the Orlando Postmaster, and then leaves Loot and goes to make the call.

I make the now familiar trip to the Casa de Zaidi in almost no time flat. I have my Lightning hat and shades on. I am not very optimistic about my chances, but I really need to talk to Emilia. I park my rented Impala in the hotel parking lot and take my cellphone out and dial the hotel. I ask to speak with the general manager on some urgent hotel related matter. I do not get the GM but rather an underling, the Front Office Manager. Again I push my agenda to speak with the GM Emilia. The Front Office Manager informs the caller on the phone that the GM is on a conference call. I then identify myself as a police officer and want to know when to call back. I am informed that the call should be over by 2:30 p.m. I look at my watch. Great. Twelve fifty. Well, I have to kill an hour and a half.

A push of the doorbell announces a visitor at the front door. Kate is in the shower. Diane gets up from her seat to answer it. "May I help YOU?!" There is a horrific thud as the butt of the gun comes down across the right temple of Diane and lays her out cold. There is a small puddle of blood forming right next to her head on the plush blue carpet. The trespasser walks through the house until he gets to the bathroom. Ahhh, there's nothing like the sight of a beautiful woman. She'll be a few more minutes while she gets her hair clean, so I guess we can still have a little fun. The man walks back to the newly unconscious Diane and picks her up, bringing her to the dining room. Once they get there he uses some extension cords he found by the telephone to tie her up to a dining chair. Then he uses a sock and bath towel to gag her. Some duck tape to the ankles leaves a stunning masterpiece only MacGuyver could be proud of. Don't worry my pretty; you'll be just fine after your headache goes away. "Diane" The call goes out. One more time Kate calls for her friend. Kate begins to walk across the living room from the bathroom when she comes across the bloody carpet. A frantic scream is replaced by a fear based adrenaline rush as Kate begins to look for her friend. As Kate turns the corner her adrenaline is replaced by horror as she sees her friend tied to a chair and gagged. The fear for her friend is instantly replaced by a general state of terror as she hears the clicking of the cylinder as it is being pulled back and the cold feel of steel presses against the back of her wet head. "Do not turn around." The voice is commanding and Kate is obedient. "Close your eyes and go to your bedroom."

"What do you want from me?"

The steel migrates from the back of her head to the side of her neck. The chill of the cold steel on her neck sends a shudder down her spine, but the shutter from the absolute terror is much more commanding. "Keep your eyes closed and go to your bedroom unless you want to watch me torture, maim and kill your sleeping friend. Walk." The voice talks in whispers as all Kate can comprehend is the shifting of the gun from place to place. The voice continues. "Now go over to your drawers and put on a sweatsuit." Kate tries to ask a question but she can only quiver and cry. "I can't see to get my things." The sudden crack of the muzzle follows twice as a horrific sound of shattering glass echoes through the room. Kate is positioned in front of her dresser. "Open your eyes to get your clothes. Do not turn around or you will not ever move again." Kate opens her eyes and looks in her third drawer. She grabs a pink Puma jogging suit. She goes to her top drawer and reaches for her underwear. She can see the mirror has been shot out. The voice whispers again. "You don't need them. Put the suit on." The gun is now being run up and down her spine from her buttocks to the base of her neck where it stays. Kate does her best to put the suit on without looking. When she drops the towel some sort of derogatory comment is made. She tries not to hear it, only to do what is asked.

After she is dressed she is walked back out to the dining room. "Stop." The voice says. The gun is still perfectly held at the base of her neck, just above the shoulder line. There is some kind of a noise, as if the dining room is being dragged. Maybe he is doing something to Diane. Kate turns suddenly and makes a dash. The uninvited guest reaches out and grabs her. She swings wildly and misses. Kate looks at the man but cannot see the face, instead fixating on the barrel of a gun placed two inches from her eyes. The cold steel of the guns muzzle is now moved to the base of her throat. "Sit." The whisper is eerie and calculating. Kate sits and is instantly crushed by the weight of a two ton anvil. The base of the gun pushes against her throat. "Do not move. I usually prefer knives; I find guns are much too messy. I seem to have had my knife taken from me though. I would hate to make such a mess of you and your pretty little friend." 'OH MY GOD!' the thought runs through her head. It's him. "It's you!" Kate thought out loud a little too loud.

"Of course it's me my dear. Who else were you expecting?" Kate had not thought of that question yet. "Now be still. We're almost done here." Kate felt the muzzle be lowered away from her throat. She could feel the monsters chest pressing against hers with every breath he took. Kate could feel a cloth or something being placed as a blindfold over her eyes. Then the man placed both his arms across the front of his body as if he was looking for something. Kate's arms were pinned to her body by the man's massive body and legs, and she dared not try anything further for the safety of her and her friend. She then felt the man's left hand move back and forth, rubbing against her right arm. He was leaning heavily on her right shoulder where Kate could feel the high back to the chair riding into her shoulder blade. "Perfect." The gun was back in her throat and the man was moving around doing something. She could not tell what. When he was finished he asked for her car keys. "They are in hanging by the garage through the kitchen." They walked past the kitchen to where the keys should be. They were not there. The move was swift and purposeful. She should have known better. She was doing so well. You can't play games with the chess master. The arm rapped totally around her throat. Her air supply was cut off immediately. It took about twenty seconds before her body flopped to the floor as if all the bones had been plucked from her body. She lay there as he continued to look for her keys. Once he found the pocketbook with Kate's license in it all the contents were dumped on the floor. The keys to her Cadillac were there. He dragged the body to the car and placed her in the back seat. A pair of handcuffs found hanging in the garage would prove quite handy. And the duct tape of course. Yes indeed, MacGuyver would be proud.

Willie returned to the cafeteria and informs Lieutenant Murphy that the Postmaster has given permission for the application card for Box 4892 to be pulled. Willie walks Loot down to the computer room where the applications for P.O. Boxes gets filed. Willie tells Lieutenant Murphy that all that is required usually is a driver's license and a certified receipt of the prior address. It's actually pretty easy, Willie says. Loot just hopes there is a driver's license in the file. Willie escorts Loot to records and turns him over to Lisa, the technician on duty. Willie tells Lisa that Postmaster Lundy has given permission for this transaction to occur. Willie takes his leave and Loot works with Lisa. Loot tells Lisa he is enquiring about Box 4892. Lisa types in the number. That's strange she finds. She clicks some keys on her computer and comes to another screen. "Lieutenant, this is strange."

"What is it?" Loot asks.

"According to the files, this file was opened by a cop. The comment says it was a sting. The initials are KS."

"I see." Loot was not expecting that but it makes sense, considering how careful the killer has been so far. "How do you verify the identity of the police officer? This person only left initials."

"That's easy." Lisa begins to pound some keys and goes to where she wants to. "Here we are. Badge number 743." Great, Loot says to himself. This guy has access to fake badges. OPD badges all have four numbers. Well, Loot thinks, I guess the fake badge is my next step.

"Great, thanks Lisa." With that Loot begins to walk out and down the hall. He takes ten steps and then stops and spins back around. He walks back to records and in through the door. Lisa looks surprised to see him. "Lisa, one more quick question."

"Sure."

"If a box was being bought for a patron it costs money, right?"

"Seventy-five dollars a year."

"What if it were police use, like in this case. Would they have to sign something? How would that work?"

"Well" Lisa thinks, "You would either have to have a signed voucher or a corporate card."

"Where would I find out how this particular box was paid for?" Loot is on to something.

"Accounting. It's up on four. "

"Great. Thanks." Loot starts to walk away.

"If you run into any problems have them call me." Loot waves thanks to Lisa and makes his way to the elevator. He gets in and presses four. He checks his watch. Two forty. Great. Loot dials the girls. No answer. That's funny, he thinks.

I have waited for an hour and fifty minutes. I searched up and down the parking area and walked the sidewalk out front of the Casa de Zaidi. I got a cup of coffee. I came back and hung out watching the people who walked past, hoping to see something that looked out of place. I tried calling at two thirty. Emilia was still in her conference call. I dialed the girls at Loot's. No answer. Strange, I thought. Maybe I'd try the Hurricane From Hell. He decided to call the Casa de Zaidi first. I asked for Emilia. The receptionist said she was available and put me on hold. Emilia picked up the phone and said hello. I identified myself as Lieutenant Murphy and ask if she will meet me on the loading dock. After she agrees I walk down the parking garage and wait for Emilia to arrive. Emilia arrives a few minutes later and much to her surprise finds a long haired man with a Tampa Bay Lightning hat and sunglasses. I remove my hat and Emilia stops and pauses for a minute.

"Will you still speak with me?" I ask contritely.

"I don't know what to say." Emilia is still stunned by her surprise visitor.

"I don't want to cause you any problems. I didn't do it. And I am still steadfastly committed to catch the guy who is terrorizing my town and destroying my name. I think you can help. I asked you to come down here to talk so that I don't cause you any publicity or embarrassment. If you are not comfortable speaking with me I will go away. Either way, I will find the man who is the *real* killer." Emilia senses my sincerity but is not totally convinced.

Emilia asks "You know, my sister Justyna doesn't believe you are guilty, but she has to follow the evidence. How is it exactly that you think I can help you, detective."

"I appreciate her position. What I am concerned with specifically is I was quite surprised when you said you had seen another detective on the morning that you and I last spoke. You mentioned he was rude, and for that I apologize. My concern, and hope that you may help me, is that there should have been no one else to see you that day. Then later on you get the person attacking 'The Hatman' on three. This is very unsettling, especially because I think the knife that killed these girls was planted during that day."

"What?" Emilia is shocked by the allegation.

"I'm sorry; I didn't mean to startle you. You see when we came back that night after Nancy's call I noticed a big scratch in the top of the ice machine. There wasn't one there when you and I were at the machine in the morning. That's what made me look inside and find the knife. I think the killer put the scratch there to get me to look inside knowing the knife had my finger print on it."

"How do you think your print could get on the knife?"

"I really don't know, honestly. There is little doubt this guy was following me for a while, but he must be familiar with police work to be able to lift a fingerprint. So this guy that identified himself to you as a cop, well it makes me suspicious."

Emilia followed his rationale and didn't disagree, but expressed to me that it sounded like a farfetched story. I could only nod my head in agreement. I then turned my attention, and Emilia's, to the mystery policeman from later on that morning. I asked Emilia what he asked her for, what he wanted, where he went, and how long the man was there for. I asked if she had a business card from him. I asked if the man was on the third floor. Emilia was trying to recall whatever she could. He was white and big. He went to the third floor and was alone up there for about twenty minutes. He asked for no help and was not interrupted. He displayed a badge, and said he was part of Detective Spade's team. The man asked no specific questions and said he was following up on a lead for me. He had no manners and was standoffish. Emilia did not know what he was looking for or if he found it. I wanted to know what time this person arrived. Lunch, Emilia figured, give or take.

"So the guy who was attacked that evening, he would not have seen this cop?" Spade asked.

"No," Emilia said, "Bill had just come on duty when he was attacked that night."

"OK" I thought aloud. "I am thinking these two people are working together to fool us all, so I was just reaching."

"I've seen you reach" Emilia said, "And it's not too pretty. You should have been more like him. At least he was graceful."

"I'm sorry?" I am confused.

"This obnoxious cop. He was very light on his feet. Especially for a big man. He tripped over my housekeeper who was cleaning the spot you so eloquently tried to maneuver that morning. But this guy, he moved like a dancer. Caught himself right away." I thanked Emilia, but did not want to take away any more of her time. I told her I appreciated her help and hoped to be able to prove to her and everyone else that I was innocent. I thanked her and walked back up to the parking structure. I dialed the girls again. That's weird, I thought. Still no answer. Where could they be?

Loot reaches the accounting office for the Orlando post office on the fourth floor of the central post office building. He walked in and introduced himself to the secretary. He tells the secretary he was sent up by Lisa down in records downstairs. Loot tells the lady he needs to know how box 4892 was paid for. The secretary asks when the box was opened.

"Do you want a job?" Loot is scratching his head.

"Excuse me?" She is lost by his comment.

"I was so interested in what I completely forgot to ask when. Can we call down to Lisa to find that out?" Loot can't believe his stupidity. The secretary calls down to Lisa who gives her a date.

"We're in business. June 16." The secretary walks down to a file cabinet and pulls out the file for June 16. She brings the file down to her desk. "See here, the daily file is separated into counter postage, P.O. Boxes, USPS boxes and governmental, such as money orders and the like. Right here is P.O. Boxes. We had six opened that day. Your particular one was opened at the Lee Road branch. The box was paid for by MasterCard. Here you go." Loot goes over and looks at the receipt. He hastily writes the credit-card number down then bids his helper great thanks. Loot runs down the hall onto the elevator and out to his car. Loot flies down to the Hole and calls MasterCard. He is put in contact with the fraud division who usually run identity theft issues. Loot identifies himself and asks them to run the card. They take his information and begin to work on his request.

I sat in my rental trying to get hold of Kate and Diane. He tried the Murphy's house again, as well as the girl's cell phones. None of them were being answered. I called down to the Hurricane From Hell. Rock said the place was shut but all else was quiet. I was beginning to worry. It was not like both of them to be unavailable. I pondered the information that Emilia had given me. Typical cop, big guy. I was hung up on the attack of the Hatman later that night. Did the killer have an accomplice? This question really bothered me. The fact that Emilia had seen a big man and that Hatman said it was a big guy could mean that both acts were done by the same man, but I just didn't have enough evidence to determine that. Which meant that I could not rule out the possibility of two people working together. The combination of being so much closer to catching this guy and yet to be at the same place I had been for all these months was very frustrating to me. I kept pondering everything over and over. There has got to be something I'm missing. I look at my watch. Four thirty. I consider calling Justyna, but realize her professionalism and determine she will not be able to help, even if she is sympathetic to my cause. "I've got to be missing something" I tell myself. "I've got to."

Loot sits in the Hole waiting for the phone to ring. He looks around at everything. Then Loot calls Kate. No answer. Loot calls her cell. Again, no answer. Where the hell is she? Loot is becoming edgy waiting for the phone to ring. He looks around for something, though he knows not what it is. So this is what every day of life must be like for Spade, he thinks to himself. Where the hell is Kate? She is not answering her phone. Loot is becoming increasingly concerned. Loot looks at the clock. Four forty-five. The phone rings.

Kate looks up. Where am I? She looks around. She cannot see anything. She is still blindfolded. She listens. She is in a car. What happened? The throbbing around her neck is foreign to her. It feels like when she gets rug burn on her knees. What happened to me? Kate tries to struggle but cannot move. Her hands are bound behind her back. Her feet are restricted too. She listens carefully. Heavy breathing. WHERE ARE YOU TAKING ME? She tries to scream. Her mouth is covered. Kate tries to scramble around. The thud lands hard and loud across her temple. "Stay down if you want to see tomorrow." Kate recognizes that voice.

I look at the watch again. Four fifty. It seems like it was just three to me. I sit in the car, having no real direction. I close my eyes. A silent but deadly rips through the car. That's bad. Once again I run through the evidence. The cards. One with a smudge. One with a name. One with a message. All taunting me. Someone who hates me. Oh Elizabeth, who would hate me so? Why can't I think? Jesus, Spade, think. What's the matter with you? Breathe deep. Review. Someone who hates me and would enjoy hurting me. Someone who is clever. Someone who is left handed. Someone who knows police work, and could work with fingerprints. A big man. A man who was light on his feet. HOLY SHIT! I look to my right. Elizabeth nods.

Loot answers the ringing phone. Yes, he was looking for the person assigned to that credit card number. Hold on while he got a pen. OK go ahead. WHAT?!? World Health Organization?!?

The familiar Van Halen ring fills the rented Impala. I frantically dig for the phone.

"WHAT?!?"

"SPADE, IT'S LOOT. IT'S…"

"I KNOW. WHEN WAS THE LAST TIME YOU TALKED TO THE GIRLS?"

"AT THE HOUSE."

"ME TOO. GET THERE NOW!"

I frantically hang up the phone. I fire the Impala and burst out into the street narrowly avoiding an oncoming cab. I run the car like a John Glenn ridden space flier, manipulating and navigating every inch of road given me. Michael Schumacher would be proud. I hit the crowded interstate with the five o'clock rush bogging it down. I run the shoulder at triple digits and almost wipe half a dozen cars when I forget there's a left exit on I-4 downtown. I grab the phone. I dial hysterically. I get Tolliver on the other line. Grab Ronan and get to Loot's. Now. Bring back up. I keep flying, trying to get to Maitland as fast as possible. For a fleeting second I hope whoever rented the car chose the collision rider.

Loot runs from the Hole full speed. That fucking monster knows where I live, he kept telling himself. Loot jumps in his cruiser and blasts away from the Hole toward his house. The other cars on the road are standing still as if they are in a video game. He drives like a son of a bitch. Loot, in a fleeting moment of cognizant thought, calls the Chief and informs of what he found. The Chief doesn't believe it. Loot tells him where to find the evidence and that the Chief can back track his work. Loot then hangs up. "Asshole" He says to himself. Loot makes his way to his house. The Impala is sitting on the front lawn. Spade is sitting by the front door, gun drawn.

"Where'd you get that?" Loot asks. I hold my finger up to my lips telling Loot to be quiet. I motion to Loot to grab the door handle, which he does. Loot twists slowly and feels the lock disengage. Loot holds up his fingers and counts down. Three … two … one … Loot turns the handle. I rush in covering the open living room. There is blood on the carpet. Loot follows me in, turning toward the dining room. Loot screams 'Spade,' and I again put my fingers to my lips. I deftly cover the kitchen, bathroom and main bedroom, where I find a towel and a shot out mirror. I begin to get sick to my stomach. I whip around and double back to the front door. There I find Loot attending to something in the dining room. Diane has been tied to a chair and she has a big gash on her head over her eye. "Oh my god, are you all right?" I ask my wife of less than twenty-four hours. Diane is crying hysterically. She tries to tell Loot and me what happened. There is a card on the dining room table. An ace of spades. It has a small simple note, written in red. TOO LATE SPADE. I look at Loot and show him the card. A white and blue in full statement pulls up, lights and sirens blaring. Loot runs out and tells them to secure the perimeter. About four minutes later a Crown Victoria pulls up also in full statement, followed by two more white and blues. I try to calm Diane down, but she is talking in circles. Diane apologizes for not doing a better job of being careful. I let her know it's OK. Loot asks where Kate is, but Diane does not know. She remembers very little. I run out and grab Ronan. "Get an ambulance here and take my wife to the hospital"

"Your wife?" Ronan questions.

"SHUT UP!" I scream. "DO NOT LET HER OUT OF YOUR SIGHT. PERIOD. UNLESS YOU HEAR OTHERWISE FROM LOOT OR ME!" Ronan nods understandingly. I run back inside and grab Diane's hand. "Baby, where is she?"

"I don't know. I tried to…" Diane can't handle the guilt and begins to cry uncontrollably. I attempt to comfort her. "OK, it's OK." Another siren can be heard in the background. Tolliver comes running in announcing the ambulance was here.

Loot comes out and ushers the paramedics in. Diane is examined quickly and put on the stretcher. She again tries to talk. It is just becoming dusk and the lights illuminate the block like a Fourth of July fireworks festival. As Diane is loaded into the ambulance she again tries to tell Loot and me "It was…"

"We know." we say. "Don't worry." Diane is loaded to the ambulance. I grab Ronan. "Total protection. No one near her. NO ONE! Unless you here otherwise from Loot or myself. NO ONE!" Ronan nods and Tolliver comes over and reassures me. "We got it." Loot's house is awash in cops now. I grab Loot. The sun is setting. "LET'S GO!" I scream. I fire up the rental and gun the engine. I again scream for Loot. "LET'S GO!"

Loot gives some final commands. Ronan with Diane. No one near her. Call the Chief and get him down here. Lieutenant Murphy's wife has been kidnapped. Put it on the APB. Tolliver is instructed to guard the house. Keep some uniformed officers with him. Secure it and let no one near it. I scream one more time. Loot runs over and gets in the car. I spin the car around and ride past the now blockaded road on the sidewalk before I hit the pavement, which makes the car a little wiggly and makes a god awful smell and sound of burnt up rubber. I wish I had my Vette. I begin to roar toward the main road back to the interstate. Loot looks over at me. He is on the verge of tears fearing for his beloved Kate. I zip along, passing cars all over the place in all different ways. Loot is hanging on to the hand strap. "Where the hell are you even going? Diane didn't know. Where are you going? You're wasting time." Loot's frustration has caught up with him and he is venting on me. "You don't know where she is."

I look in the rear view mirror. "I have a pretty good idea." Loot looks at me funny, and then looks in the back seat. His jaw hits the floor and his heart jumps up past his eyes. Loot is not able to speak and breaks into a chilling sweat as goose pimples form all over his body. Sitting in the back seat in total angelic white is Elizabeth Downing guiding her own guardian angel to where I need to be. I hit the interstate and throw the flashers on. I weave in and out of traffic like a maniac, riding shoulders on both sides and cutting people off in the heavy rush hour traffic. I nearly cause accidents three different times and I am driving the car so hard the hubcaps flew off the right side tires. I am in the zone but somehow crack, straight faced, "I hope you guys took insurance out on this." Loot is still petrified as he cannot get past the five year dead Elizabeth Downing sitting in the back of the car. Elizabeth turns to Loot and smiles reassuringly at him. I steer the car off West Colonial and start maneuvering through dense traffic laden bog. I run sidewalks, red lights and oncoming traffic lanes to get through. I turn to Loot. "We'll be there in a minute. Call it in. Get back up."

"Where?"

"He took her *there*." I am exceptionally intense as I maneuver the vehicle hard right and fishtail, narrowly missing a lime green beetle. Loot looks at me funny, and then looks in the back seat. It hits him. Kate was taken to the woods by Park Lake. The woods where I found Elizabeth five years ago. The ultimate finishing insult. Loot gets on the cellphone and calls the Chief, who is at Loot's house. Loot fills in the details and demands back up, which the Chief sends. I rumble the Impala into the parking lot for Park Lake Park. There is no Cadillac. "Where are they?" Loot asks.

"They're here." I am intensely focused. I drive the car past the end of the parking stop and scream it to a halt just shy of the first set of condensed trees. Loot is panicking. "Her car is not here." I fling the door open and rip out my gun. A sharp and sudden pain shoots through my right wrist. I drop the gun, but pick it up quickly. The hand had begun to throb while I was doing my best AJ Foyt getting here. Loot starts to scream to me. I holler back "shut up and let's go." I start snaking through the woods. There is a flash of light in the sky followed by the boom of thunder and a deluge of rain that is only slightly diminished by the shelter of the forest canopy. Loot tries very hard to keep up. The woods are very dark, except for the flooding moonlight and occasional lightning. The ground gets muddy and slippery. It is very unusual for a thunderstorm to strike at night, but apropos given what I anticipate. I maneuver without a hesitation. Loot had his flashlight out and was trying to keep up. Fifteen feet ahead I slammed to a dead stop. Loot was running so hard to keep up he nearly crashed right into my back. There standing in the clearing was a well dressed large man holding a police issue 9 mm. Off to our left about twenty feet was Kate Murphy. She was gagged but not blindfolded and her feet were duct taped together. Her arms were tied to two trees directly across from each other which left Kate spread like she was on a cross. She was stripped down naked. There were no visible injuries to her.

"So Spade, what do you think of my piece de resistance? It looks a little familiar, don't you think?" I stood their stone faced, gun at my side. Loot raised his gun and took aim.

"Put it down or your little wifey pooh will bite the bullet." The killer chuckles with his little joke as he points the gun directly at Kate's head. "You know I can hit her from here don't you, Dan?"

"Poncher, you son of a bitch, let her go!" Loot is becoming unglued and begins to lurch toward his wife. Poncher puts a bullet about eight inches front Kate's right shoulder.

I restrain Loot. "Lighten up, Francis." The second shot is about six inches away from her hip.

"Enough with the cute jokes, Spade." Loot raises his gun at Poncher who pulls his cock back and adjust his aim ever so slightly. "Come on Dan, be a man. Pull the trigger. Maybe you can stop me before I get one-off." Poncher wiggles his finger in the trigger chamber. I reach over and lowers Loot's arm down. I still have my gun in my right hand. The pain it was giving me before has been replaced with adrenaline as I remain fixated on Poncher. "So tell me boys, where did I go wrong?" he asks.

Loot refocuses his gaze on Poncher. "The knife." Loot says.

"The knife was fool proof. I never used my name anywhere. I bought it through the mail. The knife? Impossible!" Poncher is pleased with himself.

"You used your credit card to secure to the P.O. Box that you sent the knife to."

"You're kidding me? You tracked me through that. That's damn fine detective work there boys." Poncher is mocking us.

"Actually," I chime in, "You goofed at the hotel. It was very kind of you to attack that bellman when you wanted me to find the knife." Poncher mocks a bow of appreciation. "And you did an absolutely excellent job of remaining nondescript to the hotel employees when you planted it. You see I was in the hotel just a few hours before you. That's when I found the tip of the knife that sent us to *The Outdoorsman* and led Loot down his path. But you slipped up, or more correctly, you didn't." Poncher looks at me, confused.

"What the hell are you talking about?"

"You see," I continue, "You followed me. I was so excited after I found the tip of the knife that I stumbled going through the lobby in all my haste. Twice. But when you nearly tripped over the guy cleaning up *my* mess, you 'moved like a dancer. Caught himself right away' I believe were the words. So I was sitting thinking. This guy thinks like a cop, is a big guy, is nimble and knows how to work with fingerprints. Then it hit me. How did you lift my print, anyway?"

Poncher nods his head. "I am very impressed. I guess, Spade, that I underestimated you. After all these months you had no clue." Poncher brings his right hand over and clap's it against the base of the gun. "Bravo. The fingerprint was easy. You gave it to me."

"How?" I am all ears. The rain falls harder now, making all the leaves snap and crackle, but I remain engrossed in Poncher's every word.

"Interrogation, before your bitch lawyer showed up. You drank the cup of coffee. As soon as you left I took the cup then lifted the print. Right before I planted the knife I placed the print on it. It takes a steady hand, but if you're careful it can be done." Poncher was pleased with his work.

"Why?" I ask the long awaited question.

"WHY?" Poncher becomes increasingly angry as his face turns beet red. "WHY? BECAUSE OF THAT SON OF A BITCH RIGHT THERE!" Poncher waves his gun at Loot. "YOU RUINED MY LIFE. YOU STOLE EVERYHTING FROM ME. YOU STOLE HER FROM ME!" Poncher waves his gun at Kate. "I COULD HAVE HAD HER. BUT YOU HAD TO STEAL HER AWAY! SHE WAS MINE. I VOWED RIGHT THERE I WOULD GET YOU BACK! SO I WENT UP FOR THE FORCE! BUT YOU HAD TO BEAT ME! THEN I WENT UP FOR HOMICIDE! YOU HAD TO BEAT ME AGAIN! ALL I WAS LEFT WITH WAS THE PUTRID IAD, WHICH I ONLY GOT BECAUSE, AS YOU SO DELICIUOSLY PUT IT SPADE, BECAUSE CUTLER IS FAMILY! WELL I KNEW RIGHT THERE THAT I WOULD GET EVEN. BUT THEN A SNOOTY BEAT COP HAD TO FIND A PRETTY, TORTUTRED GIRL. AND AFTER HE WENT AWRY THE COM-PASSIONATE LIEUTENANT MURPHY HAD TO TAKE THIS SNOT NOSE COP UNDER HIS WING AND INTO HOMICIDE. THAT WAS MY JOB! *AND THEN THE GREAT DETECTIVE SPADE HAS TO HAVE A GUNFIGHT WITH A GANG AND BE-COME THE DARLING OF THE MEDIA.* FUCK YOU BOTH! YOU COST ME EVERYTHING!! I KNEW RIGHT THEN SPADE, WHAT TO DO. I COULDN'T HURT KATE, MY LOVE, BUT I COULD HURT LOOT THROUGH YOU. SO I BEGAN TO THINK. THE REST WAS EASY!" Poncher, who was screaming at the top of his very powerful lungs the whole time, then sudden-ly relaxes and breathes deep. He begins to speak, barely loud enough to be heard. The rain lessens slightly but Poncher is interrupted by a monstrous clap of thunder, which annoys him. "And so, my darling adversaries, it ends. For in less than five minutes I will be dead. The department will cover it up with a heroic gun battle in which some made up person perishes so as not to embarrass the department. But I will not go it alone. Oh no. Someone will go with me. Spade, you have impressed me a lot today, so I will let you choose. How did you know to find me here, anyway?"

"I knew you hated me. It was the obvious choice. Bring me back to my personal place of pain. Thanks for the cards, by the way." I am direct and stoic.

"They were nice, weren't they? I especially liked the Valentine's one. Well done detective. You have certainly redeemed yourself tonight. So, Spade, who will it be?"

"No one is dying tonight." I am firm and certain. And wrong. With my last words Kate violently thrashes about startling everyone. As everyone turns to look at the struggling lady I fire instantaneously, hitting Poncher in the left shoulder, causing him to drop his gun. "I told you, no one dies tonight." I walk over and kick the gun away from Poncher's hand. I stand over Poncher, gun drawn. Poncher is bleeding from his shoulder and the rain assists the blood in running down his arm. "You're under arrest." I reach down and pull handcuffs from his side. I try to cuff Poncher's hand but Poncher struggles with me, kicking me in the groin. I step on the injured shoulder and smack Poncher in the head with my cast. "Ouch" I scream. I slap the cuffs on Poncher and walk away, shaking my hand. After a few steps I then head over toward Loot, who has rushed over to Kate and now has her partially covered with his jacket and is removing her gag. Kate is wet and shivering. I begin to run to check on Kate when I hear the click. Stupid ass, I say to myself. There is another tremendous thunderclap but, remarkably, the rain has stopped falling. I spin and lunge, turning my head just as I see the flash of the muzzle. I fumble for my weapon with my slippery, agonizing hand. In slow motion while floating through the air I empty my gun once. The burning sensation strikes immediately in my chest and warms the rest of my body. You should have checked him for an ankle piece. Some cop you are, I tell myself.

Loot unties the gag from Kate's mouth and cuts her ropes. He then rushes over to see what happened. The two cracks happened so fast Loot didn't even have a chance to reach for his gun. Loot reaches me. There is a big pool of dark red soaking through the front of my blue tee shirt. Loot checks for a pulse and finds a feint one. Loot rips away my shirt. I have no vest on. Why would I, we were not planning for this today. Loot puts pressure on my wound. The bleeding is massive. Kate comes over still in shock from the ordeal. She has just freed herself from all her restraints. "Put your hands here and press hard." Kate does as she is told, not comprehending everything that happened. Loot picks up the phone and dials. "OFFICER DOWN, OFFICER DOWN, PARK LAKE WOODS. SEND PARAMEDICS, ASAP!" Loot steps over and checks on Poncher. The bullet entered directly through the right eye and left a baseball size hole in the back of his skull. Loot then looked back at Kate and I, who lay motionless. Loot then gasps and takes a deep breath. Directly behind where I lie Loot sees the ropes and tape that had held the naked Kate prisoner. He realizes I took the bullet to shield them. Loot begins to cry and rushes over to take over for Kate, who has had a traumatic day and still has nothing covering her except for her husband's jacket.

I open my eyes slightly. It is really pretty dark, I tell myself. I am glad it stopped raining. Kate is kneeling over me, while Loot is on the phone towering like the Washington Monument. 'I should have frisked him. I'm sorry" I say. I am not sure if my words are audible.

It takes about four minutes for the first cops and paramedics to find them in the woods. I remember hearing someone say 'he's gone.' Are they talking about me, I wonder. Someone tell my wife I love her and I'm sorry. I feel very warm. The flurry of activity around me is surreal. It begins to hurt as I see the paddles being lowered upon me. There is a great deal more light and Kate is crying, covered in a blanket leaning on Loot. Loot is holding a hand that I recognize as my own by the cast. It's funny, I think; I can't feel my hand anymore. It doesn't hurt right now. I do not remember closing my eyes.

NINETEEN

Diane had not left her husband's side for the four days since he had been brought in. Diane was still in the hospital when I arrived with the half naked and blood filled Kate and Loot. Diane had fainted when she saw me. Loot and an orderly had to revive her. Kate was given a thorough exam and treated for shock, then was given a set of scrubs to wear. She did not appear to be harmed in any other way. I had flat lined in the ambulance and Loot thought I was gone. But I found a way to hold on, although I never did open my eyes. Diane, a bandage over her eye and suffering from a mild concussion, stood outside the operating room doors the entire six and a half hours I was in surgery. The Chief of Police and the Mayor came to offer their prayers for me and for Diane. Kate and Loot waited with her the whole time. Ashley had also come buy and waited, but gave Diane her space to grieve and offered her whatever help Diane could want. It was a long night when I finally made it to ICU at almost 2 a.m.

The paper the next day had said it all. HERO. The article, authored by Steve Frizz, told of the stunning set of events of the prior day. It was based primarily on leaks and hearsay, and Frizz was honest of that. From what Frizz had pieced together Spade and Lieutenant Murphy had determined the killer was a police officer who had a grudge with both Spade and Lieutenant Murphy. The facts of the case were not complete, at least to a point where Frizz could honestly report them. It was believed, according to Frizz's sources, that the killer had framed Detective Spade and subsequently arranged his arrest. During the day yesterday, Frizz reported, the killer struck at both men by invading Lieutenant Murphy's house and pistol-whipping Spade's girlfriend Diane Ellisin. Then the killer kidnapped Lieutenant Murphy's wife Kate Murphy and, in a sick twist, took her to the same spot where a young Elizabeth Downing had been murdered five years earlier. It was there Patrolman Spade that had found Miss Downing right before she died in his arms. Steve Frizz then took the extraordinary step of apologizing to Detective Spade and Miss Ellisin, Lieutenant Murphy and his wife, and to the citizens of Orlando for all the sensationalist journalism he had reported over the six-month spree. It was poor journalism, Frizz wrote, and he apologized for it.

Subsequent articles and news reports over the next two days after completed the story, identifying the killer as Internal Affairs Officer Francis Poncher. It was also learned that Detective Spade and Diane Ellisin had wed the day before the shooting. The chief and mayor had announced the identity was accurate, and said it was a sad day for the Orlando Police Department in all ways associated with the case. They ordered all city flags flown at half-staff in honor of the three murdered woman and Detective Spade. Loot, Kate and Diane were angered by this, because I was not dead yet.

The outpouring from the public was phenomenal. The Hurricane From Hell had become the official outpost for the good wishes. Rock and Beth and Joey had the bar opened pretty much all day since the day after. There were flowers all over the bar, and television news crews had taken up residence. Even Steve Frizz had come by and asked how the Spades were doing. The murdered girl from Winter Park's parents had come by to offer their sympathies, and the mother apologized for striking me in court. Lisa Yeung's fiancée stopped by to say thanks and pray for me, and the Russian Embassy sent flowers.

There had been no reaction from me for four days now. When the doctors told Diane that I was in a coma she broke down crying hysterically. Kate and Loot were unable to console her. She had not eaten in those four days and only slept in cat naps while Loot took the turn being my guardian. Yesterday, the third day past the incident, doctors told Diane that the bullet just missed my heart but did massive internal damage, collapsing a lung before lodging right near my spine. The decision to remove the bullet would be made at a later time. Diane was remarkably stronger for that horrifying news.

Diane sits over me holding my hand. She whispers softly as she kisses my fingers. "I need you, Kenny. You need to come back to me. I can't do this without you. Our baby needs a father. Did you hear me, Kenny? You are going to be a daddy. So I need you to come back to me. Come back to me, please baby. Come back."

Loot looks at Kate in a state of shock. He asks her if she knew about this. Yes, she did. Loot asks her for how long. Since the arraignment, is her reply. Loot begins to protest when Kate grabs his hand and places it on her tummy. Then Kate smiles. No, Loot says. Kate just shakes her head.

I take all this in from above. I can see myself lying in the bed and I hear Diane's words. When I hear Kate tell Loot that she too is pregnant, I whisper 'Congratulations' to my best friend. Elizabeth, who is above the room with me, turns to me. "Your family down there loves you. You, my champion, have done all your fighting for me. Now, you must decide how you want to fight for you." Elizabeth floats over and gives me a kiss. "You must decide what you are going to do."

I begin to cry.